What readers are saying about
Beach Read

'When I say I want to read romance, this is what I
mean. This book. This exact book'
Netgalley reviewer ★ ★ ★ ★ ★

'The best book I've read this year so far, and easily a top 10
on my all-time favourites list. Emily Henry's writing is masterful
in *Beach Read* . . . Witty, interesting and utterly enjoyable'
Patricia, Netgalley ★ ★ ★ ★ ★

'A delightful, romantic, amusing and well written tale . . . will
have you smiling to the end. A wholly satisfying read'
Netgalley reviewer ★ ★ ★ ★ ★

'I loved this book so damn much that I don't even know
where to begin. This book made me laugh, cry, and
laugh-cry . . . I cannot recommend it enough'
Brooks, Netgalley ★ ★ ★ ★ ★

'Exceptionally well written, incredibly authentic
characters, deeply moving and entertaining'
Emer, Netgalley ★ ★ ★ ★ ★

'Loved this book!'
Rachel, Netgalley ★ ★ ★ ★ ★

'Romance at its very best. I was so invested in January and
Gus and their literary journey to love. I can't tell you how happy
this book made me! Highly, HIGHLY recommend'
Kate, Netgalley ★ ★ ★ ★ ★

'An absolutely brilliant, fresh and exciting book.
With family drama, an excellent love interest and
a great concept, it's a clear winner'
Andrea, Netgalley ★ ★ ★ ★ ★

Emily Henry studied creative writing at Hope College and the New York Center for Art & Media Studies, and now spends most of her time in Cincinnati, Ohio, and the part of Kentucky just beneath it. *Beach Read* is her debut adult novel.

Beach Read

EMILY HENRY

PENGUIN BOOKS

PENGUIN BOOKS

UK | USA | Canada | Ireland | Australia
India | New Zealand | South Africa

Penguin Books is part of the Penguin Random House group of companies
whose addresses can be found at global.penguinrandomhouse.com.

First published in the United States by Berkley, an imprint of Penguin Random House LLC 2020
First published in Great Britain by Penguin Books 2020
009

Printed at Thomson Press India Ltd, New Delhi

A CIP catalogue record for this book is available from the British Library

ISBN: 978-0-241-98952-4

www.greenpenguin.co.uk

Penguin Random House is committed to a
sustainable future for our business, our readers
and our planet. This book is made from Forest
Stewardship Council® certified paper.

For Joey:
You are so perfectly my favorite person.

1

The House

I HAVE A FATAL flaw.

I like to think we all do. Or at least that makes it easier for me when I'm writing—building my heroines and heroes up around this one self-sabotaging trait, hinging everything that happens to them on a specific characteristic: the thing they learned to do to protect themselves and can't let go of, even when it stops serving them.

Maybe, for example, you didn't have much control over your life as a kid. So, to avoid disappointment, you learned never to ask yourself what you truly wanted. And it worked for a long time. Only now, upon realizing you didn't *get* what you didn't *know* you wanted, you're barreling down the highway in a midlife-crisis-mobile with a suitcase full of cash and a man named Stan in your trunk.

Maybe your fatal flaw is that you don't use turn signals.

Or maybe, like me, you're a hopeless romantic. You just can't stop telling yourself the story. The one about your own life, complete with melodramatic soundtrack and golden light lancing through car windows.

It started when I was twelve. My parents sat me down to tell me the news. Mom had gotten her first diagnosis—suspicious cells in her left breast—and she told me not to worry so many times I suspected I'd be grounded if she caught me at it. My mom was a do-er, a laugher, an optimist, *not* a worrier, but I could tell she was terrified, and so I was too, frozen on the couch, unsure how to say *anything* without making things worse.

But then my bookish homebody of a father did something un-expected. He stood and grabbed our hands—one of Mom's, one of mine—and said, *You know what we need to get these bad feelings out? We need to dance!*

Our suburb had no clubs, just a mediocre steak house with a Friday night cover band, but Mom lit up like he'd just suggested taking a private jet to the Copacabana.

She wore her buttery yellow dress and some hammered metal earrings that twinkled when she moved. Dad ordered twenty-year-old Scotch for them and a Shirley Temple for me, and the three of us twirled and bobbed until we were dizzy, laughing, tripping all over. We laughed until we could barely stand, and my famously reserved father sang along to "Brown Eyed Girl" like the whole room wasn't watching us.

And then, exhausted, we piled into the car and drove home through the quiet, Mom and Dad holding tight to each other's hands between the seats, and I tipped my head against the car window and, watching the streetlights flicker across the glass, thought, *It's going to be okay. We will always be okay.*

And that was the moment I realized: when the world felt dark and scary, love could whisk you off to go dancing; laughter could take some of the pain away; beauty could punch holes in your fear. I decided then that my life would be full of all three. Not just for my own benefit, but for Mom's, and for everyone else around me.

There would be purpose. There would be beauty. There would be candlelight and Fleetwood Mac playing softly in the background.

The point is, I started telling myself a beautiful story about my life, about fate and the way things work out, and by twenty-eight years old, my story was perfect.

Perfect (cancer-free) parents who called several times a week, tipsy on wine or each other's company. Perfect (spontaneous, multilingual, six foot three) boyfriend who worked in the ER and knew how to make coq au vin. Perfect shabby chic apartment in Queens. Perfect job writing romantic novels—inspired by perfect parents and perfect boyfriend—for Sandy Lowe Books.

Perfect life.

But it was just a story, and when one gaping plot hole appeared, the whole thing unraveled. That's how stories work.

Now, at twenty-nine, I was miserable, broke, semi-homeless, very single, and pulling up to a gorgeous lake house whose very existence nauseated me. Grandly romanticizing my life had stopped serving me, but my fatal flaw was still riding shotgun in my dinged-up Kia Soul, narrating things as they happened:

January Andrews stared out the car window at the angry lake beating up on the dusky shore. She tried to convince herself that coming here hadn't been a mistake.

It was *definitely* a mistake, but I had no better option. You didn't turn down free lodging when you were broke.

I parked on the street and stared up at the oversized cottage's facade, its gleaming windows and fairy tale of a porch, the shaggy beach grass dancing in the warm breeze.

I checked the address in my GPS against the handwritten one hanging from the house key. This was it, all right.

For a minute, I stalled, like maybe a world-ending asteroid would take me out before I was forced to go inside. Then I took a deep breath and got out, wrestling my overstuffed suitcase from the back seat along with the cardboard box full of gin handles.

I pushed a fistful of dark hair out of my eyes to study the corn-flower blue shingles and snow-white trim. *Just pretend you're at an Airbnb.*

Immediately, an imaginary Airbnb listing ran through my head: *Three-bedroom, three-bath lakeside cottage brimming with charm and proof your father was an asshole and your life has been a lie.*

I started up the steps cut into the grassy hillside, blood rushing through my ears like fire hoses and legs wobbling, anticipating the moment the hellmouth would open and the world would drop out from under me.

That already happened. Last year. And it didn't kill you, so neither will this.

On the porch, every sensation in my body heightened. The tingling in my face, the twist in my stomach, the sweat prickling along my neck. I balanced the box of gin against my hip and slipped the key into the lock, a part of me hoping it would jam.

That all this would turn out to be an elaborate practical joke Dad had set up for us before he died.

Or, better yet, he wasn't actually dead. He'd jump out from behind the bushes and scream, "Gotcha! You didn't *really* think I had a secret second life, did you? You couldn't possibly think I had a second *house* with some woman other than your mother?"

The key turned effortlessly. The door swung inward.

The house was silent.

An ache went through me. The same one I'd felt at least once a day since I got Mom's call about the stroke and heard her sob those words. *He's gone, Janie.*

No Dad. Not here. Not anywhere. And then the second pain, the knife twisting: *The father you knew never existed anyway.*

I'd never really had him. Just like I'd never really had my ex Jacques or his coq au vin.

It was just a story I'd been telling myself. From now on, it was the ugly truth or nothing. I steeled myself and stepped inside.

My first thought was that the ugly truth wasn't super ugly. My dad's love nest had an open floor plan: a living room that spilled into a funky, blue-tiled kitchen and homey breakfast nook, the wall of windows just beyond overlooking a dark-stained deck.

If Mom had owned this place, everything would've been a mix of creamy, calming neutrals. The bohemian room I'd stepped into would've been more at home in Jacques's and my old place than my parents'. I felt a little queasy imagining Dad here, among these things Mom never would've picked out: the folksy hand-painted breakfast table, the dark wooden bookshelves, the sunken couch covered in mismatched pillows.

There was no sign of the version of him that I'd known.

My phone rang in my pocket and I set the box on the granite countertop to answer the call.

"Hello?" It came out weak and raspy.

"How is it?" the voice on the other end said immediately. "Is there a sex dungeon?"

"Shadi?" I guessed. I tucked the phone between my ear and shoulder as I unscrewed the cap from one of my gin bottles, taking a swig to fortify myself.

"It honestly worries me that I'm the *only* person who might call you to ask that," Shadi answered.

"You're the only person who even knows about the Love Shack," I pointed out.

"I am *not* the only one who knows about it," Shadi argued.

Technically true. While I'd found out about my father's secret lake house at his funeral last year, Mom had been aware much longer. "Fine," I said. "You're the only person I *told* about it. Anyway, give me a second. I just got here."

"Literally?" Shadi was breathing hard, which meant she was walking to a shift at the restaurant. Since we kept such different hours, most of our calls happened when she was on her way into work.

"Metaphorically," I said. "Literally, I've been here for ten minutes, but I only just feel that I have *arrived*."

"So wise," Shadi said. "So deep."

"Shh," I said. "I'm taking it all in."

"Check for the sex dungeon!" Shadi hurried to say, as if I were hanging up on her.

I was not. I was simply holding the phone to my ear, holding my breath, holding my racing heart in my chest, as I scanned my father's second life.

And there, just when I could convince myself Dad couldn't *possibly* have spent time here, I spotted something framed on the wall. A clipping of a *New York Times* Best Sellers list from three years ago, the same one he'd positioned over the fireplace at home. There I was, at number fifteen, the bottom slot. And there, three slots above me—in a sick twist of fate—was my college rival, Gus (though now he went by Augustus, because Serious Man) and his highbrow debut novel *The Revelatories*. It had stayed on the list for five weeks (not that I was counting (I was absolutely counting)).

"Well?" Shadi prompted. "What do you think?"

I turned and my eyes caught on the mandala tapestry hanging over the couch.

"I'm led to wonder if Dad smoked weed." I spun toward the windows at the side of the house, which aligned almost perfectly with the neighbor's, a design flaw Mom would never have overlooked when house shopping.

But this wasn't her house, and I could clearly see the floor-to-ceiling bookshelves that lined the neighbor's study.

"Oh, God—maybe it's a grow house, not a love shack!" Shadi sounded delighted. "You should've read the letter, January. It's all been a misunderstanding. Your dad's leaving you the family business. That Woman was his business partner, not his mistress."

How bad was it that I wished she were right?

Either way, I'd fully intended to read the letter. I'd just been waiting for the right time, hoping the worst of my anger would settle and those last words from Dad would be comforting. Instead, a full year had passed and the dread I felt at the thought of opening the envelope grew every day. It was so unfair, that he should get the last word and I'd have no way to reply. To scream or cry or demand more answers. Once I'd opened it, there'd be no going back. That would be it. The final goodbye.

So until further notice, the letter was living a happy, if solitary, life in the bottom of the gin box I'd brought with me from Queens.

"It's not a grow house," I told Shadi and slid open the back door to step onto the deck. "Unless the weed's in the basement."

"No way," Shadi argued. "That's where the sex dungeon is."

"Let's stop talking about my depressing life," I said. "What's new with you?"

"You mean the Haunted Hat," Shadi said. If only she had fewer than four roommates in her shoebox apartment in Chicago, then maybe I'd be staying with her now. Not that I was capable of getting anything done when I was with Shadi. And my financial situation was too dire *not* to get something done. I had to finish my next book in this rent-free hell. Then maybe I could afford my own Jacques-free place.

"If the Haunted Hat is what you want to talk about," I said, "then yes. Spill."

"Still hasn't spoken to me." Shadi sighed wistfully. "But I can, like, *sense* him looking at me when we're both in the kitchen. Because we have a connection."

"Are you at all worried that your connection isn't *with* the guy who's wearing the antique porkpie hat, but perhaps with the ghost of the hat's original owner? What will you do if you realize you've fallen in love with a ghost?"

"Um." Shadi thought for a minute. "I guess I'd have to update my Tinder bio."

A breeze rippled off the water at the bottom of the hill, ruffling my brown waves across my shoulders, and the setting sun shot golden spears of light over everything, so bright and hot I had to squint to see the wash of oranges and reds it cast across the beach. If this were just some house I'd rented, it would be the perfect place to write the adorable love story I'd been promising Sandy Lowe Books for months.

Shadi, I realized, had been talking. More about the Haunted Hat. His name was Ricky, but we never called him that. We always spoke of Shadi's love life in code. There was the older man who ran the amazing seafood restaurant (the Fish Lord), and then there was some guy we'd called Mark because he looked like some other, *famous* Mark, and now there was this new coworker, a bartender who wore a hat every day that Shadi loathed and yet could not resist.

I snapped back into the conversation as Shadi was saying, "Fourth of July weekend? Can I visit then?"

"That's more than a month away." I wanted to argue that I wouldn't even be here by then, but I knew it wasn't true. It would take me at least all summer to write a book, empty the house, and sell both, so I could (hopefully) be catapulted back into relative comfort. Not in New York, but somewhere less expensive.

I imagined Duluth was affordable. Mom would never visit me there, but we hadn't done much visiting this past year anyway, apart from my three-day trip home for Christmas. She'd dragged me to four yoga classes, three crowded juice bars, and a *Nutcracker* performance starring some kid I didn't know, like if we were alone for even a second, the topic of Dad would arise and we'd burst into flames.

All my life, my friends had been jealous of my relationship with her. How often and freely (or so I thought) we talked, how much fun we had together. Now our relationship was the world's least competitive game of phone tag.

I'd gone from having two loving parents and a live-in boyfriend to basically just having Shadi, my much-too-long-distance best friend. The one blessing of moving from New York to North Bear Shores, Michigan, was that I was closer to her place in Chicago.

"Fourth of July's too far off," I complained. "You're only three hours away."

"Yeah, and I don't know how to drive."

"Then you should probably give that license back," I said.

"Believe me, I'm waiting for it to expire. I'm going to feel so free. I *hate* when people think I'm able to drive just because, legally, I am."

Shadi was a terrible driver. She screamed whenever she turned left.

"Besides, you know how scheduling off is in the industry. I'm lucky my boss said I could have Fourth of July. For all I know, he's expecting a blow job now."

"No way. Blow jobs are for major holidays. What you've got on your hands is a good old-fashioned foot job quid pro quo."

I took another sip of gin, then turned from the end of the deck and nearly yelped. On the deck ten feet to the right of mine, the back of a head of curly brown hair peeked over a lawn chair. I silently prayed the man was asleep—that I wouldn't have to spend an entire summer next door to someone who'd heard me shout *good old-fashioned foot job*.

As if he'd read my mind, he sat forward and grabbed the bottle of beer from his patio table, took a swig, and sat back.

"So true. I won't even have to take my Crocs off," Shadi was saying. "Anyway, I just got to work. But let me know if it's drugs or leather in the basement."

I turned my back to the neighbor's deck. "I'm not going to check until you visit."

"Rude," Shadi said.

"Leverage," I said. "Love you."

"Love you more," she insisted and hung up.

I turned to face the curly head, half waiting for him to acknowledge me, half debating whether I was obligated to introduce myself.

I hadn't known any of my neighbors in New York well, but this was Michigan, and from Dad's stories about growing up in North Bear Shores, I fully expected to have to lend this man sugar at some point (note: must buy sugar).

I cleared my throat and pasted on my attempt at a neighborly smile. The man sat forward for another swig of beer, and I called across the gap, "Sorry for disturbing you!"

He waved one hand vaguely, then turned the page of whatever book was in his lap. "What's disturbing about foot jobs as a form of currency?" he drawled in a husky, bored voice.

I grimaced as I searched for a reply—*any* reply. Old January would have known what to say, but my mind was as blank as it was every time I opened Microsoft Word.

Okay, so maybe I'd become a bit of a hermit this past year. *Maybe* I wasn't entirely sure what I'd spent the last year doing, since it wasn't visiting Mom and it wasn't writing, and it wasn't charming the socks off my neighbors.

"Anyway," I called, "I'm living here now."

As if he'd read my thoughts, he gave a disinterested wave and grumbled, "Let me know if you need any sugar." But he managed to make it sound more like, *Never speak to me again unless you notice my house is on fire, and even then, listen for sirens first.*

So much for Midwestern hospitality. At least in New York, our neighbors had brought us cookies when we moved in. (They'd been gluten-free and laced with LSD, but it was the thought that counted.)

"Or if you need directions to the nearest Sexual Fetish Depot," the Grump added.

Heat flared through my cheeks, a flush of embarrassment and anger. The words were out before I could reconsider: "I'll just wait for your car to pull out and follow." He laughed, a surprised, rough sound, but still didn't deign to face me.

"*Lovely* to meet you," I added sharply, and turned to hurry back through the sliding glass doors to the safety of the house, where I would quite possibly have to hide all summer.

"Liar," I heard him grumble before I snapped the door shut.

2

The Funeral

WASN'T READY TO look through the rest of the house, so I settled down at the table to write. As usual, the blank document
stared accusingly at me, refusing to fill itself with words or characters, no matter how long I stared back.

Here's the thing about writing Happily Ever Afters: it helps if
you believe in them.

Here's the thing about me: I did until the day of my father's
funeral.

My parents, my family, had been through so much already, and
somehow we always came through it stronger, with more love and
laughter than before. There was the brief separation when I was a
kid and Mom started feeling like she'd lost her identity, started
staring out windows like she might see herself out there living life
and figure out what she needed to do next. There was the kitchen-

dancing, hand-holding, and forehead-kissing that followed when Dad moved back in. There was Mom's first cancer diagnosis and the wildly expensive celebratory dinner when she kicked its ass, eating like we were millionaires, laughing until their overpriced wine and my Italian soda sprayed from our respective noses, like we could afford to waste it, like the medical debt didn't exist. And then the second bout of cancer and the new lease on life after the mastectomy: the pottery classes, ballroom dancing classes, yoga classes, Moroccan cooking classes that my parents filled their schedules with, like they were determined to pack as much life into as little time as possible. Long weekend trips to see me and Jacques in New York, rides on the subway during which Mom begged me to stop regaling her with stories of our pothead neighbors Sharyn and Karyn (not related; regularly slid informational "Flat Earth" pamphlets under our door) because she was afraid she was going to pee herself, all while Dad debunked the flat Earth theory under his breath for Jacques.

Trial. Happy ending. Tribulation. Happy ending. Chemo. Happy ending.

And then, right in the middle of the happiest ending yet, he was just gone.

I was just standing there, in the foyer of his and Mom's Episcopalian church, in a sea of black-clad people whispering useless words, feeling like I'd sleepwalked there, barely able to recall the flight, the ride to the airport, packing. Remembering, for the millionth time in the last three days, that he was *gone*.

Mom had slipped into the bathroom, and I was alone when I saw her: the only woman I didn't recognize. Dressed in a gray dress and leather sandals, a crocheted shawl tied around her shoulders and her white hair wind-tossed. She was staring right at me.

After a beat, she swept toward me, and for some reason, my stomach bottomed out. As if my body knew first that things were about to change. This stranger's presence at Dad's funeral was going to wrench my life off track as much as his death had.

She smiled hesitantly as she stopped in front of me. She smelled like vanilla and citrus. "Hello, January." Her voice was breathy, and her fingers twirled anxiously through the fringe on her shawl. "I've heard so much about you."

Behind her, the bathroom door swung open and Mom walked out. She stopped short, frozen with an unfamiliar expression. *Recognition? Horror?*

She didn't want the two of us to talk. What did that mean?

"I'm an old friend of your father's," the woman said. "He means . . . *meant* a lot to me. I've known him all my life, just about. For quite some time, we were thick as thieves, and—he never shut up about *you*." Her laugh tried for easy, missed it by a light-year.

"I'm sorry," she said, hoarse. "I promised I wouldn't cry, but . . ."

I felt like I'd been shoved off a building, like the dropping would never end.

Old friend. That was what she said. Not *lover* or *mistress*. But I knew, from the way she was crying—some funhouse mirror version of Mom's tears during the funeral. I recognized the look on her face as the same one I'd seen on mine this morning while I tapped concealer under my eyes. Dad's death had irreparably broken her.

She fished something out of her pocket. An envelope with my

15

name scrawled across it, a key resting atop it. A tab hung from the key with an address scribbled in the same unmistakable handwriting as the chicken scratch on the envelope. Dad's.

"He wanted you to have this," she said. "It's yours."

She pushed it into my palm, holding on for a second. "It's a beautiful house, right on Lake Michigan," she blurted. "You'll love it. He always said that you would. And the letter is for your birthday. You can open it then, or . . . whenever."

My birthday. My birthday wasn't for another seven months. My dad would not be there for my birthday. My dad was gone.

Behind the woman, Mom unfroze, moving toward us with a murderous expression. *"Sonya,"* she hissed.

And then I knew the rest.

That while I'd been in the dark, Mom had not.

I closed the Word document, like clicking that little X in the corner would shut out the memories too. Looking for a distraction, I scrolled through my inbox to the latest email from my agent, Anya.

It had arrived two days ago, before I left New York, and I'd found increasingly ridiculous reasons for putting off opening it. Packing. Moving things into storage. Driving. Trying to drink as much water as I could while peeing. "Writing," heavy on the scare quotes. Drunk. Hungry. Breathing.

Anya had a reputation for being tough, a bulldog, on the publishers' end of things, but on the writers' end, she was something like Miss Honey, the sweet teacher from *Matilda*, mashed together with a sexy witch. You always desperately wanted to please her, both because you had the sense that no one had loved and admired you so purely before *and* because you suspected she could sic a herd of pythons on you, if she so chose.

I drained my third gin and tonic of the night, opened the email, and read:

> Helloooo, you beautiful and miraculous jellyfish,
> angelic artist, money-maker mine,
>
> I know things have been SO crazy on your end, but
> Sandy's writing again—really wants to know how the
> manuscript's coming slash whether it will still be ready by
> the end of the summer. As ever, I'm more than happy to
> hop on the phone (or instant message, or a Pegasus's
> back as need be) to help you brainstorm/hash out plot
> details/WHATEVER it takes to help bring more of your
> beautiful words and unparalleled swoon into the world!
> Five books in five years was a tall order for anyone (even
> someone with your spectacular talent), but I do believe
> we've reached a breaking point with SLB, and it's time to
> grin and birth it, if at all possible.
>
> xox,
> Anya

Grin and birth it. I suspected it'd be easier to deliver a fully formed human baby out of my uterus at the end of this summer than to write and sell a new book.

I decided that if I went to sleep now, I could pop out of bed early and crank out a few thousand words. I hesitated outside the downstairs bedroom. There was no way to be sure which beds Dad and That Woman had partaken of.

I was in a funhouse of geriatric adultery. It might've been funny, if I hadn't lost the ability to find anything funny in the last year spent penning rom-coms that ended with a bus driver falling asleep and the whole cast going off a cliff.

It's SUPER interesting, I always imagined Anya saying, if I were to actually send in one of these drafts. *I mean, I would read your GROCERY list and laugh-cry doing it. But it's not a Sandy Lowe book. For now, more swoon and less doom, babycakes.*

I was going to need help sleeping here. I poured myself another G&T and closed my computer. The house had gotten hot and stuffy, so I stripped to my underwear, then circled the first floor opening windows before draining my glass and flopping onto the couch.

It was even more comfortable than it looked. Damn That Woman with her beautifully eclectic tastes. It was also, I decided, too low to the ground for a man with a bad back to be climbing on and off of, which meant it was probably *not* used for S-E-X.

Though Dad hadn't always had a bad back. When I was a kid, he'd take me out on the boat most weekends that he was home, and from what I'd seen, boating was 90 percent bending over to tie and untie knots and 10 percent staring into the sun, your arms thrown wide to let the wind race through your swishy jacket and—

The ache rose with a vengeance in my chest.

Those early mornings, on the man-made lake thirty minutes from our house, had always been just for the two of us, usually the morning after he got back from a trip. Sometimes I didn't even know he was home yet. I'd just awake to my still-dark room, Dad tickling my nose, whisper-singing the Dean Martin song he'd named me for: *It's June in January, because I'm in love*... I'd jolt awake, heart trilling, knowing it meant a day on the boat, the two of us.

Now I wondered if all those precious chilly mornings had been literal guilt trips, time for him to readjust to life with Mom, after a weekend with That Woman.

I should save the storytelling for my manuscript. I pushed it all out of my mind and pulled a throw pillow over my face, sleep swallowing me like a biblical whale.

When I jerked awake, the room was dark, and there was music blasting through it.

I stood and ambled, dazed and gin-fogged, toward the knife block in the kitchen. I hadn't heard of a serial killer who began each murder by rousing the victim with R.E.M.'s "Everybody Hurts" but I really couldn't rule out the possibility.

As I moved toward the kitchen, the music dimmed, and I realized it was coming from the other side of the house. From the Grump's house.

I looked toward the glowing numbers on the stove. Twelve thirty at night, and my neighbor was blasting a song most often heard in dated dramedies wherein the protagonist walks home alone, hunched against the rain.

I stormed toward the window and thrust my upper body through it. The Grump's windows were open too, and I could see a swath of bodies lit up in the kitchen, holding glasses and mugs and bottles, leaning lazy heads on shoulders, looping arms around necks as the whole group sang along with fervor.

It was a raging party. So apparently the Grump didn't hate *all* people, just me. I cupped my mouth around my hands and yelled out the window, "EXCUSE ME!"

I tried twice more with no response, then slammed the window closed and circled the first floor, snapping the others shut. When I was finished, it still sounded pretty much like R.E.M. was playing a concert on my coffee table.

And then, for a beautiful moment, the song stopped and the sounds of the party, laughter and chatter and bottles clinking, dipped to a static murmur.

And then it started again.

The same song. Even louder. Oh, God. As I pulled my sweatpants back on, I contemplated the advantages of calling the police with a noise complaint. On the one hand, I might maintain plausible deniability with my neighbor. (Oh, 'twas not I who called the constable! I am but a young woman of nine and twenty, not a crotchety old spinster who loathes laughter, fun, song, and dance!) On the other, ever since I'd lost my dad, I'd had a harder and harder time forgiving small offenses.

I threw on my pizza-print sweatshirt and stormed out the front door, marching up the neighbor's steps. Before I could second-guess myself, I'd reached for the doorbell.

It rang out in the same powerful baritone as a grandfather clock, cutting through the music, but the singing didn't stop. I counted to ten, then rang it again. Inside, the voices didn't even waver. If the partygoers heard the doorbell, they were ignoring it.

I pounded on the door for a few more seconds before accepting no one was coming, then turned to stomp home. One o' clock, I decided. I'd give them until one before I called the cops.

The music was even louder in the house than I remembered,

and in the few minutes since I'd shut the windows, the temperature had risen to a sticky swelter. With nothing better to do, I grabbed a paperback from my bag and headed for the deck, fumbling for the light switches beside the sliding door.

My fingers hit them but nothing happened. The bulbs outside were dead. Reading by phone light, at one in the morning, on the deck of my father's second home it was! I stepped out, skin tingling from the refreshing chill of the breeze coming off the water.

The Grump's deck was dark too, except for a lone fluorescent bulb surrounded by clumsy moths, which was why I nearly screamed when something moved in the shadows.

And by nearly screamed, I of course mean *definitely screamed*.

"Jesus!" The shadowy thing gasped and shot up from the chair where it had been sitting. And by shadowy thing, I of course mean *man who'd been chilling in the dark until I scared the shit out of him*. "What, what?" he demanded, like he expected me to announce that he was covered in scorpions.

If he had been, this would be less awkward.

"Nothing!" I said, still breathing hard from the surprise. "I didn't see you there!"

"You didn't see me here?" he repeated. He gave a scratchy, disbelieving laugh. "Really? You didn't see me, on my own deck?"

Technically, I didn't see him now either. The porch light was a few feet behind and above him, transforming him into nothing but a tallish, person-shaped silhouette with a halo ringing his dark, messy hair. At this point, it would probably be better if I managed to go the whole summer without having to make eye contact with him anyway.

"Do you also scream when cars drive past on the highway or

you spot people through restaurant windows? Would you mind blacking out all our perfectly aligned windows so you don't accidentally *see me* when I'm holding a knife or a razor?"

I crossed my arms viciously over my chest. Or tried to. The gin was still making me a little fuzzy and clumsy.

What I meant to say—what the old January would've said—was *Could you possibly turn your music down a little bit?* Actually, she probably would've just slathered herself in glitter, put on her favorite velvet loafers, and shown up at the front door with a bottle of champagne, determined to win the Grump over.

But so far, this was the third-worst day of my life, and that January was probably buried wherever they put the old Taylor Swift, so what I actually said was "Could you turn off your sad-boy-angsting soundtrack?"

The silhouette laughed and leaned against his deck railing, his beer bottle dangling from one hand. "Does it look like I'm the one running the playlist?"

"No, it looks like you're the one sitting in the dark alone at his own party," I said, "but when I rang the doorbell to ask your frat brothers to turn down the volume, they couldn't hear me over the Jell-O wrestling, so I'm asking you."

He studied me through the dark for a minute—or at least, I assumed that was what he was doing, since neither of us could actually see the other.

Finally, he said, "Look, no one will be more *thrilled* than me when this night ends and everyone gets out of my house, but it *is* a Saturday night. In summer, on a street full of vacation homes. Unless this neighborhood got airlifted to the little town from *Footloose*, it doesn't seem crazy to play music this late. And maybe—just maybe—the brand-new neighbor who stood on her deck scream-ing *foot job* so loud birds scattered could afford to be lenient if one miserable party goes later than she'd like."

Now it was *my* turn to stare at the dark blob.

God, he was right. He was a grump, but so was I. Karyn and Sharyn's vitamin-powder-pyramid-scheme parties went later than this, and those were on weeknights, usually when Jacques had a shift at the ER the next morning. Sometimes I'd even *attended* those parties, and now I couldn't even handle Saturday-night group karaoke?

And worst of all, before I could figure out what to say, the Grump's house went miraculously silent. Through his illuminated back doors, I could see the crowd breaking up, hugging, saying goodbyes, setting down cups, and putting on jackets.

I'd argued with this guy for nothing, and now I'd have to live next to him for months. If I needed sugar, I was going to be shit out of luck.

I wanted to apologize for the *sad-boy angst* comment, or at least for these goddamn pants. These days, my reactions always felt out-sized, and there was no easy way to explain them when strangers had the bad fortune of witnessing them.

Sorry, I imagined myself saying, *I didn't mean to transform into a crotchety grandmother. It's just my dad died and then I found out he had a mistress and a second house and that my mom knew but never told me and she still won't talk to me about any of it, and when I finally came apart, my boy-friend decided he didn't love me anymore, and my career has stalled, and my best friend lives too far away, and PS* this *is the aforementioned Sex House, and I used to like parties but lately I don't like anything, so please forgive my behavior and have a lovely evening. Thank you and good night.*

Instead, that knife-twisting pain hit my gut, and tears stung the back of my nose, and my voice squeaked pathetically as I said to no one in particular, "I'm *so* tired."

Even silhouetted as he was, I could tell he went rigid. I'd learned it wasn't uncommon for people to do that when they intuited a woman was on the verge of emotional collapse. In the last few weeks of our relationship, Jacques was like one of those snakes that can sense an earthquake, going taut whenever my emotions rose, then deciding we needed something from the bodega and rushing out the door.

My neighbor didn't say anything, but he didn't rush away either. He just stood there awkwardly, staring at me through the pitch-dark. We faced off for easily five seconds, waiting to see what would happen first: me bursting into tears or him running away.

And then the music started blaring again, a Carly Rae Jepsen banger that, under different circumstances, I loved, and the Grump startled.

He glanced back through the sliding doors, then to me again. He cleared his throat. "I'll kick them out," he said stiffly, then turned and went inside, a unanimous cheer of "EVERETT!" rising from the crowd in the kitchen at the sight of him.

They sounded ready to hoist him up into a keg stand, but I could see him leaning over to shout to a blonde girl, and a moment later, the music fell silent for good.

Well. Next time I needed to make an impression, I might be better off with a plate of LSD cookies.

3

The Pete-Cute

AWOKE, HEAD THROBBING, to a text from Anya: Hey, babycakes! Wanted to make sure you got my email re: your glorious mind and the summer deadline we chatted about.

That period reverberated through my skull like a death knell.

I'd gotten my first true hangover when I was twenty-four, the morning after Anya sold my first book, *Kiss Kiss, Wish Wish*, to Sandy Lowe. (Jacques had bought his favorite French champagne to celebrate, and we drank it from the bottle as we walked the Brooklyn Bridge, waiting for the sun to rise, because we thought it seemed hugely romantic.) Later, lying on the bathroom floor, I'd sworn I'd fall on a sharp knife before I let my brain feel like an egg frying on a rock in the Cancún sun again.

And yet! Here I was, face pressed into a beaded throw pillow, brain sizzling in the saucepan of my skull. I ran to the downstairs bathroom. I didn't need to throw up, but I was hoping that if I pretended I did, my body would fall for it and evacuate the poison in my gut.

I threw myself onto my knees in front of the toilet and lifted my eyes to the framed picture that hung from a ribbon on the wall behind it.

Dad and That Woman were on a beach, dressed in windbreakers, his arms wrapped around her shoulders, the wind pulling at her pre-white blonde hair and pushing his only-just-graying curls flat against his forehead as they grinned.

And then, in a more understated but equally hilarious joke from the universe, I spotted the magazine rack beside the toilet, which contained exactly three offerings.

A two-year-old *Oprah Magazine*. A copy of my third book, *Northern Light*. And that damn *The Revelatories*—a hardcover with one of those shiny AUTOGRAPHED stickers, no less.

I opened my mouth and retched heartily into the toilet bowl. Then I stood, rinsed out my mouth, and turned the picture frame around so it faced the wall.

"Never again," I said aloud. Step one to a hangover-free life? Probably *not* moving into a house that drives you to drink. I would have to find other coping mechanisms. Like . . . nature.

I went back to the living room, fished my toothbrush from my bag, and brushed at the kitchen sink. The next essential step for me to go on existing was a coffee IV.

Whenever I drafted a book, I pretty much lived in my illustrious give-up pants, so aside from a collection of equally terrible sweatpants, I'd packed pretty lightly for this trip. I'd even watched a handful of lifestyle vloggers' videos about "capsule wardrobes" in an attempt to maximize the amount of "looks" I could "build" from a pair of Daisy Dukes I mostly wore when I was stress-cleaning and a collection of ratty T-shirts with celebrities' faces on them—remnants from a phase in my early twenties.

I pulled on a somber black-and-white Joni Mitchell, stuffed my booze-bloated body into the denim cutoffs, and put on my floral-embroidered ankle boots.

I had a thing about shoes, from the very cheap and tacky to the very expensive and dramatic. As it turned out, this "thing" of mine was fairly incompatible with the whole capsule wardrobe concept. I'd only packed four pairs, and I doubted anyone would consider my sparkly Target tennis shoes or the over-the-knee Stuart Weitzman boots I'd splurged on to be "classic."

I grabbed my car keys and was heading out into the blinding summer sun when I heard my phone buzzing from within the couch cushions. A message from Shadi: Made out with the Haunted Hat, followed by a bunch of skulls.

As I stumbled outside again, I typed back: SEE A PRIEST IMMEDIATELY.

I tried not to think about last night's humiliating face-off with the neighbor as I jogged down the steps to the Kia, but that just freed up my mind to wander to my least favorite subject.

Dad. The last time we'd gone boating together, he'd driven us to the man-made lake in the Kia and told me he was giving it to me. It was also the day he told me I should go for it: move to New York. Jacques was already there for medical school, and we were doing the long-distance thing so I could be with Mom. Dad had to travel a lot for "work," and even if I ultimately believed my own story—that our lives would always, ultimately, work out—a big

27

part of me was still too scared to leave Mom alone. As if my absence would somehow make room for the cancer to creep back in a third time.

"She's fine," Dad had promised as we sat in the frigid, dark parking lot.

"It could come back," I'd argued. I didn't want to miss a second with her.

"Anything could happen, January." That was what he'd said. "Anything could happen to Mom, or me, or even you, at any point. But right now, nothing is. Do something for yourself for once, kiddo."

Maybe he thought my moving to New York to live with my boyfriend was, at its core, the same as him buying a second house to hide away with his mistress. I'd given up grad school to help take care of Mom during that second round of chemo, put every cent I could toward helping with medical bills, and where had he been then? Wearing a windbreaker and drinking pinot noir on the beach with That Woman?

I pushed the thought away as I slid into the car, the leather hot against my thighs, and pulled away from the curb, cranking down the window as I went.

At the end of the street, I turned left, away from the water, and headed into town. The inlet that reached down along the right side of the road threw slivers of sparkling light against my window, and the hot wind roared in my ears. For a minute, it was like my life had ceased to exist around me. I was just floating past hordes of scantily clad teenagers milling around the hot dog stand on my left, parents and kids lined up out the door of the ice cream shop on my right, packs of cyclists riding back toward the beach.

As I cruised down the main drag, the buildings clumped closer until they were pressed shoulder to shoulder: a tiny Italian restaurant with vine-covered terraces flush with a skate shop, pressing it into the Irish pub next door, followed by an old-fashioned candy shop, and finally a café called Pete's Coffee—not to be confused with Peet's, though the sign looked, actually, like it was specifically trying to be confused with Peet's.

I pulled into a parking spot and ducked into the sweet chill of Pete Not Peet's air-conditioning. The floorboards were painted white and the walls were a deep blue, speckled with silver stars that swirled between tables, interrupted by the occasional framed platitude attributed to "Anonymous." The room opened directly into a well-lit bookstore, the words PETE'S BOOKS painted in that same auspicious silver over the doorway. An elderly couple in fleece vests sat in the half-collapsed armchairs in the back corner. Aside from the late-middle-aged woman at the register and me, they were the only people here.

"Much too nice of a day to be inside, I s'pose," the barista said, as if reading my thoughts. She had a gruff voice to match her blonde crew cut, and her tiny gold hoop earrings winked in the soft lighting as she waved me forward with a set of pale pink fingernails. "Don't be shy. We're all family at Pete's."

I smiled. "God, I hope not."

She slapped the counter as she laughed. "Oh, family's tricky," she agreed. "Anyway, what can I get you?"

"Jet fuel."

She nodded sagely. "Oh, you're one of those. Where are you from, honey?"

"New York most recently. Ohio before that."

"Oh, I've got family in New York. The state, not the city. You're talking about the city though, aren't you?"

"Queens," I confirmed.

"Never been," she said. "You want any milk? Any syrup?"

"I'd do some milk," I said.

"Whole? Half? One-sixteenth?"

"Surprise me. I'm not picky when it comes to fractions."

She threw her head back and laughed again as she moved lackadaisically between machines. "Who has time to be? I swear, even North Bear Shores moves too fast for me most days. Maybe if I took up drinking this 'jet fuel' of yours it'd be a different story."

Having a barista who did *not* drink espresso wasn't ideal, but I liked the woman with the tiny gold earrings. Honestly, I liked her so much that it sent a little pang of longing through me.

For the old January. The one who loved throwing themed parties and coordinating group costumes, who couldn't go to the gas station or stand in line at the post office without winding up making plans to grab coffee or hit up a gallery opening with someone I just met. My phone was riddled with contacts like *Sarah, the anchor bar, cute dog* and *Mike, runs that new vintage store*. I'd even met Shadi in a pizza shop bathroom when she came out of the stall wearing the best Frye boots I'd ever seen. I missed feeling that deep curiosity about people, that spark of excitement when you realized you had something in common or admiration when you uncovered a hidden talent or quality.

Sometimes, I just missed *liking* people.

But this barista, she was thoroughly likable. Even if the coffee sucked, I knew I'd be back. She tucked the plastic lid on the cup and plopped it down in front of me. "No charge for first-timers," she said. "I just ask that you return."

I smiled, promised I would, and stuffed my last dollar bill into the tip jar as she went back to mopping up the counters. On my way back to the door, I froze, Anya's voice running through my head: *Heeeeeeey, sugar cube! SERIOUSLY not trying to overstep, but you know, book clubs are your DREAM market. If you're literally IN a small-town bookstore, you should pop over and say hey!*

I knew Imaginary Anya was right. Right now, every sale mattered to me.

Plastering a smile on my face, I passed through the doorway into the bookstore. If only I could travel back in time and choose to put on *any* outfit *besides* the 2002 Jessica Simpson music video extra costume I was sporting.

The store was small oak shelves along the outside walls and a hodgepodge labyrinth of shorter bookshelves tunneling back and forth between them. The register was unattended, and as I waited, I glanced toward the trio of braces-wearing preteens in the romance section to make sure it wasn't one of *my* books they were giggling over. All four of us would be irrevocably traumatized if the bookseller led me over to sign stock only to discover a copy of *Southern Comfort* in the redhead's hands. The girls gasped and tittered as the redhead clutched the book to her chest, revealing the cover: a topless man and woman embracing as flames leapt around them. Definitely not one of mine.

I took a sip of the latte and promptly spit it back into the cup. It tasted like mud.

"Sorry about the wait, hon." The scratchy voice came from over my shoulder, and I spun to face the woman zigzagging toward me through the crooked rows of shelves. "These knees don't move like they used to."

At first, I thought she must be the barista's identical twin, sisters who'd opened the business together, but then I realized the woman was untying her gray PETE's apron from her waist as she made her way to the register.

"Do you believe I used to be a roller derby champion?" she said as she dropped the wadded apron on the counter. "Well, believe it or not, I did."

"At this point I'd hardly be surprised to find out you're the mayor of North Bear Shores."

She gave a rattling laugh. "Oh, no, can't say that I am! Though maybe I could get some shit done around here, if they'd have me! This town is a nice little pocket of progressivism here in the Mitten, but the people with the purse strings are still a bunch of pearl-clutching golf bags."

I fought a smile. It sounded so much like something Dad would've said. The ache seared through me, fire-poker sharp and hot.

"Anyway, don't mind me and my O-PIN-YUNS," she enunciated, lifting her thick ash-blonde brows. "I'm just a lowly entrepreneur. What can I do you for, sugar?"

"I just wanted to introduce myself," I admitted. "I'm a writer, actually, with Sandy Lowe Books, and I'm here for the summer, so I figured I'd say hi, sign stock if you have any."

"Ohhh, another writer in town!" she cried. "How exciting! You know, North Bear brings in a lot of artist types. It's our way of life, I think. And the college. All sorts of freethinkers over there. A beautiful little community. You're going to love it here . . ." The way her words dropped off suggested she was waiting for me to insert my own name at the end of her sentence.

"January," I chimed in. "Andrews."

"Pete," she said, shaking my hand with the vigor of a green beret who's just said, *Put 'er there, son!*

"Pete?" I said. "Of Pete's Coffee fame?"

"The very same. Legal name's Posy. What kind of a name is that?" She pantomimed gagging. "Seriously, do I look like a Posy to you? Does anyone look like a Posy?"

I shook my head. "Maybe, like, a baby wearing a polyester flower costume?"

"Soon as I could talk, I set that one straight. Anyway, January Andrews." Pete stepped up to the computer and plugged my name into the keyboard. "Let's see if we've got your book."

I never corrected people when they said singular "book" rather than plural "books," but sometimes the assumption dug under my skin. It made me feel like people thought my career was a fluke. Like I'd sneezed and a romance novel came out.

And then there were the people who acted like we were in on some secret joke together when, after a conversation about Art or Politics, they found out I wrote upbeat women's fiction: *Whatever pays the bills, right?* they'd say, practically begging me to confirm I didn't *want* to write books about women or love.

"Looks like we don't have any in stock," Pete said, looking up from the screen. "But I tell ya what, you'd better believe I'm ordering them in."

"That'd be great!" I said. "Maybe we could host a workshop later this summer."

Pete gasped and clutched my arm. "Idea, January Andrews! You should come to our *book club*. We'd love to have ya. Great way to get involved in the community. It's Mondays. Can you do Monday? Tomorrow?"

In my head, Anya said, *You know what made* The Girl on the Train *happen? Book clubs.*

That was a stretch. But I liked Pete. "Mondays work."

"Fan*tastic*. I'll send you my address. Seven PM, lots of booze, always a hoot." She pulled a business card from the desk and passed it across the counter. "You do email, don't you?"

"Almost constantly."

Pete's smile widened. "Well, you just shoot me a message and we'll make sure you're all set for tomorrow."

I promised her I would and turned to go, nearly colliding with the display table. I watched the pyramid of books tremble, and as I stood there, waiting to see if they'd fall, I realized the entire thing was made out of the same book, each marked with an AUTO-GRAPHED sticker.

An uncanny tingle climbed my spine.

There, on the abstract black-and-white cover, in square red letters, beneath *The Revelatories*, was his name. It was all coming together in my mind, a domino trail of realizations. I didn't mean to say it aloud, but I might have.

Because the bells over the bookshop door tinkled, and when I looked up, there he was. Olive skin. Cheekbones that could cut you. Crooked mouth and a husky voice I'd never forget. Messy, dark hair I could immediately picture haloed in fluorescent light.

Augustus Everett. Gus, as I'd known him back in college.

"Everett!" as Pete was calling affectionately from behind the desk.

My neighbor, the Grump.

I did what any reasonable adult woman would do when confronted with her college rival turned next-door neighbor. I dove behind the nearest bookshelf.

4

The Mouth

THE WORST PART of being college rivals with Gus Everett? Probably the fact that I wasn't sure he knew we were. He was three years older, a high school dropout who'd gotten his GED after spending a few years working as a literal gravedigger. I knew all of this because every story he turned in our first semester was part of a collection centering on the cemetery where he'd worked.

The rest of us in the creative writing program were pulling fodder from our asses (and childhoods: soccer games won in the last instant, fights with parents, road trips with friends), and Gus Everett was writing about the eight kinds of mourning widows, analyzing the most common epitaphs, the funniest, the ones that subtly betrayed a strained relationship between the deceased and the person footing the headstone's bill.

Like me, Gus was at U of M on a slew of scholarships, but it was unclear how he'd gotten them, since he played no sports and hadn't technically graduated from high school. The only explanation was that he was atrociously good at what he did.

To top things off, Gus Everett was stupidly, infuriatingly attractive. And not the universal kind of handsome that almost dulls itself with objectivity. It was more of a magnetism he emanated. Sure, he was just barely on the tall side of average, with the lean muscle of someone who never stopped moving around but also never intentionally exercised—a lazy kind of fit that came from genetics and restlessness rather than good habits—but it was more than that.

It was the way he talked and moved, how he looked at things. Not, like, how he saw the world. Literally how he *looked* at things, his eyes seeming to darken and grow whenever he focused, his eyebrows furrowing over his dented nose.

Not to mention his crooked mouth, which should've been outlawed.

Before she dropped out of U and M to become an au pair (a pursuit soon abandoned), Shadi would ask me nightly at dinner for updates on Sexy, Evil Gus, sometimes abbreviated as SEG. I was minorly besotted with him and his prose.

Until we finally spoke for the first time in class. I was passing out my latest short story for critique, and when I handed it to him, he looked me dead in the eyes—his head tilted curiously—and said, "Let me guess: Everyone lives happily ever after. Again."

I wasn't writing romance yet—I didn't even realize how much I loved *reading* romance until Mom's second diagnosis two years later, when I needed a good distraction—but I was definitely writing *romantically*, about a *good world*, where things happened for a reason, where love and human connection were all that really mattered.

And Gus Everett had looked at me with those eyes, deepening and darkening like they were sucking every bit of information about me into his skull, and he'd determined that I was a balloon in need of popping.

Let me guess: Everyone lives happily ever after. Again.

We spent the next four years taking turns winning our school's writing prizes and contests but managed to barely speak again, unless you counted workshops, during which he rarely critiqued anyone's stories except mine and nearly always showed up late without half his stuff and asked to borrow my pens. And there was one wild night at a frat party where we'd . . . not quite talked, but definitely interacted.

Frankly, we crossed paths *constantly*, partly because he dated two separate roommates of mine and plenty of other girls on my floor—though I use the term *dated* loosely. Gus was notorious for having a two-to-four-week dating shelf life, and while the first roommate had started things up with him hoping to be the exception, the second (and plenty of the others) went in fully aware Gus Everett was just someone you could have fun with, for up to thirty-one days.

Unless you wrote short stories with happy endings, in which case you were apparently far more likely to spend four years as rivals, pass another six occasionally Googling him to compare your careers, and then run into him here while dressed like a teen cheerleader at a car wash fundraiser.

As in, here. Now. Walking into Pete's Books.

I was already planning what I would text Shadi as I power walked down the side of the store, chin tucked and face angled into the shelves like I was casually browsing (whilst practically jogging, as one does).

"January?" Pete was calling. "January, where'd you go? I want you to meet someone."

I'm not proud to admit that when I froze, I was looking at the door, judging whether I could make it out of there without responding.

It's important to note that I knew for a fact there were bells over the door, and I *still* couldn't make an immediate decision.

Finally, I took a deep breath, forced a smile, and stepped out from between the shelves, clutching my god-awful latte like it was a handgun. "Hiiiiiiiiii," I said, then waved in a distinctly animatronic way.

I had to force myself to look directly at him. He looked just like he did in his author photo: all sharp cheekbones, furiously dark eyes, and the leanly muscled arms of a gravedigger turned novelist. He was wearing a rumpled blue (or faded black) T-shirt and rumpled dark blue (or faded black) jeans, and his hair had started streaking through with gray, along with the just-past-five-o'clock shadow around his crooked mouth.

"This is January Andrews," Pete announced. "She's a *writer*. Just moved here."

I could practically see the same realization dawning on his face that had just crashed down on mine, his eyes homing in as he pieced together whatever bits of me he'd caught in the dark last night.

"We've met, actually," he said. The fire of a thousand suns rushed to my face, and probably my neck and chest and legs and every other exposed inch of my body.

"Oh?" Pete said, delighted. "How's that?"

My mouth fell open silently, the word *college* somehow evading grasp, as my eyes shifted back to Gus's. "We're neighbors," he said. "I believe?"

Oh, God. Was it possible he didn't remember me at all? My name was January, for shit's sake. It wasn't like I was a Rebecca or a Christy/Christina/Christine. I tried not to think too hard about how Gus could have forgotten me, because doing so would only take my complexion from overcooked lobster to eggplant. "Right," I think I said. The phone beside the register began to ring, and Pete held up a finger excusing herself as she turned to answer it, leaving us alone.

"So," Gus said finally.

"So," I parroted.

"What sort of thing do you write, January Andrews?"

I did my best not to glance sideways at the stadium of *Revelatories* curling around the table behind me. "Romance, mostly."

Gus's eyebrow arched. "Ah."

"Ah, what?" I said, already on the defensive.

He shrugged. "Just 'ah.'"

I folded my arms. "That was an awfully knowing 'just ah.'"

He leaned against the desk and folded his arms too, his brow furrowing. "Well, that was fast," he said.

"What was?"

"Offending you. One syllable. Ah. Pretty impressive."

"Offended? This isn't my offended face. I look like this because

I'm tired. My weird-ass neighbor was blasting his crying soundtrack all night."

He nodded thoughtfully. "Yeah, must've been the 'music' that was making it so hard for you to walk last night too. Hey, if you think you might have a 'music' problem, there's no shame in getting help."

"Anyway," I said, still fighting a blush. "You never told me what *you* write, *Everett*. I'm sure it's something really groundbreaking and important. Totally new and fresh. Like a story about a disillusioned white guy, wandering the world, misunderstood and coldly horny."

A laugh barked out of him. "'Coldly horny'? As opposed to the very artfully handled sexual proclivities of your genre? Tell me, which do you find more fascinating to write: love-struck pirates or love-struck werewolves?"

And now I was seething again.

"Well, it's not really about *me* so much as what my *readers* want. What's it like writing Hemingway circle-jerk fan fiction? Do you know all your readers by name?" There was something sort of freeing about new January.

Gus's head tilted in that familiar way and his brow knit as his dark eyes studied me, the intensity of them making my skin prickle. His full lips parted as if he was about to speak, but just then Pete hung up the phone and slipped into our circle, cutting him off.

"What are the odds, eh?" Pete asked, clapping her hands together. "Two published writers on the same little street in North Bear Shores! I bet you two will be shooting the shit all summer. I told you this town was full of artists, didn't I, January? How do you like that?" She laughed heartily. "No sooner had I said it than Everett marches right in! The universe is on my side today, looks like."

The ringing of my phone in my pocket saved me from having to answer. For once, I scrambled to answer the call, eager to escape this conversation. I was hoping for Shadi, but the screen read ANYA, and my stomach sank.

I looked up to find Gus's dark eyes burning into me. The effect was intimidating. I glanced toward Pete. "Sorry—I've got to take this, but it was lovely meeting you."

"Back atcha!" Pete assured me as I retreated through the maze of shelves. "Don't forget to mail me an email!"

"See you at home," Gus called after me.

I answered Anya's call and slipped outside.

5

The Labradors

"S WEAR YOU CAN do this, January," Anya was saying as I zoomed out of town. "If I promise Sandy a book by September first, we have *got* to have *a book by September first*."

"I've written books in half that time," I shouted over the wind.

"Oh, I know you have. But we're talking about *this* manuscript. We're talking specifically about the one that's now taken fifteen months and counting. How far are you?"

My heart was racing. She was going to know I was lying to her. "It's not written," I said. "But it's planned. I just need some time to hammer it out, no distractions."

"I can do no distractions. I can be the Queen of Not Distracting You, but please. Please, please, please, don't lie to me about this. If you want a break—"

"I don't want a break," I said. And I couldn't afford one. I had to do whatever it took. Empty the beach house so I could sell it. Write a romance despite having recently lost close to all faith in love and humanity. "It's coming along great, actually."

Anya pretended to be satisfied, and I pretended to believe she was satisfied. It was June second and I had just under three months to write a book-like thing.

So of course, rather than heading straight home to work, I was driving to the grocery store. I'd had two sips of Pete's latte, and it was three sips too many. I dumped it in the trash can on my way into Meijer and replaced it with a giant iced Americano from the Starbucks kiosk inside before stocking up on enough drafting food (macaroni, cereal, anything that didn't require much prep) to last me a couple of weeks.

By the time I got home, the sun was high, the heat thick and sticky, but at least the iced espresso had softened the pounding in my skull. When I'd finished unloading the groceries, I carried my computer onto the deck, only to realize I'd let the battery die last night. I went back inside to plug it in and caught my phone buzzing on the table. A text from Shadi: No WAY. Sexy, Evil GUS? Did he ask about me? Tell him I miss him.

I typed back, Still sexy. Still EVIL. I will NOT tell him as I will NOT be speaking to him again, for as long as we both shall live. He didn't remember me.

Shadi answered immediately. Hmmmm, there is LITERALLY no way that's true. You are his fairy princess. His shadow self. Or he's yours or whatever.

She was referring to another humiliating Gus moment I'd tried to forget. He'd ended up in a general math class with Shadi and mentioned that he'd noticed we were friends. When she confirmed, he asked her what my "deal" was. When she asked him to elaborate on what the hell that meant, he'd shrugged and mumbled something about how I acted like a fairy princess who'd been raised by woodland creatures.

Shadi told him I was actually an empress who'd been raised by two very sexy spies.

Seeing him in the wild after all this time was horrifying, I told her. I'm traumatized. Please come nurse me back to health.

Soon, habibi, she wrote back.

I was aiming to write fifteen hundred words that day. I only made it to four hundred, but on the bright side, I also won twenty-eight consecutive games of spider solitaire before I stopped to stir-fry some veggies for dinner. After I'd eaten, I sat in the dark, folded up at the kitchen table, with a glass of red wine caught in the glow of my laptop. All I needed was a bad first draft. I'd written dozens of those, spat out faster than I could type and then painstakingly rewritten in the months following.

So why couldn't I just make myself *write* this *bad book*?

God, I missed the days when the words poured out. When writing those happy endings, those kisses in the rain and music-swelling, knee-on-the-ground proposal scenes had been the best part of my day.

Back then, true love had seemed like the grand prize, the one thing that could weather any storm, save you from both drudgery and fear, and writing about it had felt like the single most meaningful gift I could give.

And even if that part of my worldview was taking a brief sabbatical, it *had* to be true that sometimes, heartbroken women found their happy endings, their rain-falling, music-swelling moments of pure happiness.

My computer pinged with an email. My stomach started flipping and didn't stop until I'd confirmed it was just a reply from Pete, with the address for her book club and a one-sentence message: Feel free to bring your favorite drink or just yourself :)))

I smiled. Maybe some version of Pete would make it into the book.

"One day at a time," I said aloud, then swiped up my wine and wandered to the back door.

I cupped my hand around my eyes to block the glare on the glass and peered toward Gus's deck. Smoke had been pluming out of the firepit earlier, but it was gone now, the deck abandoned.

So I slid the door open and stepped out. The world was cast in shades of blue and silver, the gentle rush of the tide breaking on sand made louder by the silence of the rest of the world. A gust of wind blew off the treetops, making me shiver, and I tightened the robe around me, draining my wineglass, then turned back to the house.

At first, I thought the blue glow that caught my eye was coming from my own laptop, but the light wasn't coming from my house. It shone from the otherwise dark windows of Gus's place, bright enough that I could see him pacing in front of his table. He stopped suddenly and bent to type for a moment, then picked a beer bottle up off the table and began to pace again, his hand running through his hair.

I recognized that choreography well. He could *love-struck pirates and werewolves* me all he wanted, but when it came down to it,

Augustus Everett was still pacing in the dark, making shit up like the rest of us.

PETE LIVED IN a pink Victorian on the edge of the college campus. Even in the thunderstorm that had whipped off the lake that Monday evening, her home looked sweet as a dollhouse.

I parked along the curb and stared up at its ivy-encroached windows and charming turrets. The sun hadn't totally set yet, but the soft gray clouds that filled the sky diffused any light to a dim greenish glow, and the garden that sprawled from Pete's porch to her white picket fence looked lush and magical beneath its shroud of mist. This was the perfect escape from the writing cave I'd been hiding in all day.

I grabbed the tote bag full of signed bookmarks and *Southern Comfort* quote-pins from the passenger seat and jumped out of the car, pulling my hood up as I bolted through the rain and eased the gate open to slip in along the cobbled path.

Pete's garden was, quite possibly, the most picturesque place I'd ever been, but the best part might've been that, over the rumble of thunder, "Another Brick in the Wall" by Pink Floyd was playing so loudly that the porch was shivering as I stepped onto it.

Before I could knock, the door swung open and Pete, very full plastic blue wineglass in hand, sang out, "Jaaaaaaaaaaaaaanuary Andrews!"

Somewhere behind her, a chorus of voices sang back, "January Annnnnndrews!"

"Peeeeete," I sang in response, holding out the bottle of char-

47

donnay I'd grabbed from the store on the way over. "Thanks so much for having me."

"Ohhhh." She accepted the bottle of wine and scrunched up her eyes as she examined the label, then chuckled. It was called POCKETFUL OF POSIES, but I'd scratched POSIES out and written PETES in its place. "Sounds French!" she joked. "Which is the Dutch word for *fancy*!" She waved for me to follow her down the hall, toward the music. "Come on in and meet the girls."

There was a pile of shoes, mostly sandals and hiking boots, arranged neatly on a rug by the door, so I kicked off my heeled green rain boots and followed the barefoot trail Pete cut down the hall. Her toenails were painted lavender to match her fresh manicure, and in her faded jeans and white linen button-up, she struck a softer image than she had at the store.

We swept past a kitchen whose granite countertops were crowded with liquor bottles and stepped into the living room at the back of the house. "Normally, we use the garden, but normally God isn't bowling a perfect game overhead, so inside will have to do tonight. We're just waiting on one more."

The room was small enough to feel crowded with the five people total inside it. Of course, the three black Labradors snoozing on the couch (two of them) and armchair (the third) didn't help. Bright green wooden chairs had been dragged in, ostensibly for the humans to sit in, and arranged to form a small semicircle. One of the dogs jumped up and wandered, tail wagging, through the sea of legs to greet me.

"Girls," Pete said, touching my back, "this is January. January brought wine!"

"Wine, how lovely!" a woman with long blonde hair said,

48

sweeping forward to give me a hug and a kiss on the cheek. When the blonde pulled back, Pete passed her the bottle of wine, then edged around the room toward the sound system. "I'm Maggie," the blonde said. Her tall, willowy stature was made more striking by the sea of drapey white things she'd dressed herself in. She smiled down at me, equal parts Galadriel Lady of the Golden Wood and aging Stevie Nicks, and the wrinkled corners of her brown eyes crinkled sweetly. "So lovely to meet you, January."

Pete's voice came a bit too loudly as the music dropped out from under it: "She's Mrs. Pete."

Maggie's serene smile seemed to be a version of an affectionate eye roll. "Just Maggie will do. And this is Lauren." She opened an arm to make room for me to shake hands with the dreadlocked woman in the orange sundress. "And back there, on the couch, is Sonya."

Sonya. The name hit my stomach like a hammer. Before I'd even seen her, my mouth went dry. My vision fuzzed at the corners.

"Hi, January," That Woman said meekly from under the snoring Labradors. She forced a smile. "Nice to see you."

6

The Book Club

WAS THERE A dignified way to happen upon your dead father's lover? If so, I imagined it wasn't blurting *I have to pee*, jerking free the bottle of wine you'd handed your host, and running back down the hall in search of a bathroom. But that was the best I could come up with.

I twisted the top off the wine and poured it down my throat, right there in the nautical-themed bathroom. I considered leaving, but for some reason, that seemed like the most embarrassing option. Still, it occurred to me that I could walk out the door, get into the car, and drive to Ohio without stopping. I'd never have to see any of these people again. I could get a job at Ponderosa Steakhouse. Life could be grand! Or I could just stay in this bathroom, forever. I had wine; I had a toilet; what else did one need?

Admittedly, it was not my good attitude and strength of spirit that got me out of the bathroom. It was the shuffle of steps and conversation moving down the hallway, the sound of Pete saying, "Oh, you're *sure* you can't stay?" in a voice that made it sound much more like *What the hell, Sonya? Why is that weird little girl afraid of you?* and of Sonya saying, "No, I wish I could, but I totally forgot this work call—my boss won't stop emailing until I'm in the car and on my Bluetooth."

"Bluetooth shmootooth," Pete was saying.

"Indeed," I said into my wine bottle. The chardonnay was hitting me fast. I thought my way backward through my day, recounting my meals in an attempt to understand my immediate tipsiness. The only thing I could be *sure* I'd eaten was the fistful of mini marshmallows I'd grabbed on my way to a much-needed pee break.

Whoops.

The front door was opening. Goodbyes were being said over the pitter-patter of rain against the roof, and I was still locked in a bathroom.

I set the bottle on the sink, looked at myself in the mirror, and pointed fiercely at my small brown eyes. "This will be the hardest night you have all summer," I whispered. It was a lie, but I totally bought it. I smoothed my hair, shrugged out of my jacket, hid the wine bottle in my tote bag, and stepped back into the hallway.

"Sonya had to dip out," Pete said, but it sounded more like *What the hell, January?*

"Oh?" I said. "That's too bad." But it sounded more like *Praise be to the Bluetooth Shmootooth!*

"Indeed," Pete said.

I followed her back to the living room, where the Labradors

had rearranged themselves, along with the ladies. One of the dogs had moved over to the far side of the couch, Maggie having taken the vacant spot left behind, while the second one had relocated to the armchair, mostly on top of the third. Lauren was sitting in one of the high-backed green chairs, and Pete gestured for me to take the one next to her as she slid into a third. Pete checked the time on her leather watch. "Should be here any minute. Must've gotten caught in the storm! I'm sure we'll be able to get started soon."

"Great," I said. The room was still spinning a bit. I could barely look toward where Sonya had been curled on the couch, willowy and relaxed with her white curls piled on her head, the opposite of my tiny, straight-banged mother. I took the opportunity to dig through my bag (careful not to upend the wine) for the bookmarks.

Someone knocked on the door, and Pete leapt up. My heart stuttered at the thought that Sonya might've changed her mind and doubled back. But then a low voice was scratching down the hall, and Pete was back, bringing in tow a damp and disheveled Augustus Everett. He ran a hand through his peppered hair, shaking rain from it. He looked like he'd rolled out of bed and wandered here through the storm, drinking from a paper bag. Not that I was one to judge at this precise moment.

"Girls," Pete said, "I believe you all know the one and only Augustus Everett?"

Gus nodded, waved. Smiled? That seemed too generous a word for what he was doing. His mouth *acknowledged* the room, I would say, and then his eyes caught on mine, and the higher of his mouth's two corners twisted up. He nodded at me. "January."

My mind spun its feeble, wine-slick wheels trying to figure out what bothered me so much about the moment. Sure, there was smug Gus Everett. There was stumbling upon That Woman and the bathroom wine. And—

The difference in Pete's introductions.

This is January was how a parent forced one kindergartner to befriend another.

The one and only Augustus Everett was how a book club introduced its special guest.

"Please, please. Sit here, by January," Pete said. "Would you like a drink?"

Oh, God. I'd misunderstood. I wasn't here as a guest. I was here as a potential book club member.

I'd come to a book club that was discussing *The Revelatories*.

"Would you like something to drink?" Pete asked, looping back to the kitchen.

Gus scanned the blue plastic glasses in Lauren and Maggie's hands. "What are you having, Pete?" he asked over his shoulder.

"Oh, first round at book club's always White Russians, but January brought some wine, if that sounds better."

I balked both at the thought of *starting* a night with a White Russian and at the prospect of having to shamefully fish out my purse-wine for Gus.

I could tell by the huge grin on her face that nothing would delight Pete more.

Gus leaned forward, resting his elbows on his thighs. The left sleeve of his shirt rose with the motion, revealing a thin black tattoo on the back of his arm, a twisted but closed circle. A Möbius strip, I thought it was called.

"A White Russian sounds great," Gus answered.

Of course it did.

People liked to imagine their favorite male authors sitting down at a typewriter with a taste of the strongest whiskey and a hunger for knowledge. I wouldn't be surprised if the rumpled man sitting beside me, the one who'd mocked *my* career, was wearing dirty day-of-the-week underwear inside out and living on Meijer-brand cheese puffs.

He could show up looking like a college junior's backup pot dealer (for when the first one was in Myrtle Beach) and still get taken more seriously than I would in my stuffy Michael Kors dress. I could get author photos taken by the senior photo editor of *Bloomberg Businessweek* and *he* could use his mom's digital camera from 2002 to snap a shot of himself scowling on his deck and still garner more respect than me.

He might as well have just sent in a dick pic. They would've printed it on the cover flap, right over that two-line bio they'd let him shit out. *The shorter, the fancier,* Anya would say.

I sensed Gus's eyes on me. I imagined *he* sensed my brain tearing him to pieces. I imagined Lauren and Maggie sensed this night had been a terrible mistake.

Pete returned with another blue wineglass full of milky vodka, and Gus thanked her for it. I took a deep breath as Pete slid into a chair.

Could this night get any worse?

The Labrador nearest to me audibly farted.

"Okay, then!" Pete said, clapping her hands together.

What the hell. I slid my purse-wine out and took a gulp. Maggie giggled on the couch, and the Labrador rolled over and stuffed his face in between the cushions.

"Red, White Russians, and Blue Book Club is now in session, and I'm dying to hear what everyone thought of the book."

Maggie and Lauren exchanged a look as they each took a slurp of their White Russians. Maggie set hers on the table and lightly slapped her thigh. "Heck, I loved it."

Pete's laugh was gruff but warm. "You love everything, Mags."

"Do not. I didn't like the man spy—not the main one, but the other one. He was snippy."

Spies? There were *spies* in *The Revelatories*? I looked over at Gus, who looked as puzzled as I felt. His mouth was ajar and his White Russian rested against his left thigh.

"I didn't care for him either," Lauren agreed, "especially in the beginning, but he came around by the end. When we got the backstory about his mother's ties to the USSR, I started to understand him."

"That was a nice touch," Maggie agreed. "All right, I take it back. By the end, I sort of liked him too. I still didn't care for the way he treated Agent Michelson though. I won't make excuses for that."

"Well, no, of course not," Pete chimed in.

Maggie waved her hand lightly. "Total misogynist."

Lauren nodded. "How did you all feel about the twin reveal?"

"Honestly, it bored me a bit, and I'll tell ya why," Pete said. And then she did tell us why, but I barely heard it because I was so absorbed in the subtle gymnastics Gus's expression was performing.

This could not possibly be his book they were talking about. He didn't look horrified so much as bemused, like he thought someone was playing a prank on him but he wasn't confident enough to call it out yet. He'd drained his White Russian already and was glancing back at the kitchen like he was hoping another might carry itself out here.

"Did anyone else cry when Mark's daughter sang 'Amazing Grace' at the funeral?" Lauren asked, clutching her heart. "That got to me. It really did. And you *know* my heart of stone! Doug G. Hanke is just a phenomenal writer."

I looked around the room, to the credenza, the bookshelves on the far side of the couch, the magazine rack under the coffee table. Names and titles jumped out at me from dozens, if not hundreds, of dark paperbacks.

Operation Skyforce. The Moscow Game. Deep Cover. Red Flag. Oslo After Dark.

Red, White Russians, and Blue Book Club.

I, January Andrews, romance writer, and literary wunderkind Augustus Everett had stumbled into a book club trafficking primarily in spy novels. It took some effort to stifle my laughter, and even then I didn't do an amazing job.

"January?" Pete said. "Is everything all right?"

"Spectacular," I said. "Think I've just had too much purse-wine. Augustus, you'd better take it from here." I held the bottle out to him. He lifted one stern, dark eyebrow.

I imagined I wasn't quite smiling but managed to look victorious nonetheless as I waited for him to accept the two-thirds-drunk chardonnay.

"I've thought about it some more," Maggie said airily. "And I think I *did* like the identical twin twist."

Somewhere, a Labrador farted.

7

The Ride

T HANK YOU SOOOO much for having us, Pete," I said as I
pulled her into a hug in the foyer.

She patted my back. "Any time. Any Monday, especially! Heck,
every Monday. Red, White Russians, and Blue could use fresh
blood. You see how things get stale in there. Maggie likes to hu-
mor me, but she's not much of a fiction person, and I think Lauren
comes for the socializing. She's another faculty wife, like me."

"Faculty wife?" I said.

Pete nodded. "Maggie works at the university with Lauren's
husband," she answered quickly, then said, "How are you getting
home, dear?"

I wasn't feeling the wine nearly as much as I would've liked to
at that point, but I knew I shouldn't risk driving anyway.

"I'll take her," Gus said, stern and unamused.

"I'll Uber," I said.

"Uber?" Pete repeated. "Not in North Bear Shores, you won't. We've got about one of those, and I doubt he's out driving around after ten o'clock!"

I pretended to look at my phone. "Actually, he's here, so I should go. Thanks again, Pete. Really, it was . . . extremely interesting."

She patted my arm and I slipped out into the rain, opening the Uber app as I went. Beneath the rain, I heard Gus and Pete exchanging quiet goodbyes on the porch behind me, and then the door shut and I knew he and I were alone in the garden.

So I walked very fast, through the gate and down the length of the fence, as I stared at the blank map on my Uber app. I closed the app and opened it again.

"Let me guess," Gus drawled. "It's exactly as the person who actually lives here says: there aren't any Ubers."

"Four minutes away," I lied. He stared at me. I pulled my hood up and turned away.

"What is it?" he said. "Are you worried it's a slippery slope from getting into my car to going down the Slip 'N Slide on my roof and competing in my heavily publicized Jell-O wrestling matches?"

I folded my arms. "I don't know you."

"Unlike the North Bear Shores Uber driver, with whom you're quite close."

I said nothing, and after a moment, Gus climbed into his car, its engine sputtering awake, but he didn't pull away. I busied myself with my phone. Why wasn't he leaving? I did my best not to look at his car, though it was looking more appealing every moment I stood there in the cold rain.

I checked the app again. Still nothing.

The passenger window rolled down, and Gus leaned across the seat, ducking his head to see me. "January." He sighed.

"Augustus."

"It's been four minutes. No Uber's coming. Would you please get in the car?"

"I'll walk."

"Why?"

"Because I need the exercise," I said.

"Not to mention the pneumonia."

"It's like sixty-five degrees out," I said.

"You're literally shivering."

"Maybe I'm trembling with the anticipation of an exhilarating walk home."

"Maybe your body temperature is plummeting and your blood pressure and heart rate are dropping and your skin tissue is breaking up as it freezes."

"Are you kidding? My heart is positively *racing*. I just sat in on a *three-hour-long* book club meeting about *spy novels*. I *need* to run some of this adrenaline off." I started down the sidewalk.

"Wrong way," Gus called.

I spun on my heel and started in the other direction, back past Gus's car. His mouth twisted in the dim light of the console. "You do realize we live seven miles from here. At your current pace that puts your arrival at about . . . never. You're going to walk into a bush and quite possibly spend the rest of your life there."

"That's actually the perfect amount of time I'll need to sober up," I said. Gus pulled slowly down the road alongside me. "Besides, I can*not* risk waking up with another hangover tomorrow. I'd rather walk into traffic."

"Yeah, well, I'm worried you're going to do both. Let me take you home."

"I'll fall asleep tipsy. Not good."

"Fine, I won't take you home until you're sober, then. I know the best trick for that in all of North Bear Shores."

I stopped walking and faced his car. He stopped too, waiting.

"Just to be clear," I said, "you're not talking about sex stuff, are you?"

His smile twisted. "No, January, I'm not talking about sex stuff."

"You'd better not be." I opened the passenger door and slid onto the seat, pressing my fingers to the warm vents. "Because I carry pepper spray in this tote. And a gun."

"What the *fuck*," he cried, putting the car in park. "You're drunk with a *gun* flopping around in your wine bag?"

I buckled my seat belt. "It was a joke. The gun part, not the 'killing you if you try something' part. I meant that."

His laugh was more shocked than amused. Even in the dark of the car, I could see his eyes were wide and his crooked mouth was tensed. He shook his head, wiped the rain off his forehead with the back of his hand, and put the car back into drive.

"THIS IS THE trick?" I said, when we pulled into the parking lot. The rain had slowed but the puddles in the cracking asphalt's potholes glowed with the reflection of the neon sign over the low, rectangular building. "The trick for sobering up is . . . donuts." That was all the sign said. For all intents and purposes, it was the diner's name.

"What did you expect?" Gus asked. "Was I supposed to *almost* drive off a cliff, or hire someone to fake-kidnap you? Or wait, was that sex-stuff comment sarcastic? Did you *want* me to seduce you?"

"No, I'm just saying, next time you're trying to convince me to get in your car, you'll save a lot of time if you cut right to *donuts*."

"I'm hoping I won't have to coax you into my car very often," he said.

"No, not very often," I said. "Just on Mondays."

He cracked another smile, faint, like he'd rather not reveal it. It instantly made the car feel too small, him a little too close. I tore my gaze away and got out of the car, head clearing immediately. The building glowed like a bug zapper, its empty, seventies-orange booths visible through the windows along with a fish tank full of koi.

"You know, you should consider driving for Uber," I said.

"Oh?"

"Yeah, your heat works great. I bet your air-conditioning's decent too. You don't smell like Axe, and you didn't say a word to me the whole way here. Five stars. Six stars. Better than any Uber driver I've had before."

"Hm." Gus pulled the smudgy door open for me, bells jangling overhead. "Maybe next time you get into an Uber, you should try announcing that you have a loaded gun. You might get better service."

"Truly."

"Now don't be alarmed," he said under his breath as I stepped past him.

"What?" I turned back to ask.

"Hello!" a voice called brightly over the Bee Gees song crackling through the place.

I spun to face the man behind the illuminated display case. The radio sat there on the counter, producing at least as much static fuzz as crooning disco. "Hi," I replied.

"Howdy," the man said with a deep nod. He was at least as old as my parents and wire-thin, his thick glasses held to his face with neon-yellow Croakies.

"Hi," I said again. My brain was caught in a hamster wheel, the same realization playing over and over: this elderly gentleman was in his underwear.

"Welllll, hello there!" he chirped, apparently determined not to lose this game. He leaned his elbows on top of the case. His underwear, thankfully, included a white T-shirt, and he had mercifully opted for white boxers rather than briefs.

"Hi," I said one last time.

Gus sidestepped between my open jaw and the counter. "Can we just do a dozen day-olds?"

"Shore!" The underwear-baker grapevined down the length of the display and grabbed a to-go box from the stack on top of it. He carried it back to the old-school register and tapped out a couple of numbers. "Five dollars flat, my man."

"And coffee?" Gus said.

"Can't in good conscience charge you for that stuff." The man jerked his head toward the carafe. "That shit's been sitting in there sizzling for three good hours. Want me to make you the new stuff?"

Gus looked to me pointedly.

"What?" I asked.

"It's for you. What do you think? Free and bad? Or a dollar and . . ." He couldn't bring himself to say *good*, which told me everything I needed to know.

"That shit" was *always* sitting in there, sizzling.

"Free," I said.

"Five flat, then, as discussed," the man said.

I reached for my wallet, but Gus headed me off, slapping five dollar bills down on the counter. He tipped his head, gesturing for me to accept the foam cup and box of donuts the man was holding. To fit twelve into this box, they'd been compacted into one box-shaped mash of fried dough. I grabbed them and plopped into a booth.

Gus sat across from me, leaned across the table, and pried the box open. He stared down at the donut guts between us. "God, those look disgusting."

"Finally," I said. "Something we agree on."

"I bet we agree on a lot." He plucked a mangled maple-nut donut out and sat back, examining it in the fluorescent light.

"Such as?"

"All the important stuff," Gus said. "The chemical composition of Earth's atmosphere, whether the world needs six Pirates of the Caribbean movies, that White Russians should only be drunk when you're already sure you're going to vomit anyway."

He managed to fit the whole donut into his mouth. Then, without an ounce of irony, he made eye contact with me. I burst out laughing.

"Fffwaht?" he said.

I shook my head. "Can I ask you something?"

He chewed and swallowed enough to answer. "No, January, I'm not going to tell this guy to turn his music down." He reached over and snatched another donut clump from the box. "Now I have a question for you, Andrews. Why'd you move here?"

I rolled my eyes and ignored his question. "If I were going to ask you to encourage this guy to make one small change to his business practices, it would definitely not be the radio volume."

Gus's grin split wide, and even now, my stomach flipped traitorously. I wasn't sure I'd seen him smile like that before, and there was something intoxicating about it. His dark eyes flitted toward the counter and I followed his gaze. The underwear-clad man was positively boogying back and forth between his ovens. Gus's eyes came back to mine, hyperfocused. "Are you going to tell me why you moved here?"

I stuffed a donut chunk into my mouth and shook my head.

He half shrugged. "Then I can't answer your question."

"That's not how conversations work," I told him. "They're not just even trades."

"That's exactly what they are," he said. "At least, when you're not into foot jobs."

I covered my face with my hands, embarrassed, even as I said, "You were extremely rude to me, by the way."

He was silent for a minute. I flinched as his rough fingers caught my wrists and tugged my hands away from my face. His teasing smile had faded, and his brow was creased, his gaze inky-dark and serious. "I know. I'm sorry. It was a bad day."

My stomach flipped right side up again. I hadn't expected an apology. I'd certainly never gotten an apology for that *happily ever after* comment. "You were hosting a raging party," I said, recovering. "I'd love to see what a good day looks like for you."

The corner of his mouth twitched uncertainly. "If you removed the party, you'd be a lot closer. Anyway, will you forgive me? I've been told I make a bad first impression."

I crossed my arms, and, emboldened by the wine or his apology, I said, "That wasn't my first impression."

Something inscrutable passed across his face, vanishing before I could place it. "What was your question?" he said. "If I answer it, will you forgive me?"

"Not how forgiveness works either," I said. When he began to rub his forehead, I added, "But yes."

"Fine. One question," he said.

I leaned across the table. "You thought they were doing your book, didn't you?"

His brows knit together. "'They'?"

"Spies and Liquified Pies," I said.

He pretended to be aghast. "Do you perhaps mean Red, White Russians, and Blue Book Club? Because that nickname you just gave it is an affront to literature salons everywhere, not to mention Freedom and America."

I felt the smile break out across my face. I sat back, satisfied. "You totally did. You thought they were reading *The Revelatories*."

"First of all," Gus said, "I've lived here five years and Pete's never invited me to that book club, so yeah, it seemed like a fairly reasonable assumption at the time. Secondly"—he snatched a glazed cake donut from the box—"you might want to be careful, January Andrews. You just revealed you know the title of my book. Who knows what other secrets are on the verge of spilling out of you?"

"How do you know I didn't just Google it?" I countered. "Maybe I'd never heard of it before."

"How do you know that your Googling me wouldn't be even more amusing to me?" Gus said.

"How do you know I wasn't Googling you out of suspicion you had a criminal background?"

Gus replied, "How do you know I won't keep answering your questions with other questions until we both die?"

"How do you know I'll care?"

Gus shook his head, smiling, and took another bite. "Wow, this is terrible."

"The donuts or this conversation?" I asked.

"This conversation, definitely. The donuts are good. I Googled you too, by the way. You should consider getting a rarer name."

"I'll pass that suggestion along to the higher-ups, but I can't make any promises," I said. "There's all kinds of red tape and bureaucratic bullshit to go through."

"*Southern Comfort* sounds pretty sexy," he said. "You have a thing for Southern boys? No teeth and overalls really rev your engine?"

I rolled my eyes. "I'm led to believe you've never been to the South and possibly couldn't locate 'south' on a compass. Besides, why does everyone try to make women's writing semiautobiographical? Do people generally assume your lonely, white, male—"

"Coldly horny," Gus inserted.

"—*coldly horny* protagonists are you?"

He nodded thoughtfully, his dark eyes intent on me. "Good question. *Do* you assume I'm coldly horny?"

"Definitely."

This seemed to amuse him and his crooked mouth.

I glanced out the window. "If Pete wasn't planning on using either of our books, how did she just forget to tell us what the book club's pick was? I mean, if she just wanted us to join, you'd think she'd give us a chance to actually read the book."

"This wasn't an accident," Gus said. "It was an intentional manipulation of the truth. She knows there's no way I would've come tonight if I'd known what was really happening."

I snorted. "And what was the end goal of this nefarious plan? To become an eccentric side character in the next Augustus Everett novel?"

"What exactly do you have against my books, which you have allegedly not read?" he asked.

"What do you have against *my* books," I said, "which you have *certainly* not read?"

"What makes you so sure?"

"The pirate reference." I dug in to a strawberry frosted covered in sprinkles. "That's not the kind of romance I write. In fact, my books aren't even shelved as romance, technically. They're shelved as women's fiction."

Gus slumped against the booth and stretched his lean olive arms over his head, rolling his wrists to make them crack. "I don't understand why there'd need to be a full genre that's just books for women."

I scoffed. Here it was, that always-ready anger rising like it had been waiting for an excuse. "Yeah, well, you're not the only one who doesn't understand it," I said. "I know how to tell a story, Gus, and I know how to string a sentence together. If you swapped out all my Jessicas for Johns, do you know what you'd get? *Fiction.* Just fiction. Ready and willing to be read by anyone, but somehow by *being* a woman who *writes* about women, I've eliminated half the Earth's population from my potential readers, and you know what? I don't feel *ashamed* of that. I feel *pissed.* That people like you will assume my books couldn't possibly be worth your time, while meanwhile you could shart on live TV and the *New York Times* would praise your bold display of humanity."

Gus was staring at me seriously, head cocked, rigid line between his eyebrows.

"Now can you take me home?" I said. "I'm feeling nice and sober."

8

The Bet

GUS SLID OUT of the booth, and I followed, gathering the donut box and my cup of sizzling shit. It had stopped raining, but now heavy fog hung in clumps. Without another word, we got into the car and drove away from DONUTS, the word glowing teal in the rearview mirror.

"It's the happy endings," Gus said suddenly as he pulled onto the main drag.

"What?" My stomach clenched. *They all live happily ever after. Again.*

Gus cleared his throat. "It's not that I don't take romance seriously as a genre. And I like reading about women. But I have a hard time with happy endings." His eyes cautiously flashed my way, then went back to the road.

"A hard time?" I repeated, as if that would make the words make sense to me. "You have a hard time . . . *reading happy endings?*"

He rubbed at the curve of his bicep, an anxious tic I didn't remember. "I guess."

"Why?" I asked, more confused than offended now.

"Life is pretty much a series of good and bad moments right up until the moment you die," he said stiffly. "Which is arguably a bad one. Love doesn't change that. I have a hard time suspending my disbelief. Besides, can you think of a single real-life romance that actually ended like Bridget fucking Jones?"

There it was, the Gus Everett I knew. The one who'd thought I was hopelessly naive. And even if I had some evidence he'd been right, I wasn't ready to let him trash the thing that had once meant more to me than anything else, the genre that had kept me afloat when Mom relapsed and our whole imagined future disappeared like smoke on a breeze.

"*First* of all," I said, "'Bridget fucking Jones' is an ongoing series. It is literally the *worst* example you could have chosen to prove that point. It's the antithesis of the oversimplified and inaccurate stereotype of the genre. It does *exactly* what I aim to: it makes its readers feel known and understood, like their stories—*women's stories*—matter. And secondly, are you honestly saying you don't believe in love?"

I felt a little desperate, like if I let him win this fight, it would be the final straw: there'd be no getting back to myself, to believing in love and seeing the world and the people in it as pure, beautiful things—to loving writing.

Gus's brow furrowed, his dark eyes flashing from me to the road with that intent, absorbing look Shadi and I had spent so much time trying to put into words. "Sure, love happens," he said finally. "But it's better to be realistic so shit's not constantly blowing up in your face. And love is *way* more likely to blow up in your face than to bring eternal happiness. And if it doesn't hurt *you*, then you're the one hurting someone else.

"Entering a relationship is borderline sadomasochistic. Especially when you can get *everything* you would from a romantic relationship from a friendship, without destroying anyone's life when it inevitably ends."

"Everything?" I said. "Sex?"

He arched an eyebrow. "You don't even need *friendship* to get sex."

"And what, it never turns into more for you?" I said. "You can keep things that detached?"

"If you're realistic," he said. "You need a policy. It doesn't turn into more if it only happens once."

Wow. The shelf life had shortened. "See?" I said. "You *are* coldly horny, Gus."

He glanced sidelong at me, smiling.

"What?"

"That's the second time you've called me Gus tonight."

My cheeks flushed. Right, *Everett* seemed to be his preference these days. "So?"

"Come on, January." His eyes went back to the road, the twin spears of the headlights reaching over the asphalt and catching blips of the evergreens whipping past. "I remember you." His gaze settled on me again, his eyes nearly as solid and heavy as if they were hands.

I was grateful for the dark as heat rushed to my face. "From?"

"Stop. It wasn't that long ago. And there was that one night."

Oh, God. We weren't going to talk about *that one night*, were we?

The only night we'd talked outside of class. Well, not talked. We'd been at the same frat party. The theme had been a very vague "Classics."

Gus and his friend Parker had come as Ponyboy and Johnny and spent the night getting called "Greased Lightning" by drunk frat boys. Shadi and I had gone as truck-stop Thelma (her) and Louise (me).

Gus's girl-of-the-hour, Tessa, had gone home for the weekend. She and I lived in the same student apartments and wound up at a lot of the same parties. She was the latest reason Gus and I had been crossing paths, but *that* night was different.

It was the beginning of the school year, not quite fall. Shadi and I had been dancing in the basement, whose cement walls were sweating. All night, I'd been watching Gus, fuming a little because his last short story had been so good and he was still ridiculously attractive and his criticism was still on point and I was tired of him asking to borrow my pens, and furthermore, he'd caught me staring at him, and ever since, I'd felt—or thought (hoped?) I'd felt—him watching me too.

At the makeshift bar in the next room. At the beer pong table upstairs. In the kitchen at the keg. And then he was standing still in the throng of bodies jumping and frantically dancing to "Sandstorm" (Shadi had hijacked the iPod, as she was wont to do), only a few yards away from me, and we were both staring at each other, and somehow I felt vindicated by this, sure that all this time, he'd seen me as his competition after all.

I didn't know if I'd made my way to him, or if he'd made his way to me, or if we'd met in the middle. All I knew was that we'd ended up dancing with (on?) each other. There were flashes of memory from that night that still made me buzz: his hands on my hips, my hands on his neck, his face against my throat, his arms around my waist.

Coldly horny? No, Gus Everett had been all hot breath and sparking touches.

Rivalry or not, it had been palpable how much we wanted each other that night. We had both been ready to make a bad decision.

And then Shadi had saved the day by shaving her head in the bathroom with clippers she'd found under the sink and getting us both kicked out and banned from that particular frat's parties for life. Although we hadn't tried to go back in the last few years and I suspected frats had a rather short memory. Four years, max.

Apparently, I had a much longer memory.

"January?"

I looked up and startled at the dark gaze I'd been remembering, now here in the car with me. I'd forgotten the tiny white scar to the right of his Cupid's bow and now wondered how I'd managed it.

I cleared my throat. "You told Pete we just met the other night."

"I told her we were neighbors," he allowed. Eyes back on the road. Eyes back on me. It felt like a personal attack, the way he kept looking at me then away after just a second too long. His mouth twitched. "I wasn't sure you remembered me."

Something about that made my insides feel like a ribbon being drawn across scissors until it curled. He went on: "But no one calls me Gus except people I knew before publishing."

"Because?" I asked.

"Because I don't like every whack job next-door neighbor I've ever had to be able to Google me and leave me scathing reviews?" he said. "Or ask me for free books."

"Oh, I don't need free books," I assured him.

"Really?" he teased. "You don't want to add a fifth level to your shrine?"

"You're not going to distract me," I said. "I'm not done with this conversation."

"Shit. I honestly didn't mean to offend you," he promised. "Again."

"You didn't offend me," I said uncertainly. Or maybe he had, but his apology had caught me off guard yet again. More so, I was baffled. "I just think you're being silly."

We'd reached our houses without me even noticing, and Gus parked along the curb and faced me. For the second time I noticed how small the car was, how close we were, how the dark seemed to magnify the intensity of his eyes as they fixed on mine. "January, why did you come here?"

I laughed, uncomfortable. "Into the car you begged me to get into?"

He shook his head, frustrated. "You're different now."

I felt the blood rush into my cheeks. "You mean I'm not a fairy princess anymore."

Confusion rippled across his face.

"That's what you called me," I said, "back then. You want me to say you were right. I got my wake-up call and things don't work out like they do in my books, right?"

His head tilted, the muscle in his jaw leaping. "That's not what I was saying."

"It's exactly what you were saying."

He shook his head again. "Well, it's not what I meant," he said. "I meant to say . . . You were always so . . ." He huffed. "I don't know, you're drinking wine out of your purse. I'm guessing there's a reason for that."

My mouth jammed shut, and my chest tightened. Probably Gus Everett was the last person I'd expect to read me like that.

I looked out the window toward the beach house as if it were a glowing red emergency exit sign, a savior from this conversation. I could hear waves breaking on the shore behind the houses, but the fog hung too thick for me to see anything.

"I'm not asking you to tell me," Gus said after a second. "I just . . . I don't know. It's weird to see you like this."

I turned toward him and folded my legs up on the seat as I studied him, searching his expression for irony. But his face was serious, his dark eyes narrowed and his brow pinched, his head doing that particular half tilt that made me feel like I was under a microscope. The Sexy, Evil stare that suggested he was reading your mind.

"I'm not writing," I said. I wasn't sure why I was admitting it, least of all to Gus, but better him than Anya or Sandy. "I'm out of money, and my editor's *desperate* to buy something from me—and all I've got is a handful of bad pages and three months to finish a book someone other than my mom will spend US dollars on. That's what's going on."

I batted away thoughts of my tattered relationship with Mom and the conversation we'd had after the funeral to focus on the lesser evil of my situation.

"I've done it before," I said. "Four books, no problem. And it's bad enough that I feel like I'm incapable of doing the *one* thing I'm good at, *the* thing that makes me feel like *me*, and then there's the added fact that I'm totally out of money."

Gus nodded thoughtfully. "It's always harder to write when you *have* to. It's like . . . the pressure turns it into a job, like anything else, and you might as well be selling insurance. The story suddenly loses any urgency to be told."

"Exactly," I agreed.

"But you'll figure it out," he said coolly after a second. "I'm sure there are a million Happily Ever Afters floating around in that brain."

"Okay, A, no, there aren't," I said. "And B, it's not as easy as you think, Gus. Happy endings don't matter if the *getting there* sucks."

I tipped my head against the window. "At this point, it honestly might be easier for me to pack it in on the upbeat women's fiction and hop aboard the Bleak Literary Fiction train. At least it would give me an excuse to describe boobs in some horrifying new way. Like *bulbous succulents of flesh and sinew*. I never get to say *bulbous succulents of flesh* in my books."

Gus leaned back against the driver's side door and let out a laugh, which made me feel simultaneously bad for teasing him and ridiculously victorious for having made him laugh yet again. In college, I'd barely seen him crack a smile. Clearly I wasn't the only one who'd changed.

"You could *never* write like that," he said. "It's not your style."

I crossed my arms. "You don't think I'm capable?"

Gus rolled his eyes. "I'm just saying it's not who you are."

"It's not who I *was*," I corrected. "But as you've pointed out, I'm different now."

"You're going through something," he said, and again, I felt an uncomfortable prickle at him seeming to x-ray me like that, *and* at the spark of the old competitive flame Gus always ignited in me. "But I'd wager you're about as likely to churn out something dark and dreary as I am to go all *When Harry Met Sally*."

"I can write whatever I want," I said. "Though I can see how writing a Happily Ever After might be hard for someone whose happy endings usually happen during one-night stands."

Gus's eyes darkened, and his mouth hitched into an uneven smile. "Are you challenging me, Andrews?"

"I'm just saying," I parroted him, "it's not who you are."

Gus scratched his jaw, his eyes clouding as he recessed into thought. His hand dropped to rest over the steering wheel and his focus shifted sharply to me. "Okay," he said. "I have an idea."

"A *seventh* Pirates of the Caribbean movie?" I said. "It's so crazy it might work!"

"Actually," Gus said, "I thought we could make a deal."

"What sort of deal, Augustus?"

He visibly shuddered at the sound of his full name and reached across the car. A spark of anticipation—of what, I wasn't sure—rushed through me. But he was only opening the box in my lap and grabbing another donut. Coconut.

He bit into it. "You try writing bleak literary fiction, see if that's who you are now, if you're capable of being that person"—I rolled my eyes and snatched the last bite of donut from his hand. He went on, unbothered—"and I'll write a Happily Ever After."

My eyes snapped up to his. The fringes of the porch light were making their way through the fog now, brushing at the car window and catching at the sharp angle of his face and the dark wave that fell across his forehead. "You're kidding."

"I'm not," he said. "You're not the only one who's been in a rut. I could use a break from what I'm doing—"

"Because writing a romance will be *so* easy it will essentially be a nap for you," I teased.

"And *you* can lean into your bleak new outlook and see how it fits. If *this* is the new January Andrews. And whoever sells their book first—with a pen name, if you prefer—wins."

I opened my mouth to say something, but no words came out. I closed it and tried again. "Wins *what*?"

Gus's brow lifted. "Well, first of all, you'll have sold a book, so you can pay your bills and keep your purse stocked with wine. Secondly . . ." He thought for a moment. "The loser will promote the winner's book, write an endorsement for the cover, recommend it in interviews, choose it when guest judging for book clubs, and all that, guaranteeing sales. And thirdly, if you win, you'll be able to rub it in my face forever, which I suspect you'd consider nearly priceless."

I couldn't come close to hiding the smile blooming across my face. *"True."* Everything he was saying made at least *some* sense. Wheels were turning in my head—wheels that had been out of order for the past year. I really *did* think I could write the kind of book Gus wrote, that I could mimic The Great American Novel.

It was different with love stories. They meant too much to me, and my readers had waited too long for me to give them something I didn't wholeheartedly believe in.

It was all starting to add up. Everything except one detail. I narrowed my eyes. Gus exaggeratedly narrowed his back. "What do *you* stand to gain here?" I asked.

"Oh, all the same things," he said. "I want something to lord over you. And money. Money's always helpful."

"Uh-oh," I said. "Is there trouble in Coldly Horny Paradise?"

"My books take a long time to write," Gus said. "The advances have been good, but even with my scholarships, I had a lot of student loans, and some old debt, and then I put a lot into this house. If I can sell something quick, it will help me out."

I gasped and clutched my heart. "And you would stoop to peddling the sadomasochistic American dream of lasting love?"

Gus frowned. "If you're not into the plan, just forget it."

But now I couldn't forget it. Now I needed to prove to Gus that what I did was harder than it looked, that I was just as capable as he was. Besides, having Augustus Everett promote a book of mine would have benefits I couldn't afford to pass up.

"I'm in," I said.

His eyes bored into me, that evil smile climbing the corner of his top lip. "You sure? This could be truly humiliating."

An involuntary laugh sprang out of me. "Oh, I'm counting on it," I said. "But I'll make it a *little* easier on you. I'll throw in a rom-com crash course."

"Fine," Gus said. "Then I'll take you through my research process. *I'll* help you lean into your latent nihilism, and *you'll* teach me how to sing like no one's listening, dance like no one's watching, and love like I've never been hurt before."

His faint grin was contagious, if overconfident.

"You really think you can do this?" I asked.

He lifted one shoulder. "You think *you* can?"

I held his gaze as I thought. "And you'll endorse the book? If I win and sell the book, you'll write a shiny pull quote to slap on the cover, no matter how bad it is."

His eyes were doing the thing again. The sexy/evil thing where they expanded and darkened as he lost himself in thought. "I remember how you wrote when you were twenty-two," he said carefully. "It won't be bad."

I fought a blush. I didn't understand how he could do that, bounce between being rude, almost condescending, and disarmingly complimentary.

"But yes," he added, leaning forward. "Even if you give me a novelization of the sequel to *Gigli*, if you sell it, I will endorse it."

I sat back to put some distance between us. "Okay. So what about this? We spend our weekdays writing, and leave the end of the week for *education*."

"Education," he repeated.

"On Fridays, I'll go with you to do whatever research you would usually do. Which would include . . ." I gestured for him to fill in the blank.

He smiled crookedly. It was extremely evil. "Oh, all sorts of riveting things," he supplied. "And then on Saturdays, we'll do whatever you usually do for research—hot-air balloon trips, sailing lessons, two-person motorcycle rides, candlelit restaurants with patio seating and bad cover bands, and *all that* shit."

Heat spread up my neck. He had just nailed me, again. I mean, I hadn't done the two-person motorcycle rides (I had no death wish), but I *had* taken a hot-air balloon ride to prepare for my third novel, *Northern Light*.

The corner of his mouth twitched, apparently delighted by my expression.

"So. We have a deal?" He held out his hand to me.

My mind spun in dizzying circles. It wasn't like I had any *other* ideas. Maybe a depressed writer could only make a depressing book. "Okay." I slid my hand into his, pretending not to feel the sparks leaping from his skin straight into my veins.

"Just one more thing," he said soberly.

"What?"

"Promise not to fall in love with me."

"Oh my *God*!" I shoved his shoulder and flopped back into my seat, laughing. "Are you slightly misquoting *A Walk to Remember* at me?"

Gus cracked another smile. "Excellent movie," he said. "Sorry, *film*."

I rolled my eyes, still shivering with laughter.

A half laugh rattled out of him too. "I'm serious. I think I got to second base in the theater during that one."

"I refuse to believe anyone would cheapen the greatest love story involving Mandy Moore ever told by letting a teenage Gus Everett cop a feel."

"Believe whatever you want, January Andrews," he said. "Jack Reacher risks his life every day to guarantee you that freedom."

9

The Manuscript

WHEN I WOKE, I did *not* have a hangover, but I did have a text from Shadi, reading, He has a whole RACK of vintage hats!!!

And how would you know that? I texted back.

I climbed off the couch and went into the kitchen. While I still hadn't gathered enough courage to go upstairs, or even start sleeping in the downstairs guest bedroom, I'd started to find my way around the cupboards. I knew the rose-speckled kettle was already on the burner, that there was no coffeemaker in the kitchen, and that there was a French press and grinder down in the lazy Susan. This, I had to assume, was one of Sonya's contributions, because I'd never seen Dad drink anything but the Starbucks Keurig cups Mom bought in bulk or the green tea she begged him to have instead.

I wasn't a coffee snob myself—I could get behind flavored syrups and whipped toppings—but I started most mornings with something drinkable enough to have it black. I filled the kettle and turned the burner on, that warm, earthy smell of gas leaping to life with the flame. I plugged the grinder in and stared out the window as it worked. Last night's mist had held out, cloaking the strip of woods between the house and the beach in deep grays and blues. The house had chilled too. I shivered, pulling my robe tighter.

As I waited for the coffee to steep, my phone vibrated against the counter.

WELL, Shadi began, a bunch of us went out after work, and AS USUAL, he was totally ignoring me EXCEPT whenever I wasn't looking and then I could feel him just absolutely staring at me. So eventually he went to the bathroom and I also had to go so I was back in the hallway waiting and then he came out and was like "hey shad" and I was like "wow, I honestly thought you didn't speak until this moment" and he just like shrugged. So I was like "ANYWAY I was thinking about leaving." And he was like "oh, shit, really?" And he was just like, obviously disappointed, and then I was like, "Well, I was thinking about leaving with you." And he was SO nervous!! And like, excited like, "Yeah? That sounds good. When do you want to go?" and I was like "Duh. Now." And as you can see, the rest is history.

Wow, I typed back. It's a tale as old as time.

Truly, Shadi responded. Girl meets boy. Boy ignores girl except when she's not looking. Girl goes home with boy and sees him hang his haunted hat on a crowded rack.

The timer went off and I pressed the coffee and poured some into a mug shaped like a cartoonish orca whale, then took it and my computer out onto the deck, mist pleasantly chilling every bare inch of my skin. I curled up in one of the chairs and started to make a mental checklist for the day, and for the rest of the summer.

First and foremost, I needed to figure out where exactly this book was going, if not in the direction of a feel-good summer romance with a single father. Then I needed to plan out Saturday's romantic-comedy scenario for Gus.

My stomach flipped at the thought. I'd half expected to wake up in a panic about our agreement. Instead I was excited. For the first time in years, I was going to write a book that absolutely *no one* was waiting for. *And* I'd get to watch Gus Everett try to write a love story.

Or I was going to make a huge fool of myself and, far worse, disappoint Anya. But I couldn't think about that right now. There was work to do.

Aside from working on the book and scheduling the (actual only) Uber driver to take me to get my car from Pete's, I decided I'd conquer the second upstairs bedroom today and divide whatever was in there into throwaway, giveaway, and sell piles.

I also vowed to move my stuff into the downstairs bedroom. I'd done okay on the couch the first few nights but had awoken this morning to some serious kinks in my neck.

My gaze wandered toward the swath of windows along the back of Gus's house. At that precise moment, he walked into his kitchen, pulling a (shocker!) rumpled, dark T-shirt over his head. I spun back in my deck chair.

He couldn't have seen me watching him. But the more I thought about it, the more I worried that I might've stared for a couple of seconds before looking away. I could vividly picture the curves of Gus's arms as he tugged the shirt over his head, a flat length of stomach framed by the sharp angles of hip bones. He was a little softer than he'd been in college (not that it took much), but it suited him. Or maybe it just suited me.

Well. I had definitely stared.

I glanced back quickly and started. Gus was standing in front of the glass doors now. He lifted his mug as if to toast me. I lifted mine in response, and he shuffled away.

If Gus Everett was getting to work already, I also needed to. I opened my computer and stared at the document I'd been picking at for the last few days. A meet-cute. There weren't meet-cutes in Augustus Everett novels, that was for damn sure.

What was there? I hadn't read either of them, not *Rochambeau* and not *The Revelatories*, but I'd read enough reviews of them to satiate my curiosity.

People doing the wrong thing for the right reasons. People doing the right thing for the wrong reasons. Only getting what they wanted if it would ultimately destroy them.

Twisted, secretive families.

Well, I had no experience there! The ache shot through me. It felt like the first few seconds of a burn, when you couldn't tell whether it was heat or cold burrowing into your skin but knew either way it would leave damage.

The memory of my fight with Mom after the funeral rose up like a tidal wave.

Jacques had left for the airport the second the service was over to make it back for work, missing the showdown with Sonya entirely, and once *she'd* fled, Mom and I didn't stick around for long either.

We fought the whole drive back to the house. No, that wasn't true. I fought. Years' worth of feelings I'd chosen not to feel. Years of betrayal forcing them out.

"How could you keep this from me?" I'd shouted as I drove.

"She wasn't supposed to come here!" Mom had said, then buried her face in her hands. "I can't talk about this," she'd sobbed, shaking her head. "I *can't*."

From then on, anything else I said was answered with this: *I can't talk about this. I can't talk about him like this. I'm not going to talk about it. I can't.*

I should have understood. I should have cared more what Mom was feeling.

This was meant to be the moment that I became the adult, hugging her tight, promising everything would be okay, taking her pain. That's what grown daughters did for their mothers. But back in the church, I'd torn in half and everything had spilled out of me into plain view for the first time.

Hundreds of nights I'd chosen not to cry. Thousands of moments I'd worried about *worrying*. That if I did it, I'd make things worse for my parents. That I needed to be strong. That I *needed* to be happy so I wouldn't drag them down.

All those years when I was *terrified* my mother would die, I'd tucked every ugly thing out of sight to transform my life into a shiny window display for her benefit.

I'd made my parents laugh. I'd made them proud. I'd brought home solid grades, fought tooth and nail to keep up with Gus Everett. I'd stayed up late reading with Dad and gotten up early to pretend I liked yoga with Mom. I'd told them about my life, asked them endlessly about theirs so I'd never regret wasting time with them. And I hid the complicated feelings that came with trying to memorize someone you loved, just in case.

I fell in love at twenty-two, just like they had, with a boy named Jacques who was the singularly most beloved and interesting person I'd met, and I paraded our happiness past them as often as I could. I gave up on grad school to be close to them but proved I hadn't *really* missed out on anything by publishing at twenty-five.

Look! I'm fine! Look! I have every beautiful thing you wanted for me! Look! This hasn't affected me at all!

Look, they all live happily ever after. Again.

I'd done everything I could to prove that I was okay, that I wasn't worrying. I did everything I could for *that* story. The one where the three of us were unbreakable.

On the drive home from the funeral, I didn't want to be okay anymore.

I wanted to be a kid. I wanted to scream, to slam doors, to yell, "I hate you! You're ruining my life!" like I never had.

I wanted Mom to ground me, then sneak into my room later and kiss my forehead, whisper, "I understand how scared you are."

Instead, she wiped away her tears, took a deep breath, and repeated, "I'm not going to talk about this."

"Fine," I said, defeated, broken. "We won't talk about it."

When I flew back to New York, everything changed. Mom's calls became rare, and even when they *did* happen, they hit like a tornado. She'd cyclone through every detail of her week, then ask how I was doing, and if I hesitated too long she'd panic and excuse herself for some exercise class she'd forgotten about.

She'd spent years preparing for her own death without any time to brace herself for *this*. For him to leave us and for the ugly truth to walk into his funeral and tear all our pretty memories in half. She was in pain. I knew that.

But I was in pain too, so much of it that for once I couldn't laugh or dance any measure of it away. I couldn't even write myself a happy ending.

I didn't want to sit here in front of my laptop outside this house full of secrets and exorcise my father's memory from my heart. But apparently I'd found the one thing I *could* do. Because I'd already started typing.

> *The first time she met the love of her father's life was at his funeral.*

MY LOVE AFFAIR with romance novels had started in the waiting room of my mother's radiologist's office. Mom didn't like for me to go in with her—she insisted it made her feel senile—so I'd sat with a well-worn paperback from the rack, trying to distract myself from the ominous ticking of the clock fixed over the sign-in window.

I'd expected to stare at one page for twenty minutes, caught in the hamster wheel of anxiety. Instead I'd read 150 pages and then accidentally stuffed the book in my purse when it was time to go home.

It was the first wave of relief I'd felt in weeks, and from there, I binge-read every romance novel I could get my hands on. And then, without any true plans, I started writing one, and that feeling, *that* feeling of falling head over heels in love with a story and its characters as they sprang out of me, was unlike anything else.

Mom's first diagnosis taught me that love was an escape rope, but it was her second diagnosis that taught me love could be a life vest when you were drowning.

The more I worked on my love story, the less powerless I felt in the world. I may have had to ditch my plan to go to grad school and find a teaching job, but I could still help people. I could give them something *good*, something funny and hopeful.

It worked. For years, I had a purpose, something good to focus on. But when Dad died, suddenly writing—the one thing that had always put me at ease, a verb that felt more like a place only for me, the thing that had freed me from my darkest moments and brought hope into my chest in my heart's heaviest—had seemed impossible.

Until now.

And okay, this was more of a diary written in third person than a novel, but words were coming out of my hands and it had been so long since that had happened I would've rejoiced to find *ALL WORK AND NO PLAY MAKES JACK A DULL BOY* filling up the Word document a thousand times over.

This had to be better than *that* (????):

> She had no idea whether her father had actually loved That Woman. She didn't know whether he'd loved her mother either. The three things she knew, without doubt, that he'd loved were books, boats, and January.

It wasn't just that I'd been born then. He'd always acted like I'd been born in January *because* it was the best month and not the other way around.

In Ohio, I'd largely considered it to be the worst month of the year. Oftentimes we didn't get snow until February, which meant January was just a gray, cold, lightless time when you no longer had a major holiday to look forward to.

"In West Michigan, it's different," Dad had always said. There was the lake, and the way it would freeze over, covered in feet of snow. Apparently you could walk across it like it was some Martian tundra. In college, Shadi and I had planned to drive out one weekend and see it, but she'd gotten a call that their sheltie had died, and we'd spent the weekend watching *Masterpiece Classic* and making s'mores on the stove top instead.

I got back to typing.

> *If things had been different, she might've gone to the lakeside town in winter instead of summer, sat behind the wall of windows staring at the white-capped blues and strange frozen greens of the snowy beach.*
>
> *But she'd had this uncanny feeling, a fear she'd come face-to-face with his ghost if she'd shown up there at just the right time.*

I would've seen him everywhere. I would've wondered how he'd felt about every detail, remembered a particular snowfall he'd described from his childhood: *All these tiny orbs, January, like the whole world was made out of Dippin' Dots. Pure sugar.*

He'd had a way of describing things. When Mom read my first book she told me she could see him in it. In the way I wrote.

It made sense. I'd learned to love stories from him, after all.

She used to pride herself on all the things she had in common with him, regard the similarities with affection. Night owls. Messy. Always late, always carrying a book.

Careless about sunblock and addicted to every form of potatoes. Alive when we were on the water. Arms thrown wide, jackets rustling, eyes squinting into the sun.

Now she worried those similarities betrayed the terrible wrongness that lived in her. Maybe she, like her father, was incapable of the love she'd spent her life chasing.

Or maybe that love simply didn't exist.

10

The Interview

'D READ SOMEWHERE that it took 10,000 hours to be an expert at something. Writing was different, too vague a "something" for 10,000 hours to add up to much. Maybe 10,000 hours of lying in an empty bathtub brainstorming added up to being an expert on brainstorming in an empty bathtub. Maybe 10,000 hours of walking your neighbor's dog, working out a plot problem under your breath, would turn you into a pro at puzzling through plot tangles.

But those things were parts of a whole.

I'd probably spent more than 10,000 hours *typing* novels (those published as well as those cast aside), and I still wasn't an expert at *typing*, let alone an expert on writing books. Because even when you'd spent 10,000 hours writing feel-good fiction and another 10,000 reading it, it didn't make you an expert at writing any other kind of book.

I didn't know what I was doing. I couldn't be sure I was doing *anything*. There was a decent chance I'd send this draft to Anya and get an email back like, *Why did you just send me the menu for Red Lobster?*

But whether or not I was actually *succeeding* at this book, I *was* writing it. It came in painful ebbs and desperate flows, as if timed to the waves crashing somewhere behind that wall of fog.

It wasn't my life, but it was close. The conversation between the three women—Ellie, her mother, and Sonya's stand-in, Lucy—might've been word for word, although I knew not to trust memory quite so much these days.

If memory were accurate, then Dad *couldn't* have been here, in this house, when Mom's cancer came back. He couldn't have been because, until he died, I had memories of them dancing barefoot in the kitchen, of him smoothing her hair and kissing her head, driving her to the hospital with me in the back seat and the playlist he'd enlisted me to help him piece together playing on the car stereo.

Willie Nelson's "Always on My Mind."

Mom and Dad's hands clasped tightly on the center console.

Of course I remembered the "business trips" too. But that was the point. I remembered things as I'd thought they'd been, and then the truth, That Truth, had ripped the memories in half as easily as if they had been images on printer paper.

The next three days were a fervor of writing, cleaning, and little else. Aside from a box of wrapping paper, a handful of board games, and a great deal of towels and spare bedding, there was nothing remotely personal in the upstairs guest bedroom. It could've been any vacation home in America, or maybe a model home, a half-assed promise that your life too could be this kind of generically pretty.

I liked the upstairs decor significantly less than the warm boho vibe downstairs. I couldn't decide whether I felt relieved or cheated by that.

If there had been more of him, or of *her*, here, she'd already done the heavy lifting of scrubbing it clear.

On Wednesday, I photographed the furniture and posted it on craigslist. On Thursday, I packed the extra bedding, board games, and wrapping paper into boxes for Goodwill. On Friday, I stripped all the bedding and the towels from the racks in the second upstairs bathroom and carried them down to the laundry closet on the first floor, dumping them into the washer before sitting down to write.

The mist had finally burned off and the house was hot and sticky once again, so I'd opened the windows and doors and turned on all the fans.

I'd gotten glimpses of Gus over the last three days, but they'd been few. As far as I could tell, he moved around while drafting. If he was working at the kitchen table in the morning, he was never there by the time I poured my second cup of coffee. If he was nowhere to be seen all day, he'd appear suddenly on the deck at night, writing with only the light of his laptop and the swarm of moths batting around it.

Whenever I spotted him, I instantly lost focus. It was too fun imagining what he could be writing, brainstorming the possibilities. I was praying for vampires.

On Friday afternoon, we lined up for the first time, sitting at our tables in front of our matching windows.

He sat at his kitchen table, facing my house.

I sat at my kitchen table, facing his.

When we realized this, he lifted his bottle of beer the same way he'd mock-toasted with his coffee mug. I lifted my water glass.

Both windows were open. We could've talked but we would have had to scream.

Instead Gus smiled and picked up the highlighter and notebook beside him. He scribbled on it for a second, then held the notebook up so I could read it:

LIFE IS MEANINGLESS, JANUARY. GAZE INTO THE ABYSS.

I suppressed a laugh, then fished a Sharpie out of my backpack, dragged my own notebook toward me, and flipped to a blank page. In large, square letters, I wrote:

THIS REMINDS ME OF THAT TAYLOR SWIFT VIDEO.

His smile leapt up his face. He shook his head, then went back to writing. Neither of us said another word, and neither of us relocated either. Not until he knocked on my front door for our first research outing, a steel travel mug in each hand.

He gave my dress—the same itchy black thing I'd worn to book club—and boots one slow up-and-down, then shook his head. "That . . . will not work."

"I look great," I fired back.

"Agreed. If we were going to see the American Ballet Theatre, you'd be perfect. But I'm telling you, January, that will *not* work for tonight."

———

"IT'S GOING TO be a late night," Gus warned. We were in his car, heading north along the lake, the sun slung low in the sky, its last feverish rays painting everything to look like backlit cotton candy. When I'd demanded he pick out my new outfit and save me the trouble, I'd expected him to be uncomfortable. Instead he followed me into the downstairs guest room, looked at the handful of things hanging in the closet, and picked out the same denim shorts I'd worn to Pete's bookstore and my Carly Simon T-shirt, and with that we'd set off.

"As long as you don't make me listen to you sing 'Everybody Hurts' twice in a row," I said, "I think I can deal with a late night."

His smile was faint. It made his eyelids sink heavily. "Don't worry. That was a special occasion I let a friend talk me into. Won't happen again."

He was tapping restlessly against the steering wheel as we pulled up to a red light, and my eyes slid down the veins in his forearms, up along the back of his bicep to where it met his sleeve. Jacques had been handsome like an underwear model, perfectly toned with a winning smile and golden-brown hair that fell the same exact way every day. But it was all of Gus's minor imperfections—his scars and ridges, crooked lines and sharp edges—and how they added up that had always made it hard for me to stop looking at him, and made me want to see more.

He leaned forward to mess with the temperature controls, his eyes flicking toward me. I jerked my gaze out the window, trying to clear my mind before he could read it.

"Do you want to be surprised?" he said.

My heart seemed to trip over its next beat. "What?"

"About where we're going."

I relaxed. "Hm. Surprised by something disturbing enough that *you* think it belongs in a book. No thanks."

"Probably wise," he agreed. "We're going to interview a woman whose sister was in a suicide cult."

"You're kidding."

He shook his head.

"Oh my God," I said through a shock of laughter. All at once, the tension I'd imagined dissipated. "Gus, are you writing a *rom-com* about a suicide cult?"

He rolled his eyes. "I scheduled this interview before our bet. Besides, the point of this outing is helping *you* learn to write literary fiction."

"Well, either way, you weren't kidding about staring into the abyss," I said. "So the point of this lesson is basically *Everything sucks, now get to work writing about it*?"

Gus smirked. "No, smart-ass. The points of this lesson are character and detail."

I faux-gasped. "You're never going to believe this crazy coincidence, but we have those in women's fiction too!"

"You know, you're the one who initiated this whole lesson-plan element of the deal," Gus said. "If you're going to make fun of me the whole time, I'm happy to drop you off at the nearest suburban comedy club open mic and pick you up on the way back."

"Okay, okay." I waved him on. "Character and detail. You were saying . . ."

Gus shrugged. "I like writing about outlandish scenarios. Characters and events that *seem* too absurd to be real, but still work. Having specificity helps make the unbelievable believable. So I do a lot of interviews. It's interesting what people remember about a situation. Like if I'm going to write a cult-leading zealot who believes he's an alien consciousness reincarnated as every great world leader for centuries, I also need to know what kind of shoes he wears, and what he eats for breakfast."

"But do you *really*?" I teased. "Are the readers honestly begging for that?"

He laughed. "You know, maybe the reason you haven't been able to finish your book is that you keep asking what someone else wants to read instead of what you want to write."

I crossed my arms, bristling. "So tell me, Gus. How are you going to put a romantic spin on your suicide-cult book?"

His head tilted against the headrest, his knife-edged cheekbones casting shadows down his face. He scratched his jaw. "First of all, when did I say this interview was for my rom-com? I could just as easily set aside all my notes from this until I win our bet, then get back to work on my next *official* novel."

"And is that what you're doing?" I asked.

"I don't know yet," he admitted. "Trying to figure out if I can combine the ideas."

"Maybe," I said doubtfully. "Tell me the specifics. I'll see if I can help."

"Okay. So." He adjusted his grip on the steering wheel. "The original premise was basically that this journalist finds out his high school sweetheart, a former drug addict, has joined a cult, so he decides to infiltrate it and take it down. But while he's there, he starts moving up through the ranks really quickly, like waaaay past the woman he went there to *save*. And as he does, he starts seeing all this stuff, this proof, that the leader's right. About everything. Eventually, the girl was going to get scared and try to back out, try to talk *him* into leaving with her."

"So I'm guessing," I said, "they leave, honeymoon in Paris, and settle down in a small villa in the south of France. Probably become winemakers."

"He was going to murder her," Gus said flatly. "To save her soul. I hadn't decided if that was going to be what finally brought the cult down—got all the leaders arrested and everything—or if he was going to become the new prophet. I liked the first option because it feels more like a closed loop: he wants to get her out of the cult; he does. He wants to bring the cult down; he does. But the second one feels more cyclical in a way. Like every damaged person with a hero complex could end up doing exactly what the original leader of the cult does. I dunno. Maybe I'd have a young man or woman with a drug habit show up at the very end."

"Cute," I said.

"Exactly what I was going for," he answered.

"So. Any ideas for the not-terrible version of this book?"

"I mean, I liked that south-of-France pitch. That shit's fire."

"Glad you see things my way."

"Anyway," he said. "I'll figure it out. A cult rom-com does *sound* like a thing. What about you? What's your book?"

I pretended to puke in my lap.

"Cute," he echoed, flashing me a grin. Speaking of fire, sometimes his eyes seemed to be reflecting it, even though there wasn't any. The car was nearly pitch-black, for God's sake. His eyes shouldn't be allowed, physically or morally, to glint like that. His pupils were disrespectful to the laws of nature. My skin started burning under them.

"I have no idea what my book was," I said when he finally looked back to the road. "And little idea what it is. I think it's about a girl."

He waited for me to go on for a few seconds, then said, "Wow."

"I know." There was more. There was the father she adored. There was his mistress and his beach house in the town he grew up in, and his wife's radiation appointments. But even if things between Gus Everett and me had warmed (the fault of his eyes), I wasn't ready for the follow-up questions this conversation might yield.

"Why did you move here anyway?" I asked after a lengthy silence.

Gus shifted in his seat. Clearly there was plenty he didn't want to talk to *me* about either. "For the book," he said. "I read about this cult here. In the nineties. It had this big compound in the woods before it got busted. There was all kinds of illegal shit going on there. I've been here about five years, interviewing people and researching and all that."

"Seriously? You've been working on this for five years?"

He glanced my way. "It's research heavy. And for part of that time I was finishing up my second book and touring for that and everything. It wasn't like, five uninterrupted years at a typewriter with a single empty water bottle to pee in."

"Your doctor will be relieved to hear that."

We drove in taut silence for a while before Gus rolled down his window, which gave me permission to roll mine down. The warm whip of the air against the open windows dissolved any discomfort from the silence we'd fallen into. We could've just been two strangers on the same beach or bus or ferry.

As we drove, the sun vanished inch by inch. Eventually, Gus fiddled with the radio, stopping to crank up an oldies station playing Paul Simon.

"I love this song," he told me over the wind cycloning through the car.

"Really?" I said, surprised. "I figured you'd make me listen to Elliott Smith or Johnny Cash's cover of 'Hurt' the whole way."

Gus rolled his eyes, but he was smiling. "And I figured *you'd* bring a Mariah Carey playlist with you."

"Damn, I wish I'd thought of that."

His gruff laugh was mostly lost in the wind, but I heard enough of it to make my cheeks go warm.

It was two hours before we got off the highway and then another thirty minutes of ice-damaged back roads, lit only by the car's brights and the stars overhead.

Finally, we pulled from the winding road through the woods into the gravel lot of a bar with a corrugated tin roof. Its glowing marquee read, THE BY-WATER. Aside from a few motorcycles and a junker of a Toyota pickup, the lot was empty, but the windows, illuminated by glowing BUDWEISER and MILLER signs, revealed a dense crowd inside.

"Be honest," I said. "Did you bring me here to murder me?"

Gus turned off the car and rolled up the windows. "Please. We drove three hours. I've got a perfectly good murder spot back in North Bear Shores."

"Are all your interviews at spooky dive bars in the forest?" I asked.

He shrugged. "Only the good ones."

We climbed out of the car. Without the fifty mph wind, it was hot and sticky out, every few feet punctuated by a new cloud of mosquitoes or fireflies. I thought maybe I could hear the "water" the bar's name referred to somewhere in the woods behind it. Not the lake itself, I didn't think. A creek, probably.

I always felt a bit anxious going to neighborhood spots like this when I wasn't a part of the neighborhood, but Gus appeared to be at ease, and hardly anyone looked up from their beer or pool tables or trysts against the wall beside the old-school jukebox. It was a place full of camo hats and tank tops and Carhartt jackets.

I was extremely grateful Gus had encouraged me to change my outfit.

"Who are we meeting?" I asked, sticking close to him as he surveyed the crowd. He tipped his chin toward a lone woman at a high-top near the back.

Grace was in her midfifties and had the rounded shoulders of someone who'd spent a lot of time sitting, but not necessarily relaxed. Which made sense. She was a truck driver with four sons in high school and no romantic partner to lean on.

"Not that that matters," she said, taking a sip from her Heineken. "We're not here to talk about that. You want to know about Hope."

Hope, her sister. Hope and Grace. Twins from northern Michigan, not quite the Upper Peninsula, she'd already told us.

"We want to talk about whatever you think is relevant," Gus said.

She wanted to be sure it wasn't for a news story. Gus shook his head. "It's a novel. None of the characters will have your names or look like you, or be you. The cult won't be the same cult. This is to help us understand the characters. What makes someone join a cult, when you first noticed something off with Hope. That sort of thing."

Her eyes glanced off the door then back to us, an uncertainty in her expression.

I felt guilty. I knew she'd come here of her own volition, but this couldn't be easy, scraping the muck out of her heart and holding it out to a couple of strangers.

"You don't have to tell us," I blurted, and I felt the full force of Gus's eyes cut to me, but I kept my focus on Grace, her watery eyes, slightly parted lips. "I know talking about it won't undo any of it. But not talking about it won't either, and if there's anything you need to say, you can. Even if it's just your favorite thing about her, you can say it."

Her eyes sharpened into slivers of sapphire and her mouth tightened into a knot. For a second, she was stock-still and somber, a midwestern Madonna in a stone pietà, some sacred memory cradled in her lap where we couldn't quite see it.

"Her laugh," she said finally. "She snorted when she laughed."

The corner of my mouth inched up but a new heaviness settled across my chest. "I love when people do that," I admitted. "My best friend does it. I always feel like she's drowning in life. In a good way. Like it's rushing up her nose, you know?"

A soft, wispy smile formed on Grace's thin lips. "A good way," she said quietly. Then her smile quivered sadly, and she scratched her sunburned chin, her sloped shoulders rising as she set her forearms on the table. She cleared her throat.

"I didn't," she said thickly. "Know anything was off. That's what you wanted to know?" Her eyes glossed and she shook her head once. "I had no idea until she was already gone."

Gus's head tilted. "How is that possible?"

"Because." Tears were rushing into her eyes even as she shrugged. "She was still laughing."

WE WERE SILENT for most of the drive home. Windows up, radio off, eyes on the road. Gus, I imagined, was mentally sorting the information he'd gotten from Grace.

I was lost in thoughts about my dad. I could so easily see myself avoiding the questions I had about him until I was Grace's age. Until Sonya was gone, and Mom too, and there was no one left to give me answers, even if I wanted them.

I wasn't prepared to spend my life avoiding any thought of the man who'd raised me, feeling sick whenever I remembered the envelope in the box atop the fridge.

But I was also tired of the pain inside my rib cage, the weight pressing on my clavicles and anxious sweat that cropped up whenever I considered the truth for too long.

I closed my eyes and pressed back into the headrest as the memory surged forward. I tried to fight it off, but I was too tired, so there it was. The crocheted shawl, the look on Mom's face, the key in my palm.

God, I didn't want to go back to that house.

The car stopped and my eyes snapped open.

"Sorry," Gus stammered. He'd slammed the breaks to avoid plowing into a tractor at a dark four-way stop. "Wasn't paying attention."

"Lost in that beautiful brain of yours?" I teased, but it came out flat, and if Gus heard, he gave no indication. The more animated corner of his mouth was twisted firmly down.

"You okay?" he asked.

"Yeah."

He was quiet for another beat. "That was pretty intense. If you want to talk about it . . ."

I thought back to Grace's story. She'd thought Hope was doing better than ever when she first fell in with her new crowd. She'd gotten off heroin, for one thing—a nearly insurmountable challenge. "I remember her skin looked better," Grace had said. "And her eyes. I don't quite know what about them, but they were different too. I thought I had my sister back. Four months later, she was dead."

She'd died by accident, internal bleeding from "punishments." The rest of the trailer compound that was New Eden had gone up in flames as the FBI investigation was closing in.

Everything Grace had told us was probably great for Gus's original plot line. It didn't leave a lot of room for meet-cutes and HEAs. But that was sort of the point. Tonight's research had been for *me*, to take my brain down the trails that led to the kind of book I was supposed to be writing.

I couldn't understand how people did this. How Gus could bear to follow such dark paths just for the sake of a story. How he could keep asking questions when *all* I'd wanted all night was to grab Grace and hold her tight, apologize for what the world had taken from her, find some way—any way—to make the loss one ounce lighter.

"Have to stop for gas," Gus said, and pulled off the highway to a deserted Shell station. There was nothing but parched fields for miles in every direction.

I got out of the car to stretch my legs while Gus pumped the gas. Night had cooled the air, but not much. "This one of your murder spots?" I asked, walking around the car to him.

"I refuse to answer that on the grounds that you might try to take it from me."

"Solid grounds," I answered. After a moment, I couldn't hold the question in any longer. "Doesn't it bother you? Having to live in someone else's tragedy? Five years. That's a long time to put yourself in that place."

Gus tucked the nozzle back into the pump, all his focus on twisting the gas cap closed. "Everybody's got shit, January. Sometimes, thinking about someone else's is almost a relief."

"Okay, fine," I said. "Let me have it."

Gus's eyebrows lifted and his Sexy, Evil mouth went slack. "What?"

I folded my arms and pressed my hip into the driver's side door. I was tired of being the most delicate person in the room. The girl drunk on purse-wine, the one trying not to tremble as someone else poured their pain out on a high-top in a crummy bar. "Let's hear this mysterious shit of yours. See if it gives me an effective break from mine." And now Grace's, which weighed just as heavily on my chest.

Gus's liquidy dark eyes slid down my face. "Nah," he said finally, and moved toward the door, but I stayed leaning against it. "You're in my way," he said.

"Am I?"

He reached for the door handle, and I slid sideways to block it.

His hand connected with my waist instead, and a spark of heat shot through me.

"Even more in my way," he said, in a low voice that made it sound more like *I dare you to stay there*.

My cheeks itched. His hand was still hanging against my hip like he'd forgotten it was there, but his finger twitched, and I knew he hadn't.

"You just took me on the world's most depressing date," I said. "The least you could do is tell me a single thing about yourself, and why all this New Eden stuff matters to you."

His brow lifted in amusement and his eyes flickered in that bonfire-lit way. "Wasn't a date."

Somehow, he managed to make it sound filthy.

"Right, you don't date," I said. "Why is that? Part of your dark, mysterious past?"

His Sexy, Evil mouth tightened. "What do I get?"

He stepped a little closer, and I became hyperaware of every molecule of space between us. I hadn't been this close to a man since Jacques. Jacques had smelled like high-end cologne by Commodity; Gus smelled smoky and sweet, like nag champa incense mixed with a salty beach. Jacques had blue eyes that twinkled over me like a summer breeze through chimes. Gus's dark gaze bored into me like a corkscrew: *What do I get?*

"Lively conversation?" My voice came out unfamiliarly low.

He gave a slight shake of his head. "Tell me why you moved here, and I'll tell you *one* thing about my dark, mysterious past."

I considered the offer. The reward, I decided, was worth the cost. "My dad died. He left me his beach house."

The truth, if not all of it.

For the second time, an unfamiliar expression fluttered—sympathy? Disappointment, maybe?—across his face too fast for me to parse out its meaning. "Now your turn," I prompted.

"Fine," he said, voice scratchy, "one thing."

I nodded.

Gus leaned in toward me and dropped his mouth beside my ear conspiratorially, his hot breath pulling goose bumps up the side of my neck. His eyes flashed sideways across my face, and his other hand touched my hip so lightly it could've been a breeze. The heat in my hips spread toward my center, curling around my thighs like kudzu.

It was crazy that I remembered that night in college so vividly that I knew he'd touched me just like this. That first touch when we met on the dance floor, featherlight and melting-point hot, careful, intentional.

I realized I was holding my breath, and when I forced myself to breathe, the rise and fall of my chest was ridiculous, the stuff of Regency-era erotica.

How was he *doing* this to me? *Again?*

After the night we'd had tonight, this feeling, this hunger in me shouldn't have been possible. After the *year* I'd had, I hadn't thought it was anymore.

"I lied," he whispered against my ear. "I *have* read your books."

His hands tightened on my waist and he spun me away from the car, opened the door, and got in, leaving me gasping at the sudden cold of the parking lot.

11

The Not Date

I SPENT FAR TOO much of my Saturday trying to choose a perfect destination for Gus's first Adventure in Romance. Even though I'd been suffering from chronic writer's block, I was still an expert in my field, and my list of possible settings for his introduction to meet-cutes and Happily Ever Afters was endless.

I'd pounded out another thousand words first thing in the morning, but since then I'd been pacing and Googling, trying to choose the *perfect* place. When I still couldn't make up my mind, I'd driven myself to the farmer's market in town and walked the sunny aisle between the stands, searching for inspiration. I picked through buckets of cut flowers, longing for the days when I could afford a bundle of daisies for the kitchen, calla lilies for the night-stand in the bedroom. Of course, that had been back when Jacques and I were sharing an apartment. When you were renting in New

York by yourself, there wasn't much money for things that smelled good for a week, then died in front of you.

At the booth of a local farm, I filled my bag with plump tomatoes, orange and red, along with some basil and mint, cucumbers, and a head of fresh butter lettuce. If I couldn't pick something to do with Gus tonight, maybe we'd cook dinner.

My stomach grumbled at the thought of a good meal. I wasn't big on cooking myself—it took too much time I never felt like I had—but there was definitely something romantic about pouring two glasses of red wine and moving around a clean kitchen, chopping and rinsing, stirring and sampling tastes from a wooden spoon. Jacques had loved to cook—I could follow a recipe okay, but he preferred a more intuitive, cook-all-night approach, and kitchen intuition and food-patience were both things I sorely lacked.

I paid for my veggies and pushed my sunglasses up as I entered the enclosed part of the market in search of some chicken or steak and fell back into brainstorming.

Characters could fall in love anywhere—an airport or auto body shop or hospital—but for an anti-romantic, it would probably take something more obvious than that to get the ideas going. For me, the best usually came from the unexpected, from mistakes and mishaps. It didn't take inspiration to dredge up a list of plot points, but to find that moment—the perfect moment that defined a book, that made it come alive as something greater than the sum of its words—that required an alchemy you couldn't fake.

The last year of my life had proven that. I could plot all day, but it didn't matter if I didn't fall into the story headfirst, if the story itself didn't spin like a cyclone, pulling me wholly into itself. *That* was what I'd always loved about reading, what had driven me to write in the first place. That feeling that a new world was being spun like a spiderweb around you and you couldn't move until the whole thing had revealed itself to you.

While the interview with Grace hadn't given me any of those all-consuming tornadoes of inspiration, I *had* awoken with a glimmer of it. There were stories that deserved to be told, ones I'd never considered, and I felt a spark of excitement at the thought that maybe I could tell one of them, and *like* doing it.

I wanted to give Gus that feeling too. I wanted him to wake up tomorrow itching to write. Proving how difficult it was to write a rom-com was one thing, and I was confident Gus would see that, but getting him to understand what I loved about the genre—that reading and writing it was nearly as all-consuming and transformative as *actually* falling in love—would be a different challenge entirely.

I was too distracted to write when I got home, so I put myself to better use. I twisted my hair into a topknot, put on shorts and a Todd Rundgren tank top, and went to the guest bathroom on the second floor with trash bags and boxes.

Dad or That Woman had kept the closet stocked with towels and backup toiletries, which I piled into donation boxes and carried to the foyer one at a time. On my third trip, I stopped before the kitchen window facing into Gus's house. He was sitting at the table, holding an oversized note up for me to see. Like he'd been waiting.

I balanced the box against the table and swiped my forearm up my temple to catch the sweat beading there as I read:

JANUARY, JANUARY, WHEREFORE ART THOU, JANUARY?

The message was ironic. The butterflies in my chest were not. I pushed the box onto the table and grabbed my notebook, scribbling in it. I held the note up.

New phone who dis?

Gus laughed, then turned back to his computer. I grabbed the box and carried it out to the Kia, then went back for the rest. The humidity of the last few days had let up again, leaving nothing but breezy warmth behind. When I'd finished loading the car, I poured myself a glass of rosé and sat on the deck.

The sky was bright blue, an occasional fluffy cumulus cloud drifting lazily past, and the sunlight painted the rustling treetops a pale green. If I closed my eyes, shutting myself off from what I could see, I could hear squeals of laughter down by the water.

At home, Mom and Dad's yard had backed up to another family's, one with three young kids. As soon as they moved in, Dad had planted a grove of evergreens along the fence to create some privacy, but he'd always loved that on late summer nights, as we sat around the firepit, we'd hear the screams and giggles of the kids playing tag, or jumping on the trampoline, or lying in a tent behind their house.

Dad loved his space, but he also always said he liked to be reminded that there were other people out there, living their lives. People who didn't know him or care to.

I know feeling small gets to some people, he had once told me, *but I kind of like it. Takes the pressure off when you're just one life of six billion at any given moment. And when you're going through something hard—*at the time, Mom was doing chemo—*it's nice to know you're not even close to the only one.*

I'd felt the opposite. I was harboring a private heartbreak. About the universe, about Mom's body betraying her again. About the life I'd dreamed of dissipating like mist. I'd watched my U of M classmates over Facebook as they went on to grad school and (mysteriously funded) international travel. I'd watched them post doting Mother's Day tributes from far corners of the world. I'd listened to the kids who lived behind my parents' house shriek and giggle as they played Ghost in the Graveyard.

And I'd felt secretly heartbroken that the world could do this to *us* again, and even worse because I knew saying any of that would only make things harder for Mom.

And then she'd kicked it the second time. And I'd been so grateful. More relieved than I knew a person could feel. Our life was back on track, the three of us stronger than ever. Nothing could tear us apart ever again, I was sure.

But still, I was mourning those years lost to doctor visits and shed hair and Mom, the do-er, lying sick on the couch. Those feelings didn't fit with our beautiful post-cancer life, I knew—they added nothing helpful or good—so I'd tamped them down once more.

When I found out about Sonya, they'd all sprung out, fermented into anger over time, like an overzealous jack-in-the-box pointed straight at Dad.

"Question."

I looked up and found Gus leaning against the railing on his deck. His gray T-shirt was as rumpled as everything else I'd seen him wear. His clothes very likely never made it from the hamper to drawers, assuming they made it to the laundry in the first place, but the muss of his hair also suggested he could have just rolled out of a nap.

I went to stand against the railing on my side of the ten-foot divide. "I hope it's about the meaning of life. That or which book is first in the Bridget Jones series."

"That, definitely," he said. "And also, do I need to wear a tuxedo tonight?"

I fought a smile. "I would pay one hundred dollars to see what a tuxedo under your laundry regimen looks like. And I'm extremely broke, so that says a lot."

He rolled his eyes. "I like to think of it as my laundry *democracy*."

"See, if you let something inanimate vote on whether it wants to be washed, it's not going to answer."

"January, are you taking me to a reenactment of the *Beauty and the Beast* ball or not? I'm trying to plan."

I studied him. "Okay, I'll answer that question, but on the condition that you tell me, honestly, do you *own* a tuxedo?"

He stared back. After a long pause, he sighed and leaned into the railing. The sun had started to set and the flexed veins and muscles in his lean arms cast shadows along his skin. "Fine. Yes. I own a tuxedo."

I erupted into laughter. "Seriously? Are you a secret Kennedy? No one *owns* a tuxedo."

"I agreed to answer one question. Now tell me what to wear."

"Considering I've only seen you in almost imperceptibly different variations of one outfit, you can safely assume I wouldn't plan anything requiring a tuxedo. I mean, until now, when I found out you owned a tuxedo. Now all bets are off. But for tonight, your grumpy bartender costume should do."

He shook his head and straightened up. "Phenomenal," he said, and went inside.

In that moment, I knew exactly where I was going to take Gus Everett.

"WOW," GUS SAID.

The "carnival" I'd found eight miles from our street was in a Big Lots parking lot, and it fit there a bit too easily.

"I just counted the rides," Gus said. "Seven."

"I'm really proud of you for getting that high," I teased. "Maybe next time see if you can aim for ten."

"I *wish* I were high," Gus grumbled.

"It's perfect," I replied.

"For what?" he said.

"Um, duh," I said. "Falling in love."

A laugh barked out of Gus, and again I was a little too proud of myself for my own liking. "Come on." I felt a pang of regret as I handed over my credit card at the ticket booth in exchange for our all-you-can-ride bracelets, but was relieved when Gus interrupted to insist on buying his own. That was one of many horrible parts of being broke: having to think about whether you could afford to share sucked.

"That wasn't very romantic of me, I guess," I said as we wandered into the throng of bodies clustered around a milk can toss.

"Well, lucky for you, *that* is pretty much my exact definition of romance." He pointed to the teal row of porta potties at the edge of the lot. A teenage boy with his hat turned backward was gripping his stomach and shifting between his feet as he waited for one of the toilets to open up while the couple beside him hardcore made out.

"Gus," I said flatly. "That couple is so into each other they're making out a yard away from a literal row of shit piles. *That* juxtaposition is basically the entire rom-com lesson for the night. It really does nothing to your icy heart?"

"Heart? No. Stomach, a little. I'm getting sympathy diarrhea for their friend. Can you imagine having such a *bad* time with your friends that a porta potty becomes a beacon of hope? A bedrock! A place to rest your weary head. We're definitely looking at a future existentialist. Maybe even a coldly horny novelist."

I rolled my eyes. "That guy's night was pretty much my entire high school—and much of college—experience, and somehow I survived, tender human heart intact."

"Bullshit!" Gus cried.

"Meaning?"

"I knew you in college, January."

"That seems like the biggest in a series of vast exaggerations you've made tonight."

"Fine, I knew *of* you," he said. "The point is, you weren't the diarrhea-having third wheel. You dated plenty. Marco, right? That guy from our Fiction 400 workshop. And weren't you with that premed golden boy? The one who was addicted to studying abroad and tutoring disadvantaged youth and, like, rock climbing shirtless."

I snorted. "Sounds like you were more in love with him than I was."

Something sharp and appraising flashed over Gus's eyes. "But you *were* in love with him."

Of course I was. I'd met him during an impromptu snowball fight on campus. I couldn't imagine anything more romantic than that moment, when he'd pulled me up from the snowdrift I'd fallen into, his blue eyes sparkling, and offered his dry hat to replace my snow-soaked one.

It took all of ten minutes as he walked me home for me to determine that he was the most interesting person I'd ever met. He was working on getting his pilot's license and had wanted to work in the ER ever since he'd lost a cousin in a car accident as a kid. He'd done semesters in Brazil, Morocco, and France (Paris, where his paternal grandparents lived), and he'd also backpacked a significant portion of the Camino de Santiago by himself.

When I told him I'd never been out of the country, he immediately suggested a spontaneous road trip to Canada. I'd thought he was kidding basically until we pulled up to the duty-free shop on the far side of the border around midnight. "There," he said with his model grin, all shiny and guileless. "Next we need to get you somewhere they'll actually stamp your passport."

That whole night had taken on a hazy, soft-focus quality like we were only dreaming it. Looking back, I thought we sort of had been: him pretending to be endlessly interesting; me pretending to be spontaneous and carefree, as usual. Outwardly we were so different, but when it came down to it, we both wanted the same thing. A life cast in a magical glow, every moment bigger and brighter and tastier than the last.

For the next six years, we were intent on glowing for each other.

I tucked the memories away. "I was never with Marco," I answered Gus. "I went to *one* party with him, and he left with someone else. Thanks for reminding me."

Gus's laugh turned into an exaggerated, pitying *"awh."*

"It's fine. I persevered."

Gus's head cocked, his eyes digging at mine like shovels. "And Golden Boy?"

"We were together," I admitted.

I'd thought I was going to marry him. And then Dad had died and everything had changed. We'd survived a lot together with Mom's illness, but I'd always held things together, found ways to shut off the worrying and have fun with him, but this was different. Jacques didn't know what to do with this version of me, who stayed in bed and couldn't write or read without coming apart, who slugged around at home letting laundry pile up and ugliness seep into our dreamy apartment, who never wanted to throw parties or walk the Brooklyn Bridge at sunset or book a last-minute getaway to Joshua Tree.

Again and again he told me I wasn't myself. But he was wrong. I was the same me I'd always been. I'd just stopped trying to glow in the dark for him, or anyone else.

It was our beautiful life together, amazing vacations and grand gestures and freshly cut flowers in handmade vases, that had held us together for so long.

It wasn't that I couldn't get enough of him. Or that he was the best man I'd ever known. (I'd thought that was my dad, but now it was the dad from my favorite 2000s teen drama, *Veronica Mars*.) Or that he was my favorite person. (That was Shadi.) Or because he made me laugh so hard I wept. (He laughed easily, but rarely joked.) Or that when something bad happened, he was the first person I wanted to call. (He wasn't.)

It was that we met at the same age my parents had, that the snowball fight and impromptu road trip had felt like fate, that my mother adored him. He fit so perfectly into the love story I'd imagined for myself that I mistook him for the love of my life.

Breaking up still sucked in every conceivable way, but once the initial pain wore off, memories from our relationship started to seem like just another story I'd read. I hated thinking about it. Not because I missed him but because I felt bad for wasting so much of his time—and mine—trying to be his dream girl.

"We were together," I repeated. "Until last year."

"Wow." Gus laughed awkwardly. "That's a long time. I'm . . . really regretting making fun of his shirtless rock climbing now."

"It's okay," I said, shrugging. "He dumped me in a hot tub." Outside a cabin in the Catskills, three days before our trip with his family was scheduled to end. Spontaneity wasn't always as sexy as it was cracked up to be. *You're just not yourself anymore,* he'd told me. *We don't work like this, January.*

We left the next morning, and on the drive back to New York, Jacques had told me he'd call his parents when we got back to let them know the news.

Mom's going to cry, he said. *So is Brigitte.*

Even in that moment, I was possibly more devastated to lose Jacques's parents and sister—a feisty high schooler with impeccable 1970s style—than Jacques himself.

"A hot tub?" Gus echoed. "Damn. Honestly, that guy was always so self-impressed I doubt he could even see you through the glare off his own glistening body."

I cracked a smile. "I'm sure that was it."

"Hey," Gus said.

"Hey, what?"

He tipped his head toward a cotton candy stand. "I think we should eat that."

"And here it finally is," I said.

"What?" Gus asked.

"The second thing we agree on."

Gus paid for the cotton candy and I didn't argue. "No, that's fine," he teased when I said nothing. "You can just owe me. You can just pay me back whenever."

"How much was it?" I asked, tearing off an enormous piece and lowering it dramatically into my mouth.

"Three dollars, but it's fine. Just Venmo me the dollar fifty later."

"Are you sure that's not too much trouble?" I said. "I'm happy to go get a cashier's check."

"Do you know where the closest Western Union is?" he said. "You could probably wire it."

"What sort of interest were you thinking?" I asked.

"You can just give me three dollars when I take you home, and then if I ever find out I need an organ, we can circle back."

"Sure, sure," I agreed. "Let's just put a pin in this."

"Yeah, we should probably loop in our lawyers anyway."

"Good point," I said. "Until then, what do you want to ride?"

"Ride?" Gus said. "Absolutely nothing here."

"Fine," I said. "What are you willing to ride?"

We'd been walking, talking, and eating at an alarming rate, and Gus stopped suddenly, offering me the final clump of cotton candy. "That," he said while I was eating, and pointed at a pathetically small carousel. "That looks like it would have a *really* hard time killing me."

"What do you weigh, Gus? Three beer cans, some bones, and a cigarette?" *And* all the hard lines and lean ridges of muscle I definitely hadn't gawked at. "Any number of those painted animals could kill you with a sneeze."

"Wow," he said. "First of all, I may only weigh three beer cans, but that's still three more beer cans than your ex-boyfriend. He looked like he did nothing but chew wheatgrass while running. I weigh easily twice what he did. Secondly, you're one to talk: you're what, four feet and six inches?"

"I'm a very tall five four, actually," I said.

He narrowed his eyes and shook his head at me. "You're as small as you are ridiculous."

"So not very?"

"Carousel, final offer," Gus said.

"This is the perfect place for our montage," I said.

"Our what now?"

"Young—extremely beautiful and *very tall for her height*—woman in sparkly tennis shoes teaches fearful, party-hating curmudgeon how to enjoy life," I said. "There'd be a lot of head shaking. A lot of me dragging you from ride to ride. You dragging me back out of the line. Me dragging you back into it. It'd be adorable, and more importantly it'll help with your super romantic suicide-cult book. It's the promise-of-the-premise portion of the novel, when your readers are grinning ear to ear. We *need* a montage."

Gus folded his arms and studied me with narrowed eyes.

"Come on, Gus." I bumped his arm. "You can do it. Be adorable."

His eyes darted to where I'd bumped him, then back to my face, and he scowled.

"I think you misunderstood me. I said *adorable*."

His surly expression cracked. "Fine, January. But it's not going to be a montage. Choose *one* death trap. If I survive that, you can sleep well tonight knowing you brought me one step closer to believing in happy endings."

"Oh my God," I said. "If you wrote this scene, would we *die*?"

"If I wrote this scene, it wouldn't be about us."

"Wow. One, I'm offended. Two, who would it be about?"

He scanned the crowd and I followed his gaze. "Her," he said finally.

"Who?"

He stepped in close behind me, his head hovering over my right shoulder. "There. At the bottom of the Ferris wheel."

"The girl in the *Screw Me, I'm Irish* shirt?" I said.

His laugh was warm and rough in my ear. Standing this close to him was bringing back flashes of the night at the frat house I'd rather not revisit.

"The woman working the machine," he said in my ear. "Maybe she'd make a mistake and watch someone get hurt because of it. This job was probably her last chance, the only place that would hire her after she made an even bigger mistake. In a factory maybe.

Or she broke the law to protect someone she cared about. Some kind of almost-innocent mistake that could lead to less innocent ones."

I spun to face him. "Or maybe she'd get a chance to be a hero. This job was her last chance, but she loves it and she's good at it. She gets to travel, and even if she mostly only sees parking lots, she gets to meet people. And she's a people person. The mistake isn't hers—the machinery malfunctions, but she makes a snap decision and saves a girl's life. That girl grows up to be a congresswoman, or a heart surgeon. The two of them cross paths again down the road. The Ferris wheel operator's too old to travel with the carnival anymore. She's been living alone, feeling like she wasted her life. Then one day, she's alone. She has a heart attack. She almost dies but she manages to call nine-one-one. The ambulance rushes her in, and who is her doctor but that same little girl.

"Of course, Ferris doesn't recognize her—she's all grown up. But the doctor never could've forgotten Ferris's face. The two women strike up a friendship. Ferris still doesn't get to travel, but twice a month the doctor comes over to Ferris's double-wide and they watch movies. Movies set in different countries. They watch *Casablanca* and eat Moroccan takeout. They watch *The King and I* and eat Siamese food, whatever that may be. They even watch— gasp!—*Bridget Jones's Diary* while bingeing on fish and chips. They make it through twenty countries before Ferris passes away, and when she does, Doctor realizes her life was a gift she almost didn't get. She takes some of Ferris's ashes—her ungrateful asshole son didn't come to collect them—and sets out on a trip around the world. She's grateful to be alive. The end."

Gus stared at me, only one corner of his very crooked mouth

at all engaged. I was fairly sure he was smiling, although the deep grooves between his eyebrows seemed to disagree. "Then write it," he said finally.

"Maybe so," I said.

He glanced back at the gray-haired woman working the machinery. "That one," he said. "I'm willing to ride that one. But only because I trust Ferris so damn much."

12

The Olive Garden

THERE WAS NO montage. It was a slow night on the warm asphalt, under the neon glow and screeching metal of cheap rides. Hours of eating deep-fried food and drinking lime-infused beer from sticky cans between visits to each of the seven rides. There was no dragging in and out of lines. There was just wandering. Telling stories.

Gus pointed at a pregnant girl with a barbed wire tattoo. "She joins the cult."

"She does not," I disagreed.

"She does. She loses the baby. It's awful. The only thing that starts to bring her back to life is this rising YouTube star she follows. She finds out about New Eden from him, then goes for a weekend-long seminar and never leaves."

"She's there for two years," I countered. "But then her little brother comes to get her. She doesn't want to see him, and security's trying to get him out of there, but then he pulls out a sonogram. His girlfriend, May, is pregnant. A little boy. Due in a month. She doesn't leave with him, but that night—"

"She tries to leave," Gus took over. "They won't let her. They lock her in a white room to decontaminate her. Her exposure to her brother's energy, they say, has temporarily altered her brain chemistry. She has to complete the five purification steps. If she still wants to leave after that, they'll let her."

"She completes them," I said. "The reader thinks they've lost her. That she's stuck. But the last line of the book is some clue. Something she and her brother used to say. Some sign that she kept a secret part of herself safe, and the only reason she's not leaving yet is because there are people trapped there she wants to help."

We went back and forth like that all night, and when we finally stopped, it was only because riding the scrambler left me so nauseated I ran from it to the nearest trash can and vomited heartily.

Even as the recently eaten chili dog was rushing back up, I had to think the night had been some kind of success. After all, Gus grabbed my hair and pulled it away from my face as I retched.

At least until he grumbled, "Shit, I hate vomit," and ran off gagging.

Hate, I found out on the ride home, was a less embarrassing way to say *fear*.

National Book Award nominee Augustus Everett was vomit-phobic, and had been ever since a girl named Ashley in his fourth grade class puked on the back of his head.

"I haven't puked in easily fifteen years," he told me. "And I've had the stomach flu twice in that time."

I was fighting giggles as I drove. In general, I didn't find phobias funny, but Gus was a former gravedigger turned suicide-cult investigator. Nothing Grace said in our interview had made him bat an eye, and yet cheap rides and puke had nearly bested him.

"God, I'm sorry," I said, regaining control of myself. I glanced over to him, slumped back in my passenger seat with one arm folded behind his head. "I can't believe my first lesson in love stories actually just unearthed multiple traumas for you. At least you didn't end up also . . . you-know-what-ing . . ." I didn't say the word, just in case.

His eyes flashed over to me and the corner of his mouth curled. "Trust me, I got out in the nick of time. One more second and *you* would've gotten Ashley Phillips'ed."

"Wow," I said. "And yet you held my hair. So noble. So brave. So selfless." I was teasing, but it actually was pretty sweet.

"Yeah, well, if you didn't have such nice hair, I wouldn't have bothered." Gus's eyes went back to the road. "But I learned my lesson. Never again will I try to be a hero."

"My parents met at a carnival." I hadn't meant to say it; it had just slipped out.

Gus looked at me, his expression inscrutable. "Yeah?"

I nodded. I fully intended to drop the subject, but the last few days had loosened something in me, and the words came pouring out. "Their freshman year, at Ohio State."

"Oh, not *The* Ohio State University," he teased. Michiganders and Ohioans had a major rivalry I often forgot about due to my total ignorance of sports. Dad's brothers had lovingly referred to him as the *Great Defector*, and he'd teased me with the same nickname when I chose U of M.

"Yes, the very one," I played along.

We fell into silence for a few seconds. "So," Gus prompted, "tell me about it."

"No," I said, giving him a suspicious smile. "You don't want to hear that."

"I'm legally obligated to," he said. "How else am I going to learn about love?"

An ache speared through my chest. "Maybe not from them. He cheated on her. A lot. While she had cancer."

"Damn," Gus said. "That's shitty."

"Says the man who doesn't believe in dating."

He ran a hand through his already messy hair, leaving it ravaged. His eyes flickered to me, then back to the road. "Fidelity was never my issue."

"Fidelity across a two-week span isn't exactly impressive," I pointed out.

"I'll have you know I dated Tessa Armstrong for a month," he said.

"Monogamously? Because I seem to remember a sordid night in a frat house that would suggest otherwise."

Surprise splashed across his face. "I'd broken up with her when that happened."

"I saw you with her that morning," I said. It probably should have been embarrassing to admit I remembered all this, but Gus didn't seem to notice that. In fact, he just seemed a little insulted by the observation.

He mussed his hair again and said irritably, "I broke up with her at the party."

"She wasn't at the party," I said.

"No. But since it wasn't the seventeenth century, I had a phone."

"You called from a party and dumped your girlfriend?" I cried. "Why would you do that?"

He looked my way, eyes narrowed. "Why do you think, January?"

I was grateful for the dark. My face was suddenly on fire. My stomach felt like molten lava was pouring down it. Was I misunderstanding? Should I ask? Did it *matter*? That was almost a decade ago, and even if things *had* gone differently that night, it wouldn't have amounted to anything in the long run.

Still, I was burning up.

"Well, shit," I said. I couldn't get anything else out.

He laughed. "Anyway, your parents," he said. "It couldn't have been all bad."

I cleared my throat. It could not have sounded any less natural. I might as well have just screamed *I DON'T WANT TO TALK ABOUT MY SAD PARENTS WHILE I'M THINKING FIERY THOUGHTS ABOUT YOU* and gotten it over with.

"It wasn't," I said, focusing on the road. "I don't think."

"And the night they met?" he pressed.

Again, the words came gushing out of me, like I'd needed to say them all year—or maybe they were just a welcome diversion from the other conversation we'd been having. "They went to this carnival at a local Catholic church," I said. "Not together. Like, they went separately to the same carnival. And then they ended up standing in line next to each other for that Esmeralda thing. You know, the animatronic psychic-in-a-box?"

"Oh, I know her well," Gus said. "She was one of my first crushes."

There was no reason that should've sent new fireworks of heat across my cheeks, and yet, here we were. "So anyway," I went on. "My mom was the fifth wheel on this, like, blatant double date trying to disguise itself as a Casual Hang. So when the others went off to go through the Tunnel-o-Love, she went to get her fortune. My dad said *he* left *his* group when he spotted this beautiful redhaired girl in a blue polka-dot dress."

"Betty Crocker?" Gus guessed.

"She's a brunette. Get your eyes checked," I said.

A smile quirked Gus's lips. "Sorry for interrupting. Go on. Your dad's just spotted your mom."

I nodded. "Anyway, he spent the whole time he was in line trying to figure out how to strike up a conversation with her, and finally, when she paid for her prediction, she started cussing like a sailor."

Gus laughed. "I love seeing where you get your admirable qualities from."

I flipped him off and went on. "Her prediction had gotten stuck halfway out of the machine. So Dad steps up to save the day. He manages to rip the top half of the ticket out, but the rest is still stuck in the machine, so Mom can't make sense of the words. So then he told her she'd better stick around and see if her fortune came out with his."

"Oh, *that* old line," Gus said, grinning.

"Works every time," I agreed. "Anyway, he put in his nickel and the two tickets came out. Hers said, *You will meet a handsome stranger*, and his said, *Your story's about to begin.*" They still had them framed in the living room. Or at least, when I was home for Christmas, they were still up.

That deep ache passed through me. It felt like a metal cheese slicer, pulled right through my center, left there midway through my body. I'd thought missing my dad would be the hardest thing I'd ever do. But the worst thing, the hardest thing, had turned out to be being angry with someone you couldn't fight it out with.

Someone you loved enough that you desperately *wanted* to push through the shit and find a way to make a new normal. I would never get a real explanation from Dad. Mom would never get an apology. We'd never be able to see things "from his point of view" or actively choose not to. He was gone, and everything of him we'd planned to hold on to was obliterated.

"They were married three months later," I told Gus. "Some twenty-five years after that, their only daughter's first book, *Kiss Kiss, Wish Wish* came out with Sandy Lowe Books, with a dedication that read—"

"'To my parents,'" Gus said. "'Who are proof of fate's strong, if animatronic, hand.'"

My mouth fell open. I'd almost forgotten what he had told me at the gas station, that he'd read my books. Or maybe I hadn't let myself think about it, because I was worried that meant he'd hated them, and somehow I was still competing with him, needing him to recognize me as his rival and equal.

"You remember that?" It came out as a whisper.

His eyes leapt toward me, and my heart rose in my throat. "It's why I asked about them," he said. "I thought it was the nicest dedication I'd ever read."

I made a face. Coming from him, that might not have been a compliment. "'Nicest.'"

"Fine, January," he said in a low voice. "I thought it was beautiful. Is that what you want me to admit?"

Again my heart buoyed through my chest. "Yes."

"I thought it was beautiful," he said immediately, sincerely.

I turned my face to the window. "Yeah, well. It turned out to be a lie. But I guess Mom thought it was a nice enough one. She knew he was cheating on her and she stayed with him."

"I'm sorry." For several minutes, neither of us spoke. Finally, Gus cleared his throat. He made it sound so natural. "You asked why New Eden. Why I wanted to write about it?"

I nodded, glad for the topic change, though surprised by his segue.

"I guess . . ." He tugged at his hair anxiously. "Well, my mom died when I was a kid. Don't know if you knew that."

I wasn't sure how I would have, but even if I didn't outright know it, it fit with the image of him I'd had in college. "I don't think so."

"Yeah," he said. "So, my dad was garbage, but my mom—she was amazing. And when I was a kid, I just thought, like, *Okay*, it's us against the world. We're stuck in this situation, but it's not forever. And I kept waiting for her to leave him. I mean—I kept a bag packed with a bunch of comic books and some socks and granola bars. I had this vision of us hopping on a train, riding to the end of the line, you know?" When his eyes flashed toward me, the corner of his mouth was curled, but the smile wasn't real.

It said, *Isn't that ridiculous? Wasn't I ridiculous?* And I knew how to read it because it was a smile I'd been practicing for a year: *Can you believe I was so stupid? Don't worry. I know better now.*

A weight pressed low in my stomach at the image: Gus, before he was the Gus I knew. A Gus who daydreamed about escape, who believed someone would rescue him.

"Where were you going to go?" I asked. It came out as little more than a whisper.

His eyes leapt back to the road and the muscle in his jaw pulsed, then relaxed, his face serene once more. "The redwoods," he said. "Pretty sure I thought we could build a tree house there."

"A tree house in the redwoods," I repeated quietly, like it was a prayer, a secret. In a way, it was. It was a tiny piece of a Gus I'd never imagined, one with romantic notions and hope for the unlikely. "But what does that have to do with New Eden?"

He coughed, checked his rearview mirror, went back to staring down the road. "I guess . . . a few years ago, I just sort of realized my mom wasn't a kid." He shrugged. "I'd thought we were waiting for the perfect time to leave, but she was never going to. She'd never said she was. She could have taken us out of there, and she didn't."

I shook my head. "I doubt it was that simple."

"That's why," he murmured. "I know it wasn't simple, and when I talk about this book, I tell people it's because I want to 'explore the reasons people stay, no matter the cost,' but the truth is I just want to understand *her* reasons. I know that doesn't make sense. This cult thing has nothing to do with her."

No matter the cost. What had staying cost his mother? What had it cost Gus? The weight in my stomach had spread, was pressing against the insides of my chest and palms. I'd started publishing romance because I wanted to dwell in my happiest moments, in the safe place my parents' love had always been. I'd been so comforted by books with the promise of a happy ending, and I'd wanted to give someone else that same gift.

Gus was writing to try to understand something horrible that had happened to him. No wonder what we wrote was so different.

"It does make sense," I said finally. "No one gets 'looking for postmortem parental answers' like I do. If I watched the movie *300* right now, I'd probably find a way to make it about my dad."

He gave me a faint smile. "Great cinema." It was so obviously a *Thank you* and a *Let's move on now.* As different as I'd thought we were, it felt a little bit like Gus and I were two aliens who'd stumbled into each other on Earth only to discover we shared a native language.

"We should have a film club," I said. "We're always on the same page about this stuff."

He was quiet for a moment, thoughtful. "It really was a beautiful dedication," he said. "It didn't feel like a lie. Maybe a complicated truth, but not a lie."

The warmth filled me up until I felt like a teakettle trying hard not to whistle.

When I got home, I turned on my computer and ordered my own copy of *The Revelatories*.

AND HERE CAME the true montage.

I did surgery on the book. I ripped it up and stored the pieces in separate files. Ellie became Eleanor. She went from being a down-on-her-luck real estate agent to a down-on-her-luck tight-rope walker with a port-wine stain the shape of a butterfly on her cheek, because Absurdly Specific Details. Her father became a sword swallower, her mother a bearded lady.

They moved from the twenty-first century to the early twentieth. They were part of a traveling circus. That was their family: a tight-knit group who ended every night smoking hand-rolled cigarettes around a fire. It was the only world she'd ever known.

They spent every moment with each other, but somehow told each other very little. There wasn't much time for talking in their line of work.

I renamed the file, from *BEACH_BOOK.docx* to *FAMILY_SECRETS.docx*.

I wanted to know whether you could ever fully know someone. If knowing *how* they were—how they moved and spoke and the faces they made and the things they tried not to look at—amounted to knowing them. Or if knowing things about them—where they'd been born, all the people they'd been, who they'd loved, the worlds they'd come from—added up to anything.

I gave them each a secret. That part was the easiest.

Eleanor's mother was dying but she didn't want anyone to know. The clowns everyone believed to be brothers were actually lovers. The sword swallower was still mailing checks to a family back in Oklahoma.

They became less and less like the people I knew, but somehow, their problems and secrets became more personal. I couldn't put my father or mother down on paper. I could never get that right. But these characters carried the truth of the people I'd loved.

I was particularly fond of writing a mechanic named Nick. I loved knowing that no one except me would ever recognize the skeleton of Augustus Everett I'd built the character around.

Gus and I made a habit of writing at our respective kitchen tables around noon, and most days we took turns holding up notes. They became more and more elaborate. It was obvious that while some were spontaneous, others were planned—written out earlier in the day, or even the night before. Whenever inspiration struck. Those written in the moment especially became non-sensical as writing-madness took us over. Sometimes I would laugh so hard I'd lose muscle control in my hands and be unable to write any more notes. We'd laugh until we both laid our heads down on our tables. He'd snort into his coffee. I'd nearly choke on mine.

It started with platitudes like IT IS BETTER TO HAVE LOVED AND LOST THAN TO HAVE NEVER LOVED AT ALL (me) and THE UNIVERSE SEEMS NEITHER BENIGN NOR HOSTILE, MERELY INDIFFERENT (him) but usually ended with things like FUCK WRITING (me) and SHOULD WE JUST DITCH THIS AND BECOME COAL MINERS? (him).

Once he wrote to tell me that LIFE IS LIKE A BOX OF CHOCOLATES. YOU REALLY DON'T KNOW WHAT YOU'RE EATING AND THE CHOCOLATE MAP IN THE LID IS FUCKING ALWAYS WRONG.

I wrote to tell him that IF YOU'RE A BIRD, I'M A BIRD.

He let me know that IN SPACE, NO ONE CAN HEAR YOU SCREAM, and I wrote back, NOT ALL WHO WANDER ARE LOST.

Going through Dad's stuff fell to the back burner, but I didn't mind procrastinating. For the first time in months, I wasn't flinching every time my phone or laptop pinged. I was making progress. Of course, a lot of that progress was research, but for every new factoid I gleaned about twentieth-century circus culture, it seemed like a new plot light bulb illuminated over my head.

At night, Gus and I sat on our separate decks, having a drink and watching the sun slide into the lake. Most nights we'd talk from across the gap, mostly about how productive we had or hadn't been, about the people we could see from our decks and the stories we could imagine for them. We'd talk about the books (and movies) we'd loved (and hated), the people we'd gone to school with (both together at U of M and before that: Sara Tulane, who used to pull my hair in kindergarten; Mariah Sjogren, who broke up with sixteen-year-old Gus—a full three months into their relationship, he was way too proud to tell me—because he smoked a cigarette in the car with her and "kissing a smoker is like licking an ashtray").

We talked about our terrible jobs (my part-time car wash position in high school, where I regularly got sexually harassed by customers and had to scrub down the tunnel before I could go home at night; his call-center job at a uniform manufacturer, where he got yelled at for incorrect embroideries and delayed shipments). We talked about the most embarrassing albums we'd owned and concerts we'd been to (redacted for the sake of dignity).

And other times, we'd sit in silence, not quite together but definitely not alone.

"So what do you think?" I asked him one night. "Are romance and happiness harder than they look?"

After a moment, he said, "I never said that they were easy."

"You implied it," I pointed out.

"I implied they were easy for *you*," he said. "For me, they're about as challenging as I'm sure you're imagining."

The possibility hung in the air: at any time, one of us could have invited the other over, and either of us would have accepted. But neither of us asked, and so things went on as they'd been.

On Friday, we left for our research excursion a bit earlier than we had the week prior and headed east, inland.

"Who are we meeting this time?" I asked.

Gus answered only, "Dave."

"Ah, yes, Dave. I'm a big fan of his restaurant, Wendy's."

"Believe it or not, different Dave," Gus said. He was lost in thought, barely playing along with our usual banter.

I waited for him to go on but he didn't. "Gus?"

His gaze flinched toward me, as if he'd forgotten I was there and my presence had startled him. He scratched at his jaw. His usual five-o'clock shadow had stretched closer toward a seven-o'clock dusk.

"Everything okay?" I asked.

His eyes bounced between me and the road three times before he nodded. I could almost see it—him swallowing down whatever he'd been considering saying. "Dave was part of New Eden," he said instead. "He was just a kid back then. His mother took him out of there a few months before the fire. His dad stayed behind. He was in too deep."

"So his father . . ."

Gus nodded. "Died in the fire."

We were meeting Dave at an Olive Garden, and on the way in, Gus warned me that Dave was a recovering alcoholic. "Three years sober," Gus said as we waited at the host stand. "I told him we wouldn't be drinking anything."

We'd beaten Dave to the table and put in an order for a couple of sodas. We'd had no problem talking in the car, but sitting across from each other in an Olive Garden booth was a different story.

"Do you feel like your mom just dropped us off here before homecoming?" I asked.

"I never went to homecoming," he said.

I pretended to play a violin, at which point I realized I had no idea how a person actually held a violin.

"What's that," Gus said flatly. "What are you doing?"

"I think I'm holding a violin," I answered.

"No," he said. "No, I can safely say you are not."

"Seriously?"

"Yes, seriously. Why is your left arm straight out like that? Is the violin supposed to balance atop it? You need that hand on the neck."

"You're just trying to distract me from the tragedy of your missed homecoming."

He laughed, rolled his eyes, scooted forward on his bench. "Somehow, I survived, tender human heart intact," he said, repeating my words from the carnival.

Now *I* rolled my eyes. Gus smiled and bumped my knee with his under the table. I bumped his back. We sat there for a minute, grinning at each other over a basket of Olive Garden breadsticks. I felt a little bit like there was water boiling in my chest. At once, I could feel his calloused hands gathering my hair off my neck as I puked into a carnival trash can. I could feel them on my hips and waist, pressing me closer as we danced in the sweaty frat house basement. I could feel the side of his jaw scrape my temple.

He broke eye contact first, checked his phone. "Twenty minutes late," he said without looking at me. "I'll give him ten more before I call."

But Dave didn't answer Gus's call. And he didn't answer Gus's texts, or his voice mail, and soon we were an hour and twenty minutes into the bottomless breadsticks, and our server, Vanessa, had started seriously avoiding our table.

"Sometimes this happens," Gus said. "They get spooked. Change their minds. Think they're ready to talk about something when they're really not."

"What do we do?" I asked. "Should we keep waiting?"

Gus opened one of the menus on the table. He flipped through it for a minute, then pointed to a picture of a frozen blue drink with a pink umbrella sprouting out of it. "That," he said. "I think that's what we do."

"Well, shit," I said. "If we drink our frozen blue things *now* then I'll have to totally rethink my plan for tomorrow night."

Gus lifted an eyebrow. "Wow, I was living the lifestyle of a romance writer all along and I didn't even know it."

"See? You were born for this, Augustus Everett."

He shuddered.

"Why do you do that?"

"What?" he said.

I repeated, "Augustus Everett." His shoulders lifted, although a bit more discreetly this time. *"That."*

Gus raised the menu as Vanessa was trying to bound past and she screeched to a stop like Wile E. Coyote at the edge of a cliff. "Could we get two of these blue things?" he asked.

His eyes were doing the sexy, intimidating X-ray thing. Color rushed into her cheeks. Or maybe I was projecting what was happening to me onto her. "Sure thing." She sped away, and Gus looked back at the menu.

"Augustus," I said.

"Shit," he said, flinching again.

"You really don't like sharing things about yourself with other people, do you?"

"Not particularly," he said. "You already know about the vomit-phobia. Anything more than that and you'll have to sign a nondisclosure."

"Happily," I said.

Gus sighed and leaned forward, forearms resting on the table. His knee grazed mine beneath the table, but neither of us moved away, and all the heat in my body seemed to focus there. "The only person who called me that was my father." He shrugged. "That name was usually said with a disapproving tone. Or screamed in a rage."

My stomach twisted and a sour taste crept across the back of my mouth as I grasped for something to say. I couldn't help searching his pupils for signs of the history he'd been piecing together for days. His mother had stayed with his father, *no matter the cost*, and part of that had been her son learning to hate his own name.

Gus's gaze lifted from the menu. He looked calm, serious. But it was a practiced look, unlike the alluring openness that sometimes overtook his face when he was deep in thought, working to understand some new information.

"I'm sorry," I said helplessly. "That your dad was an asshole."

Gus gave a breathless laugh. "Why do people always say that? You don't need to be sorry. It's in the past. I didn't tell you so you'd be sorry."

"Well, you told me because I asked. So at least let me be sorry for that."

He shrugged. "It's fine."

"Gus," I said.

He looked me in the eye again. It felt like a warm tide rushing over me, feet to head. His expression had shifted to open curiosity. "What were *you* like?" he said.

"What?"

"You know enough about my childhood. I want to know about baby January."

"Oh, God," I said. "She was a lot."

His laugh vibrated through the table, and my insides started fizzing like champagne. "Let me guess. Loud. Precocious. Room full of books, organized in a way that only you understood. Close with your family and a couple of tight-knit friends, all of whom you probably still talk to regularly, but casual friends with anyone else with a pulse. A secret overachiever, who had to be the best at something even if no one else knew. Oh, and prone to juggling or tap-dancing for attention in any crowd."

"Wow," I said a little stunned. "You both nailed *and* roasted me—though the tap lessons were my mom's idea. I just wanted the shoes. Anyway, you missed that I briefly had a shrine to Sinéad O'Connor, because I thought it made me seem Interesting."

He laughed and shook his head. "I bet you were an adorable little freak."

"I *was* a freak," I said. "I think being an only child did that. My parents treated me like a living TV. Like I was just this hilarious, interesting baby genius. I seriously spent most of my life delusively confident in myself and my future."

And that no matter what else, home would always be a safe place, where all three of us belonged. A burning sensation flared in my chest. When I looked up and met Gus's eyes, I remembered where I was, who I was talking to, and half expected him to gloat. The bright-eyed ingenue with all the happy endings had finally gotten chewed up, the rose-colored glasses ground to dust.

Instead, he said, "There are worse things to be than delusively confident."

I studied his dark, focused eyes and lax, crooked mouth: a look of complete sincerity. I was more convinced than ever that I wasn't the only one who'd changed since college, and I wasn't sure what to say to this new Gus Everett.

At some point the frozen blue cocktails had appeared on the table, as if by magic. I cleared my throat and lifted my glass. "To Dave."

"To Dave," Gus agreed, clinking his plastic cup to mine.

"The greatest disappointment of this evening by far," I said, "is that they didn't actually include the paper umbrellas."

"See," Gus said. "It's shit like this that makes it impossible for me to believe in happy endings. You never get the paper umbrellas you were promised in this world."

"Gus," I said. "You must *be* the paper umbrellas you wish to see in this world."

"Gandhi was a wise man."

"Actually, I was quoting my favorite poet, Jewel."

His knee pressed into mine, and heat pooled between my legs. I pressed back. His rough fingertips tentatively touched my knee, slid up until he found my hand. Slowly, I turned my palm up to him, and his thumb drew heavy circles on it for a minute.

When I slid it closer, he folded his fingers into mine, and we sat there, holding hands under the table, pretending we weren't. Pretending we weren't acting sixteen years old and a little bit obsessed with each other.

God, what was happening? What was I doing and why couldn't I make myself stop? What was *he* doing?

When the check came, Gus jerked back from me and pulled his wallet out. "I got it," he said, without looking at me.

13

The Dream

I DREAMED ABOUT GUS Everett and woke up needing a shower.

14

The Rule

'D HAD SATURDAY planned for three days, which freed me up to spend the morning working on the book. It was slow going, not because I didn't have ideas, but because it required such painstaking research to confirm that each scene was historically possible.

I'd started working at eight and had managed to write about five hundred words by the time Gus came to sit at his kitchen table, facing mine. He wrote his first note of the day and held it up. I squinted to read.

SORRY I GOT WEIRD LAST NIGHT.

My notebook and marker were already ready. They always were. I didn't know exactly what he meant, but I imagined it had something to do with being adults who weren't dating but were holding hands under a table at Olive Garden. I fought a sinking feeling in my stomach. Yes, it had been weird.

I had also loved it.

From watching Shadi's love life, I knew how relationship-phobes like Gus Everett reacted when boundaries broke down, when things went from friendly to intimate, or from sexual to romantic. Guys like Gus were *never* the ones to pump the brakes when the emotional-entanglement train started moving, and they were *always* the ones to jump out and roll clear of the tracks once they realized they'd reached top speed.

I needed to keep my head straight and eyes clear—no romanticizing allowed. As soon as things got complicated, Gus would be gone, and in this moment, I was realizing how *not* ready for that I was. He was my only friend here. I had to protect that. Besides, there was the bet, which I couldn't fully benefit from if he ghosted me before I even won.

I wrote back:

DON'T BE RIDICULOUS, GUS. YOU WERE ALWAYS WEIRD.

The corner of his mouth twitched into a smile. He held my gaze for a beat too long, then turned his focus back to the notebook. When he held it up next, it showcased a series of numbers. I recognized the first three as the local area code.

My stomach flipped. I scribbled the numbers down small at the top of the page, then wrote my own phone number much larger beneath it, followed by, *I'M STILL GOING TO WRITE THESE NOTES.*

Gus replied, *GOOD.*

I wrote another five hundred words by three thirty in the afternoon, at which point I drove over to Goodwill to drop off the load of boxes I'd filled from the upstairs guest room and bath. When I got back, I scrubbed the upstairs bathroom clean, then padded back downstairs to shower in the bathroom I'd been using for the past two weeks. The picture of my dad and Sonya still hung on the wall, photo facing inward.

I'd felt too guilty to destroy it, but I figured it was only a matter of time until I worked up the courage. For now it was a bleak reminder that the hardest work was still ahead of me: the basement I hadn't even peeked into and the master bedroom I'd thoroughly avoided.

I still hadn't really been down to the beach, which seemed like a shame, so after I'd made a pot of macaroni to tide me over until tonight, I picked my way down the wooded trail to the water. The light bouncing over the waves from the setting sun was incredible, all reds and golds blazing over the lake's back. I slipped out of my shoes and carried them to the edge of the water, gasping out a swear as the icy tide rushed over my feet. I scrambled back, laughing breathlessly from the sheer shock of it.

The air was warm but not even close to hot enough to make the chill pleasant. Most of the people left on the beach had pulled sweatshirts on or wrapped themselves in towels and blankets. Everyone, all those wind-beaten and sunburned faces, all that lake-tangled hair, those eyes squinting into the fierce light. Looking at the same setting sun.

It made me ache. I felt suddenly more alone than ever. There was no floppy-haired, romantic Jacques waiting for me in Queens—no one to cook me a real meal or whisk me away from the computer. No missed calls or *Was just thinking about Karyn and*

Sharyn and almost peed again texts from Mom, and no way for me to send her a picture of the sunlight dripping onto the lake without opening the wound that was the lake house.

I'd only seen Shadi twice since the funeral, and with her work schedule, most texts from her came in long after I'd gone to bed, and most of my replies went out long before she'd wake up.

My writer friends had stopped checking in too, as if sensing that every note from them, every call and text, was just one more reminder of how terribly far behind I had fallen. Was falling. Every moment of every day, I was tripping backward while the rest of the world marched forward.

Honestly, I even missed Sharyn and Karyn: sitting on their colorful rag rug drinking the nasty-ass bathtub moonshine they were so proud of while they hawked homemade essential oils that smelled great, even if they didn't actually cure cancer.

My world felt empty. Like there was no one in it, except sometimes Gus, and nothing in it except this book, and the bet. And no matter how much better *this* book felt than every iteration of it that had come in the last twelve months, it wasn't enough.

I was on a beautiful beach, in a beautiful place, and I was alone. Worse, I wasn't sure I'd ever stop being alone again. I wanted my mom, and I missed my lying dad.

I sat down in the sand, folded my legs to my chest, rested my forehead against my knees, and cried. I cried until my face was hot and red and soaking wet, and I would've kept crying if a seagull didn't shit on my head, but of course, it did.

And so I stood and turned back to the path only to find someone frozen in the middle of it, watching me ugly cry like Tom Hanks in *Cast Away*.

It was like something out of a movie, the way Gus was standing there, except that there was nothing romantic or magical about it. Even though I'd been sobbing about being alone, he was one of the last people I would've chosen to see me like this. Momentarily forgetting the pile of bird excrement on my head, I wiped at my face and eyes, trying to make myself look more . . . something.

"Sorry," Gus said, visibly uncomfortable. He glanced sidelong down the beach. "I saw you come down here, and I just . . ."

"A bird pooped on my head," I said tearily. Apparently there was nothing more to say than *that*.

His look of painful empathy cracked under a soundless laugh. He closed the gap between us and pulled me roughly into a hug. The action seemed uncomfortable, if not painful, for him at first, but even so it was something of a relief to be held.

"You don't have to tell me," he said. "But just so you know . . . you can."

I buried my face in his shoulder, and his hands' clumsy patting against my back settled into slow, gentle circles, before they stopped moving at all, just curled in against my spine, easing me closer. I let myself sink into him. The crying had stopped as fast as it had started. All I could think about was the press of his hard stomach and chest, the sharp ridges of his hips and the almost smoky smell of him. The heat of his body and his breath.

It was a bad idea to stand here like this with him, touch him like this, but it was also intoxicating. I decided to count to three and then let go.

I got to two before his hand slid into my hair, cradling the back of my head, then jerked suddenly clear as he took an abrupt step back. "Wow. That's a lot of shit."

He was staring at his hand and the goop dripping off of it.

"Yeah, I said 'bird' but it very well could have been a dinosaur."

"No kidding. I guess we should get cleaned up before we take off for the night."

I sniffed and wiped the residual tears away from my eyes. "Was *take off* an intentional bird pun or . . . ?"

"Hell no," Gus said, turning back toward the trail with me. "I said that because I assumed we would be taking a helicopter ride over the lake."

A ripple of timid laughter went through me, breaking up the residual knot of emotion and heat in my chest. "Is that your final guess?"

He looked me up and down, as if weighing my outfit against some widely recognized helicopter-date uniform. "Yeah, I think so."

"Sooo close."

"Really?" he said. "What is it, then? Tiny airplane over the lake? Tiny submarine *under* the lake?"

"You'll have to wait and find out."

We parted ways between our houses, agreeing to meet at my car in twenty minutes. When I'd washed my hair for the second time that day, I threw it into a bun and put the same (poop-free) outfit back on. I'd packed most of the supplies for our trip earlier that day, so all I had left to do was grab the rest out of the fridge and stuff it into the cooler I'd found on one of the kitchen's bottom shelves.

It was 7:30 when Gus and I finally set out and 8:40 when we finally pulled in to Meg Ryan Night at Big Boy Bobby's Drive-In.

"Oh my God," Gus said as we drove up to the booth to hand over the tickets I'd bought online. "This is a triple feature." He was reading the glowing marquee to our right: *When Harry Met Sally*, *Sleepless in Seattle*, and *You've Got Mail*. "Aren't half of those Christmas movies?"

The attendant raised the gate and I pulled through. "Half of three is one and a half, so no, half of these movies aren't Christmas movies."

"Have I mentioned that Meg Ryan's face pisses me off?"

I scoffed. "One, no. Two, that's impossible. Her face is adorable and perfect."

"Maybe that's what it is," Gus said. "I couldn't tell you, and I know it's not logical, but I . . . just can't stand her."

"Tonight that's all going to change," I promised. "Trust me. You just have to open your heart. If you can do that, your world's going to be a much brighter place from now on. And *maybe* you'll even stand a chance at writing a sellable rom-com."

"January," he said solemnly as I backed into an open parking spot, "just *imagine* what you'd do to me if I took you to a six-hour-long Jonathan Franzen reading."

"I cannot and I will not," I said. "And if you choose to use one of our Friday nights in such a way, there's nothing I can do to stop you, but it's Saturday and thus I'm the captain of this ship. Now come help me figure out where we can buy the Big Bobby Ice Cream Surprise I read about online. According to the website it is 'SOOO Worth It!'"

"It had better be." Gus sighed, climbing out of the Kia to join me. As the previews flashed clunkily across the screen, we made our way through the field to the concession stands. I beelined for the wooden sign painted to look like an ice cream sundae, but Gus touched my arm, stopping me from getting in line right away. "Will you just promise me one thing?"

"Gus, I won't fall in love with you."

"One more thing," he said. "Please just try your hardest not to puke."

"If I start to, I'll just swallow it."

Gus cupped his hand over his mouth and gagged.

"Kidding! I won't puke. At least not until you take me to that six-hour reading. Now come on. I've spent all week looking forward to eating something other than cold Pop-Tarts."

"I don't think this is going to be the vitamin- and nutrient-rich smorgasbord you seem to be imagining."

"I don't need vitamins. I need nacho cheese and chocolate sauce."

"Ah, in that case, you planned the perfect night."

Because I'd bought the tickets, Gus paid for the popcorn and the Ice Cream Surprises ($6 each, decidedly un-worth it), and he tried to buy us sodas before I completely indiscreetly cut him off, doing my best to signal that we had other options in the car.

When we got back, I opened the tailgate and put the middle seats flat, revealing the setup of pillows and blankets I'd packed earlier, along with the cooler full of beer. "Impressed?" I asked Gus.

"By your car's trunk space? Absolutely."

"Har-har-har," I said.

"Har-har-har," Gus said back.

We climbed through the open trunk and I turned the car on, tuning the radio to the right channel to pick up the movie's audio before settling in beside Gus just as the opening credits began. Despite what he'd said about trunk space, the Kia wasn't exactly big. Lying on our stomachs, chins propped up on our hands, we were very nearly touching in several places, and our elbows *were* touching. This position wouldn't be comfortable for long, and re-arranging with both of us in the car was going to be a challenge. Being this close to him was also going to be a challenge.

As soon as Meg Ryan appeared onscreen, he leaned a little closer and whispered, "Her face really doesn't bother you?"

"I think you should see a doctor," I hissed. "That's not a normal reaction." As soon as I got my first book advance, I'd bought Shadi and myself both like twenty Meg Ryan movies so we could watch them together long-distance whenever we wanted, starting them at the same exact moment so we could text about what was happening in real time and pausing whenever one of us had to pee.

"Just wait until you hear how Meg Ryan pronounces *horses* when she sings 'Sleigh Ride,'" I whispered to Gus. "Your life will be irrevocably changed."

Gus gave me a look like I wasn't helping my case. "She just looks so damn *smug*," he said.

"A lot of people have told me I look like her," I said.

"There's no way that's true."

"Okay, they haven't, but they *should* have."

"That's ridiculous," he said. "You look nothing like her."

"On the one hand, I'm offended. On the other, I'm relieved you probably don't loathe my face."

"There's nothing to loathe about your face," he said matter-of-factly.

"There's nothing to loathe about Meg Ryan's face either."

"Fine, I take it back. I love her face. Does that make you happy?"

I turned toward him. His head was propped in his hand, his body angled toward me, and the light from the screen just barely caught his eyes, drawing liquidy slivers of color in them. His dark hair was as messy as ever, but his facial hair was back under control, and that smoky smell still hung on him.

"January?" he murmured.

I maneuvered onto my side, facing him, and nodded. "It makes me happy."

His knee bumped mine. I bumped his back.

A shadow of a smile passed over his serious face, there and gone so fast I might've imagined it. "Good," he said.

We stayed like that for a long time, pretending to watch the movie from an angle where neither of us could possibly see more than half the screen, our knees pressed into one another.

Whenever one of us rearranged, the other followed. Whenever one of us could no longer bear the discomfort of one position, we both shifted. But we never stopped touching.

We were in dangerous territory.

I hadn't felt like this in years—that almost painful weight of *wanting*, that paralyzing fear that any wrong move would ruin everything.

I glanced up when I felt his gaze on me, and he didn't look away. I wanted to say something to break the tension, but my mind was mercilessly blank. Not the blinking-cursor-on-a-white-screen blank of trying to concoct a novel from thin air. The color-popping-in-darkness blank of scrunching your eyes shut. Of staring at flames too long.

The pulsing blank of *feeling* so much you're incapable of *thinking* anything.

The staring contest stretched an uncomfortable distance without either of us breaking it. His eyes looked nearly black, and when the light from the screen hit them, the illusion of flames sparked in them, then vanished.

Somewhere deep in my mind, a self-preservation instinct was screaming, *THOSE ARE THE EYES OF A PREDATOR*, but that was exactly why nature gave predators eyes like that. So dumb little rabbits like me wouldn't stand a chance.

Don't be a dumb bunny, January!

"I have to go to the bathroom," I said abruptly.

Gus smiled. "You just went to the bathroom."

"I have a really tiny bladder," I said.

"I'll go with you."

"That's okay!" I chirped and, forgetting I was in a car, sat up so fast I slammed my head into the roof.

"Shit!" Gus said at the same time I hissed out a confused, "WHAT?"

He bolted up and shuffled on his knees toward where I sat, clutching my head. "Let me see." His hands cradled the sides of my face, tilting my head down so he could see the crown of my skull. "It's not bleeding," he told me, then angled my face back up into his, his fingers threaded gently through my hair. His eyes wandered down to my mouth, and his crooked lips parted.

Oh, damn.

I was a bunny.

I leaned toward him, and his hands went to my waist, drawing me onto his lap so that I was straddling him where he knelt. His nose brushed the side of mine, and I lifted my mouth under his, trying to close the gap between us. Our slow breaths pressed us into each other and his hands squeezed my sides, my thighs tightening against him in reaction.

One time one time one time was all I could think. That was his policy, right? Would it really be so bad if something happened between us, just once? We could go back to being friends, neighbors who talked every day. Could I do *casual*, this one time, with my college crush turned nemesis, seven years after the fact? I couldn't think clearly enough to figure it out. My breathing was shaky and shallow; his was nonexistent.

We hovered there for a minute, like neither of us wanted to accept the blame.

You touched me first! I'd say.

You leaned in! he'd fire back.

And then you scooped me into your lap!

And you lifted your mouth toward mine!

And then—

His mouth dragged warm breath across my jaw and then up to my lips. His teeth skated across my bottom lip, and a small hum of pleasure went through me. His mouth quirked into a smile even as it sank hot and light against my mouth, coaxing it open. He tasted like vanilla and cinnamon left over from the Ice Cream Surprise, only better than the dessert itself had. His heat rushed into my mouth, into me, until it was flooding through me, racing like a river current baked hot by the sun. Want dripped through me, pooling in all the nooks that formed between our bodies.

I reached for a handful of his shirt, feeling the warmth of his skin through the thin material. I needed him closer, to remember how it felt to be pressed against him, to be wrapped around him. One of his hands swept up the side of my neck, his fingers curling under my hair. I sighed into his mouth as he kissed me again, slower, deeper, rougher. He tipped my mouth up to him for more, and I grabbed for his ribs, trying to get closer. He leaned into me until my back met the side of the car, until he pressed hard against me.

A stupid gasp escaped me at the feel of his chest unyielding against mine, and I ground my hips against his. He braced one hand on the window behind me, and his teeth caught my bottom lip again, a little harder this time. My breaths came fast and shaky as his hand swiped down the car window to my chest, feeling me through my shirt.

I raked my hands through his hair, arched into the press of his hand, and a low, involuntary groan lifted in his throat. He leaned away and flipped me onto my back, and I greedily pulled him over me. A pulse went through me at the feeling of him hard against me, and I tried to will him closer than clothes allowed. That sound rasped out of him again.

I couldn't remember the last time I'd been this turned on.

Actually, I could. It was seven years ago in a frat house basement.

His hand slipped up beneath my shirt, his thumb scraping up the length of my hip bone and seeming to melt it as he went. His mouth grazed hot and damp down my neck, sinking heavily against my collarbone. My whole body was begging him for more without any subtlety, lifting toward him as if pulled by a magnet. I felt like a teenager, and it was wonderful, and it was horrible, and—

He tightened over me as light hit us, as cold and sobering as if someone had dumped a bucket of ice water on us. We sprang apart at the sight of the surly middle-aged woman with the flashlight aimed our way. She had a frizzy triangle of gray hair and a bright blue track jacket screen printed with the BIG BOY BOBBY'S logo.

She cleared her throat.

Gus was still propped up over me with one hand tangled in the hem of my shirt.

"This is a *family* establishment," the woman hissed.

"Well, you're doing a great job." Gus's voice was thick and husky. He cleared it again and gave the woman his best Evil smile. "My wife and I were just saying we should bring the kids here sometime."

She folded her arms, apparently immune to the charms of his mouth. Must be nice.

Gus knelt back onto his heels, and I tugged my shirt down. "Sorry about that," I said, mortified.

The woman jerked a thumb down the dark, grassy aisle between cars. "Out," she barked.

"Of course," Gus said quickly and jerked the tailgate closed, shutting us off from her. I burst out in humiliated, deranged laughter, and Gus turned toward me with a faint smile, his lips bruised and swollen, his hair disastrous.

"That was such a bad idea," I whispered helplessly.

"Yeah." Gus's voice slipped back into its dangerous rasp. He leaned forward through the dark and caught me in one last viciously slow, dementedly hot kiss, his fingers spanning the side of my face. "Won't happen again," he told me, and all the sparks awake in my bloodstream fizzled out just a bit.

One time. That was his rule. But did *this* count? My gut twisted with disappointment. It couldn't. It had done nothing to satisfy me. If anything, it had left me worse off than before, and from the way Gus was staring at me, I thought he must feel the same way.

The woman banged on the back window, and we both jumped.

"We should go," Gus said.

I scrambled from the back of the car into the front seat. Gus got out the back door and back into the passenger seat.

I drove us home, feeling like my body was a heat map and everywhere he'd touched, everywhere he looked when he glanced over from the passenger seat, was glowing red.

GUS DIDN'T APPEAR at the kitchen table at noon on Sunday. I figured that was a bad sign—that what had happened had destroyed the only friendship I had in this town. Really, one of only several friendships I had the world over, since Jacques and my couple of friends, it had turned out, had no use for Just Me.

I tried to put Gus out of my mind, to work on the book with singular focus, but I went back to jumping every time my phone buzzed.

A text from Anya: Hey, love! Just wanted to check in. The house would really like to see some initial pages, to give some input.

An email from Pete: Hello! Good news! Your books will be in stock tomorrow. Is there a day this week you could stop by to sign?

An email from Sonya, which I did not open but whose first sentence I could see: Please, please don't let me scare you off from book club. I'm totally happy to stay home on Monday nights if you'd like to keep . . .

A text from Shadi: January. Help. I cannot get ENOUGH of that haunted hat. He's come over the last THREE nights and last night I let him STAY.

I texted her back, You know exactly where this is going. You're INTO him!!

I HATE falling in love, she replied. It's always ruining my bad-boy reputation!!

I sent her a sad face. I know, but you must persevere. For the good of the Haunted Hat and so I can live vicariously through you.

Memories from last night flashed across my mind as bright and hot as fireworks, the sparks landing and burning everywhere he'd touched. I could feel the ghost of his teeth on my collarbone, and my shoulder blade was a little bruised from the car door.

Hunger and embarrassment raced through me in one twisted braid.

God, what had I done? I should have known better. And then there was the part of me that couldn't stop thinking, *Am I going to get to do it again?*

It didn't *have* to mean anything. Maybe this was it: I would finally learn how to have a casual relationship.

Or maybe the deal was off and I would literally never hear from Gus Everett again.

I was out of both cereal and ramen, so after I'd painfully churned out three hundred words, I decided to break for a grocery trip and, on my way out the door, saw that Gus's car wasn't in its usual spot on the street. I forced the thought from my head. This didn't have to be a big deal.

At the grocery store, I checked my bank account again, then wandered the aisles with my phone calculator open, adding up the price of Frosted Mini-Wheats and cans of soup. I'd managed to put together a decent haul for sixteen dollars when I rounded the corner to the checkout and saw her there.

Curly white hair, willowy frame, that same crocheted shawl.

Panic coursed through me so fast I felt like I'd gotten an adrenaline shot in the heart. I abandoned my cart right there in the aisle and, head down, booked it past her toward the doors. If she saw me, she didn't say anything. Or if she did, my heart was pounding too loud for me to hear it. I jumped back into my car feeling like I'd robbed a bank and drove twenty minutes to another grocery store, where I was so shaken up and paranoid about another run-in that I barely managed to get anything.

By the time I got home, I was still shaky, and it didn't help that Gus's car hadn't reappeared. It was one thing to have to dodge Sonya in my bimonthly grocery trips. If I wound up having to avoid my next-door neighbor, I was pretty sure *Plan B: Move to Duluth* would have to take effect.

Before I crawled into bed that night, I peeked out the front windows one more time, but Gus's car was still missing. Dread inflated in my chest like the world's least fun balloon. I'd finally found a friend, someone I could talk to, who'd seemed to want to be around me as much as I wanted to be around him, and now he was just gone. Because we'd kissed. Anger reared up in me, forcing my humiliation and loneliness out of the way for just a while before they buoyed to the surface again.

I thought about texting him, but it seemed like the weirdest possible time to start, so instead I went to sleep, a sick, anxious feeling coiled in my stomach.

By Monday morning, he still wasn't back. *Tonight*, I decided. If his car wasn't along the curb tonight, I could text him. That wouldn't be weird.

I put him out of my mind and pounded out two thousand fresh words, then texted Anya: Going well (actually (seriously (I mean it this time!))) but I'd like to get a little more done before anyone reads the partial. I think it's going to be hard to tell where I'm going with this without the complete picture and I'm afraid if I jump forward to outline it will kill all momentum I've finally built up.

Next, I replied to Pete: Great! How does Wednesday work? The truth was, I could've come in on Sunday when I got the email, or on Monday when I sent the reply. But I didn't want another invitation to the Red Blood, White Russians, and Blue Jeans Book Club. Putting off my stop at the bookstore until Wednesday eliminated one more potential week of that whole experience without having to reject the invitation.

By eleven that night, Gus's car still wasn't back, and I'd talked myself into and out of texting him five times. Finally, I put my phone in the drawer of the side table, clicked off the lamp, and went to sleep.

Tuesday I awoke soaked in sweat. I'd forgotten to set my alarm, and the sun was streaking through the blinds in full force, baking me in its pale light. It had to be close to eleven. I slid out from under the thick duvet and lay there for another minute.

I still felt a little sick. And then a little furious that I felt sick. It was so dumb. I was a grown woman. Gus had told me exactly how he operated, exactly what he thought about romance, and he'd never said or done anything to suggest he'd changed his mind. I knew that no matter how attracted to him I occasionally felt, the only place our relationship could go was through a revolving door in and out of his bedroom.

Or the back of my deeply uncool car.

And even if things had gone further that night, it wouldn't have precluded him from disappearing for days. There was exactly one way that I could theoretically *have* Gus Everett, and it would leave me feeling sick like this as soon as it was over.

I needed to get him out of my head.

I took a cold shower. Or, at least, I took one second of a cold shower, during which I screamed the f-word and almost broke my ankle lunging away from the stream of water. How the hell were people in books always taking cold showers? I turned the water back to hot and fumed as I washed my hair.

I wasn't mad at *him*. I couldn't be. I was furious with myself for wandering down this path. I *knew* better. Gus wasn't Jacques. Guys like Jacques wanted snowball fights and kisses at the top of the Eiffel Tower and sunrise strolls on the Brooklyn Bridge. Guys like Gus wanted snarky banter and casual sex on top of their unfolded laundry.

In the back of your deeply uncool car at a family establishment.

Although I couldn't be sure that hadn't been *my* idea.

It was conceivable that I'd thrown myself at him. It wouldn't be the first time I was seeing through rose-colored glasses, assigning meaning where there was none.

I was being stupid. After everything with my dad, I should have known better. I'd just barely started to heal, and I'd run right out and gotten a crush on the one person who was *guaranteed* to prove right every single fear I had about relationships.

I needed to let this go.

Writing, I decided, would be my solace. It was slow going at first, every word a decision not to think about Gus disappearing, but after a while I found a rhythm, almost as strong as yesterday's.

The family circus wound up back in Oklahoma, close to where Eleanor's father's secret second family lived. A week, I decided. The bulk of this book was going to take place over the week the circus was parked in Town TBD (Tulsa?), Oklahoma. Writing in a different era presented a completely new challenge. I was leaving a lot of notes to myself like *Find out what drinks were popular then* or *Insert historically accurate insult.*

What mattered, though, was that I had a vision.

All the secrets were going to come to the surface, almost win out, and then they'd be packed back down neatly. That was how an Augustus Everett novel would go, wouldn't it? He would say it had a nice cyclical quality when I told him.

(If I got the chance to tell him.)

I wanted the readers to be cheering, begging for Eleanor's found family to tell the truth by the end, while watching through their fingers, afraid of how the situation would implode. Someone needed a gun, I realized, and a reason to have a hair-trigger reaction. Fear, of course. I needed to pressure-cook the situation.

Build and build, only to tamp it back down in time for the characters to move along to their next destination.

Eleanor's father would owe money to dangerous men back in his hometown—ostensibly the reason he'd left in the first place, why he'd abandoned his family.

Eleanor's mother would have the gun. It seemed only fair to give her something to fight with. But with it, she'd have to shoulder the weight of some PTSD, remnants of an old employer who liked to get violent with the girls who worked for him. She needed to be wound tight, ready to snap, like I'd been feeling this past year.

Like I wanted Mom to be after the full extent of Dad's lies came to light.

Eleanor, for her part, was going to fall in love with a local. Or at least fancy herself having done so, the night of their first performance in Tulsa. She would spend the week moving closer to escaping the life she'd grown up in, only to have a horrible last-minute revelation that no matter how she might sometimes despise this world, it was the only one in which she belonged.

Or maybe she would realize the world she'd lusted after, the one she'd watched from behind circus tents and atop tightropes, that filtered past while she was hard at work, was as much an illusion as the one she knew.

The boy would fall in love with someone else, just as quickly as he had with her.

Or the boy would leave for college, the military.

Or his parents would find out about Eleanor and persuade him of his recklessness.

It would be an anti-romance. And I was entirely capable of writing it.

15

The Past

A ND THERE'S THE author herself!" Pete called when I stepped into the coffee shop. "A pink eye for you, hon?"

Probably she meant red-eye. Either way, I shook my head. "What else do you recommend?"

"Green tea's good for you," Pete mused.

"Well, sign me up." My body could use some antioxidants. Or whatever was in green tea that made it "good for you." Mom had told me, but the point had been pleasing her, not cleansing myself, so I didn't totally remember.

Pete handed me the plastic cup, and this time she let me pay. I ignored the sinking in my stomach. How much money did I have left in my bank account? How long until I had to crawl back to my now-ruined childhood home with my tail between my knees?

I reminded myself that *FAMILY_SECRETS.docx* was rapidly

growing into a book-like thing. Even one I'd be curious to read. Sandy Lowe might not end up wanting it, but surely, *someone* would.

Okay, not surely. But hopefully.

Pete took off the apron as she led the way into the bookstore.

"Maybe you should get a Clark Kent trench coat," I said. "Seems like less hassle than bows and knots."

"Yes, and who doesn't want to buy their coffee from a gal in a trench coat," Pete said.

"Touché."

"So here we go." Pete stopped at *The Revelatories* display, which was now only halfway a pyramid of *Revelatories*. The other half was comprised of bubblegum pink, bright yellow, and sky blue books. Pete beamed. "Thought it would be kinda neat to do this local-authors display. Showcase the whole spectrum of what we've got goin' on here in North Bear. What do ya think? Grab a stack, by the way." Pete was already carrying an armload over to the counter, where a roll of AUTOGRAPHED stickers and a couple of Sharpies awaited.

"It's great," I said, following her with another stack.

"And Everett?" she said.

"Great," I answered, accepting the uncapped Sharpie she was pushing into my hand. She started flipping to title pages and sliding books across for me to sign, one at a time.

"Sounds like you two've been spending a lot of time together."

I balked. "Sounds like?"

Pete threw her back into her guffaw. "You know, as private as that boy is, I have to pull a lot from context out of our conversations. But yes, I've gathered the clues that you two have formed a friendship."

I tried to hide my surprise. "You talk often?"

"He probably answers about a third or so of my calls. Sure, I drive him batty calling as much as I do, but I worry. We're the only family each other's got here."

"Family?" I looked up at her, no longer hiding my confusion.

Her own features seemed to snap upward on her face, surprised. She scratched the back of her head. "I thought you knew. I never *can* tell what he thinks is private and what isn't. So much of it shows up in his books you'd think he'd be comfortable peeling off his skin and parading through Times Square. 'Course, that might just be me projecting. I know how you artist types are. He insists it's fiction, so I should read it as such."

I was barely tracking. Apparently my face revealed that, because Pete explained, "I'm his aunt. His mother was my sister."

A wave of dizziness hit me. The shop seemed to rock. This didn't make sense. Two and a half weeks of near-constant (albeit nontraditional) communication, and Gus hadn't even shared the most basic parts of his life with me.

"But you call him Everett," I said. "You're his aunt and you don't use his first name."

She stared at me for a moment, confused. "Oh! That. An old habit. When he was a little guy, I coached his soccer team. Couldn't show favoritism, called him by his last name like any other player, and it stuck. Half the time I forget he *has* a first name. Hell, I've introduced him as Everett to half the town by now."

I felt like I'd just dropped a wooden doll only to watch six more fall out and discover it had been a matryoshka. There was the Gus I knew: funny, messy, sexy. And then there was the other Gus, who disappeared for days, who had played soccer as a kid and lived in the same town as his aunt, who said no more than he absolutely had to about himself, his family, his past while I spilled wine, tears, and my guts all over him.

I bent my head and went back to signing in silence. Pete kept sliding books across the counter to me, stacking the signed ones neatly on my other side. After a handful of seconds she said, "Be patient with him, January. He really likes you."

I kept signing. "I think you're misunderstanding the—"

"I'm not," she said.

I looked into her fierce blue eyes, held her gaze. "He told me about the day you moved in. Not a wonderful first impression. It's a recurring issue of his."

"So I hear."

"But of course you have to give him a break on that one," she said. "His birthday's really hard for him ever since the split."

"Birthday?" I parroted, looking up. *Split?* I thought.

Pete looked surprised, then unsure. "She left him on it, you know. And every year since then, his friend Markham throws this huge party to try and keep his mind off it. And of course, Gus *hates* parties, but he doesn't want Markham thinking he's upset, so he lets the party happen."

"Excuse me?" I choked out. Was this some kind of joke? Had Pete woken up this morning and thought, *Hm, maybe today I shall release snippets of shocking information about Gus to January in a random yet cryptic order?*

"She left him on his birthday?" I repeated.

"He didn't tell you that was what had gotten a bee in his bonnet that night you moved in?" she said. "Now, that really does surprise me. If he'd told you he'd been thinking about his divorce, of course it would've explained how rude he was to you."

"Divorce," I said, my whole body going cold. "It was about . . . his divorce."

Gus was divorced.

Gus had been *married*.

Pete shifted uncomfortably. "I'm surprised he didn't tell you. He felt so bad about being rude."

My brain felt like a top spinning in my skull. It didn't make sense. None. Gus couldn't have been married. He didn't even date. The store seemed to wobble around me.

"I didn't mean to upset you," Pete said. "I only thought it might explain—"

"No, it's fine," I said, and then it was happening again: the word-spilling. The feeling that I'd held everything in a moment too long and now had no choice over how much I let out. "I'm probably overreacting. I just . . . This year's been weird for me. Like, in my mind marriage has always been this sacred thing, you know? Like the epitome of love, the kind that can weather anything. And I hate thinking some bad experiences justify people shitting on the entire concept."

Gus shitting on the concept. Calling relationships sadomasochistic without even telling me he'd been married. Almost making me feel stupid for wanting and believing in lasting love, just because his own attempt hadn't worked. Hiding that attempt from me.

But even so, why did I care what he thought? I shouldn't need everyone to believe in or want the things I believed in and wanted.

When it came down to it, I resented the fact that some part of him must think I was stupid for still believing in something my own father had disproven. And beyond that, I resented my*self* for not letting go of it. For still wanting that love I'd always pictured for myself.

And a small, stupid part of me even resented that Gus had secretly loved someone enough to marry her, while one brief makeout session with me had apparently been enough to make him relocate to Antarctica without so much as a *See ya!*

"I don't know," I said, shaking my head. "Does that make sense?"

"Of course it does." Pete squeezed my arm.

I had a feeling she would have said that even if it didn't. Like maybe she just knew it was what I needed to hear right then.

16

The Porch Furniture

THURSDAY AT NOON, Gus was back at his kitchen table, looking less "sexily disheveled" and more like he'd been dragged behind a dump truck with a loose tailgate. He smiled and waved, and I returned the gesture, despite the sick roiling in my stomach.

He scribbled a note: SORRY I'VE BEEN MIA THIS WEEK.

I wished that hadn't replaced the nausea with the zero-gravity rush of a roller coaster loop. I looked around: I hadn't brought my notebook in today. I went into the bedroom and grabbed it, writing, NOTHING TO BE SORRY ABOUT as I ambled back into the room. I held the note aloft. Gus's smile wavered. He nodded, then jerked his attention back to his laptop.

It was harder to focus on writing now that he was back but I did my best. I was about a quarter of the way through the book, and I needed to keep up.

Around five, I (discreetly, at least I hoped) watched Gus get up and move around the kitchen, making some semblance of a meal. When he'd finished, he sat back down at his computer. At about eight thirty, he looked up at me and tipped his head toward the deck. This had been our signal, as close to an invitation as either of us got before we moseyed onto our respective decks and not quite hung out at night.

Now that seemed like a blatantly obvious metaphor—his keeping a literal gulf between us, my readily meeting him each night. No wonder I'd gotten so confused. He'd been keeping careful boundaries and I'd been ignoring them. I was so bad at this, so unprepared to find myself drawn to someone completely emotionally unavailable.

I shook my head to Gus's invitation, then added a written note to my pass: SORRY—TOO MUCH TO DO. ANYA ON MY ASS.

Gus nodded understanding. He stood, mouthing something along the lines of *If you change your mind* . . . then disappeared from sight for a moment and reappeared on his deck.

He walked to its farthest point and leaned across the railing. The breeze fluttered through his shirt, lifting his left sleeve up against the back of his arm. At first I thought he'd gotten a new tattoo—a large black circle, solidly filled in—but then I realized it was exactly where his Möbius strip had been, only that had been blotted out entirely since I last spotted it. He stayed out there like that until the sun had gone down and night cloaked everything in rich blues, the fireflies coming to life around him, a million tiny night-lights switched on by a cosmic hand.

He glanced over his shoulder toward my deck doors, and I looked sharply toward my screen, typing the words *PRETEND-*

ING TO BE BUSY, VERY BUSY AND FOCUSED to complete the illusion.

Actually, I'd been at my computer for nearly twelve hours and I'd only typed a thousand new words. Though I'd managed to open fourteen tabs on my web browser, including two separate Facebook tabs.

I needed to get out of the house. When Gus looked away again, I sneaked from the table out to the front porch. The air was dense with humidity, but not uncomfortably hot. I perched on the wicker couch and surveyed the houses across the street. I hadn't spent much time out here, since the water was *behind* Gus's and my side of the street, but the cottages and dollhouses on the other side were cute and colorful, every porch packed with its own variation on the lawn furniture theme. None was so homey or eclectic as the set Sonya had chosen.

If I'd had no negative ties to this furniture, I'd be sad to have to sell it, but I figured now was as good a time as any. It'd be one less thing to worry about later. I stood and flicked on the porch light, snapping pictures of each individual piece, and some of the whole set, then pulled up craigslist on my phone.

I stared at it for a moment, then exited the browser and opened my email. I could still see the bolded words from Sonya's last message. I hadn't deleted any of them, but I didn't want to read them either. I opened a new email and addressed it to her.

SUBJECT: Porch furniture.

Hi,

I'm beginning to sort out things at the house. Did you want the furniture on the porch, or should I sell it?

I tried out three separate signatures but none seemed right. In the end, I decided not to leave so much as a *J* behind. I hit *SEND*.

That was it. All the emotional labor I had in me for the day. So I washed my face, brushed my teeth, and climbed into bed, where I watched *Veronica Mars* until the sun came up.

ON FRIDAY, THE knocking on my door came hours earlier than I'd expected. It was two thirty in the afternoon, and as I'd fallen asleep at five that morning, I'd only been awake for a couple of hours by then.

I grabbed my robe off the couch and pulled it over my outfit (boxers stolen from Jacques and my worn-out David Bowie shirt minus a bra). I drew back the linen curtain that covered the window set into the door and saw Gus pacing on the porch, his hands locked behind his head and pulling it down, as if stretching his neck.

He stopped, wide-eyed, and spun toward me as I opened the door.

"What's wrong?" I asked. In that moment, I saw the part of his gene pool that overlapped with Pete's in the way that his expression shifted from confusion to surprise.

He shook his head quickly. "Dave's here."

"Dave?" I said. "Dave as in . . . *Dave*? Of Olive Garden fame?"

"It's definitely not *Wendy's* Dave," Gus confirmed. "He called me a minute ago and said he was in town. He drove out on an impulse, I guess—he's in my house right now. Can you come over?"

"Now?" I said dumbly.

"Yes, January! Now! Because he's in my house! Now!"

"Yes," I said. "Just let me get dressed."

I shut the door and ran back to the bedroom. I'd fallen behind on laundry this week. The only clean thing I had was the stupid black dress. So naturally I wore a dirty T-shirt and a pair of jeans.

Gus's door was unlocked, and I let myself in without thinking. When I stepped inside, it all struck me. We'd been friends almost a month and I was finally in the house I'd peered curiously into that first night. I was tucked between those dark shelves, far overstuffed with books, Gus's smoky incense smell in the air. The space was lived-in—books left open on tables, stacks of mail on top of anthologies and literary journals, a mug here or there on a coaster—but compared to his usual level of sloppiness, the room was meticulously neat.

"January?" The narrow hall that veered straight into the kitchen seemed to swallow his voice. "We're in here."

I followed it as if it were bread crumbs leading to some fantastical place. That or a trap.

I stopped in the kitchen, a mirror image of mine: on the left a breakfast nook, where the table I'd seen Gus sit behind so often was pushed almost flush to the window, and the counters and cupboards on the right. Gus waved at me from the next room over, a little office.

I wanted to take my time, to examine every inch of this house full of secrets, but Gus was watching me in that focused way that made it seem like he might be reading my thoughts, so I hurried into the office. A minimalist desk, all sleek Scandinavian lines and utterly free of clutter, was pushed against the back window.

Where Gus's house sat, his deck overlooked the woods, but the trees fell away before the furthest right side of the building, and here the view of the beach was unobstructed, the silvery light filtering through the clouds, bouncing along the tops of the waves like skipped stones.

Dave wore a red T-shirt and a mesh-backed hat. Bags hung under his eyes, giving him the look of a sleepy Saint Bernard. He took his hat off and stood as I entered the room but didn't stretch out his hand, which gave me the disorienting feeling of having wandered into a Jane Austen novel.

"Hi," I said. "I'm January."

"Pleasure," Dave said with a nod. There was a desk chair (turned away from the desk so Gus could face the rest of the tiny room), an armchair wedged into the corner (which Dave had evacuated when he stood), and a kitchen chair Gus had clearly brought in especially for the occasion. Dave sat back in that one, gesturing for me to take the armchair.

"Thanks." I sat, inserting myself into the triangle of chairs and knees. "And thanks so much for talking to us."

Dave put his hat back on and swiveled the bill anxiously. "I wasn't ready before. Sorry for wasting you all's time, driving out my way. Feel awfully bad."

"No need," Gus assured him. "We know how sensitive all this is."

He nodded. "And my sobriety—I just wanted to be sure I could handle it. I went to a meeting that night—when we were supposed to meet at the Olive Garden, that's where I was."

"Totally understandable," Gus said. "This is just a book. You're a person."

Just a book. The phrase caught me off guard coming from Gus's mouth. Gus "Books with Happy Endings Are Dishonest" Everett. Gus "Drinking the Goddamn Literary Kool-Aid" Everett had said the words "just a book," and for some reason that unraveled me a bit.

Gus has been married.

He caught me staring. I looked away.

"That's just it," Dave said. "It's a book. It's a chance to tell a story that might help people like me."

The corner of Gus's mouth twisted uncomfortably. I still hadn't read my new copy of *The Revelatories*—I was afraid of how it might dim or exacerbate my crush on him—but from everything Gus had said, I knew he wasn't writing to save lives so much as to understand what had destroyed them.

Gus's rom-com was supposed to be different, but I couldn't imagine him using anything Dave had said to tell a story with a meet-cute and a Happily Ever After. The contents of this interview would be far more at home in his next literary masterpiece.

Then again, this was Gus. When we'd started down this path, I'd thought I'd be writing bullshit, just mimicking what I'd seen other people do, but really, my new project was as quintessentially *me* as anything else I'd written; maybe Gus's rom-com really *would* have a place like New Eden as a backdrop, all kinds of horrible things happening between kisses and professions of love.

Maybe he was finally going to give someone the happy ending they deserved, in a book about a cult.

Or maybe Dave was barking up the wrong tree.

"It will be honest," Gus told him. "But it won't be New Eden. It won't be you. It will—*hopefully*—be a place you can imagine existing, characters you believe could be real." He paused, thinking. "And if we're lucky, maybe it will help someone. To feel known and understood, like *their* story matters."

Gus glanced at me so fast I almost missed it. My stomach somersaulted as I realized he was quoting me, something I'd said that night we'd made our deal, and I didn't think he was teasing me. I thought he meant it.

"But even if not," he went on, focusing on Dave, "just knowing you told it might help you."

Dave pulled at a stray thread peeling out of the hole in the knee of his jeans. "I know that. I just had to make sure my ma understood. She still feels bad. Like she could've maybe talked my dad out of staying, gotten him to leave with us. He'd still be alive, she thinks."

"And you?" Gus asked.

Dave scrunched up his lips. "Do you believe in fate, Augustus?"

Gus hid his grimace at the name. "I think some things are . . . inevitable."

Dave slumped forward, tugged on his hat bill. "Used to sleepwalk as a kid. Real bad habit. Scary stuff. Once, before we went to New Eden, my mom found me standing at the edge of our apartment's pool with a butter knife in my hand. Naked. I didn't even sleep naked.

"Two weeks before we joined New Eden, we'd been at a park, just Ma and me, when a storm started up. She always liked the rain, so we stayed out too long. Thunder got going. Big, scary clashes. So we started running home. There was a chain-link fence around the park, and when we reached it, she yelled for me to wait. She wasn't sure how lightning worked but she figured it was a bad idea to let her six-year-old grab a fistful of metal. She wrapped her hand in her shirt and opened the gate for me.

"We got all the way home. We were on the front steps when it happened. A crack like a giant ax had hit the world. Honest to God, I thought the sun was crashing into Earth. That's how bright the light was."

"What light?" Gus said.

"The bolt of lightning that hit me," Dave said. "We weren't religious people, Augustus. Especially not my dad. But that scared Ma. She decided to make a change. We went to church that next week—the strictest one she could find—and on our way out, someone handed her a flier. *NEW EDEN*, it said. *God is inviting you to a new beginning. Will you answer?*"

Gus was writing notes, nodding as he went. "So she took that as a sign?"

"She thought God had saved my life," Dave said. "Just to get her attention. A week later we were moving into the compound, and Dad went along with it. He didn't believe, but he considered a child's 'spiritual upbringing' to be the job of the mother. I don't know what got him. What changed his mind. But over the next two years he got in deeper than Ma ever had. And then, one night, she woke up in our trailer with a bad feeling. There was a storm raging outside and she peeked her head into the living room where I slept and the fold-out was empty, just a bunch of rumpled blankets.

"She tried to wake my dad, but he slept like a rock. So she went out into the storm. Found me standing there, naked as can be, in the middle of the woods, lightning touching down around me like falling fireworks. And you know what happened next?"

Dave looked at me, paused. "It hit the trailer. The whole thing went up in flames. That was the first fire at New Eden, and it wasn't a bad one, not like the one that killed my dad. They got that first one out before it could do much damage. But my mom took me out of there the next day."

"She took it as another sign?" Gus confirmed.

"See, here's the thing," Dave said. "My mom believes in fate, in destiny—in the divine hand of God. But not so much that there's no room to blame herself for what happened to my dad. She was the one who brought us there. And she was the one who took me out. She didn't tell him, because she knew he was in too deep. He wouldn't have just refused to leave—he would've atoned for us."

"Atoned?" I said.

"Lingo," Dave explained. "It's a confession on someone else's behalf. They didn't want us to think of it as reporting, keeping tabs on your neighbors. It was 'atoning.' It was making the selfless sacrifice of putting a wedge in your own relationship with a person in order to save them from sin. Deep down she knew that if she told Dad she wanted out, we both would've been punished. She would've gotten at least two weeks in isolation. I would've been beaten, then stuck with another family until her 'wavering faith had been restored.' They said they didn't like the violence. That it was their own sacrifice to discipline us out of love. But you could always tell the ones who did.

"She knew all that. So fated or not, my mom saw the future. She couldn't have saved him. But she did what she had to do to save me."

Gus was silent, thoughtful. Lost in thought, he looked suddenly younger, a little softer. I felt a rush of anger low in my stomach. *Why didn't someone save you?* I thought. *Why didn't someone scoop you up and run you out in the middle of the night?*

I knew it was complicated. I knew there must've been reasons, but it still sent a pang through me. It wasn't the story I would've written for him. Not at all.

GUS SHUT THE door behind Dave with a quiet click and turned to face me. For a moment we said nothing, both exhausted from the four-hour interview. We just looked at each other.

He leaned against the door. "Hey," he said finally.

"Hey," I answered.

A wisp of smile sneaked up the corner of his mouth. "It's good to see you."

"Yeah." I shifted between my feet. "You too."

He straightened and went toward the walnut sideboard in the corner, pulling two crystal highball glasses from below and setting them beside the careful arrangement of dark liquor bottles. "Want a drink?"

Of course I wanted a drink. I'd just heard a harrowing tale of a child beaten for imaginary crimes, and aside from that, I was alone with Gus for the first time since our kiss. Even from across the room, the heat in the house felt like a stand-in for our tension. For the thorny jumble of feelings today had stirred up in me. Anger with all the broken parents, heartache that they too must've felt like kids—helpless, unsure how to make the right decisions, terrified of making the wrong ones. I felt sick for Dave and what he'd been through, sad for my mother and how lost I knew she must feel without Dad, and still, even with all that, being in the same room as Gus made me feel a little warm and heavy, like from across the room he was still a physical force pressing into me.

I heard the soft clink of ice against the glasses. (He kept ice in a bucket on a tray with his liquor? How Moneyed Connecticutian of him.)

I wanted answers about Pete, and about Gus's parents and his marriage, but those were the sorts of tidbits a person had to offer up, and Gus hadn't. He hadn't even let me into his house until one of his research subjects had shown up here unannounced. Not that he'd been in my house either, but my house wasn't a part of me. It wasn't even really mine—it was just baggage. Gus's house was his *home*.

And Dave had been inside before I had.

Gus turned then to look at me, brow furrowed.

"You got a tattoo." It was the first thing I could think to say when we'd been silent too long.

His eyes darted toward his arm. "I did."

That was it. No explanation, no information about where he'd been. I was welcome to sit here, to have a drink with him and talk about books and meaningless memories of girls puking on the backs of our heads, but that was it.

My heart sank. I didn't want that, not now that I'd had glimpses of more. If I wanted casual, surface-level chitchat and conversational land mines, I'd call my mom. With him, I wanted more. It was who I was.

"Scotch?" Gus asked.

"I didn't get much done today. I should get back to it."

"Yeah." He started nodding, slowly, distractedly. "Yeah, okay. Tomorrow then."

"Tomorrow," I said.

For once I was dreading planning our Saturday night. He left the glasses on the sideboard and came to open the door for me. I stepped onto the porch but hesitated at the sound of my own name. When I looked back, his left temple was resting against the doorjamb.

He was always leaning on something, like he couldn't bear to hold all his own weight upright for more than a second or two. He lounged, he sprawled, he hunched and reclined. He never simply stood or sat. In college, I'd thought he was lazy about everything except writing. Now I wondered if he was simply tired, if life had beaten him into a permanent slouch, folded him over himself so no one could get at that soft center, the kid who dreamed of running away on trains and living in the branches of a redwood.

"Yeah?" I said.

"It's good to see you," he said.

"You said that already."

"Yeah," he replied. "I did."

I fought a smile, stifled a flutter in my stomach. A smile and a flutter weren't enough for me. I was done with secrets and lies, no matter how pretty. "Good night, Gus."

17

The Dance

*T*UX TONIGHT? GUS wrote at noon on Saturday.

Anxiety crept up every time I thought about being alone in the car with him, but I'd also had tonight planned since *last* Saturday, and I wasn't ready to bow out of our deal, not when I was finally writing for the first time in months. OH, DEFINITELY, I wrote back.

SERIOUSLY? Gus asked.

NO, I wrote. DO YOU HAVE COWBOY BOOTS?

WHAT DO YOU THINK? Gus said. FROM EVERYTHING YOU KNOW ABOUT ME, TAKE A WILD GUESS WHETHER I OWN COWBOY BOOTS.

I stared at the blank page then went for it: YOU'RE A MAN OF MANY SECRETS. YOU COULD HAVE A WHOLE CLOSET FULL OF TEN-GALLON HATS. AND IF YOU DO, WEAR ONE. 6 PM.

When Gus appeared at my door that night, he was wearing his

usual uniform, plus a wrinkly black button-up. His hair was swept up his forehead in a way that suggested it had been forced there via him anxiously running his hand through it while he wrote. "No hat?" I said.

"No hat." He pulled his other hand from behind his back. He was holding two flasks, the thin, foldable kind you could tuck under your clothes. "But I brought these in case you're taking me to a Texan church service."

I crouched by the front door, tugging my embroidered ankle boots on. "And once again, you reveal that you know *much* more about romance than you've previously let on."

Even as I said it, my stomach clenched.

Gus has been married.

Gus is divorced.

That was why he was so sure love could never last, and he'd told me none of these key details, because he hadn't *really* let me in.

If my comment reminded him of any of that, he didn't let on. "Just so you know," he said, "if I actually have to wear a cowboy hat at some point tonight, I will probably die."

"Cowboy hat allergy." I grabbed my keys from the table. "Got it. Let's go."

This date would've been perfect, if it had been a date.

The parking lot of the Black Cat Saloon was jammed and the rough-hewn interior was just as packed. "A lot of flannel," Gus mused as we made our way in.

"What do you expect on line-dancing night, Gus?"

"You're kidding, right?" Gus said, freezing. I shook my head. "This has been an exact recurring nightmare I'm only just realizing was actually a premonition."

On the low stage at the front of the barnlike room, the band picked up again, and a crush of bodies moved past on our left, knocking me into him. He caught me around the rib cage and righted me as the group pushed toward the dance floor. "You good?" he shouted over the music, his hands still on my ribs.

My face was hot, my stomach flipping traitorously. "Fine."

He leaned in so I could hear him. "This seems like a dangerous environment for someone your size. Maybe we should leave and go . . . literally anywhere else."

As he eased back to look me in the face, I grinned and shook my head. "No way. The lesson doesn't even *start* for another ten minutes."

His hands slid off me, leaving pulsing points behind on my skin. "I guess I survived Meg Ryan."

"Barely," I teased, then blushed as flashes of memory seared across my mind. Gus's mouth tipping mine open. Gus's teeth on my clavicle. Gus's hands tightening against my hips, his thumb scraping over the jut of bone.

The moment stretched out between us. Or rather, it seemed to tighten between us, and since we didn't move any closer, the air grew taut. The song was winding down now and a lanky man with a horsey face bounded onto the stage with a microphone, summoning beginners to the floor for the next song.

I grabbed Gus's wrist and cut a path through the crowd to the dance floor. For once, his cheeks were flushed, his forehead dented with worried wrinkles. "You honestly have to write me into your will for this," he said.

"You might not want to talk through the instructions," I replied, tipping my head toward the horse-faced caller, who was using a volunteer from the crowd to demonstrate a few key moves, all while talking with the speed of an auctioneer. "I have a feeling this guy won't be repeating much."

"Your last will and testament, January," Gus whispered fiercely.

"And to Gus Everett," I whispered back, "a closet full of ten-gallon hats!"

His laugh crackled like popping oil. I thought of its sound against my ear that night at the party. We hadn't said anything as we danced in that slick basement, not a single word, but he'd laughed against my ear and I'd known, or at least suspected, that it was because he was dimly aware that we should have been embarrassed to be all over each other like that. We should have been but there were more pressing feelings to be felt that night. Just like at the drive-in.

Heat filled my abdomen and I suppressed the thought.

Onstage, the fiddle started up, and soon the whole band was bouncing through the notes. The experts swarmed the floor, filling in the gaps between the anxiously waiting beginners, of whom we made up at least 20 percent. Gus pushed in close at my side, unwilling to be separated from the sentient safety blanket I'd become as soon as we'd walked through the metal double doors, and the caller shouted into the microphone, "You all ready? Here we go!"

At his first command, the crowd jostled to the right, carrying Gus and me with it. He snatched my hand as the mass of boots and heels reversed direction. I squealed as Gus jerked me out of the path of a man on a mission to grapevine whether it meant stomping on my foot or not.

There were no sung lyrics, just the caller's instructions with their strange, auctioneer rhythm and the sound of shoes scuffing along the floor. I erupted into laughter as Gus went forward instead of back, eliciting a nasty glare from the hair-sprayed blonde he collided with. "Sorry," he shouted over the music, holding up his hands in surrender, only to get bumped into her pink lace–covered chest as the crowd shifted once more.

"Oh, God," he said, stumbling back. "Sorry, I—"

"God has nothing to do with it!" the woman snapped, digging her hands into her hips.

"Sorry," I interceded, grabbing Gus by the hand. "Can't take him anywhere."

"Me?" he cried, half laughing. "You knocked me into—"

I pulled him through the crowd to the far side of the dance floor. When I looked over my shoulder, the woman had resumed her boot-scoot-boogying, face as stony as a sarcophagus's.

"Should I give her my number?" Gus teased, mouth close to my ear.

"I think she'd rather have your insurance card."

"Or a good police sketch."

"Or a crowbar," I shot back.

"Okay." Gus's smile spread enough for a laugh to slip out. "That's enough from you. You're just looking for an excuse not to dance."

"I'm just looking for an excuse?" I said. "You grabbed that woman's boobs to try to get kicked out of here."

"No way." He shook his head, caught my arm, and tugged me along as he clumsily fell back into the steps. "I'm in this for the long haul now. You'd better clear your Saturday schedules from here until eternity."

I laughed, tripping along with him, but my stomach was fighting a series of concurrent rises and dips. I didn't want to feel these things. It wasn't fun anymore, now that I was thinking it all through, where it would end up—with me attached and jealous and him having shared about as much about his life with me as you might with a hairdresser.

But then he would say things like that, *Clear your Saturday schedules from here until eternity.* He would grab me around the waist to keep me from smashing into a support beam I hadn't noticed in my dancing fugue state. Laughing, he would twirl me into him, and spin me around while the rest of the crowd was walking their feet into their bodies and back out, far wider than their hips, thumbs hooked into real and imagined belt loops.

This was a different Gus than I'd seen (The one who'd played soccer? The Gus who answered one third of his aunt's phone calls? The Gus who'd been married and divorced?), and I wasn't sure what to make of it or its sudden appearance.

Something had changed in him, again, and he was (whether intentionally or not) letting it show. He seemed somehow lighter than he had, less tired. He was being winsome and flirty, which only made me more frustrated after the past week.

"We need a shot," he said.

"Okay," I agreed. Maybe a shot would take the strange edge I was feeling off. We swam back to the bar and he nudged aside a pool of peanuts still in their shells to order two doubles of whiskey. "Cheers," he said, lifting his.

"To what?" I asked.

He smirked. "To your happy endings."

I'd thought we were friends, that he respected me, and now I felt like he was calling me a fairy princess all over again, laughing to himself about how naive and silly my worldview was, holding his failed marriage like a secret trump card that proved, once again, he knew more than me. A fierce, angry fuse lit in my stomach, and I threw back the whiskey without meeting his lifted shot. Gus seemed to think it was an oversight. He was still downing his whiskey as I headed back out to the dance floor.

I had to admit there was something singularly hilarious about line dancing angrily, but that didn't stop me from doing it. We finished two more songs, took two more shots.

When we went back out for the fourth song—a more complex dance for the proficient to enjoy while the caller used the toilet and rested his vocal cords—we had no hope of keeping up with the choreography, even if we hadn't been tipsy by then. During a double turn to the right, my shoe caught on an uneven floorboard and Gus grabbed me by the waist to keep me from going down. His laughter faded when he saw my face, and he leaned (of course) against the support beam, my nemesis from earlier, drawing me in toward him by my hips. His hand burned through my jeans into my skin and I fought to keep a clear head as he held me like that. "Hey," he murmured, dropping his mouth toward my ear so I could hear him over the music. "What's wrong?"

What was wrong was his thumbs twirling circles on my hips, his whiskey breath against the corner of my mouth, and how stupid I felt for its effect on me. I *was* naive.

I'd always trusted my parents, never sensed the missing pieces between Jacques and me, and now I'd started getting emotionally attached to someone who'd done everything he could to convince me not to.

I stepped back from him. I meant to say, *I think I need to go home*, or maybe *I'm not feeling well*.

But I'd never been good at hiding how I was feeling, especially this past year.

I didn't say anything. I just ran for the door.

I burst into the cool air of the parking lot and beelined toward the Kia. I could hear him shouting my name as he followed, but I was too *embarrassed*, frustrated, and I didn't know what else, to turn around.

"January?" Gus said again, jogging toward me.

"I'm fine." I dug for my keys in my pocket. "I just—I need to go home. I'm not—I don't . . ." I trailed off, fumbling the key against the lock.

"We can't go anywhere until we've sobered up," he pointed out.

"Then I'll just sit in the car until then." My hands were shaking and the key glanced off the lock again.

"Here. Let me." Gus took it from me and slipped it in, unlocking the driver's side door, but he didn't step away to let me open it.

"Thanks," I said without looking at him.

I flinched as his hand brushed at my face, swiping hair from my cheek. He tucked it behind my ear. "Whatever it is, you can tell me."

Now I looked up at him, ignoring the heavy *flip-flop* of my stomach as I met his eyes. "Why?"

His eyebrows lifted. "Why what?"

"Why can I tell you?" I said. "Why would I tell you anything?"

His mouth pressed closed. The muscle in his jaw leapt. "What is this? What did I do?"

"Nothing." I turned toward the car, but Gus's body still blocked the door. "Move, Gus."

"This isn't fair," he said. "You're mad at me and I can't even try to fix it? What could I have possibly—"

"I'm *not* mad at you," I said.

"You *are*," he argued. I tried again to open the door. This time he moved aside to let me. "Please tell me, January."

"I'm not," I insisted, voice shaking dangerously. "I'm not mad at you. We're not even close enough for that. I'm just your casual acquaintance. It's not like we're friends."

Twin grooves rose from the insides of his eyebrows and his crooked mouth twisted. *"Please,"* he said, almost out of breath. "Don't do this."

"Do *what*?" I demanded.

He threw his arms out to his sides. "I don't know!" he said. "Whatever *this* is."

"How stupid do you think I am?"

"What are you *talking* about?" he demanded.

"I guess I shouldn't be surprised you don't tell me anything," I said. "It's not like you respect me or my opinions."

"Of course I respect you."

"I know you were married," I blurted. "I know you were married and that you split up on your birthday, and not only did you not tell me any of that, but you listened to me spill my guts about why I do what I do and what it all means to me, and—and talk about my *dad* and what he did—and you sat there, on your smug little high horse—"

Gus gave an exasperated laugh. "'Little high horse'?"

"—thinking I was stupid or naive—"

"Of course I don't—"

"—keeping your own failed marriage a secret, just like everything else in your life, so you can look down on all the *cliché* people like me who still believe—"

"Stop," he snapped.

"—while you—"

"Stop." He jerked back from me, walked down the length of the car, then turned back, face angry. "You don't know me, January."

I laughed humorlessly. "I'm aware."

"No." He shook his head, stormed back toward me, and stopped no more than six inches away. "You think my marriage is a joke to me? I was married two years. *Two years* before my wife left me for the best man at our wedding. How's that for cliché? I know goldfish that lived longer than that. I didn't even want the divorce. I would've stayed with her, even after the affair, but guess what, January? Happy endings don't happen to everyone. There's nothing you can do to *make* someone keep loving you.

"Believe it or not, I don't just sit through *hours* of conversations with you silently judging you. And if it takes me a while to tell you things like 'Hey, my wife left me for my college roommate,' maybe it has nothing to do with you, okay? Maybe it's because I don't like saying that sentence aloud. I mean, your mom didn't leave when your dad cheated on her, and *my* mom didn't leave *my* dad when he broke my fucking arm, and yet *I* couldn't do *anything* to make my wife stay."

My stomach bottomed out. My throat clenched. Pain stabbed through my chest. It all made sense at once: the hesitancy and deflection, the mistrust of people, the fear of commitment.

No one had chosen Gus. From the time he was a kid, no one had chosen him, and he was *embarrassed* by that, like it meant something about him. I wanted to tell him it didn't. That it wasn't because *he* was broken, but because *everyone else* was. But I couldn't get any words out. I couldn't do anything but stare at him—standing there, out of steam, his chest rising and falling with heavy breaths—and ache for him and hate the world a little for chewing him up.

Right then, I honestly didn't care why he'd disappeared or where he'd gone.

The hard glint had left his eyes and his chin dropped as he rubbed at his forehead.

There were millions of things I wanted to say to him, but what came out was, "Parker?"

He looked up again, eyes wide and mouth ajar. "What?"

"Your college roommate," I murmured. "Do you mean Parker?"

Gus's mouth closed, the muscles along his jaw leaping. "Yeah," he barely said. "Parker."

Parker, the art student with the eccentric clothes. Parker, who'd picked most of his left eyebrow away. He'd had pretty blue eyes and a certain zaniness that my friends and I had always imagined translated to a golden-retriever-esque excitability when it came to sex. Which we were all fairly sure he was getting *a lot of*.

Gus wasn't looking at me. He was rubbing his forehead again, looking as broken and embarrassed as I'd felt thirty seconds ago.

"On your *birthday*. What an asshole."

I didn't realize I'd said it aloud until he responded: "I mean, that wasn't her plan." He looked away, staring vaguely through the parking lot. "I sort of dragged it out of her. I could tell something was wrong and . . . anyway."

Still an asshole, I thought. I shook my head. I had no idea what

196

else to say. I stepped forward and wrapped my arms around him, pressing my face into his neck, feeling his deep breaths push against me. After a moment, his arms lifted around me and we stood there, just out of reach of the parking lot's lone floodlight, holding on to each other.

"I'm sorry," I whispered into his skin. "She should have picked you." And I meant it, even if I wasn't sure exactly which *she* I was talking about.

His arms tightened around my back. His mouth and nose pressed against the crown of my head, and inside, a mournful Crosby, Stills, Nash & Young cover picked up, guitar twanging like its strings were crying. Gus rocked me side to side. "I want to know you," I told him.

"I want that," he murmured into my hair. We stood there for another moment before he spoke again. "It's late. We should grab some coffee inside so we can get home."

I didn't want to go home. I didn't want to pull away from Gus. "Sure."

He eased back from me and his hand ran down my throat, resting on the crook between my neck and shoulder, his rough thumb catching the edge of my collarbone. He shook his head once. "I've never thought you were stupid."

I nodded. I wasn't sure what to say, and even if I had been, I wasn't sure if my voice would come out thick and heavy, like my blood felt, or shaky and high, like my stomach did.

Gus's eyes dipped to my mouth, then rose to my eyes. "I thought—*think* it's brave to believe in love. I mean, the lasting kind. To try for that, even knowing it can hurt you."

"And what about you?"

"What about me?" he murmured.

I needed to clear my throat but I didn't. It would be too obvious, what I was thinking, how I was feeling. "You don't think you ever will again?"

Gus stepped back, shoes crackling against the gravel. "It doesn't matter if I believe it can work or not," he said. "Not believing in something doesn't stop you from wanting it. If you're not careful."

His gaze sent heat unfurling over me, the cold snapping painfully back into place against my skin when he finally turned back toward the bar. "Come on," he said. "Let's get that coffee."

Careful. Caution was something I had little of when it came to Gus Everett.

Case in point: my hangover the next morning.

I awoke to my first text from him.

It said only Ow.

18

The Ex

THERE WERE NO more nights on our separate decks. On Sunday Gus came to my house looking like he'd started going through a trash compactor only for it to spit him back up halfway through. I felt at least as bad as he looked.

We put the chaise lounges on the deck flat and lay out there with ice packs on our heads, chugging the bottles of Gatorade he'd brought over. "Did you write?" he asked.

"Whenever I picture words, I literally gag."

Beside me, Gus coughed. "That *word*," he said.

"Sorry."

"Should we order pizza?" he asked.

"Are you kidding? You almost just—"

"January," Gus said. "Don't say that word. Just answer the question."

"Of course we should."

By Monday, we'd mostly recovered. At least enough that we were both working at our own tables during the day (two thousand words hammered out on my end). Around 1:40, Gus held up the first note of the day: I TEXTED YOU.

I REMEMBER, I wrote back. A HISTORIC MOMENT IN OUR FRIENDSHIP.

NO, he said. I TEXTED YOU A MINUTE AGO.

I'd left my phone charging by the bed. I held up my pointer finger as I hurried from the room and grabbed my phone. The text just said, Do you know how to make a margarita?

Gus, I typed back. This is fewer words than the notes you wrote me to tell me about this message.

He responded immediately: I wanted to put in a formal request. Writing notes is a very casual form of communication.

I don't know how to make a margarita, I told him. But I know someone who does.

Jose Cuervo? he asked.

I pulled open the blinds and leaned out the window, yelling toward the back of our houses, where the kitchen windows were. "GOOGLE."

My phone buzzed with his response: Come over. I tried not to notice what those words did to me, the full-body shiver, the heat.

I went back for my computer and walked over barefoot. Gus met me on his porch, leaned against the doorjamb.

"Do you ever stand upright?" I asked.

"Not if it can be helped," he answered, and led me into his kitchen. I sat on a stool at the island as he pulled out the limes then went into the front room for his shaker, tequila, and triple sec. "Please, don't trouble yourself to help," he teased.

"Don't worry. I would never."

When he'd finished making our drinks we went out onto the front porch and worked until the last streaks of sunshine had vanished into that deep Michigan blue, the stars pricking through it like poked holes, one at a time. When our stomachs started to gurgle, I went back to my house for the rest of the pizza and we ate it cold, our legs outstretched, feet resting on the porch railing.

"Look," Gus said, and pointed up at the deep blue sky as two trails of silver light streaked through the stars. His eyes were doing the thing, the Gus thing, at the sight of them, and it made my chest flutter almost painfully. I loved that vulnerable excitement when he first caught sight of something that made him feel before he could cover it up.

He looks at me like that sometimes.

I jerked my focus to the falling stars. "Relatable," I said flatly.

Gus let out a half-formed laugh. "That's basically us. On fire and just straight up dropping out of the sky."

He looked over at me with a dark, fervent gaze that undid the careful composure I'd been rebuilding. My eyes slipped down him, and I scrambled for something to say. "What's the big black blob about?" I tipped my chin toward the updated tattoo on the back of his bicep, where the skin was a bit paler than his usual olive.

He looked confused until he followed my gaze. "Yeah," he said. "It used to be something else."

"A Möbius strip. I know," I said, a bit too quickly.

His eyes bored into mine for a few intimidating beats as he decided what to say. "Naomi and I got them." Her name hung in the air, the afterimage of a lightning strike. *Naomi.* The woman Gus Everett had married, I presumed. He didn't seem to notice my shock. Maybe in his mind he said her name often. Maybe having told me she existed felt the same to him as if he'd shown me their photo albums. "Right after the wedding."

"Ah," I said stupidly. My cheeks went even hotter and started to itch. I had a knack for bringing up things he had no interest in talking about. "Sorry."

He shook his head once, and his eyes kept their sharp, fiery focus. "I told you I wanted you to know me. You can ask me anything you want."

It sounded sort of like, *Get on top of me! Now!*

I hoped I looked *very pretty*, for an overripe tomato.

Dropping the topic was the smarter idea, but I couldn't help testing him, seeing if I, January Andrews, could *really* ask the secretive Gus Everett anything at all.

I settled on "What did it mean?"

"As it turned out, very little," he said. Disappointment wriggled through my stomach at how quickly our open-book policy had deteriorated.

But then he took a breath and went on. "If you start at one point on a Möbius strip and you follow it straight around, when you've done the full loop, you don't end up back where you started. You end up right above it, but on the other side of the surface. And if you *keep* following it around for a second time, you'll finally end up where you started. So it's this path that's actually twice as long as it should be. At the time, I guess we thought it meant that the two of us added up to something bigger than we were on our own."

He shrugged one shoulder, then absently scratched the black blot. "After she left, it seemed more like a bad joke. Oh, here we are, trapped on opposite sides of this surface, allegedly in the same place and somehow not at all together. Pinned together with these stupid tattoos that are five thousand percent more permanent than our marriage."

"Yikes," I said. *Yikes?* I sounded like a gum-popping babysitter trying to relate to her favorite Hot Divorced Dad. Which was sort of how I felt.

Gus gave me a crooked smile. "Yikes," he agreed quietly.

We stared at each other for a beat too long. "What was she like?" The words had just slipped out, and now a spurt of panic went through me at having asked something I wasn't sure Gus would want to answer, or *I* would enjoy hearing.

His dark eyes studied me for several seconds. He cleared his throat. "She was tough," he said. "Sort of . . . impenetrable."

The jokes were writing themselves, but I didn't interrupt him. I'd come this far. Now I had to know what kind of woman could capture Gus Everett's heart.

"She was this incredible visual artist," he said. "That's how we met. I saw one of her shows in a gallery when I was in grad school, and liked her work before I knew her. And even once we were together, I felt like I could never really know her. Like she was always just out of reach. For some reason that thrilled me."

What kind of woman could capture Gus Everett's heart?

My polar opposite. *Not* the kind who was always rude when she was grumpy, crying when she was happy, sad, overwhelmed. Who couldn't help but let it all hang out.

"But I also just had this thought, like . . ." He hesitated. "Here's someone I could never break. She didn't need me. And she wasn't gentle with me, or worried about saving me, or really letting me in enough to help her work things out either. Maybe it sounds shitty, but I've never trusted myself with anyone . . . *soft*."

"Ah." My cheeks burned and I kept my focus on his arm instead of his face.

"I saw that with my parents, you know? This black hole and this bright light he was always just trying to swallow whole."

My gaze flickered to his face, the sharp lines etched between his brows. "Gus. You're not a black hole. And you're not your father either."

"Yeah, I know." An unconvincing smile flitted across one corner of his mouth. "But I'm also not the bright light."

Sure, he wasn't a bright light, but he wasn't the cynic I'd thought either. He was a realist who was a little too afraid of hope to see things clearly when it came to his own life. But he was also exceptionally good at sitting with people through their shit, making them feel less alone without promises or empty platitudes. Me. Dave. Grace.

He wasn't afraid for things to get ugly, to see someone at their weakest, and he didn't fall over himself trying to talk me out of my own feelings. He just witnessed them, and somehow, that let them finally get out of my body after years of imprisonment.

"Whatever you are," I said, "it's better than a night-light. And for what it's worth, as a former fairy princess and the ultimate secret soft-girl, I think you're plenty gentle."

His eyes were so warm and intense on me that I was sure he could read all my thoughts, everything I felt and thought about him, written on my pupils. The heat in my face rushed through my whole body, and I focused on his tattoo again, nudging it with my hand. "And also, for what it's worth, I think the giant black blob suits you. Not because you're a black hole. But because it's funny, and weird."

"If you think so, then I have no regrets," he murmured.

"You got a tattoo," I said, still a little amazed.

"I have several, but if you want to see the others, you have to buy me dinner."

"No, I mean, you got a *marriage tattoo*." I chanced a glance at him and found him staring at me, as if waiting for some big reveal about my meaning. "That's some Cary Grant–level romance shit."

"Humiliating." He went to rub it again, but found my fingers resting there.

"Impressive," I countered.

His calloused palm slid on top of mine, dwarfing it. Instantly, I thought of that hand touching me through my shirt, gliding over the bare skin of my stomach. His gravelly voice dragged me out of the memory: "What about the Golden Boy?"

I balked. "Jacques?"

"Sorry," Gus said. "The Jacques. Six years is a long time. You must have thought you'd wind up with matching tattoos and a gaggle of children."

"I thought . . ." I trailed off as I sorted through the alphabet soup in my brain. Gus's fingers were warm and rough, careful and light over mine, and I had to swim through a resistance pool full of thoughts like *I bet scientists could exactly reconstruct him from this hand alone* to get to any memory of Jacques. "He was a leading man. You know?"

"Should I?" Gus teased.

"If you're taking our challenge seriously," I countered. "I mean that he was romantic. Dramatic. He lit up every room and had an incredible story for any occasion. And I fell in love with him in all these amazing moments we had.

"But then, whenever we were just sitting together—like eating breakfast in a filthy apartment, knowing we'd have to clean up after a big party . . . I don't know, when we weren't gleaming for each other, I sort of felt like we just worked okay together. Like we were costars in a movie and when the cameras weren't on, we didn't have all that much to talk about. But we wanted the same life, you know?"

Gus nodded thoughtfully. "I never thought about how Naomi's and my lives would work together, but I knew that's what it would be: two lives. You chose someone who wanted a relationship. That makes sense for you."

"Yeah, but that's not enough." I shook my head. "You know that feeling, when you're watching someone sleep and you feel overwhelmed with joy that they exist?"

A faint smile appeared in the corner of his mouth, and he just barely nodded.

"Well, I loved Jacques," I said. "And I loved his family and our life and his cooking, and that he was passionate about the ER and read a lot of nonfiction like my dad and—well, my mom was sick. You knew that, right?"

Gus's mouth pressed into a thin, serious line and his brow furrowed. "From our nonfiction class," he said. "But she was in remission."

I nodded. "Only, after I graduated, it came back. And I'd convinced myself she was going to beat it again. But a part of me was really comforted by the fact that, if she died, she would have at least met the man I was going to marry. She thought Jacques was so handsome and amazing, and Dad trusted him to give me the life I wanted. And I *loved* all that. But whenever I watched Jacques sleep, I felt nothing."

Gus shifted on the sofa beside me, his gaze dropping. "And when your dad died? Didn't you want to marry Jacques then? Since your dad had known him?"

I took a deep breath. I hadn't admitted this to anyone. It all felt too complicated, too hard to explain until now. "In a way, I think that almost set me free. I mean, firstly, my dad wasn't who I thought he was, so his opinion of Jacques meant less.

"But more than that, when I lost my dad . . . I mean, my dad was a liar, but I loved him. Really loved him, so much that just knowing he isn't on this planet still tears me in half whenever I think about it." Even as I said it, the pain pressed into me, a crushing but familiar weight on every square inch of my body.

"And with Jacques," I went on, "we loved the best versions of each other, inside our picturesque life, but once things got ugly, there was just . . . *nothing* left between us. He didn't love me when I wasn't the fairy princess, you know? And I didn't love him anymore either. There were thousands of times I'd thought, *He is the perfect boyfriend*. But once my dad was gone, and I was furious with him but also couldn't stop missing him, I realized I'd never thought, *Jacques is so perfectly my* favorite *person*."

Gus nodded. "It didn't overwhelm you to watch him sleep."

It was the kind of thing that, if he'd said it even a few weeks ago, I might've taken as mockery. But I knew Gus now. I knew that head tilt, that serious expression that meant he was in the process of puzzling something out about me.

I'd seen it on his face that day on campus when he pointed out that I gave everyone happy endings. I'd seen it again in Pete's bookstore when I made a jab about him writing Hemingway circle-jerk fiction.

That day, in class, he'd been working something out about who I was and how I saw the world. That day at Pete's he'd been realizing I loathed him.

I wanted to take it back, show him that *I* understood *him* now, that I trusted him. I wanted to give him something secret, like what he'd given me when he talked about Naomi. I wanted to tell him another true story, instead of a beautiful lie.

So I said, "Once, for my birthday, Jacques took me to New Orleans. We went to all these amazing jazz bars and Cajun restaurants and witchy shops. And the whole time, I was texting Shadi about how badly I wished we could be together, drinking martinis and watching *The Witches of Eastwick*."

Gus laughed. "Shadi," he said ruefully. "I remember Shadi."

"Yeah, well, she remembers *you*," I said.

"So you talk about me." Gus's smile inched higher and his eyes flashed. "To your perfectly favorite person, Shadi?"

"You talk about me to Pete," I challenged.

He gave one nod, confirming. "And what do you say?"

"You're the one who said I could ask anything," I shot back. "What do *you* say?"

"It's strictly need to know," he said. "The last thing I told her must've been that we got caught making out at a drive-in theater."

I laughed and pushed him away, covering my burning face with my hands. "Now I'll never be able to order another pink eye!"

Gus laughed and caught my wrists, tugging them from my face. "Did she call it that again?"

"Of course she did!"

He shook his head, grinning. "I'm beginning to suspect her coffee expertise is not what keeps her in business."

When we finally stood to go to bed that night, Gus didn't say good night. He said, "Tomorrow." And that became our nightly ritual.

Sometimes he came to my house. Sometimes I went to his. The wall between him and the rest of the world wasn't gone, but it was lower, at least between us.

On Thursday night, while sitting on Sonya's couch and waiting for our pad thai to be delivered, he finally told me about Pete. Not just that she was his aunt—and had been his coach for soccer, which he assured me he was terrible at—but also that she'd been the reason he'd moved here when Naomi left him. "Pete lived near me when I was a kid, back in Ann Arbor. She never came over—didn't get along with my dad—but she was always in my life. Anyway, when I was in high school, Maggie got the job teaching geology at the school here, so they moved out this way and they've been here ever since. She begged me to come. She knew the guy who was selling this house and went so far as to lend me a down payment. Just let me know I could pay her back whenever."

"Wow," I said. "I'm still caught on the fact that Maggie's a geology professor."

He nodded. "Never mention a rock in front of her. I mean it. Never."

"I'll try," I said. "But that's going to be extremely hard, what with how often rocks come up in everyday conversation."

"You'd be shocked," he promised. "Shocked and appalled and, more importantly, bored to the brink of death."

"Someone should invent a boredom EpiPen."

"I think that's essentially what drugs are," Gus said. "Anyway, January. Enough about rocks. Tell me why *you* moved here, really."

The words tangled in my throat. I could only get out a few at a time. "My dad."

Gus nodded, as if that were enough of an explanation if I couldn't force myself to go on. "He died, and you wanted to get away?"

I shifted forward, leaning my elbows on my knees. "He grew up here," I said. "And when he passed, I—I found out he'd been back here. Kind of a lot."

Gus's eyebrows pinched in the middle. He ran his hand back through his hair, which was, as usual, pushed messily off his forehead. "'Found out'?"

"This was his house," I said. "His *second* house. With . . . the woman." I couldn't bring myself to say her name. I didn't want Gus to know her, to have an opinion on her either way, and it was a small enough town that he probably did.

"Oh." He ran his hand through his hair again. "You mentioned her, kind of." He sat back into the couch, the beer bottle in his hand hanging along the inside of his thigh.

"Did you ever meet him?" I blurted, before I'd decided whether I even wanted the answer, and my heart began to race as I waited for him to respond. "You've been here five years. You must've seen . . . *them.*"

Gus studied me with liquidy, dark eyes, his brow tense. He shook his head. "Honestly, I'm not really into the neighbor thing. Most of the houses on this block are rentals. If I saw him, I would've assumed he was on vacation. I wouldn't remember."

I looked away quickly and nodded. On the one hand, it was a relief, knowing Gus had never watched the two of them barbecuing on the deck, or pulling weeds side by side in the garden, or doing any other normal couple things they might've done here—and that he didn't seem to know who That Woman was. But on the other, I felt a sinking in my stomach and realized a part of me had been hoping, all this time, that Gus *had* known him. That he'd have some story to tell that I'd never heard, a new piece of my father right here, and the miserably thin envelope taunting me from the gin box wasn't *really* all I had to look forward to of him.

"January," Gus said gently. "I'm so sorry."

I had begun to cry without giving myself permission to. I pressed my face into my hands to hide it, and Gus shifted closer, put an arm around my shoulders, and gathered me to him. Gently, he pulled me across his lap and held me there, one hand knotted into my hair, cradling the back of my head, as the other curled around my waist.

Once the tears had started, I couldn't stop them. The anger and frustration. The hurt and betrayal. The confusion that had been clogging my brain ever since I found out the truth. It all heaved out of me.

Gus's hand moved softly through my hair, turning slow circles against the back of my neck, and his mouth pressed into my cheek, my chin, my eye, catching tears as they fell until, gradually, I settled. Or maybe just ran out of tears. Maybe realized I was sitting in Gus's lap like a toddler, having my tears kissed away. Or that his mouth had paused, pressed into my forehead, his full lips slightly parted.

I turned my face into his chest and breathed him in, the smell of his sweat and the incense I now knew he burned when he first started writing each day, his lone prework ritual, and the occasional stress cigarette (though he'd largely quit smoking). He crushed me to him, arms tightening, fingers curling against the back of my head.

My whole body heated until I felt like lava, burning and liquid. Gus pulled me closer, and I molded to him, poured myself into every line of him. Each of his breaths brought us closer until finally he straightened, pulling me over him so my knees straddled his hips, his arm tight across my back. The feeling of him underneath me sent a fresh rush of heat up my thighs. His hand grazed along my waist as we stared at each other.

It was that night at the drive-in times ten. Because now I knew how he felt on top of me. Now I knew what the scrape of his jaw against my skin did to me, how his tongue would test the gaps between our mouths, taste the soft skin at the top of my chest. I was jealous he'd had more of me than I'd had of him. I wanted to kiss his stomach, sink my teeth into his hips, dig my fingers into his back and drag them down the length of him.

His hands slid toward my spine, skidding up it as I folded over him. My nose skated down his. I could almost taste his cinnamon breath from his open mouth. His right hand came back to the side of my face, roaming lightly down to my collarbone, then back to my mouth, where his tense fingers pressed into my bottom lip.

I had no thoughts of caution or wisdom. I had thoughts of him on top of me, under me, behind me. His hands setting fire to my skin. I was breathing hard. So was he.

The tip of my tongue brushed his finger, which curled reflexively into my mouth, tugging me closer until our lips were separated only by an inch of electric, buzzing air.

His chin tipped up, the edge of his mouth brushing mine infuriatingly lightly. His eyes were as dark as oil, slick and hot as they poured down me. His hands skated down my sides, out along my calves, and back up my thighs to cup my butt, grip tightening.

I drew a shuddering breath as his fingers climbed beneath the hem of my shorts, burning into my skin. "Fuck, January," he whispered, shaking his head.

The doorbell rang and all the motion, the momentum, crashed into a wall of reality.

We stared at each other, frozen for a moment. Gus's eyes dipped down me and back up again, and his throat pulsed. "Takeout," he said thickly.

I jumped up, the fuzz clearing from my head, and smoothed my hair, wiping my teary face as I crossed to the front door. I signed the credit card slip, accepted the bag full of foam containers, and thanked the delivery guy in a voice as thick and muddled as Gus's had been.

When I closed the door and turned back, Gus was standing uneasily, his hair messy and his shirt sticking to him where I'd cried on it. He scratched the crown of his head and his gaze flicked tentatively toward mine. "Sorry."

I shrugged. "You don't need to be."

"I should be," he said. We left it at that.

19

The Beach

ON FRIDAY, WE drove to Dave's house for the second part of the interview. The first had been so thorough Gus hadn't planned to have a second, but Dave had called him that morning. After thinking it over, his mother had things to say about New Eden.

The house was a small split-level, probably built in the late sixties, and it smelled like someone had been chain-smoking inside it ever since. Despite that, and its shabby decor, it was extremely tidy: blankets folded on couch arms, potted plants in a neat line by the door, pots hanging from hooks on the wall, and the sink scrubbed to sparkling.

Dave Schmidt had to be right around our age, give or take a few years, but Julie-Ann Schmidt looked a good ten years older than my mother. She was tiny, her face round and soft with wrinkles. I wondered if it was a lifetime of being treated as if she were sweet, because of her figure and face, that had given her the almost toothy handshake she offered.

She lived there with Dave. "I own the house, but he makes the payments." She guffawed at that and patted his back. "He's a good boy." I watched Gus's eyes narrow, appraising the situation. I thought he might be looking for hints of violence somewhere in their interactions, but Dave was mostly hunched and smiling in embarrassment. "He was always a good boy. And you should hear him on the piano."

"Can I get you anything to drink?" Dave hurried to ask.

"Water would be great," I answered, more to give Dave an excuse to hide than because I was actually thirsty. As he disappeared into the kitchen, I ambled around the living room, studying all the walnut picture frames mounted to the wall. It was like Dave had been frozen at about eight years old, in a V-neck sweater vest and dull green T-shirt. His father was in most of the shots, but even in the ones he didn't inhabit, it was easy to imagine he'd been behind the camera, snapping the tiny smiling woman and the baby on her hip, the toddler holding her hand, the gawky child sticking his tongue out next to the gorilla exhibit at the zoo.

Dave's dad had been lanky and brown-haired with bushy eyebrows and a receding chin. Dave looked just like him.

"So I understand you had more to say," Gus began. "Things you thought Dave couldn't offer."

"Of course I do." Julie-Ann took a seat on the blue plaid love seat, and Gus and I perched beside each other on the roughly woven tan couch. "I've got a well-rounded look. Dave only saw what we let him, and then when we left like we did—well, I'm afraid his opinion of the place probably swung from one extreme to the other."

Gus and I looked at each other. I leaned forward, trying to keep an open, friendly posture to combat her defensive one. "He seemed pretty fair, actually."

Julie-Ann pulled a cigarette pack off the table and lit up, then offered us the box. Gus took one, and I knew it was more to put her at ease than because he truly wanted one, which made me smile. Even though what we wrote and said we believed was so different, I'd started to feel like I was capable of knowing Gus, reading him, better than anyone else I'd ever met. Because every day we spent together, this peculiar feeling was growing in me: *You are like me.*

Julie-Ann lit the cigarette for him, then sat back, cross-legged. "They weren't bad people," she said. "Not most of them. And I couldn't let you go thinking they were. Sometimes—sometimes good, or at least decent, people do bad things. And sometimes they *actually* believe they're doing what's right."

"And you don't think that's just an excuse?" Gus asked. "You don't believe in any kind of internal moral compass."

The way he said it made it seem as if he himself *did* believe in such a thing, which would've surprised me a few weeks ago, but now made perfect sense.

"Maybe you start out with that," she said, "But if you do, it gets shaped as you age. How are you supposed to believe right's right and wrong's wrong if everyone around you says the opposite? You're supposed to think you're smarter than all of them?"

Dave returned with three water glasses balanced between his hands and passed them out one by one. Julie-Ann seemed reluctant to go on with her son in the room, but neither she nor Gus suggested he leave. Probably because Dave was approximately thirty years old and paying for the house we were in.

"A lot of these people," Julie-Ann went on, "didn't have much. I don't just mean money, although that was true too. There were a lot of orphans. People estranged from their families. People who'd lost spouses and children. At first, New Eden made me feel like . . . like the reason everything had gone wrong in my life up to that point was that I hadn't been living quite right. It was like they had the answers, and everyone seemed so happy, fulfilled. And after a lifetime of wanting—sometimes not even wanting anything specific but just *wanting*, feeling like the world wasn't big enough or bright enough—well, I felt like I was finally pushing back the curtain.

"I was getting my answers. It was like this great big scientific equation they'd solved. And you know what? To an extent, it worked. At least for a while. You followed their rules, did their rituals, wore their clothes, and ate their food and it *was* like the whole world was starting to light up from within. *Nothing* felt mundane. There were prayers for everything—while you were going to the bathroom, while you were showering, paying bills. For the first time, I felt grateful to be alive.

"That's what they could do for you. So then when the punishments started, when you began to slip up and fail, it felt like there was a giant hand on the bathtub plug, just waiting to yank it up and rip it all away from you. And my husband . . . He was a *good* man. He was a good, lost man." Her gaze skittered toward Dave and she took a slow puff.

"He was going to be an architect. Build sports stadiums and

skyscrapers. He loved to draw and he was damn good at it. And then we got pregnant in high school, and he knew all that had to go. We had to be practical. And he never once complained." Again her eyes gestured toward her son. "Of course he didn't. We were lucky. Blessed. But sometimes when life throws a wrench in your plans . . . I don't know how to explain it, but I just had this sense when we were there. Like . . . like my husband was clinging to whatever he could grab hold of. Like being right mattered less than being . . . okay."

I thought about my father and Sonya. About my mom staying with him, even knowing what he'd done. Her insistence that she'd thought it was over.

Well, why did it ever start? I'd demanded in the car before she had taken up her mantra: *I can't talk about it; I won't talk about it.*

But the truth was, I had a good guess right away.

In the seventh grade, my parents had separated. Briefly—just a couple of months—but he'd gone as far as to stay with some friends of theirs while he and Mom waited to see if they could work things out. I didn't know the whole story. They'd never gotten to that screaming-match level most of my friends' divorced parents had reached, but even at thirteen, I had seen the change in my mother. A sudden wistfulness, a proclivity for staring out windows, escaping to bathrooms and returning with puffy eyes.

The night before Dad moved out, I'd cracked my bedroom door and listened to their voices carrying up from the kitchen. "I don't know," Mom kept saying tearfully. "I don't know, I just feel like it's over."

"Our marriage?" Dad had asked after a long pause.

"My *life*," she'd told him. "I'm nothing but your wife. January's mother. I'm nothing else, and I don't think you can imagine how that feels. To be forty-two and feel like you've done everything you're going to do."

I hadn't been able to wrap my mind around it then, and obviously Dad hadn't either, because the next morning they'd explained everything to me while the three of us sat in a row on the edge of my bed and then I'd watched his car pull away with one suitcase in its back seat.

I'd believed life as I knew it was over.

Then, suddenly, Dad was back in the house: proof that nothing was unfixable! That love could conquer any challenge, that life would always, always work out. So when he and Mom sat me down to tell me about her diagnosis, and everything else in our lives changed, I *knew* it wouldn't be permanent. This was just another plot twist in our story.

After that, the two of them seemed more in love than ever. There was more dancing. More hand-holding. More romantic weekend getaways. More of Dad saying things like, "Your mother has been a lot of people in the twenty years I've known her, and I've had a chance to fall in love with every single one of them, Janie. That's the key to marriage. You have to keep falling in love with every new version of each other, and it's the best feeling in the whole world."

Their love, I had thought, had transcended time, midlife crises, cancer, all of it.

But that separation *had* happened, and when I'd yelled at my mother that day, I'd wondered. If those three months were when it had begun. When Dad and Sonya had reconnected. If, when he'd found her, he'd just needed to believe everything could be okay again. If, when Mom had taken him back afterward, *she'd* just needed to pretend it already *was* okay.

Julie-Ann shook her head slightly when her gaze settled on mine.

"Does that make sense?" she asked. "I just needed to be okay, and I could do the wrong thing if it had the right end."

I thought about Jacques and our determination to have a beautiful life, my desperation to end up with someone Mom had known and loved. I thought about my mother's diagnosis and my father's infidelity, and the story I'd been telling myself since age twelve to keep from being terrified about what might really happen. I thought about the romance novels I'd devoured when the cancer came back and I lost my shot at grad school and thought my life was falling apart again. The nights spent writing until the sun came up and my back hurt from needing to pee but not wanting to stop working because nothing felt more important than the book, than giving these fictional lovers the ending they deserved, giving my readers the ending *they* deserved.

People clinging to whatever steadfast thing they could find?

Yes. Yes, that made sense. It made perfect sense.

When we left that night, I texted my mother, something I hadn't done much of in months: I love you. Even if you can never talk about him again, I'll always love you, Mom. But I hope you can.

Twenty minutes later she responded: Me too, Janie. All of it.

ON SATURDAY WE walked down to the beach. "It's not very creative," I said as we picked our way over the root-laden path. Gus opened his mouth to reply and I cut him off. "Don't you dare make a joke about my genre of choice being unoriginal."

"I was going to say it's stupid we haven't come down here more," Gus answered.

"I assumed you'd gotten sick of it, I guess."

Gus shook his head. "I've barely used this beach."

"Seriously?"

"Root," he warned as I looked up at him, and I stepped carefully over it. "I'm not the world's biggest beach guy."

"Well, of course not," I said. "If you *were*, you'd be wearing a T-shirt or a hat that advertised that."

"Exactly," he agreed. "Anyway, I actually prefer this beach in winter."

"Really? Because in winter, I'd just prefer to be dead."

Gus's laugh rattled in his throat. He stepped off the wooded path onto the sand and offered me a hand as I hopped off the slight ledge. "It's amazing. Have you ever seen it?"

I shook my head. "When I was at U of M, I pretty much stayed at U of M. I didn't do much exploring."

Gus nodded. "After Pete and Maggie moved here, I'd visit them for my winter break. They'd buy my plane or bus tickets as presents, and I'd come for the holidays."

"I'm guessing your dad didn't mind." A sudden burst of anger at the thought of Gus as a kid, alone, unwanted, had forced the words out of me before I could stop. I glanced cautiously at him. His jaw was clenched a bit, but otherwise his face was impassive.

He shook his head. We'd fallen into step along the water and he looked sidelong at me, then back to the sand. "You don't have to worry about bringing him up. It wasn't that bad."

"Gus." I stopped and faced him. "Just the fact that you have to say *it* means it was way worse than it should've been."

He hesitated a second, then started walking again. "It wasn't like that," he said. "After my mom died, I could've gotten out. Pete wanted me to come live with her and Maggie. She was always try-ing to get me to—to talk about the fights he and I would get into, so she could get custody, but I chose not to. He had all this heart medication. Daily pills. He'd only take them if I asked him, like, three times, but God forbid I asked a fourth. He'd pick a fight. An actual fight. Sometimes I thought . . ." He trailed off. "I *wondered* if he wanted me to kill him. Or like, get himself so worked up his heart would give out. I dropped out of school to work so we could afford his prescriptions, but when I was out, he stopped doing *anything* for himself. Eating, bathing. I could barely keep him alive. Maybe he thought that would be my punishment."

"Your punishment?" I choked out. "For *what?*"

Gus shrugged. "I don't know. Maybe being on her side all the time."

"Your mom's?"

He nodded. "I think he felt like it was Us against Him. It *was* Us against Him. He'd blame her for everything that went wrong—dumb shit, like, she'd forget to put gas in the car one night and he'd realize he needed to stop for it on his way to work, so he'd be late. Or she'd throw away a receipt he wanted to keep, dump leftovers out of the fridge a few hours before he finally decided he wanted them.

"He was bad with me too, but it was a little more random. If the phone rang and woke him up, he'd hit me, or if he had plans to go out but had to cancel for snow, he'd knock me around to burn off his anger. I was always looking for the secret code, the rules I could follow so he wouldn't freak out. That's how you keep yourself safe, you know? You pay attention to how the world works. But there was no secret code for him. It was like our actions were entirely detached from his reactions to us. He acted like I was this lazy, selfish brat and like my mom thought she was a queen. Like she treated his money like toilet paper. She was constantly apologizing for *nothing*, and then when he'd really hurt her, or me, *he'd* apologize. Back off for a few days.

"Even with all that, I think losing her broke whatever was left in him. I don't know." He paused, thinking. "Maybe it wasn't love. Maybe treating her like shit made him feel like he had power. He didn't have that with me as I got older."

"Making you keep him alive was the only way left to manipulate you," I said.

"I don't know," he admitted. "Maybe. But if I'd left, he would've died sooner."

"And you think that would've been your fault?"

"It doesn't matter whose fault it would've been. He would've been dead, and I would've known I could've stopped it. Plus, *she* didn't leave. How could I, knowing it wasn't what she would have wanted?"

"You *don't* know that," I said. "You were a kid."

"Pete likes to say I was never a kid."

"That's the saddest thing I've ever heard."

"Don't act like I'm pitiful," he said. "It's in the past. It's over."

"You know what your problem is?" I asked, and this time when I stopped, he did too.

"I'm aware of several, yes."

"You don't know the difference between pity and sympathy," I said. "I'm not pitying you. It makes me sad to think of you being treated like that. It makes me mad to think you didn't have the things all kids deserve. And yeah, it makes me mad and sad that a lot of people go through the things you went through, but it's even more upsetting because it's you. And I know you and I like you and I want you to have a good life. That's not pity. That's caring about someone."

He stared at me intently, then shook his head. "I don't want you to think about me like that."

"Like *what*?" I asked.

"Like an angry, broken punching bag," he said, his face dark and tense.

"I *don't*." I took a step closer, searching for the right words. "I just think of you as Gus."

He studied me. The corner of his mouth twitched into an unconvincing smile, then faded, leaving him looking burned-out. "I am, though," he said quietly. "I *am* angry and messed up, and every time I try to get closer to you, it's like all these warning bells go off, and I try to act like a normal person, but I can't."

My stomach flip-flopped. *Closer to you.* I glanced at the lake while I got my bearings. "I thought you understood that there's no such thing as a normal person."

"Maybe not," Gus said. "But there's still a difference between people like me and people like you, January."

"Don't insult me." I looked sharply back at him. "Don't you think I'm angry? Don't you think I feel a little bit broken? It's not like my life's been perfect either."

"I have *never* thought your life was perfect," he said.

"Bullshit. You called me a fairy princess."

He coughed out a laugh. "Because *you're* the bright light! Don't you get it?" He shook his head. "It's not about what's happened. It's about how you cope with things, who you are. You've always been this fierce fucking light, and even when you're at your worst, when you feel angry and broken, you still know how to be a person. How to tell people you—you love them."

"Stop it," I said. He started to walk away, but I grabbed him by the elbows and held him in front of me. "You're not going to break me, Gus."

He stilled, his lips parting and his eyes searching my face for something. His head just slightly tilted and those grooves rose from the inside corners of his brows.

I hoped that what he was understanding right then was that I saw him. That he didn't have to do anything special, figure out a mysterious code to unlock the secret parts of him. That he just had to keep being here with me, letting me discover him bit by bit like he'd been doing with me since we met.

"I don't need you to tell me you care about me," I said finally. "Two nights ago you held me while I sobbed. I think I blew my nose on your shirt. I'm not asking you for anything except to return the favor in whatever underwhelming and mild equivalent of lap-weeping you need."

He let out a long breath and leaned forward, burying his face into the side of my neck like an embarrassed kid even as his hot breath woke something up beneath my skin. My hands skimmed down the curved muscle of his arms and knotted into his rough fingers. The sun was low on the horizon, the thin blankets of clouds streaked a pale tangerine. They looked like melted Dreamsicles floating in a sea of denim blue. Gus lifted his face and looked me in the eye again, the light leaping in great licks through the gaps in the moving clouds to paint him with color.

It was an unabashed moment, a comfortable silence. The kind of thing that, if I had been writing it, I might've thought I could skip right over.

But I would be wrong. Because here, in this moment when nothing was happening and we'd finally run out of things to say, I knew how much I liked Gus Everett, how much he was starting to mean to me. We'd let so much out into the open over the last three days, and I knew more would bubble up over time, but for the first time in a year, I didn't feel overstuffed with trapped emotions and bitten-back words.

I felt a little empty, a little light.

Happy. Not giddy or overjoyed, but that low, steady level of happiness that, in the best periods of life, rides underneath everything else, a buffer between you and the world you are walking over.

I was happy to be here, doing nothing with Gus, and even if it was temporary, it was enough for me to believe that someday I'd be okay again. Maybe not the exact same brand of it I'd been before Dad died—*probably* not—but a new kind, nearly as solid and safe.

I could feel the pain too, the low-grade ache I'd be left with if and when this thing between Gus and me imploded. I could perfectly imagine every sensation, in the pit of my stomach and the palms of my hands, the sharp pulses of loss that would remind me of how good it felt to stand here with him like this, but for once, I didn't think letting go was the answer.

I wanted to hold on to him, and this moment, for a while.

As if in agreement, Gus squeezed my hands in his. "I do, you know," he said. It was almost a whisper, a tender, rugged thing like Gus himself. "Care about you."

"I do," I told him. "Know that, I mean."

The tangerine light glinted over his teeth when he smiled, deepening the shadows in his rarely seen dimples, and we stayed there, letting nothing happen all around us.

20

The Basement

I HAVE BAD NEWS and bad news, Shadi texted me the next morning.

Which should I hear first??? I replied. I sat up slowly, careful not to rouse Gus. To say we'd fallen asleep on the couch seemed like a misrepresentation of the truth. I'd had to actively decide to go to sleep the night before.

For the first time since we'd started hanging out, we'd ventured to the world of movie marathons and binge-watching. "You choose one and then I'll choose one," he'd said.

That was how we'd ended up watching, or talking through, *While You Were Sleeping*, *A Streetcar Named Desire*, *Pirates of the Caribbean 3* (as punishment for making me watch *A Streetcar Named Desire*), and Mariah Carey's *Glitter* (as we descended further into madness). And even after that, I'd been wide awake, wired.

Gus had suggested we put on *Rear Window*, and halfway

through, not long before the first hints of sun would skate through the windows, we'd finally stopped talking. We'd lain very still on our opposite ends of the couch, everything below our knees tangled up in the middle, and gone to sleep.

The house was chilly—I'd left the windows open and they'd fogged as the temperature began to inch back up with the morning. Gus was scrunched nearly into the fetal position, one throw blanket wrapped around himself, so I draped the two blankets I'd been using over him as I crept into the kitchen to turn the burner on beneath the kettle.

It was a still, blue morning. If the sun had come up, it was caught behind a sheet of mist. As quietly as I could, I pulled the bag of ground coffee and the French press from the lazy Susan.

The ritual felt different than it had that first morning, more ordinary and thus somehow more holy.

Somewhere in the last week or so, this house had started to feel like my own.

My phone vibrated in my hand.

I have fallen in love, Shadi said.

With the haunted hat? I asked, heart thrilling. Shadi was always the very best, but Shadi in love—there was nothing like it. Somehow, she became even more herself. Even wilder, funnier, sillier, wiser, softer. Love lit my best friend up from within, and even if every one of her heartbreaks was utterly devastating, she still never closed herself off. Every time she fell in love again, her joy seemed to overflow, into me and the world at large.

Of course you have, I typed. Tell me EVERYTHING.

WELL, Shadi began. I don't know!! We've just spent every night together, and his best friend LOVES me and I love him, and the other night we just like, stayed up literally until sunrise and then while he was in the bathroom, his friend was like "Be careful with him. He's crazy about you" and I was like "lol same." In conclusion, I have more bad news.

So you mentioned, I replied. Go on.

He wants me to visit his family . . .

Yes, that's terrible, I agreed. What if they're NICE? What if they make you play Uno and drink whiskey-Cokes on their porch???!

WELL, Shadi said. I mean. He wants me to go this week. For Fourth of July.

I stared down at the words, unsure what to say. On the one hand, I'd been living on an island of Gus Everett for a month now, and I had come down with neither prairie madness nor cabin fever.

On the other, it had been months since I'd seen Shadi, and I missed her. Gus and I had that intoxicating rapid-release form of friendship usually reserved for sleepaway camps and orientation week of college, but Shadi and I had years of history. We could talk about anything without having to back up and explain the context. Not that Gus's style of communication called for much context. The bits of life he shared with me were building their framework as we went. I got a clearer picture of him every day, and when I went to sleep each night, I looked forward to finding more of him in the morning.

But still.

I know it's terrible timing, Shadi said, but I already talked to my boss, and I get off again for my bday in August and I PROMISE I will pack the entire sex dungeon up myself.

The kettle began to whistle and I set my phone aside as I

poured the water over the grounds and put the lid on the press to let it steep. My phone lit up with a new message and I leaned over the counter.

Obviously I don't HAVE to go, she said. But I feel like??? I HAVE to. But like, I don't. If you need me now, I can come now.

I couldn't do that to her, drag her away from something that was clearly making her happier than I'd seen her in months.

If you come in August, how long will you stay? I asked, opening negotiations.

An email *pinged* into my inbox and I opened it with trepidation. Sonya had finally replied to my query about the porch furniture:

January,

I would love the porch furniture but I'm afraid I can't afford to buy it from you. So if you were offering to give it to me, let me know when I could bring a truck & friends to pick it up. If you were offering to sell it to me, thank you for the offer, but I'm unable to take you up on it.

Either way, is there a time we could talk? In person would be good, I—

"Hey."

I closed my email and turned around to find Gus shuffling into the kitchen, the heel of his hand rubbing at his right eye. His wavy hair stuck up to one side and his T-shirt was creased like a piece of ancient parchment behind glass at a museum, one of the sleeves twisted up on itself to reveal more of his arm than I'd seen before. I felt suddenly greedy for his shoulders.

"Wow," I said. "This is what Gus Everett looks like before he puts on his face."

Eyes still sleepily scrunched, he held his arms out to his sides. "What do you think?"

My heart fluttered. "Exactly what I pictured." I turned my back to him as I dug through the cabinets for a couple of mugs. "In that you look exactly how you always do."

"I'm choosing to take that as a compliment."

"That's your right, as an American citizen." I spun back to him with the mugs, hoping I appeared more casual than I felt about waking up in the same house as him.

His hands were braced against the counter as he leaned, like always, into it, his mouth curled into a smile. "Thanks be to Jack Reacher."

I crossed my heart. "Amen."

"That coffee ready?"

"Very nearly."

"Porch or deck?" he asked.

I tried to imagine cabin fever. I tried to imagine this getting old: that smile, those rumpled clothes, the language only Gus and I spoke, the joking and crying and touching and not touching.

A new message came in from Shadi: I'll stay at LEAST a week.

I texted her back. See you then, babe. Keep me posted on the hauntings of your heart.

IT WAS WEDNESDAY, and we'd spent the day writing at my house (I was now a solid 33 percent into the book) while we waited for the buyer to come pick up the furniture from the upstairs bedroom. I'd held off on selling the porch furniture now that Gus and I had gotten in the habit of using it some nights. I'd started boxing up knickknacks from the entire downstairs and dropping them off at Goodwill and even selling off the less necessary furniture downstairs. The love seat and armchair from the living room were gone, the clock from the mantel was gone, the place mats and tapered candles and votives in the armoire by the kitchen table all donated.

Maybe because it was starting to feel less like a home than a dollhouse, it had become our de facto office, and when we'd finished work that day, we'd relocated to Gus's.

He was in the kitchen, getting more ice, and I took the opportunity to peruse (snoop through) his bookshelves as thoroughly as I'd wanted to ever since the night I moved in and saw them lit up through my living room window. He had quite the collection, classics and contemporary alike. Toni Morrison, Gabriel García Márquez, William Faulkner, George Saunders, Margaret Atwood, Roxane Gay. For the most part he'd arranged them in alphabetical order, but he obviously hadn't kept up on shelving new purchases for a while, and these sat in stacks in front of and on top of other books, the receipts still poking out from under their covers.

I crouched to get a better look at the bottom row on the shelf furthest from the door, which was entirely out of order, and audibly gasped at the sight of a thin spine reading GREGORY L. WARNER HIGH SCHOOL.

I opened the yearbook and flipped to the E surnames. A laugh burst out of me as my eyes fell on the black-and-white shot of a shaggy-haired Gus standing with one foot on either side of a dilapidated set of train tracks. "Oh my God. Thank you. Thank you, Lord."

"Oh, come on," Gus said as he stepped back into the room. "Is nothing sacred to you, January?" He set the ice bucket on the sideboard and tried to pry the book from my hands.

"I'm not done with this," I protested, pulling it back. "In fact, I doubt I'll ever be done with this. I want this to be the first thing I see when I wake up and the last thing I look at before I go to bed."

"Okay, pervert, stick to your underwear catalogues." He tried again to pluck it from my hands, but I turned away and clutched it to my chest, forcing him to reach around me on either side.

"You can take my life," I yelped, dodging his hands, "you can take my freedom, but you'll never take this goddamn yearbook from me, Gus."

"I would much rather just have the yearbook," he said, lunging for it again. He caught either side of the book, his arms wrapped around me, but still I didn't release it.

"I was *not* kidding. This is too bright a light to hide under a bushel or a lampshade. The *New York Times* needs to see this. *GQ* needs to see this. You need to submit this to *Forbes*'s sexiest men contest for consideration."

"And again, I'm seventeen in that picture," he said. "Please stop objectifying child-me."

"I would've been obsessed with you," I told him. "You literally look like you bought that outfit in a packaged Teen Rebel costume from a Halloween shop. Wow, it's true what they say. Some things really don't ever change. I swear you're wearing the exact same outfit today as you are in that picture."

"That is one hundred percent untrue," he argued, still pressed up against my back, his arms folded around me to rest on the book. I'd managed to keep the page marked with my finger, and as

I opened the book again, his grip relaxed. He leaned over my shoulder to get a better look, his hands scraping down my arms to rest on my hips.

As if for balance. As if to keep from falling over my shoulder.

How many times could we possibly end up in situations like this? And how long until I lost what little self-control I'd managed to maintain?

As soon as something concrete happened between us, that would be it. I was going to lose him. He'd be freaked out, afraid that I was too into him, wanted too much from him, that he was bound to destroy me. And meanwhile I'd be . . . too into him, bound to be destroyed.

I was too much of a romantic for anything to stay casual, and even if we were totally incompatible, I was already in deeper with Gus than a purely physical attraction.

And it seemed like neither of us could stop pushing the boundaries.

As we stared at the yearbook, or pretended to, his hands ran lightly back and forth along my hips, pulling me into him then pushing me away, in a terribly appropriate metaphor. I could feel the tightness of his stomach against my back, and I chose to focus on his photo instead.

My initial giddiness faded, and the picture struck me anew. Probably 30 percent of the boys in my own high school yearbook had gone for the same angsty look, but Gus's was different. The crooked line of his mouth was tense and unsmiling. The white scar that bisected his top lip was darker, fresher, and his eyes were ringed with tired circles. Even if Gus was constantly surprising me in small ways, there was also an instinctual level at which I felt I knew him, recognized him. At book club, Gus had known that something had changed me, and looking at this photo, *I* knew something had happened to him not long before the picture was taken.

"Was this after your mom . . ." I trailed off, unable to get the words out.

Gus's chin nodded against my shoulder. "She died when I was a sophomore. That's my senior photo."

"I thought you dropped out," I said, and he nodded again.

"My dad's brother was a groundskeeper at this huge cemetery. I knew he was going to hire me full-time the second I was eighteen—insurance and everything—but my friend Markham insisted we take the photo and submit it anyway."

"Thank you, Markham," I whispered, trying to keep things light, despite the sadness welling in my chest. I wondered if my eyes looked like that now, so lost and empty, if after Dad's funeral my face had been this hollowed out. "I wish I'd known you," I said helplessly. I couldn't have changed anything, but I could have been there. I could have loved him.

My dad might've been a liar, a philanderer, and a traveling businessman, but I didn't have a single memory of feeling truly alone as a kid. My parents were always there, and *home* was always my safe place.

NO WONDER I'D seemed like a fairy princess to Gus, skipping through life with my glittery shoes and deep trust in the universe, my insistence that *anyone* could *be* who they wanted, *have* what they wanted. It made me ache, not being able to go back and see him clearly, be more patient. I should've seen the loneliness of Gus Everett. I should've stopped telling myself a story and actually looked around at the world.

His hands kept moving. I realized I was moving with them, like he was a wave I was rocking with. Whenever he pulled me toward him, I found myself pressing back against him, arching to feel him against me. His hands slid down to my legs, curled into my skin, and I did everything I could to keep my breathing even.

We were playing a game: how far can we go without admitting we've gone?

"I had a thought," he said.

"Really?" I teased, though my voice was still thick with a half dozen conflicting emotions. "Do you want me to grab the video camera to document?"

Gus's hands tightened against me, and I leaned back against him. "Hilarious," he said flatly. "As I was saying, I had an idea, but it affects our research."

Ah. Research. The reminder that we still had to couch whatever this was in the terms of our deal. That, ultimately, this still was some kind of game.

"Okay, what's up?" I turned to him, and his hands skidded across my skin as I shifted, but he didn't let go.

"Well." He grimaced. "I told Pete and Maggie I'd go to their Fourth of July, but that's on Friday."

"Oh." I stepped back from him. There was something disorienting about remembering the rest of the world existed when his hands were on me. "So you need to skip one of our research nights?"

"Well, the thing is, I also really need to get out to see New Eden soon if I'm going to keep drafting," he said. "So since I can't go on Friday, I was hoping I could do it on Saturday."

"Got it," I said. "So we skip Rom-Com 101 this week and take a Lit Fic field trip?"

Gus shook his head. "You don't have to go—I can do this one on my own."

I raised an eyebrow. "Why wouldn't I go?"

Gus's teeth worried at his bottom lip, the scar beside his cupid's bow going even whiter than usual. "It's going to be awful," he said. "You sure you want to see it?"

I sighed. This again. The old fairy-princess-can't-handle-this-cruel-world song and dance. "Gus," I said slowly, "if you're going, I'm going too. That's the deal."

"Even though I'm skipping out on Romance Hero boot camp for the week?"

"I think you've done more than enough line dancing this month," I said. "You deserve a break and a Fourth of July party."

"What about you?" he said.

"I always deserve a break," I said. "But my breaks largely *consist* of line dancing."

He cleared his throat. "I meant Friday."

"Friday what?"

"Do you want to go to Pete's on Friday?"

"Yes," I answered immediately. Gus gave his trademark closed-mouthed smile. "Wait. Maybe." His expression fell and I hurried to add, "Is there a way to . . ." I thought and rethought how to phrase it. "Pete's friends with my dad's mistress."

"Oh." Gus's mouth juddered open. "I . . . wish she'd mentioned that when I asked her if I could invite you. I wouldn't have agreed if I'd realized . . ."

"I'm not sure she knows."

"Or she was trying to get a promise from me by omitting important information," he said.

"Well, you *should* go," I said. "I'm just not sure if *I* can."

"I'll find out," Gus said quickly. "But if she's not?"

"I'll come," I said. "But I'm *definitely* bringing up rocks to Maggie."

"You're sick and twisted, January Andrews," Gus said. "That's what I love about you."

My stomach dipped and rose higher than it had started out. "Oh, *that's* what it is."

"Well," he said. "*One* thing. It seemed too crass to invite you to my aunts' house and then bring up your ass."

USUALLY WHEN I went to a party, I used it as an excuse to buy a thematically appropriate outfit. Or at least new shoes. But even after selling a good amount of furniture, when I logged in to my bank account on Friday morning, the site practically frowned at me.

I texted Gus. I don't think I can come to the party as I have recently discovered I cannot afford to bring even a single serving of potato salad.

I watched the ". . ." appear onscreen as he typed. He stopped. Started again. After a full minute, the symbol vanished and I went back to staring the basement door down.

I'd held off sorting through the master bedroom and bath and taken down pretty much everything (including the things nailed to the wall) on the first floor, and that left the basement.

Inhaling deeply, I opened the door and gazed down the dark staircase. Cement at the bottom. That was good—no reason to suspect it was finished, full of *more* furniture whose removal I'd have to coordinate. I flicked the switch, but the bulb was dead. It wasn't pitch-black by any means—there were glass block windows I'd seen from outside that must've let in some natural light. I brandished my phone like a flashlight and descended. A few red and green plastic tubs were stacked along the wall beside a metal rack full of tools and a stand-alone freezer. I wandered toward the rack, touching a dust-coated box of light bulbs. My fingers furled around the lid, tugged it open.

One of the light bulbs had already been taken.

Maybe the one that had burned out on the basement stairs.

Maybe Dad had come down here to do something else and realized, like I had, that the switch wasn't working. He'd taken the bulb out and climbed halfway back up the stairs to where he could replace it without going onto tiptoes.

This time the ache was like a harpoon. Wasn't the pain supposed to get better over time? When would handling something my dad had touched stop making my chest hurt so badly I couldn't get a good breath? When would the letter in the gin box stop filling me with dread?

"January?"

I spun toward the voice, truly expecting to find a ghost, a murderer, or a murderous ghost that had been hiding down here in the belly of the house all along.

Instead I found Gus, backlit from the hall light spilling down the stairs as he leaned down to see me from under the partial wall that lined the top half of the steps.

"Shit," I gasped, still thrumming with adrenaline.

"The door was unlocked," he said, padding down the steps. "Kind of freaked me out seeing the basement door open."

"Freaked *me* out hearing someone's voice in the basement when I thought I was alone."

"Sorry." He looked around. "Not much down here."

"No sex dungeon," I agreed.

"Was that ever on the table?" he asked.

"Shadi was hopeful."

"I see." After a beat of silence, he said, "You know, you don't have to go through all this. You don't have to go through any of it, if you don't want to."

"Kind of weird to sell a house with dusty tools and a single box of light bulbs in it," I pointed out. "Falls in the gray zone between fully furnished and empty as shit. Besides, I need the money. Everything must go. It's a fire sale, of sorts. In that this is my alternative to lighting the house on fire and trying to score the insurance money."

"That's actually what I came to talk to you about," he said.

I gaped at him. "You were going to suggest we burn my house down as part of an arson insurance scam?"

"Potato salad," he said. "I should've mentioned that there is absolutely no need to bring *anything* to Pete and Maggie's Fourth of July party. In fact, anything you bring will just end up sitting underneath a table that's already too full of everything they've provided and then they'll send it home with you at the end of the night. If you try to leave it as a gesture, you'll find it in your purse, hot and moldy, three days from now."

"They'll provide *everything*?" I said.

"Everything."

"Even White Russians?"

Gus nodded.

"What about rocks? Will there *be* rocks, or should I bring my own? Just as casual conversation starters."

"I just realized something," Gus said. "You're no longer invited."

"Oh, I'm definitely invited," I said. "They won't turn someone with rocks away."

"Okay, in that case, I'm coming down with something. You'll have to go alone."

"Relax." I grabbed his arm. "I won't engage in rock talk. Much."

He smirked and stepped in closer to me, shaking his head. "I'm not going. Too sick."

"You'll survive." My hand was still in the crook of his arm, his skin burning hot under my fingers. When my hand tensed on him, he edged closer, shaking his head again. My back met the cold edges of the tool rack, and his eyes swept down me and back up, leaving goose bumps in their wake. I pulled him closer, and our stomachs met, heavy want gathering behind my ribs and belly button and all the places we were touching.

He lightly held my hips and eased them up to his, and heat raced down me like flames on a streak of gasoline. My breath hitched. My blood felt like it was slowing, thickening in my veins, but my heart was racing as I watched his expression change, his smile seeming to singe off at the corners of his mouth, his eyes darkening with focus.

If he could see into me right then, I didn't care. I even wanted him to.

One time one time one time rushed through my brain on repeat, like tumbleweeds through a desert.

And then Gus slowly bent, his nose grazing down mine until his breath hit my lips, somehow parting them without so much as a touch, and my fingers burrowed into his skin as his lips caught mine roughly, so fierce and hot and slow I felt like I would melt against him before that first kiss had ended.

He tasted like coffee and the tail end of a cigarette and I couldn't get enough. My hands knotted into his hair as his tongue slipped into my mouth. He flattened me into the tool rack as his hands rose to my jaw, angling my mouth up to his as he kissed me again, even deeper, like we were desperate to plumb the depths of each other.

Every kiss, every touch was rough and warm, like him. His hands slid down my chest and then they were under my shirt, his fingers light as falling snow against my waist, against my bra, making my skin tingle as we rocked into each other. The rack whined as he slowly pushed me back against it, and Gus laughed into my mouth, which somehow made me feel even more desperate for him.

I twisted my hands into his shirt and his mouth drifted down my throat, slow and hungry. One of his hands grasped at my waist while the other slipped beneath the lace of my balconette, turning heavy circles on me. He was gentle at first, every movement languid and purposeful, but as I arched under his touch, his grip tightened, making me gasp.

He pulled back, breathing hard. "Did I hurt you?"

I shook my head, and Gus touched the side of my face again, gingerly turned it to kiss each of my temples. I caught the hem of his shirt and lifted it over him, chest fluttering at the sight of his lean, hard lines. As soon as I'd dropped his shirt on the ground he grabbed me, his calloused palms brushing up my sides, gathering fabric as they went. He tossed my shirt aside, then studied me intensely. "God," he said, voice deep, raspy.

I fought a smile. "Are you praying to me, Gus?"

His inky gaze scraped up my body to my eyes. The muscles in his jaw leapt and I arched against him as his hands skimmed around my back to unhook my bra. "Something like that."

He moved one of my bra straps down my arm, his eyes tracing the slow path of his fingers as they skated down the side of my breast, following the curve of it. When they skated back up, his rough palm cupped me, sending chills out through me. Again his touch was infuriatingly light, but his gaze was so furiously dark it seemed to dig into me, and I rocked with his motion, responding to his touch.

The corner of his mouth twitched as his eyes moved back to mine. He freed my other bra strap and the fabric fell away. The intensity of his dark eyes on my chest, drinking me in and taking his time doing it, made me shift and squirm as if I could grind against it. The muscle in his jaw pulsed and he tugged me hard against him.

There would be consequences. This had to be a bad idea.

He stepped in closer, pinning me to the shelf. I reached for his hips.

21

The Cookout

GUS'S HANDS TRACED down the sides of my body, feeling every exposed line and curve.

"You're so beautiful, January," he whispered, kissing me more tenderly. "You're so fucking beautiful, you're like the sun."

His mouth moved down my body, tasting all the places he'd touched. It wasn't enough. My fingernails dug into his back and he jerked me away from the rack and guided me onto the freezer beside it, fumbling with the button on my shorts. I lifted myself so he could slide them down my thighs, and as he straightened, his hands crawled back up my legs, slipped under the sides of my underwear to burrow into my skin. I arched against him and he pulled my thighs up against his hips, his mouth moving hard against mine. "God, January," he said.

My want throttled my voice into a breathy gasp when I tried to reply. I ground myself against him and his touch sharpened.

We stopped being gentle with each other. I couldn't slow myself down enough to be careful with him, and I didn't want him to be careful with me. I undid his pants and jerked them down. One of his hands slid between my legs and he groaned. The other dug into my hip as his mouth trailed down my stomach. His hands squeezed my thighs, and I gripped the sides of the freezer as he lowered himself between my legs. My breaths came faster, his fingers sank into the creases of my hips and his name slipped between my lips. He cupped my hips harder. It wasn't enough. I wanted *him*. I only realized I said it aloud when he said it back to me—*"I want you, January."*

He straightened and yanked me to the edge of the freezer, lifting my hips against him as I tightened my thighs against the sides of his body.

"Gus," I gasped and his gaze rolled up me, heat pulsing under my skin. "Do you have a condom?"

It took him a minute to answer, like his brain was translating from a second language. His eyes were still dark and hungry, his hands wrapped tight around my thighs. "Here?" he said. "In your father's spare house's basement?"

"I was thinking more along the lines of in your pocket," I said, still out of breath.

He laughed, a throaty rattle. "How would you feel if I'd brought condoms with me to tell you about the potato salad?"

"Thankful," I said.

"I didn't know this was going to happen." Gus ran a hand

through his hair in distress as the other maintained its nearly painful grip on me. "Next door. I have some."

We stared at each other for a moment, then started grabbing our clothes off the floor and pulling them on. As we ran up the stairs, Gus grabbed my ass. "God," he said again. "Thank you for this day, Lord. Also Jack Reacher."

We didn't bother with shoes, just ran out the door and across the yard. I reached his front door first and turned back just as Gus was coming up the steps. He let out a gruff laugh at the sight of me and shook his head as he seized me by the hips and kissed me again, flattening me against the door.

I threaded my fingers through his hair, forgetting where we were, forgetting everything but his hands sliding over me, dipping into my clothes, his tongue coaxing my lips apart as I touched as much of him as I could get to. A small, dissatisfied noise slipped out of me, and he reached around my hip to twist the doorknob, leading me backward into the house.

We barely made it three feet before he pulled my shirt off and peeled off his again. In a flash, I was on his console table, his hands undoing my shorts, sifting down over my hips and thighs as he pulled them down me and let them fall to the floor. He walked in between my knees.

I lifted myself against him as he dragged his hands down my breasts, catching my nipples, massaging me until everything in me pinched tight. He scooped me off the table as I wrapped my legs around him and spun to pin me against the bookcase. His hands twisted into my thighs, and I arched against the bookcase to work my hips against his.

Not enough, not even close.

He undid his pants and pulled them down from right under me. My hand scraped down his front to push ineffectually at his briefs. He adjusted me against the shelf and pushed them down.

It was almost too much feeling him against me. A gasp escaped me as I rolled my hips on him. He clutched me with one broad hand and groaned into my skin, "*Fuck*, January."

The rumble of his voice sent goose bumps racing over me. His free hand reached along the shelf at my shoulder level until it met a blue jar in my peripheral vision.

He fished a condom out of it, and I laughed, despite myself. "Oh my God," I murmured against his ear. "Do you *always* have sex against your bookshelves? Are your books behind me right now? Is this an ego thing?"

He drew back, smiling wryly as he tore the wrapper with his teeth. "It's for on my way out the door, smart-ass." His grip loosened and he drew back a few inches. "This is a first for me, but if it's not doing it for *you*, we can always wait until we stumble across a good beach cave on a rainy day."

I greedily grabbed for him, catching his bottom lip with my teeth, before he could pull away any further. He closed the gap between us, kissing me hungrily as he worked the condom on. His hands came back to my waist, tender and light this time, and he coaxed me into a slow, sensual kiss as I trembled with anticipation.

His first thrust was mind-meltingly slow, and everything in my body pulled taut around him as he sank deep into me. My breath caught, stars popping behind my eyes and the wave of pleasure racing through me.

"Oh, *God*," I gasped as he rocked into me.

"Are you praying to me?" he teased against my ear, sending a tingle down my spine. I couldn't take going this slow. I pushed against him, fast, eager, and he matched my intensity.

He pulled me away from the bookshelves and spun around to sit on the couch, drawing me on top of him as he lay back. I gasped his name as he pushed into me again, his hands spanning my ribs. I leaned over him, my hands splayed against his chest as I tried to keep from coming undone. His mouth roved over my breast, and an intoxicating pulse of heat and want went through me.

"I've wanted you for so long," he hissed, hands tightening on my ass.

A thrill rippled through my chest at the rasp of his voice. "I have too," I admitted in a hush. "Since that night at the drive-in."

"No," he said firmly. "Before that."

My chest fluttered like there was a box fan blowing glitter around in it, and everything in me mounted—tightrope-taut and quivering—as Gus went on whispering into my skin: "Before you answered the door in that black dress with those thigh-high boots, and before I saw your hair all wet and frizzy at that book club."

Gus looped an arm around my waist and flipped us over, and I wrapped my leg around his hip, my other foot sliding down the back of his calf as he murmured against my cheek, his husky voice shimmering through me like electric current.

He brushed a kiss across my jaw. "And before that goddamn frat party."

My stomach somersaulted, and I tried to say it back, but one of Gus's hands had wound around the back of my neck and the other was trailing down my center, lancing through my thoughts like a warm knife through butter. We undulated against each other, lost ourselves in each other, everything else blurry and unnecessary around us.

"Oh," I bit out as he thrust harder, deeper, and all at once, I came undone, rush after rush of pleasure rippling out through me as I clutched tight around him. He braced himself over me, burying his mouth into my neck as we unraveled together, breath hitching, muscles shivering.

He collapsed beside me, breathing hard, but kept one arm draped over me, fingers curled against my ribs, and a faint, gruff laugh rose out of him as he threw his other arm over his eyes and shook his head.

"What?" I asked, still catching my breath. I turned onto my side and Gus did the same, his hand falling from in front of his face to race up the side of my thigh and hip. He leaned forward and kissed my sweat-sheened shoulder, nuzzling his face into that side of my neck now.

"I just remembered what you said about the bookshelf," he said in a gravelly voice. "You can't even stop roasting me when I'm losing my mind over your body."

Warmth flooded through me—embarrassment and giddiness and something softer and harder to name. *Before that*, I heard him whisper in my mind. I lay back, dropping my head onto a throw pillow. Gus's hand trailed from my hip bone to my stomach, spreading wide as he leaned over and pressed a slow kiss to it.

My limbs felt exhausted and limp but my heart was still racing. Even if I'd known something had to give between Gus and me, I never would have imagined him like this, keeping his hands on me at all times, his eyes on my mouth and body and eyes, kissing my stomach and laughing into my skin as we lay naked, wrapped together like we'd done this a hundred times.

What does it mean? I thought, followed by, *Stop trying to make everything mean something!* But my chest was pulling tight as the full force of everything that had just happened settled on me. I had loved touching Gus, being touched by him, like I'd known I would, but *this* . . . this was unexpected, and it was possible I loved it even more.

He rested his head on my chest, his hand tracing a lazy, featherlight path back and forth in the slight valley between my hip bones. He kissed the gap between my breasts, the side of my ribs, and even in my state of near-total relaxation, a shiver went through me. "I love your body," his voice thrummed against me.

"I'm a fan of yours too," I said. I prodded the scar on his lip. "And your mouth."

He broke into a smile and propped himself up on his elbow, hand still splayed across my belly button. "I really didn't show up to your sex dungeon to seduce you."

I sat up. "How do you know *I* didn't seduce *you*?"

His smile crooked higher. "Because you wouldn't have had to."

His words reverberated through me again: *I've wanted you for so long. No. Before that.* My heart leapt in my chest, then jolted again at the sudden sound of a phone ringing.

"Shit." Gus groaned and kissed my stomach one last time before rolling off the couch. He snatched his pants from the floor and pulled his phone out of his pocket.

The smile melted off his face as he stared at it, lines of consternation rising between his dark brows.

"Gus?" I said, sudden worry coursing through me.

When he looked up, he seemed a little off balance. He jammed his mouth shut and jerked his gaze back to the phone. "I'm really sorry," he said. "I have to take this."

"Oh." I sat up, immediately aware of how thoroughly naked I was. "Okay."

"Shit," he said, this time under his breath. "This will only take a few minutes. Can I meet you at your house?"

I stared back at him, fighting the hurt building in my chest.

So what if he was kicking me out right after sex to take a mysterious call?

This was fine. It had to be. I had to be fine.

He was out of my system now. That was how it was supposed to work anyway. It had never been the plan to lie naked with him while he catalogued every piece of me with slow, careful kisses. Still, my stomach was sinking as I stood and gathered my clothes.

"Sure," I said. Before I'd gotten my shirt on, Gus was halfway down the hall.

"Hello?" I heard him say, and then a bedroom door closed, shutting me out.

It was eleven when I walked back into my house. Gus and I were supposed to leave for the cookout soon. Pete had told Gus that Sonya couldn't make it until later anyway so our best bet was to come for the first half of the day-to-night affair (pun unintended) and leave long before dessert wine and fireworks. When Gus had told me, I'd suggested I drive separately so he could stay until the bitter end.

"Are you kidding?" he'd said. "You can't possibly imagine how much cheek-pinching you're saving me from by coming. I'm not going to be alone with that crowd for more than thirty seconds."

"What if I have to use the bathroom?" I'd asked.

Gus had shrugged. "I'll make a getaway and leave you behind if I have to."

"Aren't you like four hundred years old?" I'd replied. "That seems a little old for both cheek-pinching *and* such a deep-seated fear of cheek-pinching."

"I may be four hundred, but they've got at least a thousand years on me, and the talons of vultures."

It was strange that that conversation had only happened about twelve hours before what had happened just now. More goose bumps rose along my spine.

The thought of never being with him again sent a new ache pinballing through my body, hitting every part of me he'd studied with his eyes and mouth and hands. The thought of never seeing him like that, naked and vulnerable and without any walls, whispering secrets straight into my bones, made my stomach drop.

One time, that was Gus's rule. And this would definitely count.

He just had an important phone call, I told myself. *It's not about the rule or you or anything.* But I couldn't be sure.

I didn't hear from Gus again until 11:45, when he texted me, Ready in 5?

Hardly. Even burning off energy walking back and forth, I was still thrumming with the memory of what had happened and anxiety about what came next. I hadn't expected him to just drop it, text me like it had never happened, but probably I should have.

I sighed and texted back, sure, then hurried into the bedroom to change into a white sundress and a pair of red sandals I'd gotten during my last Goodwill run. I threw my hair up, then took it back down before putting on as much makeup as I could in the two minutes I had left.

Gus had cleaned up a bit. His hair was the same matted mess, but he'd put on a reasonably wrinkle-free blue button-up, the sleeves rolled up around his rigid-veined forearms. A nod was my only greeting before he climbed into the driver's seat.

I got in beside him, feeling at least twice as awkward as I'd worried I would when I'd imagined some version of this scenario. *Dumb bunny, dumb bunny, dumb bunny!* I chastised myself.

But then I thought about the way he'd kissed my stomach, so tenderly, so sweetly. Were there really one-night—*one-morning* stands that felt that . . . *real?*

I looked out the window and put on my best (horribly inaccurate; 0/10) carefree voice. "Everything okay?"

"Mhm," Gus answered.

I tried to read his features. They told me enough to know I should be worried but no more.

By the time we reached Pete and Maggie's street, it was already crowded with cars. Gus parked around the corner and led the way through a side gate that opened onto one of the paths through their garden.

We bypassed the front door, instead winding around the house to the backyard.

A chorus of voices rose up, calling his name. When it ended, Pete sang, "Jaaaanuary!" and the rest of her guests followed suit. There were at least twenty people crowded around a couple of card tables under an ivy-draped trellis. Beer bottles and red cups littered the star-spangled paper tablecloths and, as promised, a long table at the edge of the patio was not only crowded but *stacked* with aluminum trays of food and cans of beer.

"Now there's my handsome nephew and his lovely companion." Pete was standing at the barbecue, flipping burgers in a KISS THE COOK apron. She'd added in Sharpie *(JK! Happily married!)* and Maggie was wearing her own white apron, whose message was entirely handwritten: KISS THE GEOLOGIST. Guests were crowded around a card table on the cedar-stained deck in the center of their whimsical garden, and past the edge of the deck, a few more were splashing around in the giant blue swimming pool.

"Hope you kids brought your suits!" Pete told Gus as he bent to hug her around her spatula. She loudly kissed his cheek and pulled back. "Water's just perfect today."

I glanced Gus's way. "Does Gus *own* a bathing suit?"

"Technically speaking," Maggie said, drifting forward to kiss her nephew on the cheek, "no, he does not." She turned to plant one on me next, then went on, "But we keep one here for him all the same—he was an absolute *fish* when he was little! We'd take him to the YMCA and have to set a timer to drag him out of the pool, to keep him from peeing in it. We knew he'd never get out of his own volition."

"This story's completely made up," Gus said. "That never happened."

"Cross my heart," Maggie said in her wistful, airy way. "You couldn't have been more than five. Remember that, Gussy? When you were a little guy, you and Rose would come to the pool with us once or twice a week."

Gus's face changed, something behind his eyes, like he was

sliding a metal door closed behind them. "Nope. Doesn't ring any bells."

Rose? Pete's real name was Posey, a little bouquet. Rose must've been her sister, Gus's mom.

"Well, the fact remains," Maggie went on. "You loved to swim, whether you do it now or not, and your suit's just waiting in the spare room." Maggie looked me up and down next. "I'm sure we could find something that would fit you too. It'd be long in the upward direction. And the across direction. You're a tiny thing, aren't you?"

"I never thought so until this summer."

Maggie rubbed my arm and smiled serenely. "That's what living among the Dutch will do to you. We're hardy stock out this-a-way. Come meet everyone. Gussy, you say hi too."

And with that, we were spirited through Pete and Maggie's back garden. Gus knew everyone—mostly faculty and the partners and children of faculty from the local university, along with two of Maggie's sisters—but seemingly had very little to say to any of them beyond a polite greeting. Darcy, Maggie's youngest sister, was a good three inches taller than Maggie with yellow, straw-like hair and giant blue eyes, while Lolly was a good foot shorter than Maggie with a blunt gray bob. "She's got horrible middle child syndrome," Maggie whispered to me as she guided me and Gus to another nook in the garden where they'd set up a beanbag toss. Two of the Labradors ran amiably back and forth, making half-assed attempts to catch the beanbags as the kids threw them.

"I'm sure they'd let you join in," Maggie told us, waving toward the game.

Gus's smile split wide in that rare, unrepentant way as he turned toward her. "I think we'll just start with a drink."

She patted his arm gently. "Oh, you're Pete's godson all right, Gussy. Let's get you two some of my world-famous blue punch!"

She went on ahead, and as we followed, Gus cast a conspiratorial look my way that warned the drink would be terrible, but after our strained drive over, even that was enough to send heat down through my body, all the way to my toes. "World-*infamous*," he whispered.

"Hey, do you know what kind of stone this path is made of?" I whispered back.

He shook his head in disbelief. "Just so you know, asking that question is the one thing I can never forgive you for."

We'd stopped walking on the path, in a nook formed by lush foliage, out of view of both the beanbag toss and the deck.

"Gus," I said. "Is everything okay?"

For a moment, his gaze was intense. He blinked and the expression vanished, a careful indifference replacing it. "Yeah, it's nothing."

"But there is an 'it,'" I said.

Gus shook his head. "No. There's no 'it' except the blue punch, and there will be a lot of that. Try to pace yourself."

He started toward the deck again, leaving me to follow. When we reached it, Maggie already had two full-to-the-brim cups ready for us. I took a sip and did my best not to cough. "What's in this?"

"Vodka," Maggie said airily, ticking the ingredients off on her fingers. "Coconut rum. Blue curaçao. Tequila. Pineapple juice. A splash of regular rum. Do you like it?"

"It's great," I said. It smelled like an open bottle of nail polish remover.

"Gussy?" she asked.

"Wonderful," he answered.

"Better than last year, isn't it?" Pete said, abandoning her post at the grill to join us.

"At least more likely to strip the paint from a car if spilled," Gus said.

Pete guffawed and smacked his arm. "You hear that, Mags? I told you this stuff could power a jet."

Maggie smiled, unbothered by their teasing, and the light caught Gus's face just right to reveal his secret dimple and lighten his eyes to a golden amber. Those eyes cut to me and his mild smile rose. He didn't look like a different person. He looked more at ease, more sure, like all this time I'd only ever come face-to-face with his shadow.

Standing there in that moment, I felt like I'd stumbled on something hidden and sacred, more intimate even than what had passed between us at his house. Like Gus had pulled back the curtains in the window of a house I'd been admiring, whose insides I'd been dreaming about but even so, underestimated.

I liked seeing Gus like this, with the people he knew would always love him.

We'd just had sex like the world was burning down around us, but if I ever got to kiss Gus again, I wanted it to be this version of him. The one who didn't feel so weighted down by the world around him that he had to lean just to stay upright.

". . . Maybe that first weekend in August?" Pete was saying.

She, Maggie, and Gus were all looking right at me, awaiting an answer whose question I hadn't heard.

"Works for me," Gus said. "January?" He still seemed relaxed, happy. I weighed my options: agree to something without having any concept of *what* that something was, admit that I hadn't been listening, or fish for more information with some (possibly damning) questions.

"What . . . what time?" I said, hoping I'd chosen the right option. And a question that made any sense.

"On weeknights, we usually do seven, but given that it's a weekend, we could do whatever time we like. Evening might still be best—this is a beach town, after all, and people might read, but they do it on their bellies in the sand."

"I think this could just be so interesting," Maggie said, clapping her hands together softly. "What you two do seems—externally—to be so different, but I imagine the internal mechanics are still very similar. It's like labradorite and—"

"Bless you," Gus said.

"No, Gussy, I wasn't sneezing," Maggie offered helpfully. "Labradorite is a stone—just beautiful—"

"It really is," Pete agreed. "Looks like something from outer space. If I were to make a sci-fi movie, I'd have the whole world made out of labradorite."

"Speaking of," Gus said. His eyes flicked toward mine and I knew he'd found a way to divert the conversation from rocks. "Have any of you seen *Contact* with Jodie Foster? That's a batshit fucking movie."

"Everett," Pete said. "Language!"

Maggie chortled behind her hand. Her nails were painted a creamy off-white speckled with light blue stars. Today, Pete's were painted dark red. I wondered if manicures were something Maggie had gotten her into, a bit of her wife that had rubbed off on her over the years. I always liked that thought, the way two people really did seem to grow into one. Or at least two overlapping parts, trees with tangled roots.

"Back to the event," Pete said, turning to me again. "Maybe seven would be good, so we're not cutting into too much beach time."

"Sounds great," I said. "Would you mind emailing me all the details to confirm? I can double-check my calendar when I get home."

"I don't know about details. All you really need to know is what time to show up! Maggie and I will come up with some good questions," Pete said.

My hesitancy must've shown, because Gus leaned in a bit. "*I'll* email you."

"Gus Everett, I've seen even less proof that you have email than I've seen that you own a bathing suit," I said.

He shrugged, his eyebrows flicking upward.

"Well, I'm glad I'm not the only one," Pete said. "You can only send so many unanswered dog videos before you start wondering if the addressee is trying to tell you something with his silence!"

Gus hooked an arm around Pete's neck. "I've told you. I don't check my email. That doesn't mean I'm incapable of sending one when asked. In person. For a good reason."

"Dog videos are a good reason for just about anything," Maggie mused.

"What do we need with those, with your own dogs running around?" Gus asked.

"Speaking of Labradors," Maggie said. "What I was saying about labradorite . . ."

Gus looked at me, grinning. As it turned out, he was entirely right. We should have, at all costs, avoided the topic of rocks. I lost track of the conversation fairly quickly as she moved from one stone to the next, spurred by interesting tidbits of information that reminded her of *other* interesting tidbits. After a while, even Pete's (mostly adoring) gaze seemed to glaze over.

"Oh, good!" she said, a bit indiscreetly, as someone else came around the side of the house. "I'd better greet the guests."

"If you want to go say hi," Gus told Maggie, "don't let us stop you!"

Maggie made a face of exaggerated shock. "Never!" she cried, taking hold of Gus's arm. "Your aunt may be fickle, but to me, *no* one is more important than *you*, Gussy! Not even the Labradors— don't tell them, of course."

I leaned into Gus and whispered, "Not even the *labradorite*." His face turned an inch toward mine and he smiled. He was so close that most of his face looked blurry to me, and the smell of the blue punch on his blue lips made my blood feel like it was spiked with Pop Rocks.

"So I'm right after the Labradors?" a man at the table teased Maggie.

"No, don't be silly, Gilbert," Pete said, striding back with the newcomers and a beautiful bouquet in her hands. "You're *tied* with the Labradors."

Gus looked down at me and his smile faded into a crooked,

thoughtful expression. I was watching him retreat into himself and felt a sudden desperation to scrabble for purchase, grab fistfuls of him to keep him there.

His eyes cut to me. "I've got to get some of this blue punch out of my body. You okay here by yourself?"

"Sure," I said. "Unless you're actually going inside to hide baby pictures of yourself. In which case, no, I am not okay here by myself."

"I'm not doing that."

"Are you sure?" I pressed, trying to make him smile, to bring Happy Safe Gus back to the surface. "Because Pete will tell me. There's no hiding them."

The corner of his mouth hitched up, and his eyes sparked. "If you want to follow me into the bathroom to be sure, that's your prerogative."

My stomach sang up through my throat. "Okay."

"Okay?" he said.

Already, heat was flooding my body under his sharp stare. "Gus," I said, "would you like me to come to the bathroom with you?"

He laughed, didn't move. His eyes skirted down me and back up, then flashed sidelong toward Pete. When he looked back to me, his smile had fallen, the gleam in his eyes gone without a trace. "That's okay," he said. "I'll be right back."

He touched my arm gently, then turned and went inside, leaving me more mortified than I'd been in a long time. Or at least than I'd been since the night I drank wine out of my purse at book club. Unfortunately, I imagined I would now be going that route again, trying to blot out the memory of what had just happened.

Gus had turned me down. Hours after he'd had me against a bookshelf, he'd turned me down.

This was somehow so much worse than the worst-case scenario my brain had concocted when I'd weighed the pros and cons of starting something with Gus.

Why did he say that thing about wanting me for so long? It had seemed so sexy in the moment, but now it made me feel like I was a loose end he'd finally gotten to tie up. My stupid fatal flaw had struck again.

I waited beside the sliding glass door, face burning and buried in my drink, for a few minutes. I jumped when my phone buzzed with an email from Gus. My heart began to race, then sank miserably when I opened it. There was nothing in it except: Event at Pete's Books, Aug 2, 7 PM.

I thought back to what Maggie had said, about how what Gus and I did was so different externally that "this" would be interesting. I was fairly sure I'd just committed to doing a book event with him.

Dumb bunny, dumb bunny, dumb bunny. I'd spent a month in near-constant contact with Gus. If I'd spent a month solid with nothing but a blood-drenched volleyball, I imagined I too would be crying as the tide swept it out to sea.

But no, that wasn't true. It wasn't just loneliness and a tendency to romanticize that had gotten me here.

I knew Gus. I knew his life was messy. I knew that his walls were so thick it would take years to chisel through them and that his mistrust of the world went nearly core-deep. I knew I was not the Magical One who could fix it all just by Being Me.

When it came down to it, I knew exactly who Gus Everett was, and it didn't change a thing. Because even though he would probably never learn to dance in the rain, it was Gus I wanted. Only Gus. Exactly Gus.

I had set myself up for heartbreak and now I suspected there was nothing I could do but brace myself and wait for it to hit.

22

The Trip

"OH, COME ON, Gussy. Get in!" Maggie splashed water toward the edge of the pool, but Gus merely stepped back, shaking his head and grinning.

"What, are you afraid it will mess up your perm?" Pete teased from the grill.

"And then we'll find out you have a perm?" I added. When his eyes cut to me, a thrill went through me, followed by the disappointing realization that the saggy one-piece Maggie had lent me made me look like a waterlogged Popsicle tangled in toilet paper.

"Maybe I'm afraid that once I get in, no one will set a timer and remind me to get out and use the bathroom," Gus said.

At the far end of the pool, a stringy little boy and girl cannon-balled in from opposite sides, their splash soaking us. Gus looked back to me. "And then there's that."

"What?" I said. "Fun? Are you afraid it's contagious?"

"No, I'm afraid the pool's already totally full of pee. You two enjoy bathing in it." Gus went back inside and I tried not to keep checking every minute or so whether he'd emerged again.

Maggie found a beach ball, and we started hitting it back and forth. Soon enough, it was four o'clock, and since Sonya was coming at five, I excused myself to change. Maggie hopped spryly out too and grabbed the yellow towels we'd left on the cement around the pool.

She draped one over my shoulders before I could grab it from her and led the way inside. "You can use the upstairs bathroom," she said with a sweet smile that seemed *almost* like a wink.

"Oh," I said uncomfortably. "Okay." I gathered my clothes and went to the stairs.

The steps were creaky, wooden, and narrow. They turned back on themselves halfway before depositing me into the upstairs hall-way. The bathroom sat at the end, a pink tile monstrosity that was so ugly it became cute again. There were two doors on one side of the hall and a third on the other, all of them closed.

It was almost time to leave. I was going to have to knock on them until I found him. I tried not to feel embarrassed or hurt, but it wasn't easy.

From your first real conversation, Gus made it clear he wasn't the type to expect anything from, January. The kind not even you were capable of roman-ticizing.

I toweled off and dressed in the bathroom, then came out and knocked softly on the first door. No answer, so I moved to the one across the hall.

A mumbled "Yeah?" came through it, and I eased it open.

Gus was on the twin bed in the corner, legs stretched out and back propped up by the wall. To his right, the blinds were partly open, letting in streaks of light between the shadows on the floor. "Time to head out?" he asked, scratching the back of his head.

I looked around the room at the mismatched furniture, the lack of plants. On the bedside table there was a lamp that looked like a soccer ball, and across from the foot of the bed, the little blue bookcase there was full of copies, US editions and foreign ones, of Gus's books. "Come here to ponder your own mortality?" I asked, tipping my head toward the bookshelf.

"Just had a headache," he said. I went toward the bed to sit beside him but he stood before I reached it. "I'd better say bye. You should too, if you don't want Pete to blacklist you." And then he was leaving the room and I was left there alone. I went closer to the bookshelf. Four framed pictures sat along the top. One of a baby with dark eyes surrounded by fluffy fake clouds and under a soft focus. The next was Pete and Maggie, a good thirty years younger, with sunglasses on top of their heads and a little boy in sandals standing between them. Over his head, between Pete's and Maggie's shoulders, a sliver of the Cinderella Castle was visible.

The third picture was much older, a sepia-toned portrait of a grinning little girl with dark curls and one dimple. The fourth was a team picture, little boys and girls in purple jerseys all lined up next to a younger, slimmer Pete, wearing a whistle around her neck and a cap low over her eyes. I found Gus right away, thin and messy with a bashful smile that favored one side.

Voices filtered up from downstairs then. ". . . sure you can't stay?" Pete was saying.

I set the photo down and left the room, closing the door on my way out.

We were quiet for the first couple of minutes of the drive home, but Gus finally asked, "Did you have fun?"

"Pete and Maggie are wonderful," I answered noncommittally.

Gus nodded. "They are."

"Okay," I said, unsure where to go from there.

His hard gaze shifted my way, softening a little, but he jammed his mouth shut and didn't look my way again.

I stared at the buildings whipping past the window. The businesses had mostly closed for the day, but there'd been a parade while we were at Pete's, and vendor carts still lined either side of the street, families clad in red, white, and blue milling between them with bags of popcorn and American-flag pinwheels in their hands.

I had so many questions but all of them were nebulous, unaskable. In my own story, I didn't want to be the heroine who let some silly miscommunication derail something obviously good, but in my real life, I felt like I'd rather risk that and keep my dignity than keep laying everything out for Gus until he finally came right out and admitted he didn't want me the way I wanted him.

More than once, I thought miserably. *Something real, even if a little misshapen.*

When we reached the curb in front of our houses (markedly later than we would have, due to the increased pedestrian traffic), Gus said, "Let me know about tomorrow."

"Tomorrow?" I said.

"The New Eden trip." He unlocked the car door. "If you still want to go, let me know."

This was all it had taken? He was now *totally* disinterested in me, even as a research companion?

He climbed out of the car. That was it. Five PM, and we were going our separate ways. On the Fourth of July, when I knew no one in town apart from him and his aunts.

"Why wouldn't I want to go?" I asked, fuming. "I said I wanted to." He was already halfway to his porch. He turned back and shrugged.

"Do you want me to?" I demanded.

"If you want," he said.

"That's not what I asked you. I asked you if you want me to come with you tomorrow."

"I want you to do whatever you want to."

I folded my arms over my chest. "What time," I barked.

"Nine-ish," he said. "It'll probably take all day."

"Great. See you then."

I went into my house and paced angrily, and when that didn't do the trick, I sat at my computer and wrote furiously until night fell. When I couldn't get out another bitter word, I went onto the deck and watched the fireworks streak over the lake, their glitter raining down on the water like falling stars. I tried not to look Gus's way, but the glow of his computer in the kitchen caught my eye every once in a while.

He was still working at midnight when Shadi texted me: Well, that's it. I'm in love. RIP me.

Same.

———

I AWOKE TO a house-shaking boom of thunder and rolled out of bed. It was eight o'clock, but the room was still dark from the storm clouds.

Shivering, I dragged my robe off the chair at the vanity and hurried into the kitchen to put the water on. Great slashes of lightning leapt from the sky to hit the churning lake, the light fluttering against the back doors like a series of camera flashes. I watched it in a stupor. I'd never seen a storm out over a massive body of water, at least outside of a movie. I wondered if it would affect Gus's plans.

Maybe it'd be better if it did. If he could effectively ghost me. I'd call and cancel the event at the bookstore, and we'd never see each other, and he could stick to his precious once-only non-dating rule, and I could go to Ohio and marry an insurance man, whatever that meant.

Behind me, the kettle whistled.

I made myself some coffee and sat down to work, and again the words poured out of me. I had reached the forty-thousand-word mark. The family's world was coming apart. Eleanor's father's second family had shown up at the circus. Her mother had had a rough encounter with a guest and was more on edge than ever. Eleanor had slept with the boy from Tulsa and been caught sneaking back into her tent, only for the mechanic, Nick, to cover for her.

And the clowns. They'd nearly been outed after a tender moment in the woods behind the fairgrounds, and they'd gotten into a huge argument because of it. One of them had left for the bar in town and wound up sleeping it off in a holding cell.

I didn't know how things were going to come together but I knew they needed to get worse. It was nine fifteen by then, and I hadn't heard from Gus. I went and sat on the unmade bed, staring out the window toward his study. I could see warm golden light pouring from lampshades through his window.

I texted him. Will this weather interfere with research?

It probably won't be a comfortable trip, he said. But I'm still going.

And I'm still invited? I asked.

Of course. A minute later he texted again. Do you have hiking boots?

Absolutely not, I told him.

What size do you wear?

7 ½, why? Do you think we wear the same size?

I'll grab some from Pete, he said, then, If you still want to come.

Dear GOD, are you trying to kick me out of this? I typed back.

It took him much longer to answer than usual and the wait started making me feel sick. I used the time to get dressed. Finally he replied, No. I just don't want you to feel obligated.

I waffled, debating what to do. He texted me again: Of course I want you to come, if you want to.

Not of course, I replied, simultaneously angry and relieved. You haven't made that clear at all.

Is it clear now? he asked.

Clear-ER.

I want you to come, he said.

Then go get the shoes.

Bring your laptop if you want, he replied. I might need to be there for a while.

Twenty minutes later, Gus honked from the curb, and I put on my rain jacket and ran through the storm. He leaned over to open the door before I'd even gotten there and I slammed it shut again behind me, pulling the hood down. The car was warm, the windows were foggy, and the back seat was loaded with flashlights, an oversized backpack, a smaller waterproof one, and a pair of muddy hiking boots with red shoelaces. When he saw me looking at them, Gus said, "They're eights—will that work?"

When I looked back at him, he almost seemed to startle, but it was such a small gesture I might've imagined it. "Lucky for you I brought a pair of thick socks, just in case." I pulled the balled-up socks from my jacket pocket and tossed them at him. He caught them and turned them over in his hands.

"What would you have done if the boots were too small?"

"Cut off my toes," I said flatly.

Finally he cracked a smile, looking up at me from under his thick, inky eyelashes. His hair was swept off his forehead per usual and a few raindrops had splattered across his skin when I'd jumped into the car. As he swallowed, the dimple in his cheek appeared, then vanished from sight.

I hated what that did to me. A tiny carrot should really not overpower the instinct in my dumb bunny brain screaming, *RUN*.

"Ready?" Gus said.

I nodded. He faced forward in his seat and pulled away from our houses. The rain had slowed enough that the windshield wipers could squeak across the glass at an easy pace, and we fell into a fairly comfortable rhythm, talking about our books and the rain and the blue punch. We moved off that last topic fairly quickly, neither of us apparently willing to broach Yesterday.

"Where are we going?" I asked, an hour in, when he pulled off the highway. From my online search, I knew New Eden was at least another hour off.

"Not a murder spot," he promised.

"Is it a surprise?"

"If you want it to be. But it might be a disappointing one."

"The world's largest ball of yarn?" I guessed.

His gaze cut toward me, narrowed in appraisal. "That would disappoint you?"

"No," I said, heart leaping traitorously. "But I thought you might *think* it would."

"There are certain wonders that no man can face without weeping, January. A giant ball of yarn is one of those."

"Okay, you can tell me," I said.

"We're getting gas."

I looked at him. "Okay, that is disappointing."

"Much like life."

"Not this again," I said.

It was another sixty-three minutes before Gus pulled off the highway again near Arcadia, and then another fifteen miles on wooded two-lane roads before he pulled over onto a muddy shoulder and told me to stuff my computer in the dry bag.

"Now *this* is definitely a murder spot," I said when we got out. As far as I could tell there was nothing here but the steep bank to our right and the trees above it.

"It's probably *someone's*," Gus said. He leaned back into the car. "But not mine. Now change your shoes. We have to walk the rest of the way."

Gus pulled on the bigger backpack and took one of the flashlights, leaving me to grab the other bag once I'd gotten the socks and shoes on. "This way," he called, climbing straight up the muddy ridge to the woods. He turned to offer me a hand, and after I slipped in the mud thrice, he managed to hoist me up onto the path. At least, it appeared to be a path, although there were no signs or visible reasons for a path to start there.

The forest was quiet apart from our tromping and our breaths and the underlying drizzling of rain speckling the leaves. I kept my hood up, but in here, the rain mostly made it to us in the form of fine mist. I'd gotten used to the blues and grays of the lake, the yellow-golds of the sun spilling over the water and the tops of the trees, but in here, everything was rich and dark, every shade of green the most saturated version of itself.

This was the most at peace I'd felt in two days, if not all year. Whatever weirdness was between Gus and me was placed on hold as we wandered through the silent temple of the woods. Sweat built up around my armpits, along my hairline, and through my underwear, until I stopped and took the jacket off. Without a word, Gus stopped and peeled his off too. I watched an olive sliver of his flat stomach appear as his shirt caught around his shoulders. I looked away as he pulled it back down.

We picked our backpacks up and kept walking. My thighs began to burn, and the gathering sweat and rain plastered my tank top and my jeans to my skin. At one point, the rain picked up again, and we ducked into a shallow pseudocave for a few minutes until the showers let up. The gray sky made it hard to tell how much time had passed, but we must have spent at least a couple of hours marching through the woods until the trees finally thinned and the charred skeleton of New Eden came into sight ahead.

"Holy shit," I whispered, stopping beside Gus. He nodded. "Have you seen it before?"

"Only in pictures," he said, and started toward the nearest smoke-blackened trailer. The second fire, unlike the one from the lightning strike, hadn't been an accident. The police investigation had found that every building had been doused in gasoline. The Prophet, a man who called himself Father Abe, had died outside the last building to catch flames, leading authorities to speculate that he'd been the one to light the place up.

Gus swallowed. His voice came out hoarse as he pointed toward a trailer on the right. "That was the nursery. They went first."

Went, I thought.

Burned, I thought. I turned to hide that I was gagging.

"People are awful," Gus said behind me.

I swallowed my stomach bile. My eyes stung. The back of my nose burned. Gus glanced over his shoulder at me, and his gaze softened. "Want to set up the tent?"

He must've seen the face I made, because he added quickly, "So we can use our computers." He nodded toward the darkly churning sky as he slid his backpack off. "Don't think this is going to let up any time soon."

"Not here though," I said. "It feels wrong to put a tent in all this."

He nodded agreement and we kept moving, hiked off until the site was no longer visible. Until I could almost pretend we were in a different forest, far away from what had happened at New Eden. As Gus pulled tent poles from the bag, I came forward to help. My hands were shaking, from both the cold and the unease of being here, and I poured all of my focus into piecing the tent together, blocking out the memory of the burned remnants of the cult.

The distraction only lasted a few minutes, and then the tent was finished, all our stuff tucked safely inside, except the little notepad and pencil Gus pulled from his pocket as we made our way back to the site.

He shot me a tentative look I couldn't interpret, then started toward one of the trailers, or rather three that had been cobbled together with plywood-and-tarp hallways. I swallowed a knot and followed, but after a few steps, he stopped and turned back to me. "You can go back to the tent," he said gruffly. "You don't need to see this."

A knot rose in my throat. Obviously I didn't want to see this. But it bothered me that he'd say *I* didn't need to while still planning to explore it himself. I could tell he hated being here too. And yet here he was, facing it.

That was how it always was. He never looked away from any of it. Maybe he thought *someone* had to bear witness to the dark, or maybe he hoped that if he stared into the pitch-black long enough, his eyes would adjust and he'd see answers hiding in it.

This is why bad things happen, the dark would say. *This is how it all makes sense.*

I couldn't go hide from this. I couldn't leave Gus here alone. If he was descending into the darkness, I was going to tie a rope between our waists and go down with him.

I shook my head and went to stand behind him, his dark eyes dipping to study me, his rain-speckled lashes curved low and dark and heavy against his olive cheeks.

There was so much I wanted to say, but all I could get out was, "I'm here."

And when I said it, his brow furrowed and his jaw tensed, and he peered at me in that particular Gus way that made the knot in my throat inch higher.

He nodded and turned back to the trailer, tipping his chin toward it. "Father Abe's place. Apparently he'd seek counsel from a group of angels, so he needed the room."

I tore my gaze from Gus to the sooty trailer. It instantly made me feel woozy and unmoored, like the air here was still overloaded with carbon dioxide and ash.

Why do bad things happen? I thought. *How will it all make sense?* But no great truth appeared to me. There was no good reason this horrible thing had happened, and no reason Gus's life had been what it was either. Dammit, R.E.M. was right: Every single person on the planet had to take turns hurting. Sometimes all you could do was hold on to each other tight until the dark spat you back out.

Gus blinked clear of his solemn haze and crouched, balancing his notepad on his knee and scribbling notes, and I stood beside him, legs wobbling but eyes open. *I'm here,* I thought at him. *I'm here and I see it too.*

We moved around the site like that, silent as ghosts, Gus guarding his notes from the rain as it soaked through our clothes and skin right down to the bone.

When we'd circled the whole plot of land once, he headed back toward Father Abe's Frankensteined trailer, glancing at me for the first time in the last two hours. "It's freezing," he said. "You should go back to the tent."

It *was* freezing—the wind had picked up, and the temperature had begun dropping until my jeans felt like ice packs against my skin. But no part of me thought that was why he was pushing me away.

"Please, January," Gus said quietly, and it was the *please* that unraveled me. What was I doing? I cared about Gus, but if he didn't want me to hold on to him, I had to let go.

"Okay," I said through chattering teeth. "I'll wait in the tent."

Gus nodded, then turned and trudged off. Heart stung, I walked back to the tent, knelt, and crawled inside. I curled into the fetal position to warm myself up and closed my eyes, listening to the barrage of rain on the fabric overhead. I tried to let all my thoughts and feelings slip away from me, but instead they seemed to swell as I drifted toward sleep, a dark, frothy wave of emotions pulling me toward a restless dream.

And then the whine of the zipper was tugging me out of it, and I opened my unfocused eyes to find Gus stooped in the tent's doorway, dripping.

"Hey." My voice came out gravelly. I sat up, smoothing my wet hair.

"Sorry that took so long," he said, climbing in and zipping the door up behind him. "I needed to get thorough pictures, draw a map, all that." He sat beside me and unzipped his rain jacket, which he'd put back on since we parted ways.

I shrugged. "It's fine. You said it would be an all-day thing."

His gaze lifted to the tent ceiling. "And I meant that," he said. "All *day*. The tent was just a precaution for the weather. Too many years in Michigan."

I nodded as if I understood. I thought I might.

"Anyway." He looked back toward my feet. "If you're ready, we can hike back."

We sat in silence for a moment. "Gus," I said, tired.

"Yeah?"

"Will you just tell me what's going on?"

He folded his legs in and leaned back on his palms, staring steadily at me. He took a deep breath. "Which part?"

"All of it," I said. "I want to know all of it."

He shook his head. "I told you. You can ask me anything."

"Okay." I swallowed a fist-sized knot. "What was the deal with that phone call?"

"The deal?"

"Don't make me say it," I whispered miserably. But he still seemed confused. I gritted my teeth and closed my eyes. "Was it Naomi?"

"No," he said, but it wasn't *No, how could you think that?* It sounded more like *No, but she still calls me.* Or *No, but it was someone else I love.*

My stomach cinched tight but I forced myself to open my eyes.

Gus's brow had wrinkled, and a raindrop slid down his sharp cheekbone. "It was my friend Kayla Markham."

"Kayla?" My voice sounded so shaky, pathetic. Gus's best friend since high school, Markham, was a woman?

Sudden understanding crossed Gus's face. "It's not like—she's my *lawyer.* She's friends with Naomi too—she's handling our divorce."

"Oh." It sounded small and stupid, exactly how I felt. "Your *mutual friend* is handling your divorce?"

"I know it's weird." He mussed his hair. "I mean, it's like she's

279

totally impartial. She throws me this big-ass birthday party every year but then I have to see pictures of her and Naomi in Cancún for a week. We never talk about it, and yet she's handling the divorce, and it's just . . ."

"So weird?" I guessed.

He let out his breath in a rush. "So weird."

A little bit of the pressure in my chest released, but regardless of who Kayla Markham was to Gus, it didn't change how he'd acted yesterday. "If it's not about her, then why are you trying to get rid of me?" I asked, voice trembling and quiet.

Gus's eyes darkened. "January." He shook his head. "I'm not doing that."

"You are," I said. I'd been telling myself not to cry, but it was no use. As soon as I said it, the tears were welling, voice wrenching upward. "You ignored me yesterday. You tried to cancel today. You sent me back to the tent when I tried to stay with you and—you didn't want me to come. I should have listened."

"January, no." Gus roughly cupped the sides of my face, holding my tear-filled gaze to his. "Not at all." He kissed my forehead. "It wasn't about you. Not even a little bit." He kissed my tear-streaked left cheek, caught another falling tear with his mouth on my right.

He pulled me in against his chest and wrapped his arms around me, covering me with rain-dampened heat as he nuzzled his nose and mouth against the top of my head.

"I feel so stupid," I whimpered. "I thought you really—"

"I *do*," he said quickly, drawing back from me. "January, I didn't want you here today because I knew it was going to be hard. I didn't want to be the reason you spent a whole day in a torched-out graveyard. I didn't want to put you through this. That's all."

He brushed some hair behind my ear, and the sweetness of the gesture only made my tears fall faster. "But you didn't want me at Pete's either," I said, voice breaking. "You invited me, and then we slept together and you changed your mind."

His mouth juddered into a look of open hurt. "I wanted you there," he all but whispered, and when a fresh tear slipped down my cheek, he caught it with his thumb.

"Look," he said, "this divorce has been so stupidly drawn out. I waited for her to file, and she just didn't, and I don't know—it didn't matter to me, so I didn't pursue it until a few weeks ago. She told me she'd sign the papers if I met her for a drink, so I went to Chicago to see her, and when I left, I thought it was settled. Yesterday, Markham called and told me Naomi changed her mind. She wants 'some details hammered out'—I mean, the only things we *owned* together were some overpriced copper pots, which she has, and our cars. It shouldn't be complicated, but I put it off too long, and . . ."

He rubbed at his forehead. "And then Markham asked what was new with me, and I told her about you, about how you were here for the summer, and she thought it was a bad idea—"

"Bad idea?" My gut roiled. That didn't sound impartial. It sounded very partial.

"Because you're leaving," Gus said in a rush. "And she knows—she knows how stupid I am when it comes to you, how crazy I was for you in college, and—"

"What are you *talking* about?" I challenged. "You never even spoke to me."

He let out a humorless laugh. "Because you hated me!" he blurted. "I'd come late to class so I could choose my seat based on where you sat, and I'd rush out afterward so I could walk with you, ask to borrow pens every day for a week, fucking drop books Three Stooges–style when you hung back so it would just be the two of us, and you'd never even look at me! Even when we were workshopping your stories and I was talking right *to* you, you wouldn't look at me. I could never figure out what I'd done, and then I saw you at that party, and you were finally looking at me and—that's my point! I'm an idiot when it comes to you!"

I was reeling with the information, replaying every interaction I could remember and trying to see them how he'd described. But almost all of those had just been me staring at him, looking away when he noticed, burning with jealousy and frustration and a little lust. I could believe that maybe Gus *had* wanted me since before the infamous frat party, because I'd been attracted to him too, but anything more than that didn't compute.

"Gus," I said, "you *only* critiqued my stories. I was a joke to you."

It was possible I'd never seen such a blatant expression of shock. "Because I was an asshole!" he said, which didn't exactly explain things, but then he went on. "I was a twenty-three-year-old elitist dick who thought everyone in our class was wasting my time except you! I thought it was *obvious* how I felt about you, *and* your writing. That's the point! I never knew what you were thinking then, and I still have no idea—"

"What do you *think* me taking your pants off means?" I said.

He tugged at the hair at the crown of his head. "That's what I'm trying to tell you, what I've been trying to tell you since you got here," he said breathlessly. "I don't remember how any of this is supposed to work or what I'm supposed to do. Even before Naomi and I— January, I'm not like Jacques."

"What is that supposed to mean?" I asked, stung.

"I'm not the kind of guy women try to date," he said, frustrated. "I never have been. I'm the one they want to hook up with and drunk text and hang out with for a change of pace when they've just gotten out of seven-year relationships with doctors, and that's fine, but I don't want that with you, okay? I can't do that."

My throat squeezed tight, strangling my voice into something flimsy and weak. "That's what you think? That this is all some kind of identity crisis for me?"

His eyes fell heavily on me, and for once I felt like I could see straight through them. That was *exactly* what he thought: that like our bet, Gus was something I was trying on for size while I took a break from the *real me*. Like I was on my own reverse *Eat, Pray, Love* tear that would fizzle out as quickly as it had flared up.

"I want to be your perfect fucking Fabio, January, but I can't," Gus went on. "I'm not."

I'm not like Jacques, he'd said, and I'd thought he was insulting Jacques or making a dig at me for dating someone like him, but that wasn't it at all.

Gus still thought he was missing something, some special piece other people had, the thing that made people *stay*, and it broke my heart a little. It broke my heart that when we were younger, he'd thought I'd never even looked at him.

I shook my head. "I don't need you to be Fabio," I said, voice thick with emotion, like it wasn't the single stupidest sentence I'd uttered in my life.

"Yes, you do," Gus said urgently. "Everything I've done in the last twenty-four hours has hurt you, January. You want me to be able to read you, and I can't. You want me to know how to do this, and I don't."

"No," I said. "I just want you to tell me how you feel. I want to know what it is you want."

"I'm going to mess this up," he said helplessly.

"Maybe!" I cried. "But that's not what I asked. Tell me what you want, Gus. Not why you can't have it, or what you think *I* want, or why you can't give *that* to me. Just tell me what you want for once. That's all I'm asking you to do."

"I want *you*," he said quietly. "I want you, in every way. I *want* to take you on dates and play with a fucking beach ball in a pool with you, but I'm a wreck, January.

"I'm trapped in a marriage with a woman who lives with another man, just waiting to be done. I'm on medicine. I'm in therapy. I'm trying to give up smoking for good and even to learn how to *meditate*—and while that's going on, while I'm a walking dumpster fire, I want you in a way I'm not sure either of us can handle. I don't want to hurt you and I don't want to feel what it would be like to lose you."

He stopped for a beat. In the dim half-light of the tent his face was all stark shadows, but his liquidy dark eyes glinted as if lit from within. He took a few breaths, then said in a soft murmur, "It doesn't mean I don't want you, January—I've always wanted you. It just means I also want you to be happy, and I'm scared I could never be the person who could give you that."

The intensity in his gaze settled, like he'd burned through every spark he had, and I loved his eyes like this too, all warm and raw and quiet. I touched the sides of his face and he looked into my eyes, still breathing hard. Warmth bubbled in my chest, spilling into my fingers as they curled around his sharp jaw.

"Then let me be happy with you, Gus," I said and kissed him softly, like the rare and tender thing he was.

His hands swept across my back, and he pulled me closer.

23

The Lake

G US LAID ME gently down, his hand still tucked beneath my neck, fingers tangling in my hair. I pulled him over me as his hands caught the bottom edge of my shirt and lifted it around my ribs. When he'd peeled the damp tank top over my head, he tossed it aside and cradled my jaw, kissing me again, slow and heavy, thick and rough and perfectly Gus. His palm skated up my center and back down to undo my wet jeans, and together we managed to get my shoes and pants off before he lifted me across his lap.

"January," he whispered through the dark, like an incantation, like a prayer.

I wanted to say his whole name back like that. To make *Augustus* mean something different to him than it had. But I knew that would take time, and for Gus, I thought I could be patient. So instead I just kissed him, slipped my fingers up his warm stomach to lift his sopping shirt over his head and discard it into the pile with mine. We sat back in the dark, looking at each other, unhurried and unembarrassed.

In the basement it had felt like we were racing to devour each other. This was different. Now I could study Gus how I'd always wanted to, savoring every hard line and sharp edge of his I'd ever stolen glances of, and his hands traced the curves of my hips and ridges of my ribs with the same quiet awe, his warm gaze trailing purposefully after them. Every piece of me he looked at seemed to light up in response, all the blood in my body rushing to the surface, jostling there, eager to be dispelled by his mouth or hands.

His mouth sank against the side my neck, again at the front of my throat, once more in the gap between my breasts. "Perfect," he whispered into my skin. His fingertips grazed every place his lips had been, and his eyes lifted to mine. "You're perfect," he rasped and brushed a kiss over my lips so slow and hot it seemed to melt me from within.

He undid my bra and pulled me flush against him, a prickle of need starting low in my belly at the feel of his chest against mine, his hands running down my sides. We were both soaked to the bone, and our mouths and skin were slick and warm against each other as we wound ourselves together, fingers and lips and tongues and hips slipping and catching, tangling and unraveling.

He tasted like the outdoors, like pine and dew and cinnamon and himself. We untwined long enough to get his pants and briefs off and then he was over me, his mouth skirting up the inside of my thigh as his hands twisted into my underwear and hitched them down my hips. His lips nestled into my stomach, scraped down the curve of it. I gasped as his mouth finally met me, and my hands found their way into his hair, onto his neck, as he cupped my hips to his mouth, every nerve in my body rushing to meet it, every sensation gathering in that one point.

I dragged him up the length of me, and his hands circled my breasts as I wrapped my thighs tight around his hips and moved against him, feeling him shiver. "Condom?" I whispered, and he leaned over to snatch his backpack, digging through it as I arched under him. He found the foil package and tore it open, and then within seconds, he was pushing into me, his mouth unraveling mine, his hands in my hair and on my skin, his breath against my ear, his name rolling through me like a tide, his voice murmuring mine into my neck as he rocked deeper, sending full-body pulses of bliss through me.

The rain fell all around us, and I let go of everything that wasn't Gus, wasn't this moment. I lost myself in him, and instead of trying to convince myself that someday everything would be okay, I focused on the fact that, right now, it already was.

Gus's hands found mine as the mounting pressure shuddered through us, and we locked together, gasping and clutching and shivering. When we were finished, he didn't let go. We lay beside each other, under the blanket he pulled out of his backpack, our hands knotted together and our heavy breath in sync.

We had sex twice more that night—an hour or so later when he interrupted our conversation about the event at Pete's to kiss me, and then again later, in a dreamy daze, when we awoke still tangled together naked in the dark, me already arching, him already hard.

When we'd finished, he pulled a bag of tortilla chips and a

couple of Clif Bars out of the pack along with the same two flasks he'd taken to line dancing.

I propped myself up on my elbow to watch him, and he turned one of the lanterns on, the light casting him in reds and golds. He held the chips out to me. "Just a precaution?" I said, nodding toward the provisions.

Gus's dimple deepened. His hand skimmed up the side of my arm and down across my collarbone. "An optimistic one. I'm an optimist now." His fingers drifted to my chin, and he tilted it up to kiss my throat again. His other hand came up and he caught both sides of my jaw as he kissed me deeply, slowly, drank me in. When he pulled back, his fingers threaded through my hair, his thumb roving over my bottom lip, he asked, "Are you happy, January?"

"Extremely," I said. "Are you?"

He gathered me against him and kissed my temple. His voice crackled against my ear. "I'm so happy."

IN THE MORNING, we pulled on our damp clothes, packed up, and walked back to the car. The skies were clear and bright, and Gus turned on the radio, then held my hand against the gearshift, the light dappling us through the trees and windshield.

I felt like I had the Gus of Pete's house right then. And I felt a little more like the January of before too, the one who could fall fearlessly. I searched my stomach for that tight feeling, the sensation of waiting for the other shoe to drop. I could find it, if I tried hard enough, but for once, I didn't want to. This moment felt worth whatever pain it might bring later, and I tried to repeat that to myself until I was sure I'd be able to remember it if I needed to.

Gus lifted my hand from the gearshift and pressed it to his mouth without looking over at me.

Last night I'd known all this could slip away, dissolve around me. I'd half expected it to by the time the first cold streaks of morning light hit the tent and Gus realized what he'd done, and more importantly, everything he'd said. But instead, when his eyes opened, he'd given me a closed-mouthed smile and pulled me against him, nuzzling his face into the side of my head, kissing my hair.

Instead, here we were in the car, Gus Everett holding on to my hand and not letting go.

What happened two days ago in his study had seemed like an inevitability, a crash course we'd been set on since the beginning of the summer. This, however—this was something I hadn't even let myself daydream about. I wouldn't have known how to. He didn't look like anyone from the story.

On the drive back, we stopped for breakfast at a greasy spoon diner along the highway, at which point I slipped away to call Shadi from the bathroom. The Haunted Hat's (Ricky's—we were going to have to start calling him by his name soon, if this kept up) little sisters were sharing their room with Shadi, at their mothers' insistence, and she'd sneaked away to talk to me at the bottom of their cul-de-sac but was still whispering like the whole family was sleeping in a pile on top of her.

"Oh my *God*," she hissed.

"I know," I said.

"My *GOOOOOOOD*," she repeated.

"Shad. I know."

"Wow."

"Wow," I agreed.

"I can't wait to visit and watch him be completely smitten with you," she said.

The thought made my stomach feel like it was fizzing. "We'll see."

"No," she said with finality. "How could he not be? Not even Sexy, Evil Gus could be that deranged, habibi." A lady was knocking on the bathroom door then, so we said our quick "I love you" and "Goodbye" and I went back to the sticky vinyl booth and the pile of pancakes and Gus. Sexy, disheveled, lazily smiling Gus, who gripped my knee beneath the table again and sent sparks down my belly and up my thighs.

I wanted to go back to the bathroom, him in tow.

Our breakfast stop turned into a trip to the bookstore in town, where they had none of my books in stock except the first, and no special display for their two copies of *The Revelatories*, and that turned into a stop at a bar with an outdoor patio.

"What's your favorite bad review?" I asked him.

He smiled to himself as he thought, stirring the whiskey and ginger ale in front of him. "Like in a magazine or from a reader?"

"Reader first."

"I've got it," he said. "It was on Amazon. One star: 'Did not order book.'"

I threw my head back, laughing. "I love the ones where they accidentally ordered the wrong book, then review based on how different it was from the book they *meant* to order."

Gus's laugh rattled. He touched my knee beneath the table. "I like the ones that explain what I was *trying* to do. Like, 'The author was trying to write Franzen, but he's no Franzen.'"

I pantomimed gagging myself and Gus covered his eyes until I stopped. "But were you?"

"Trying to write Franzen?" He laughed. "No, January. I'm just trying to write good books. That sound like Salinger."

I erupted into laughter, and he grinned back. We fell into easy silence again as we sipped on our drinks. "Can I ask you something?" I said, after a minute.

"No," Gus answered, deadpan.

"Great," I said. "Why did you try to keep me away from New Eden? I mean, I know you said you didn't want me to have to see it, and I get that. Except that the whole point of this bet was for you to convince me the world was how you said it was, right? And that was the perfect opportunity."

He was quiet for a long moment. He ran his hand through his messy hair. "Do you really think that was what this was about?"

"I mean, I hope it was at least *partially* an elaborate ruse to sleep with me," I teased, but the expression on his face was serious, even a little anxious. He shook his head and glanced toward the window.

"I never wanted you to see the world like I see it," he said.

"But the bet . . ." I said, trying to work it out.

"The bet was your idea," he reminded me. "I just thought maybe if you tried to write what I write—I don't know, I guess I hoped you'd realize it wasn't right for you." He hurried to add, "Not because you're not capable! But because it's not you. The way you think about things, it's not like that. I always thought the way you saw the world was . . . incredible." A faint flush crept into his olive cheeks and he shook his head. "I never wanted to see you lose that."

A jumble of emotion caught in my throat. "Even if what I'm seeing isn't real?"

Gus's brow and mouth softened. "When you love someone," he said haltingly, ". . . you want to make this world look different for them. To give all the ugly stuff meaning, and amplify the good. That's what *you* do. For your readers. For me. You make beautiful things, because you love the world, and maybe the world doesn't always look how it does in your books, but . . . I think putting them out there, that changes the world a little bit. And the world can't afford to lose that."

He scratched a hand through his hair. "I've always admired that. The way your writing always makes the world seem brighter, and the people in it a little braver."

My chest felt warm and liquidy, like the block of ice that had been lodged there since Dad died was breaking up, just a little, its hunks melting down. Because the truth was, learning the truth about my dad had made the world seem dark and unfamiliar, but discovering Gus bit by bit had done the opposite. "Or maybe I'm just right," I said quietly. "And sometimes people are brighter and braver than they know."

A faint smile flickered across his lips, then fell as he thought. "I don't think I've ever loved the world like you do. I remember being afraid of it. And then angry with it. And then just—deciding not to feel too strongly about it. But I don't know. Maybe when I do this shit, when I talk to people like Dave and walk through burned buildings, there's a part of me that's hoping I'm going to find something."

"Like what?" It came out as a whisper.

He put his elbows on the table. "Like the kind of world you

write about. Like proof. That it isn't as bad as it looks. Or it's more good than bad. Like if we added up all the—all the *shit* and all the wildflowers, the world would come out positive."

I reached for his hand and he let me take it, his dark eyes soft and open. "When I first found out about my dad's affair, I tried to do that kind of math," I admitted. "How much lying and cheating could he have done and still have been a good father? How deep could he have gotten himself in with That Woman and still loved my mom? Still *liked* his life. I tried to figure out how happy he could've been, how much he could've missed us when he was away, and when I was feeling particularly bad, how much he must've hated us to be willing to do what he did. And I never got my answers.

"And sometimes I still want them, and other times I'm terrified of what I'd find out. But people aren't math problems." I gave a heavy shrug. "I can miss my dad and hate him at the same time. I can be worried about this book and torn up about my family and sick over the house I'm living in, and still look out at Lake Michigan and feel overwhelmed by how big it is. I spent all last summer thinking I'd never be happy again, and now, a year later, I still feel sick and worried and angry, but at moments, I'm also happy. Bad things don't dig down through your life until the pit's so deep that nothing good will ever be big enough to make you happy again. No matter how much shit, there will always be wildflowers. There will always be Petes and Maggies and rainstorms in forests and sun on waves."

Gus smiled. "And sex on bookshelves and in tents."

"Ideally," I said. "Unless the world freezes over in a second ice age. And in that case, there will at least be snowflakes, until the bitter end."

Gus touched the side of my face. "I don't need snowflakes." He kissed me. "As long as there's January."

HEYYYYY, BABYCAKES. JUST wanted to make sure we're still on for a September 1 manuscript delivery. Sandy keeps checking in, and I will gladly be the human barricade that keeps her off your back, but she's desperate to buy something from you and if I keep promising her a book . . . well, then there really does need to be a book in the end.

Gus had spent the night, and when I shifted away from him to reach for the phone, he rolled over, still asleep, to follow me, nestling his face into the side of my boob, his hand sprawled out across my bare stomach.

My heart began to race both from the still-new thrill of his body *and* from Anya's text. I couldn't send her the incomplete book. It was miraculous she hadn't dumped me yet, and I couldn't put her in a less-than-ideal situation with Sandy Lowe without something to soften the blow. I slid out from under Gus, ignoring his grumbles, and grabbed my robe as I headed into the kitchen, texting Anya as I went: I can do it. Promise.

September 1, she replied. Hard deadline this time.

I didn't mess with the coffee. I was wide awake as it was.

I sat at the table and began to write. When Gus got up, he put the kettle on, then walked back to the table and took a swig from the beer bottle he'd left there last night.

I looked up at him. "That's disgusting."

He held it out to me. "Do you want some?"

I took a swig. "Even worse than I imagined."

He smiled down at me. His hand grazed my clavicle and

skimmed down me, parting my robe as he went. His fingers caught on the tie, and he tugged it loose, letting the fabric fall open. He reached through to touch my waist, drawing me onto my feet.

He turned me against the table and eased me onto it as he walked in between my legs. He caught the collar of my open robe and slid it down my arms, leaving me bare on the table. "I'm working," I whispered.

He lifted one of my thighs against his hip as he pushed in closer. "Are you?" His other hand rolled across my breast, catching my nipple. "I know you have a bet to win. This can wait."

I dragged him closer. "No. It can't."

FOCUS WAS A problem. Or rather, focusing on anything but Gus was a problem. We decided to go back to writing in our separate houses during the day, which might've been a more successful solution if either of us had enough self-control to *not* write notes back and forth all day.

I want you, he once wrote.

When did writing get so hard? I wrote back.

Hard, he wrote.

He wasn't always the instigator. On Wednesday, after resisting as long as I possibly could, I wrote, *Wish you were here* and drew an arrow down toward myself.

You're not the only one, he wrote back. Then, *Write 2,000 words and then we can talk.*

This proved to be the key to getting anything done. We changed the goalposts. Two thousand words and we could be in the same room. Four thousand words and we could touch.

Our whole arrangement was seeming less like a sprint and more like a three-legged race, full of teamwork and encouragement. Ultimately, I was still determined to win, though I was no longer sure what I was trying to prove, or to whom.

At night, we went out sometimes. To the Thai restaurant we'd ordered from so many times, a cute little place where everything was gilded and you sat on cushions on the floor and ordered from a menu whose cover was mock papyrus. To the pizza place we'd ordered from so many times, a less cute little place with plasticky red booths and interrogation-room lighting. We went to the Tipsy Fish, a bar in town, and when someone Gus knew from town walked in, he nodded hello without jerking his hand away from me.

Even as we played darts and, later, pool, we stayed connected, visibly *together*, Gus's hand curled casually around my hips or resting gently under my shirt at the small of my back, my fingers laced through his or snagged on his belt loop.

The next night, when we were leaving Pizza My Heart, we walked past Pete's Book Shop and saw her and Maggie inside, having a glass of wine in the armchairs in the café.

"We should say hi," Gus said, and so we ducked inside.

"It's our anniversary," Maggie explained airily.

"With North Bear," Pete added. "The day we moved here. Not *our* anniversary—our anniversary's January thirteenth."

"No kidding," I said. "That's my birthday."

"Really?!" Maggie seemed delighted. "Well, of course it is! The best day of the year—it only makes sense God would pull that."

"A perfectly good day," Pete agreed.

Maggie nodded. "And so is today."

"I'd move here all over again," Pete said. "Best thing we ever did, apart from falling in love."

"And adopting the Labradors," Maggie added thoughtfully.

"*And* extending a certain invitation to book club, which seems to have worked out all right," Pete added with a wink.

"Tricking us, you mean," Gus said, smiling.

He looked at me, and I wondered if we were thinking the same thing. It might not've been the *best* thing I ever did, moving here, showing up at Pete's house that night for book club. But it was a good one. The best in a few years at least.

"Just stay for one quick glass, Gussy," Maggie insisted, already pouring into the clear plastic cups they used for iced coffee.

One glass grew to two, two grew to three, and Gus pulled me onto his lap in the armchair across from them. Their hands were draped loosely between their chairs, knotted together, and Gus's were rubbing idle circles on my back as we talked and laughed into the night.

We left at midnight, when Pete finally pronounced that they should be getting home to the Labradors and Maggie started whisking around to clean up, but we were too tipsy to drive, so we walked through the heat and mosquitoes.

And as we did, I thought over and over again, *I almost love him. I'm starting to love him. I love him.*

And when we reached our houses, we ignored them and followed the path down to the lake instead. It was a Friday, after all, and we were still bound to our deal.

We stripped off our clothes and ran, shrieking, into the cold bite of the water, hand in hand. Out until it hit our thighs, our waists, our chests. Our teeth were chattering, our skin was alive with chills as the icy water batted us back and forth. "This is terrible," Gus gasped.

"It was warmer in my imagination!" I shrieked back, and Gus pulled me in against him, wrapping his arms around my back and rubbing it to bring warmth into my skin.

And then he kissed me deeply and whispered, "I love you." And then again, with his hands in my hair and his mouth on my temples and cheeks and jaw, as a ratty plastic bag drifted past on the surface of the water. "I love you, I love you."

"I know." I sank my fingers into his back as if my grip could stop time and keep us there. Us and the too-cold lake and the litter swimming through it. "I love you too."

"And to think," he said, "you promised you wouldn't fall in love with me."

24

The Book

DON'T WANT TO do this," I said. Gus and I were standing at the top of the stairs outside the master bedroom.

"You don't have to," he reminded me.

"If you can learn how to dance in the rain—"

"Still haven't done that," he interrupted.

"—then I can stare the ugly things down," I finished.

I opened the door. It took me a few breaths before I could calm myself enough to move. A California King sat against the far wall, flanked by matching turquoise end tables and lamps with blue and green beaded shades. A framed Klimt print hung over the high gray headboard. Opposite the bed, a mid-century-style dresser stretched along the wall, and a small round table sat in the corner, draped in a yellow tablecloth and decorated with a clock and a stack of books—*my books.*

The room was otherwise ordinary and impersonal. Gus opened one of the drawers. "Empty."

"She's already cleared it out." My voice shook.

Gus gave me a tentative smile. "Isn't that a good thing?"

I went forward and opened the drawers one by one. Nothing in any of them. I went to the side table on the left. No drawers, just two shelves. A porcelain box sat on the top one.

This had to be it. The thing I'd been waiting for. The deep, dark answer that I'd expected to spring out at me all summer. I opened it.

Empty.

"January?" Gus was standing beside the round table, holding the tablecloth up. From below, an ugly gray box stared back at me, complete with a numbered keypad on its face.

"A safe?"

"Or a really old microwave," Gus joked.

I approached it slowly. "It's probably empty."

"Probably," Gus agreed.

"Or it's a gun," I said.

"Was your dad the gun type?"

"In Ohio, he wasn't." In Ohio, he was all biographies and cozy nights in, dutiful hand-holding at doctors' appointments, and Groupon Mediterranean cooking classes. He was the father who woke me up before the sun to take me out on the water and let me steer the boat. As far as I knew, letting an eight-year-old drive through the empty lake for twenty seconds at a time was the peak of his impulsiveness and recklessness.

But anything was possible here, in his second life.

"Wait right here," Gus said. Before I could protest, he'd fled the room. I listened to his steps on the staircase, and then a moment later, he returned with a bottle of whiskey.

"What's that for?" I asked.

"To steady your hand," Gus said.

"What, before I pry a bullet out of my own arm?"

Gus rolled his eyes as he unscrewed the top. "Before you crack the safe."

"If we drank green smoothies like we drink alcohol, we would live forever."

"If we drank green smoothies like we drink alcohol, we would never leave the toilet, and that would do nothing to help you right now," Gus said.

I took the bottle and sipped. Then we sat on the carpet in front of the safe. "His birthday?" Gus suggested.

I scooted forward and entered the number. The lights flickered red and the door stayed locked. "At home all our codes were their anniversary," I said. "Mom and Dad's. I doubt that applies here."

Gus shrugged. "Old habits die hard?"

I entered the date with low expectations but my stomach still jarred when the red lights flashed.

I wasn't prepared for the fresh wave of jealousy that hit me. It wasn't fair that I hadn't gotten to know him through and through. It wasn't fair Sonya had parts of him that, now, I never would. Maybe the safe's code had even been some significant landmark for them, an anniversary or her birthday.

Either way, she would know the combination.

All it would take would be one email, but it wasn't one I wanted to send.

Gus rubbed the crook of my elbow, drawing me back to the present.

"I don't have time for this right now." I stood. "I have to finish a book." *This week,* I decided.

THE IMPORTANT THING, I told myself, was that the house could easily be sold. A safe was nothing, no big curveball. The house was practically empty. I could sell it and go back to my life.

Of course now when I thought about this, I had to do everything I could to avoid the question of where that would leave me and Gus. I had come here to sort things out and instead had made them messier, but somehow, in the mess, my work was thriving. I was writing at a speed I hadn't reached since my first book. I felt the story racing ahead of me and did everything I could to keep pace.

I banned Gus from the house for all but an hour each night (we set a literal timer) and spent the rest of my time writing in the second bedroom upstairs, where all I could see was the street below me. I wrote late into the night, and when I woke up, I picked up where I left off.

I lived in the give-up pants and even swore to start calling them something better if I could just finish this book, as if I were bargaining with a god who was deeply invested in my (thoroughly non-capsule) wardrobe.

I didn't shower, barely ate, chugged water and coffee but nothing harder.

At two in the morning on Saturday, August second, the day

of our event at Pete's, I reached the final chapter of *FAMILY_ SECRETS.docx* and stared down the blinking cursor.

It had all played out more or less how I'd imagined it. The clown couple was safe but still living with their secrets. Eleanor's father had stolen her mother's wedding ring and sold it to give his other family the money they needed. Eleanor's mother still had no idea the other family existed, and she believed she had only misplaced the ring, that perhaps when they unpacked in their next town, it would fall out of a pocket or a fold of towels. In her heart, the bit of colorful yarn her husband had tied around her finger more than replaced it. Love, after all, was often made not of shiny things but practical ones. Ones that grew old and rusted only to be repaired and polished. Things that got lost and had to be replaced on a regular basis.

And Eleanor. Eleanor's heart had been thoroughly broken.

The circus was moving on. Tulsa was shrinking behind them, their week there fogging over like a dream upon waking. She was looking back, with an ache she thought would never stop spearing through her.

There; there was where I was supposed to leave it. I knew that.

It had a nice cyclical quality to it. A temporary neatness that the reader could see unraveling somewhere far ahead off the page. Or perhaps not.

There it was, exactly as it was meant to be, and my chest felt heavy and my body felt chilled and my eyes were damp, although possibly more from exhaustion and the fan overhead than anything else.

But I couldn't leave it there. Because no matter how beautiful the moment was, in its own sad way, I didn't believe it. This wasn't the world I knew. You lost beautiful things—years of your mother's good health, your shot at the dream career, your father way too soon—but you found them too: a coffee shop with the world's worst espresso; a bar with a line-dancing night; a messy, beautiful neighbor like Gus Everett. I set my hands on the keyboard and started typing.

> *White flurries began to drift down around her, snagging in her hair and clothes. Eleanor looked up from the dusty road, marveling at the sudden snowfall. Of course it wasn't snow. It was pollen. White wildflowers had sprung up on either side of the road, the wind shaking their buds out into itself.*
>
> *Eleanor wondered where she was going next, and what the flowers would look like there.*

I saved the draft and emailed it to Anya.

Subject: Something Different.

Please don't hate me. Love, J.

I GOT UP early and drove twenty minutes to print the draft at the nearest FedEx, just so I could hold it in my hand. When I got back, Gus was waiting on my porch for me, sprawled on the couch with his forearm thrown over his eyes. He lifted it to peer at me, then smiled and sat up, making room for me to sit.

He pulled my legs over his lap and scooted me closer to him. "And?" he said.

I dropped the stack of paper in his lap. "Now I just have to wait and see if Anya fires me. And how mad Sandy is. And whether we can sell the book and I have something to 'lord over you.'"

"Anya won't fire you," Gus said.

"And Sandy?"

"Will probably be mad," Gus said. "But you wrote another book. And you'll write more. Probably even one she wants. You'll sell the book, though not necessarily before I sell mine, and either way, I'm sure you'll find *something* to lord over me."

I shrugged. "I'll try my best anyway. What about you—are you close to done?"

"Actually, yeah. With a draft anyway. Another week or two should do it."

"That should be about how long it takes me to do the dishes I've left around the house this week."

"Perfect timing," Gus said. "Look at fate, taking charge."

"Fate is wont to do that."

We parted ways before the event to get ready, and when my hair was dry after a much-needed shower, I lay on my bed, exhausted, and watched the fan twirl. The room felt different. My body felt different. I could have convinced myself I'd snatched someone else's limbs and life and fallen in love with them.

I drifted off to sleep and woke with an hour to spare. Gus knocked on my door thirty minutes later, and we headed to the shop on foot—normally I would hate to get sweaty before an event, but here, it seemed to matter less. Everyone was a little sweaty in North Bear Shores, and the stiff black event dress hadn't appealed to me after a summer in shorts and T-shirts, so I'd put the white thrift-store sundress on again, with the embroidered boots.

At the bookstore, Pete and Maggie took us into the office to have a glass of champagne. "Scare away any jitters," Maggie said sunnily.

Gus and I exchanged a knowing look. We'd both done enough events to know that in towns like this one, the turnout was pretty much local friends and family (at least when it was your first book; after that, most of *them* couldn't be bothered) and people who worked at the bookstore. Maggie and Pete had moved the display table up to the counter and set up about ten folding chairs, so clearly, they had some understanding of this too.

"Shame school's not in session," Pete said, as if anticipating my thoughts. "You'd get a full house then. The professors like to make this sort of thing mandatory. Or at least extra credit."

Maggie nodded. "*I* would've made it mandatory for *my* students."

"From now on, I'm putting labradorite in every book," I promised. "Just to give you a good excuse to do that."

She clutched her heart as if that was the sweetest thing she'd heard in months.

"Go time, kids," Pete announced and led the way out. There were four more chairs lined up behind the counter, and she ushered Gus and me in between her and Maggie, who would be "interviewing" us. Lauren and her husband were in the audience, along with a couple of other women I recognized from the cookout, and five strangers.

Generally, I preferred not to know so much of my audience. Actually, I preferred not to know anyone. But this felt nice, relaxed.

Pete was still standing, welcoming everyone to the event. I looked over at Gus and knew right away something was wrong.

His face had gone pale and his mouth was tense. All the warmth in him was gone, shut off as if by a valve. I whispered his name but he kept staring right into the "crowd." I followed his gaze to a tiny woman with nearly black curls and blue eyes that tilted up at the corners, complementing her high cheekbones and heart-shaped face. It took me a few seconds to puzzle it out, a few blissfully ignorant seconds before my stomach felt like it had dropped through my feet and into the floor.

My heart had started racing, like my body understood before my brain could admit it. I looked toward Maggie. Her lips were pursed and her hands were folded in her lap. She was stiff and still, completely unlike herself, and while Pete was carrying on confidently, I could see the change in her body language too, something of a mother bear's posture: a vicious protectiveness, a readiness to spring.

She sat and scooted her chair around while she readied herself. It was a casual enough gesture, but I thought she might be shaken.

My heart was still thudding against my chest so hard I figured the whole audience could hear it, and my hands started to sweat.

Naomi was beautiful. I should've known she would be. I probably had. But I hadn't expected to see her. Especially not alone, here, looking at Gus like that.

Apologetic, I thought, then, *hungry.*

My stomach lurched. She had come here with intent. She had something to say to Gus.

God, what if I threw up here?

Pete had kicked off the questioning. Something along the lines of, "Why don't you start by telling us about your books?"

Gus turned in his chair to face her. He was answering. I didn't hear what he said but the tone was calm, mechanical, and then he was looking at me, waiting for me to answer, and his face was entirely inscrutable.

It was like the master bedroom of Dad's house: impersonal, scrubbed clean. There was nothing for me in it. I really felt like I might vomit.

I swallowed it and started describing my last book. I'd done it enough—it was practically scripted. I didn't even have to listen to myself; I just had to let the words trickle out.

I really felt sick.

And then Pete was asking another question from a handwritten list she had in front of her (Tell us about your books. What's your writing process like? What do you start with? Who are you influenced by? etc.), and in between them, Maggie contributed her own lofty follow-ups (If your book were a beverage, what would it be? Do you ever imagine *where* your books should be read? What is the emotional process of writing a book like? Has there ever been a moment from your real life you found yourself unable to capture through words alone?).

This moment would probably be pretty damn hard, I thought.

How many different ways could you write, *Eleanor wanted badly to puke up everything she'd eaten that day*?

Possibly a lot. Time was inching past, and I couldn't decide whether I wanted it to move more quickly or if whatever came afterward would only make things worse.

The very question of that seemed to break the curse. The hour was over. The handful of people who'd come were milling forward to talk to us and get books signed, and I was gritting my teeth and trying to socially tap-dance while inside, tumbleweeds were blowing through my desolate heart.

Naomi hung back from the others, leaning against a bookcase. I wondered if she'd picked up the leaning from Gus or the other way around. I was afraid to look at her too long and recognize more of him on her, when I'd spent the last hour trying desperately to find some trace of me on him, proof that he had whispered my name fiercely into my skin even that afternoon. Pete had cornered Naomi and was trying to lead her from the store, but she was arguing, and then Lauren was joining them, trying to keep a scene from breaking out.

I couldn't hear what was being said, but I could see her curls bobbing as she nodded. The group around the table was dissolving. Maggie was ringing them up, her own clear gaze cutting between the register and the conversation by the door.

Gus looked at me finally. He seemed poised to offer an explanation but the expression on my face must've changed his mind. He cleared his throat. "I should see why she's here."

I said nothing. Did nothing. He stared back at me for no more than two seconds, then stood and crossed the store. My face was hot but the rest of my body was cold, shivering. Gus sent Pete away, and when she looked at me, I couldn't meet her gaze. I stood and hurried through the door to the office, then through the office to the back door into a back alley that was nothing more than a couple of dumpsters.

He hadn't invited her. I knew that. But I couldn't guess what seeing her did to him, or why she'd come.

Tough, beautiful Naomi, whose unknowability had thrilled Gus. Naomi who didn't need him or try to save him. Who he had never been afraid to break. Who he had wanted to spend his life with. Who he would have stayed with, despite everything, if given the chance.

I wanted to scream but all I could do was cry. I'd burned through all my anger, and fear was all that was left. Maybe that was what had been there all along, masked in thornier emotions.

Unsure what else to do, I started to walk home. It was dark out by the time I got there, and I'd forgotten to leave the porch light on, so when someone stood from the wicker couch, I nearly fell off the steps.

"I'm sorry!" came the woman's voice. "I didn't mean to scare you."

I'd only heard it twice, but the sound had worn grooves into my brain. I would never forget it.

"I was hoping we could talk," Sonya said. "No, more than hoping. I *need* to talk to you. Please. Five minutes. There's a lot you don't know. Things that will help, I think. I wrote it all down this time."

25

The Letters

DON'T WANT TO hear it," I told her.

"I know," Sonya said. "But I'll have failed your father if I don't make sure you do."

I laughed harshly. "See, that's the thing. You shouldn't have had my father to fail."

"Shouldn't have? If you started at the beginning of your father's life and predicted the whole thing, and how it *should* have played out, based only on where it started, he might never have found your mother. You might not exist."

My insides thrummed with anger. "Could you get off my porch, please?"

"You don't understand." She pulled out a piece of paper from her jeans pocket and unfolded it. "Please. Five minutes."

I started to unlock the door, but she began reading behind me.

"I met Walt Andrews when I was fifteen, in my language arts class. He was my first date, my first kiss, my first boyfriend. The first man—or boy—I said 'I love you' to."

The key stuck in the lock. I'd stopped moving, stunned. I turned toward her, my breath caught in my chest. Sonya's eyes flicked to me anxiously, then back to the page.

"We broke up several months after he went to college. I didn't hear from him for twenty years, and then one day, I ran into him here. He'd been on a business trip an hour east and had decided to extend his stay in North Bear Shores a couple days. We decided to get dinner. We'd been talking for hours before he admitted that he was newly separated.

"When we parted ways, we both believed we'd never see each other again." She looked up at me. "I mean that. But on his way out of town, your father's car broke down." She studied the note again. There were tears in her eyes. "We were both broken at the time. Some days what we had was the only good thing in my life.

"We started visiting each other every weekend. He even took a week off and came up to look for a house. Things were moving quickly. Effortlessly! I'm not saying any of this to hurt you. But I genuinely believed we had our second chance. I thought we were going to get married." She stopped talking for just a beat and shook her head. She hurried on before I could stop her.

"He put in to transfer to the Grand Rapids office. He bought the house. *This house.* It was in terrible shape back then, just falling to pieces, but I was still the happiest I'd been in years. He'd talk about bringing you up, about moving the boat up here and spending all summer on it, the three of us. I thought, *I'm going to live there until I die, with a man who loves me.*"

"He was married," I whispered. My throat felt like it was going to collapse. "He was still married."

Gus is married, I thought.

The emotion was ballooning through me. I wanted to hate her. I did hate her, and I also felt her pain mixing with mine. I felt all of the excitement of a new love, a healing one, a second chance with someone you'd almost forgotten about. And the pain when their *real* life came to call, the agony of knowing there was history with someone else, a relationship yours couldn't touch.

Sonya's eyes scrunched tight. "That didn't feel real to me until your mother's diagnosis."

The d-word still sent a shock wave through me. I tried to hide it. Went back to messing with the key, though now my eyes were so thick with tears I couldn't see.

Sonya kept reading, faster now. "We stayed in touch for a few months. He wasn't sure what was going to happen. He just knew he needed to be there for her, and there was nothing I could do about that. But the calls came less and less, and then not at all. And then one day, he sent an email, just to let me know that she was doing much better. That *they* were doing better."

I'd stopped with the door again, without meaning to. I was facing her, mosquitoes and moths whizzing around me. "But that was years ago."

She nodded. "And when the cancer came back, he called me. He was devastated, January. It wasn't about me, and I knew that. It was about her. He was so scared, and the next time he was passing through for work, I agreed to see him again. He was looking for comfort, and I—I'd started something with a friend of Maggie's, a *good* man, a widower. It wasn't serious yet, but I knew it could be. And perhaps that frightened me a bit, or perhaps a part of me would always love your father, or maybe we were just selfish and weak. I don't know. And I won't pretend to.

"But I will say this: that second time around, I had no illusions about where things were going. If your father had lost your mother, he wouldn't have been able to stand the sight of me, and I wouldn't have been able to believe he truly loved me anyway. I was a distraction, and I might even have believed I owed him that much.

"And when he started fixing up the house, I knew, without him ever telling me, it wasn't for us. And it happened again, as your mom got her health back. The visits came further and further apart. The calls slowed and stopped. And that time, I didn't even get an email. I can stand here and tell you that we had good enough intentions. There are no easy answers here. I know I *shouldn't* be allowed to be heartbroken right now, but I am.

"I'm heartbroken and angry with myself for getting into this situation and humiliated to be standing here with you . . ."

"Then why are you?" I demanded. I shook my head, another furious wave crashing over me. "If it was over, like you say it was, then *how* did you have that letter?"

"I don't know!" she cried out, tears welling instantly in her eyes, falling in quick, steady droplets down her face. "Maybe he wanted you to have this place but didn't think your mom would have the strength to tell you about it, or didn't think it was right to ask her to. Maybe he thought if he'd sent the key and letter straight to you, there'd be no one to stand here and convince you to forgive him. I don't know, January!"

Mom wouldn't *have ever told me,* I realized immediately. Even once Sonya had, Mom hadn't been able to talk about it, to confirm or explain. She wanted to remember all the good things. She wanted to cling to those so tight they couldn't fade, not loosen her grip enough to make room for the parts of him that still hurt to think about.

Sonya huffed a few teary breaths and swiped at her damp eyes. "All I know is when he died, his attorney sent me the letter and the key and a note from Walt asking *me* to pass along both to you. And I didn't want to—I've moved on. I'm finally with someone I love, I'm finally happy, but he was *gone*, and I couldn't say no. Not to him. He wanted you to know the truth, the whole thing, and he wanted you to still love him once you knew. I think he sent me here so I could make sure you forgave him."

Her voice quavered dangerously. "And maybe I came because I needed someone to know that I'm sorry too. That I will always miss him too. Maybe I wanted someone to understand I'm a complete person, and not just someone else's mistake."

"I don't care that you're a complete person," I bit out, and right then I understood that was true. I didn't hate Sonya. I didn't even know her. It wasn't about her at all. The tears were falling faster, making me gasp for breath. "It's about him. It's all the things I can never know about him or even ask him. What he put my mom through! I'll never know how to build a family, or what—if anything— I can trust of what I learned from them. I have to look back on every memory I have and wonder what was a lie. I can't know him any better now. I don't have him. I don't *have* him anymore."

The tears were really pouring now. My face was soaked. The dotted line of pain I'd been living with for a year felt like it had finally split open down my center.

"Oh, honey," Sonya said quietly. "We can never fully know the people we love. When we lose them, there will *always* be more we could have seen, but that's what I'm trying to tell you. This house, this town, this *view*—it was all a part of him he wanted to share with you. And you're here, all right? You're here and you've got the house on a beach he loved in a town he loved, and you've got all the letters, and—"

"Letters?" I said. "I have *one* letter."

She looked startled. "You didn't find the others?"

"*What* others?"

She seemed genuinely confused. "You haven't read it. The first letter. You never read it."

Of course I hadn't read it. Because *that* was the last new bit of him I could ever have, and I wasn't ready for that. Over a year since he had died, and I still wasn't ready to say goodbye. I was ready to say *a lot*, but not goodbye. The letter was at the bottom of the box where it had sat all summer.

Sonya swallowed and folded her list of talking points, stuffing it in the pocket of her oversized sweater. "You have pieces of him. You're the last person on Earth with pieces of him, and if you don't want to look at them, that's your call. But don't pretend he left you nothing."

She turned to go. That was all she had to say, and I'd let her get it out. I felt stupid, like I'd lost some game whose rules no one had explained. But at the same time, even if I was still reeling from the pain after she'd driven away, I was standing.

I'd had the conversation I'd been dreading all summer. I'd gone into the rooms I'd kept closed. I'd fallen in love and felt my heart break, and I'd heard more than I wanted to hear, and I was on my feet. The beautiful lies were all gone. Destroyed. And I was still upright.

I turned to the door with new purpose and went inside. Walked straight through the dark house to the kitchen and got the box down. A layer of dust had coated the envelope. I blew it away and flipped the loose tab up to pull out the letter. I read it there, standing over the sink with one yellow light turned on over me.

My hands were trembling so badly it was hard to make out the words.

This night. This night had almost been as bad as the night we'd lost him, or the night of his funeral. In any other situation, all I would've wanted would have been my parents.

Dammit, I *did* want my parents. I wanted Dad in his ratty pajama pants folded on the couch with a biography of Marie Curie. I wanted Mom moving around him in Lululemon, obsessively dusting the picture frames on the mantel as she hummed Dad's favorite song: *It's June in January, because I'm in love.*

That was the scene I'd walked in on when I'd surprised them that first Thanksgiving I'd been away at U of M. When a wicked wave of homesickness had prompted me to make the last-second decision to come home for break after all. When I'd unlocked the front door and stepped through with my duffel bag, Mom had screamed and dropped the Pledge on the ground. Dad had swung his legs off the couch and squinted at me through the golden light of their living room.

"Can it be?" he said. "Is that my darling daughter? Pirate queen of the open seas?"

They'd both run to me, squeezed me, and I'd started to cry, like

I could only fully comprehend how badly I'd been missing them now that we were together.

I felt broken anew right now, and I wanted my parents. I wanted to sit on the couch between them, Mom's fingers in my hair, and tell them I'd messed up. That I'd fallen in love with someone who'd done everything he could to warn me not to.

That I'd let myself go broke. That my life was falling apart, and I had no idea how to fix it. That my heart was more broken than it had ever been and I was scared I *couldn't* fix it.

I gripped the notebook paper in my hands tightly and blinked back the tears enough to start reading in earnest.

The letter, like the envelope, was dated for my twenty-ninth birthday—January thirteenth, a solid seven months *after* Dad had died, which made everything about this feel dreamy and surreal as I started to read.

Dear January,

Usually, though not always, I write these letters on your birthday, but your twenty-ninth is still a long ways off, and I want to be ready to give this, and all the other letters, to you then. So I'm starting early this year.

This one contains an apology, and I hate to give you a reason to hate me just before we celebrate your birth, but I'm trying to be brave. Sometimes I worry the truth can't be worth the pain it causes. In a perfect world, you would never know about my mistakes. Or rather, I wouldn't have made them to begin with.

But of course I have, and I've spent years going back and forth on what to tell you. I keep coming back to the fact that I want you to know me. This might sound selfish, and it is. But it isn't only selfish, January. If and when the truth comes out, I don't want it to rock you. I want you to know that bigger than my mistakes, bigger than anything good or bad I've ever done, and most completely unwavering has been my love for you.

I'm afraid what the truth will do to you. I'm afraid you won't be able to love me as I am. But your mother had the chance to make that decision for herself, and you deserve that too.

1401 Queen's Beach Lane. The safe. The best day of my life.

I ran up the stairs and thundered into the master bedroom. The tablecloth was still tucked up under the clock to reveal the safe. My heart was pounding. I needed to be right this time. I thought my body might crack in half from the weight on my chest, if I wasn't. I typed in the number, the same one scrawled in the top right corner of the letter. My birthday. The lights flickered green and the lock clicked.

There were two things in the safe: a thick stack of envelopes, wrapped in an oversized green rubber band, and a key on a blue PVC key chain. In white letters, the words SWEET HARBOR MARINA, NORTH BEAR SHORES, MI were printed across the surface.

I pulled the stack of letters out first and stared at them. My name was written on each, in a variety of pens, the handwriting getting sharper and more resolute the further back I flipped. I clutched the envelopes to my chest as a sob broke out of me. He had touched these.

I'd forgotten that about the house, somewhere along the way. But this was different. This was my name, a piece of him he'd carved out and left behind for me.

And I knew I could survive reading them because of every-thing else I'd survived. I could stare it all in the face. I staggered to my feet and grabbed my keys on the way out the door.

My phone's GPS found the marina with no trouble. It was four minutes away. Two turns and then I was in the dark park-ing lot. There were two other cars, probably employees', but as I walked down the dock, no one rushed out to shoo me away. I was alone, with the quiet sloshing of the water against the dock's supports, the gentle *thunk* and *shpp* of boats rocking into the wood.

I didn't know what I was looking for, but I knew that I was looking. I held the letters tightly in my hand as I moved down the length of the dock, up and down the off-shooting pathways.

And then there it was, pure white and lettered in blue, its sails rolled up. *January.*

I climbed unsteadily onto it. Sat on the bench and stared out at the water.

"Dad," I whispered.

I wasn't sure what, if anything, I believed about the afterlife, but I thought about time and imagined flattening it out so that every moment in this space became one. I could almost hear his voice. I could almost feel him touching my shoulder.

I felt so lost again. Every time I started to find my way, I seemed to slip further down. How could I trust what Gus and I had? How could I trust my own feelings? People *were* complicated. They weren't math problems; they were collections of feelings and decisions and dumb luck. The world was complicated too, not a beautifully hazy French film, but a disastrous, horrible mess, speckled with brilliance and love and meaning.

A breeze ruffled the letters in my lap. I brushed the hair from my teary eyes and opened the first envelope.

Dear January,

Today you were born. I knew to expect that for months. It was not a surprise. Your mother and I wanted you very much, even before you began to exist.

What I didn't know to expect is that today, I would feel like I'd been born too.

You have made me a new person: January's father. And I know this is who I will be for the rest of my life. I'm looking at you now, January, as I'm writing this, and I can barely get the words onto the page.

I am in shock, January. I didn't know I could be this person. I didn't know I could feel all this. I can't believe someday you will wear a backpack, know how to hold a pencil, have opinions on how you like to wear your hair. I'm looking at you and I can't believe you are going to become more amazing than you already are.

Ten fingers. Ten toes. And even if you had none of them, you'd still be the grandest thing I've ever seen.

I can't explain it. Do you feel it? Now that you're old enough to read this, and to know who you are, do you have a word for the thing that evades me? The thing that makes you different from anything else?

I guess I should tell you something about myself, about who I am at this very moment as I watch you sleep on your mother's chest.

Well, nice to meet you, January. I'm your father, the man you made from nothing but your tiny fingers and toes.

———

ONE FOR EVERY year, always written on the day.

January, today you are one. Who am I today, January? I'm the hand that guides you while you take your clumsy steps. Today, your mother and I made spaghetti, so I guess you could say I'm a chef too. Your personal one. I never used to like to cook much, but it has to be done.

———

Happy second birthday, January. Your hair has gotten so much darker. You wouldn't remember being a blonde, would you? I like it more this way. It suits you very much. Your mother says you look like her grandmother, but I think you take after my mother. She would have loved you. I'll try to tell you a bit about her too. She was from a place called North Bear Shores. That's where I'm from too. I lived there when I was your age. I was a nasty two-year-old, she used to tell me. I guess I screamed until I passed out. But that was probably at least in part due to Randy, my oldest brother. A bit of a jackass, but a lovable one. He lives in Hong Kong now, because he is Fancy.

———

January, I can't believe you're four. You are person-shaped now. I suppose you always were, but you're more so now than ever. When I was four, I wrecked my tricycle. I was riding down a pier toward the lighthouse at the end. My mother had gotten distracted by a friend and I thought it would be neat to ride right off the pier, see if I was going fast enough to stay atop the water. Like Road Runner. She saw me at the last minute and screamed my name. When I turned to look at her, I yanked the handlebars and smashed into the lighthouse itself. That's how I got that big pink scar on my elbow. I suppose it isn't so big now. Or else my elbow is quite a bit bigger. Last week you cracked your head on the fireplace. It wasn't too bad—didn't even need stitches, but your mother and I cried all night after you'd gone to sleep.

We felt so bad. Sometimes, January, being a parent feels like being a kid who someone has mistakenly handed another kid. "Good luck!" this unwise stranger cries before turning his back on you forever. We will always make mistakes, I'm afraid. I hope they will get smaller and smaller as we get bigger and bigger. Older, really; we're rather done growing.

———

Eight! Eight years old and smart as a whip! You never stop reading, January. I hated reading when I was eight, but then again, I was terrible at it, and both Randy and Douglas used to tease me mercilessly, though these days Douglas is as gentle as a butterfly. I imagine if I'd been better at reading, I would have liked it more. Or maybe vice versa. My dad was a busy man but he was the one who taught me how to read, January. And since he'd started, I wouldn't let my poor mother have anything to do with it. Well, when the time comes, I'm teaching you to drive, she used to tell me. Your favorite book right now is The Giving Tree, *but God, January, that book breaks my heart. Your mother is a bit like that tree and I worry you will be too. Don't get me wrong. That's a good way to be. But still. I wish you could be a bit stonier, like your old pop. Only for your own good.*

You know, when I was eight, I shoplifted for the first time. Not condoning it, of course, but the goal of this is honesty. I stole gum from the old-fashioned candy store on the main drag in North Bear Shores. I loved that shop. They had these great big fans to keep the chocolate from melting in the summer, and on days when my mother was occupied, my brothers and I would stroll down there to get out of the heat. I never found it much fun to go to the beach on my own. Perhaps now I'd feel different. I haven't been in a while. Your mother and I have been talking about taking you soon.

———

January, you are thirteen and braver than any thirteen-year-old should have to be. Today, I don't know who I am. I am your father still, of course. And the husband of your mother. But January, sometimes life is very hard. Sometimes it demands so much of you that you start losing pieces of yourself as you stretch out to give what the world wants to take. I am lost, January. Remember that lighthouse I told you about? I think I told you about it. Sometimes I think about you as that lighthouse. Keep your eyes on January, I tell myself. She won't lead you astray. If you focus on January, you won't go too far off course. But maybe I was so focused I ran smack dab into you.

Your mother too. I know this year has been frightening for you, but please know that some way or another, your mother and I are going to find our way back to ourselves, and back to each

*other. Please don't be afraid, my sweet baby, my daring pirate
queen of the open seas. Somehow everything will be okay.*

———

*I got my first kiss when I was sixteen, January. Her name was
Sonya and she was stringy and serene.*

———

*Your birthday isn't for a few more months, but I have to write
this now. Today, you are leaving for college, January, and I'm
afraid it might kill me. Of course I can't tell you that. You would
feel so guilty and you shouldn't. You are, by all accounts, doing
the right thing. You have always been so smart. This is where you
belong. And it's not forever. But when you wake up this
morning, and we start driving north, I won't be looking at you in
the rearview mirror. And when you read this (??? When will
that be???), think back to that day. Will you even notice that I
can't look at you? Probably not. You're so nervous yourself. But
if you do remember, now you'll know why. I worry I might turn
around and drive the three of us back home if you show any
ounce of hesitation. I want to keep you forever. Who am I
without you?*

———

*You should be in graduate school, and we all know it. Fuck
cancer, January. You're an adult now so that means by the time
you read this, you should be well acquainted with the word Fuck
and we both know you're already too closely acquainted with the
word Cancer. Well, fuck it. I have to be honest, January. I feel*

like our lives are imploding and a part of me wants to shove you far, far away until the implosion stops.

I told you I'd be honest with you, so here it is. If I write it here, I know I will not be able to take it back. Someday you will read this. Someday you will know.

I am cheating on your mother. Sometimes I feel like I am comforting myself and other times it feels like a punishment. Still other days I wonder if it's all a big F-U to the universe. "If you want to destroy my life, I can destroy it worse."

Some days I think I am in love with Sonya. Sonya, that's her name. I was in love with her once, when we were kids. I think I told you in your sixteenth-birthday letter. That was the year I kissed her. I'm sure you don't want to hear that. But I think I need to say it. I'm in love with a version of myself that can't exist in this hell. Do you think I'm terrible, January? It's okay if you do. I have been terrible at many different moments in my life.

I want to go back to being the man your mother made me: her new husband. The man you made me: your adoring father. I'm searching for something of myself I lost, and it's not fair to anyone.

If I could have the past back, those beautiful years before the cancer came back, I would pounce. I'm going to fix this. Don't give up on me, January. It isn't the end.

———

January, today you are twenty-eight.

When I was twenty-eight, my beautiful wife gave birth to our child. On this day. January thirteenth, widely regarded as the best day in the history of days. Sometimes I think about what your children would look like. Not your and Jacques's specifically, though that would be fine too.

I picture a girl who looks like January. Maybe she has ten fingers and ten toes, but even if she doesn't, she will be perfect. And I think about the kind of woman you will be for her. The kind of mother.

When I think about this, January, I usually cry. Because I know you will do better than I did, and I am so relieved by that thought. But even if you don't, even if you make the kinds of mistakes I made, I know you, January.

I know you so much better than you know me, and I'm sorry, but if there had to be an imbalance, I can't say I regret it going this way.

Remember your first breakup? I mentioned it in the letter for your seventeenth birthday. You were devastated. Your mother called in to your job at Taco Bell and pretended to be you, too sick to come in.

In that moment, I was so in love with her. She knew just what to do. The way she took care of you. There are no words.

She knows, by the way. She knows everything I've told you. She's let me take my time telling you. I worry she's ashamed, that she thinks everyone will pity her, and you know how she hates that. She's not sure you need to know. Maybe you don't. If that's the case, I'm sorry. But I guess I wanted you to see the whole truth so you would know.

If you think the story has a sad ending, it's because it's not over yet.

Since I started these letters, I've been a million different things, some good and some ugly.

But today, on your twenty-eighth birthday, I feel like the same man I was all those years ago.

Staring at you. Counting your fingers. Wondering what it is that makes you so different from the rest of the world. I don't know when it happened, but I'm happy again. I think, even if things don't stay like this, I will always carry this moment in me. How could I ever be sad, having watched my baby grow into the woman she is?

January, you are twenty-eight, and today I am your father.

26

The Best Friend

I LAY BACK ON the floor and stared up at the stars. Fluffy, dark clouds were drifting across the sky, blotting them out bit by bit, and I was watching them like a countdown, though to what I didn't know. The letters lay in a heap around me, all unfolded, all read. Two hours hadn't given me closure, but it was time I'd never expected to have with him. Words he hadn't said to me finally spoken. I felt like I had time traveled.

I was a wound, half-healed-over and scraped raw again. "Everybody Hurts" was running through my mind. I could see the consolation of it, the idea that your pain wasn't unique.

Something about that made it seem both bigger and smaller. Smaller because all the world was aching. Bigger because I could finally admit that every other feeling I'd been focusing on had been a distraction from the deepest hurt.

My father was gone. And I would always miss him.

And that had to be okay.

I reached for my phone and opened the YouTube app. I typed "Everybody Hurts" and I played it there, from my phone speakers. When it ended, I started it over.

The pain settled into a deep rhythm. It felt almost like exercising, a mounting burn through my muscles and joints. Once, in a bad season of tension headaches, my doctor had told me that pain was our body demanding to be heard.

"Sometimes it's a warning," she said. "Sometimes it's a billboard."

I didn't know what this pain's intent was but I thought, *If I listen to it, maybe it will be content to close back up for a while.*

Maybe this night of pain would give me even a day of relief.

The song ended again. I started it over.

The night was cold. I wondered how much colder it would be in January. I wanted to see it. If I did, I thought, that would be one more part of him I could meet.

I gathered the letters and envelopes into a neat stack and stood to go home, but now when I pictured the house on the edge of the lake, a strange new variation of that searing ache—*Gus, in D minor,* I thought—passed through me.

I felt like I was coming apart, like the connective tissue between my left and right ribs had been hacked away and I was going to split.

It had been hours now since we'd parted. I'd gotten no call, not even a text. I thought about the look on his face when he'd seen Naomi, like a ghost was standing in front of his eyes. A tiny, beautiful ghost he had once loved so madly he'd married her. So madly he wanted to work through it when she tore his heart to pieces.

I started to cry again, so hard I couldn't see.

I opened my texts with Shadi and typed: I need you.

It was seconds before she answered: First train out.

I stared at my phone for a second longer. There was only one other person I really wanted to talk to now. I tapped the contact info and held the phone to my ear.

It was the middle of the night. I didn't expect an answer, but on the second ring, the line clicked on.

"Janie?" Mom whispered in a rush. "Are you okay?"

"No," I squeaked.

"Tell me, honey," she urged. I could hear her sitting up, the rustle of sheets drawing back and the faint *click* of her bedside lamp turning on. "I'm here now, honey. Just tell me everything."

My voice wrenched upward as I started at the beginning. "Did I tell you Jacques broke up with me in a hot tub?"

Mom gasped. "That little shit-weasel!"

And then I told her the rest. I told her everything.

SHADI ARRIVED AT ten AM with a duffel bag an NBA player could've slept comfortably in and a box of fresh produce. When I opened the door to find her on the sunlit porch, I leaned first to see into the cardboard box and asked, "No booze?"

"Did you know you have an amazing farmer's market two blocks from here?" she said, whisking inside. "And that the only Uber driver seems to be legally blind?"

I tried to laugh, but just the sight of her here had tears welling up behind my eyes. "Oh, honey," Shadi said, and set the box down on the couch before enveloping me in a hug that was all rose water and coconut oil. "I'm so sorry," she said, her hand toying in my hair in a gentle, motherly way.

She pulled back and gripped my arms, examining me. "The good news is," she said softly, "your skin looks like a newborn baby's. What have you been eating out here?"

I tipped my head toward the box of squash and greenery. "None of *that*."

"Drafting diet?" she hazarded, and when I nodded, she patted my arm and turned toward the kitchen, gathering the box in her arms as she went. "I figured as much. Before the booze and the crying, you need a vegetable. And probably, like, eggs or something." She stopped short as she reached the kitchen, gasping either at size, scope, and style or at the disgusting mess I'd managed to make of it. "Okayyyy," she said, regrouping as she began to unload the veggies on the lone spare bit of countertop. "How about you change out of those pants, and I'll start on brunch."

"What's wrong with these pants?" I gestured to my sweats. "These are my official uniform now, on account of I've officially given up."

Shadi rolled her eyes and drummed her blue nails on the counter. "Honestly, Janie, it doesn't have to be a ball gown, but I will *not* cook for you until you put on pants that involve a button or zipper."

My stomach grumbled then, as if pleading with me, and I turned back to the first-floor bedroom. There were a handful of wrinkled T-shirts Gus had discarded in the past couple of weeks on the floor, never to be picked up again, and I kicked them into a pile behind the closet door where I wouldn't have to look at them, then dressed in cutoffs and an Ella Fitzgerald T-shirt.

Making brunch was an hour-and-a-half-long affair, and then there was the fact that Shadi insisted we finish all the dishes before we took a bite. "Look at this stack," I reasoned with her, gesturing at the leaning pile of cereal-crusted bowls. "It could be Christmas by the time we've gotten through all of these."

"Then I'm glad I packed a coat," Shadi replied with a casual shrug.

In the end, it only took half an hour to load the dishwasher and hand-wash everything that didn't fit. When we'd finished eating, Shadi insisted on cleaning the entire house. All I really wanted to do was lie on the couch, eating a pile of potato chips off my chest and watching reality TV, but it turned out she was right. Cleaning was a much better distraction.

For once, I didn't think about Dad's lies or Sonya approaching me at the funeral. I didn't replay tidbits of my fight in the car with Mom or picture the pretty, apologetic smile on Naomi's full lips. I didn't worry about the book, or what Anya would think, or what Sandy would do. I didn't really think at all.

Deep cleaning put me into a trance; I wished I could stay in an emotional cryogenic chamber that would allow me to sleep through the worst of whatever heartbreak I was avoiding.

The first phone call from Gus had come at about eleven, and I didn't answer. There wasn't another for twenty minutes, and when that one finally came in, making my heart knot up into my throat, he left no voice mail and sent no follow-up texts.

I turned my phone off and stuck it in the dresser drawer in my bedroom, then went back to mopping the bathroom. Shadi and I decided not to talk about it, about SEG or the Haunted Hat or anything else, until we'd finished with our work, which seemed like a good policy, since the cleaning was helping to numb me, and any time my brain even gestured toward a thought about Gus, the numbness started to unravel from my middle.

At six, Shadi determined we were done and banished me to the shower while she started on dinner. She made ratatouille, which she'd apparently been craving ever since she watched the movie *Ratatouille* with Ricky's little sisters during Fourth of July weekend.

"You can tell me about him," I promised, as we sat on either side of the table, my back turned to the window into Gus's house, despite the fact that it and its blinds were both closed. "I still want to hear about you being happy."

"After dinner," Shadi said. And again, she was right. It turned out I needed this, another meal, comprised mostly of vegetables, with nothing but comfortable small talk. Things we'd seen our old classmates post online, books she'd been reading, shows I'd been watching (only *Veronica Mars*).

After dinner, the sky clouded over, and as I was washing our plates and silverware and Shadi was making us Sazeracs, it began to rain heartily, claps of distant thunder quivering through the house like mini earthquakes. When I'd dried the serving dish and put it away in the cupboard to the right of the oven, she handed me my glass and we went to the couch I'd spent my first night on and curled up in opposite corners, our feet tucked under a blanket together.

"Now," she said. "Start at the beginning."

27

The Rain

WE TALKED ALL night, through the storms that rolled in and out like waves, always carrying a fresh batch of thunder and lightning in just when it seemed like it might let up. Our conversation took that long, with all the breaks for crying and the two Shadi took to make us fresh drinks.

In the time we'd been friends, I'd witnessed five of Shadi's life-shattering breakups. "It's about time you threw me a bone," she assured me. "I needed you to cry this much so I can come to you if and when Ricky destroys me."

"Is he going to?" I asked, through sniffles, and Shadi let out a deep sigh.

"Almost definitely."

She had a habit of falling in love with people who had no inter-est in falling in love. It always started as something casual, a fling that accidentally put down roots. In the end, there was always something standing in the way, something that had been there from the very beginning but hadn't been an issue back when things had been truly casual.

There was the pillhead cook, the alcoholic skateboarder, the extremely promising mentor in an after-school program for disadvantaged youth who, ultimately, had told Shadi he loved her in the same breath he'd admitted he wanted to be single for a few more years.

Everything about my best friend was misleading to the men of Chicago. She was eccentric and loud, prone to heavy drinking and all-night partying, comfortable with casual hookups, always the funniest and most shocking person in any room, and she posted mostly nude selfies with increasing regularity. She was enigmatic, the closest to the stereotypical male fantasy I'd ever seen outside of a movie, but deep down she was, completely, a romantic.

When she connected with someone, she opened up like a rose to expose the most tender, pure, selfless, and loyal heart I'd ever known. And when the men-children she accidentally wound up dating saw that side of her, they often wound up ass-over-toes in love with her, as she did with them. Dreaming of a future that neither of them had signed up for at the start of it all.

"I wish there was literally anything I could do to stop it," she said then.

"No you don't," I teased, and a slow smile spread across her face.

"I both love and despise falling in love."

"Same," I said. "Men are the worst."

"The wo-orst," she sang. For a few seconds we were silent. The tears on my cheeks had dried and the sun had started to rise, but the storm clouds were blocking it, diffusing the strange bluish light that came through the blinds across the couch. "Hey," she said finally. "I think it was time."

"What was?" I asked.

"I think it was time for you to fall in love," she said. "All this time I've known you and I've never gotten to see it. I think it was time."

"You knew me before Jacques. You watched that happen."

"Yeah." Shadi gave a shrug. "I know you loved Jacques. And maybe in the end, it's the same thing you wind up with, but with him, you never *fell*, Janie. You marched straight in."

"So falling's the part that hurts?" I asked with a humorless laugh. "And if you wind up in love without it hurting, then there's no falling?"

"No," Shadi said seriously. "Falling's the part that takes your breath away. It's the part when you can't believe the person standing in front of you both exists and happened to wander into your path. It's supposed to make you feel lucky to be alive, exactly when and where you are."

Tears clouded my vision. I did feel that with Gus, but I'd felt it once before.

"You're wrong that you never saw that with me," I said, and Shadi cocked her head thoughtfully. "That's how I felt when I found you."

A smile broke across her face, and she tossed one of the couch cushions at me. "I love you, Janie," she told me.

"I love you more."

After a moment, her smile faded and she gave one frank shake of her head. "I'm sure he loves you too," she said. "I can feel it."

"You haven't even seen us together," I pointed out. "You haven't even *really* met him."

"I can feel it." She waved a hand toward the wall just as another thunderous rumble shook the house, lightning slashing across the windows. "Wafting off his house. Also, I'm psychic."

"So there's that," I said.

"Right," Shadi said. "So there's that."

IT MIGHT'VE BEEN seconds between the moment I finally drifted to sleep on the couch and the one when the pounding on the door began, or it might've been hours. The living room was still masked in stormy shadows, and thunder was still shivering through the floorboards.

Shadi shot upright at the far end of the couch and clutched the blanket to her chest, her green eyes going wide at the second round of pounding. She hissed through the dark, "Are we being ax-murdered?"

Then I heard his voice coming through the door. *"January."*

Shadi scooted back against the arm of the couch. "That's him, isn't it?"

He pounded again and I stood, unsure what I was doing. What I should do, what I wanted to do. I looked at Shadi, silently asking her these questions.

She shrugged as another knock sounded. "Please," Gus said. "Please, January, I won't keep asking if you don't want me to, but please, talk to me." He fell silent, and the whine of the wind stretched out like an ellipsis begging to add more. My throat felt like it had collapsed, like I needed to swallow down the rubble a few times before I could get the words out.

"What would you do?" I asked Shadi.

She let out a long breath. "You *know* what I would do, Janie."

She'd said it last night: *I wish there was literally anything I could do to stop it.* The joke being that of course there was something she could do to stop it and yet somehow she could never bring herself to let the text messages and phone calls go unanswered, no way she could convince herself *not* to visit a new lover's family for a national holiday, no chance she could give up on the possibility of love.

I didn't—couldn't—know what Gus was going to tell me about last night, about Naomi, or where we stood. I couldn't know, but I could survive it.

I thought back to that moment in the car when I'd tried to carve the memory into my mind so that if and when I looked back on everything, I could tell myself it had been worth it.

That for a few weeks I had been happier than I had all year.

Yes, I thought. It was true.

I lost my breath then, like I'd run naked into the cold waves of Lake Michigan once more. I *was* grateful to be alive, even with trash floating past. I was grateful to have Shadi here. I was grateful to have read the letters from Dad, and I was grateful to have moved in next door to Augustus Everett.

Whatever came next, I could survive it all, like Shadi had so many times.

By the time I realized all this, a full minute must have passed without another knock on the door or any more shouts, and my heart raced as I hurried toward the door, Shadi clapping from the couch as if she were watching an Olympic race from the stands.

I threw the door open to the dark, stormy porch, but it was empty. I ran out, barefoot, to the steps and scoured the yard, the street below, the steps next door.

Gus was nowhere in sight. I jogged down the steps recklessly, and halfway down, cut through the grass instead, toes squelching in the mud. I had reached Gus's front yard when it hit me: his car wasn't here.

He was gone. I'd missed him. I wasn't sure whether I'd started to cry again, or if all my tears had been used up. My ribs ached; everything within them hurt. My shoulders were shaking and my face was wet, but that might've been from the downpour blanketing our little beach street. The whole thing was flooded now, a current carrying leaves and bits of trash away in a rush.

I wanted to scream. I'd been so patient with Gus all summer. I'd told him I would be, and I had been, and now I had closed back up in what was likely our last-chance moment.

I buried the back of my hand against my mouth as a ragged sob worked its way out of my chest. I wanted to collapse into the marshy grass, be absorbed into it. *If I were the ground,* I thought, *I'd feel even less than I did when I was cleaning.*

Or maybe I'd feel every step, every footprint walking over me, but that still might be better than the desolation I felt now.

Because I knew again, for certain, that Shadi had been right. I'd finally fallen. It had been impossibly fortuitous, fated, for me to find myself crossing paths with someone I could love like Gus Everett, and I still felt lucky even as I felt miserable.

A light flicked on in the corner of my vision, and I turned toward it, expecting to find Shadi on the front porch. But the light wasn't coming from my front porch.

It was coming from Gus's.

And then the music started, as loud as it had been that first night. Like Pitchfork or Bonnaroo was unfolding right here on our cul-de-sac.

Sinéad O'Connor's voice rang out, the mournful opening lines of "Nothing Compares 2 U."

The door opened and he stepped out under the light, as soaked as I was, though somehow, against all odds, his peppered, wavy hair still managed to defy gravity, sticking up at odd, sleepy angles.

With the song still ringing out into the street, interrupted only by the occasional distant rattle of the retreating storm, Gus came toward me in the rain. He looked as unsure whether he should laugh or cry as I now felt, and when he reached me, he tried to say something, only to realize the song was too loud for him to speak in a normal voice. I was shaking and my teeth were chattering, but I didn't feel cold exactly. I felt more like I was standing just a ways outside my body.

"I didn't plan this well at all," Gus finally shouted over the music, jerking his chin toward his house meaningfully.

A smile flickered over my face even as a pang went through my abdomen.

"I thought . . ." He ran his hand up through his hair and glanced around. "I don't know. I thought maybe we'd dance."

A laugh leapt out of me, surprising us both, and Gus's face brightened at the sound. As soon as its last trace had faded, tears sprang back into my eyes, a burning starting at the back of my nose. "You were going to dance with me in the rain?" I asked thickly.

"I promised you," he said seriously, taking my waist in his hands. "I said I would learn."

I shook my head and fought to steady my voice. "You're not beholden to any promises, Gus."

Slowly, he pulled me against him and wrapped his arms around me, the heat of him only slightly dimmed by the chill of the rain. "It's not the promise that matters," he murmured just above my right ear as he started to sway, rocking me side to side in a tender approximation of a dance, the inverse of that night we'd spent at the frat party. "It's that I told *you*."

Soft January. January who could never hide what she was thinking. January who he'd always been afraid to break.

My throat knotted. It almost hurt, being held by him like this, not knowing what he was about to tell me, or whether this would be the last time he held me at all. I tried to say something, to again insist he wasn't obligated to me, that I understood the complicated state of things.

I couldn't make a sound. His hand was in my damp hair and I closed my eyes against another stream of tears, burying my face in his wet shoulder.

"I thought you were gone. Your car . . ." I trailed off.

" . . . Is stuck on the side of the road right now," he said. "It's raining like the world is ending."

He gave a forced smile, but I couldn't match it.

The song had ended, but we were still rocking, holding on to each other, and I was terrified of the moment he'd let go, all while trying to appreciate *this* instant, the one when he still hadn't.

"I've been calling you," he said, and I nodded, because I couldn't get out *I know*.

I sucked a breath into my lungs and asked, "Was that Naomi?"

I didn't clarify that I meant *the beautiful woman at the event*, but I didn't need to.

"Yeah," Gus answered in a hush. For a few more seconds, neither of us spoke. "She wanted to talk," he finally offered. "We went for a drink next door."

I am still standing, I thought. Well, not quite. I was *leaning*, letting him take the bulk of my weight. But I was alive. And Shadi was inside, waiting for me. I would be okay.

"She wants to get back together," I choked out. I'd meant it as a question but it came out more proclamation.

Gus eased back enough to look into my eyes, but I didn't reciprocate. I kept my cheek pressed into his chest. "I guess she and Parker split up a while ago," Gus said, resting his chin on my head again. His arms tightened across my back. "She . . . she said she'd been thinking about it for a long time but she wanted to wait. To make sure I wasn't her rebound."

"How could you be her rebound?" I asked. "You're her husband."

His gruff laugh rumbled through me. "I said something like that."

My stomach squirmed.

"She's not a bad person," Gus said, like he was pleading with me.

My gut twisted. "Glad to hear it."

"Really?" Gus asked, head tilting. "Why?"

"You shouldn't be married to an asshole, I guess. Probably no one should, except maybe other assholes."

"Well, that's the thing," he said quietly. "She asked me if I could ever forgive her. And I think I could. I mean, eventually."

I said nothing.

"And then she asked if I could see myself being with her again, and—I can imagine it. I think it's possible."

I thought maybe I should say something. *Oh? Good? Well, then?* The pain didn't seem content to have been heard. It roared up in me. "Gus," I whispered, and closed my eyes as more hot tears streamed out of them. I shook my head.

"She asked if we could make our marriage work," he murmured, and my arms went limp. I stepped back from him, wiping at my face as I put distance between us. I stared at the flooded grass and my muddy toes.

"I never expected to hear her say that," Gus said breathlessly. "And I don't know—I needed time, to figure it all out. So I went home, and . . . I just started to think it all through, and I wanted to call you but it seemed so selfish, to call you like that and make you help me figure it out. So I just spent all day yesterday thinking about it," he said. "And at first I thought . . ." He stopped again and shook his head sort of manically. "I could definitely be with Naomi again, but even if we could be together, I didn't think I could ever be married again. It was all too messy and painful. And then I thought about that more, and realized I didn't mean it."

I tightened my eyes as more tears pushed out. *Please,* I wanted to beg him. *Stop.* But I felt stuck in my own body, held prisoner there.

"January," he said softly. "Look at me."

I shook my head.

I listened to his steps moving through the grass. He slipped my lifeless hands into his. "What I meant is, I *did* mean it, about her and me. I didn't mean it about you."

I opened my eyes and looked up into his face, blurred behind my tears. His throat shifted, jaw flexed. "I've never met someone who is so perfectly my favorite person. When I think about being with you every day, no part of me feels claustrophobic. And when I think about having to have the kinds of fights with you that Naomi and I used to have, there's nothing scary about it. Because I trust you, more than I've ever trusted anyone, even Pete.

"When I think about you, January, and I think about doing laundry with you and trying terrible green juice cleanses and going to antiques malls with you, I only feel happy. The world looks different than I ever thought it could be, and I don't want to look for what's broken or what could go wrong. I don't want to brace myself for the worst and miss out on being with you.

"I want to be the one who gives you what you deserve, and I want to sleep next to you every night and to be the one you complain about book stuff to, and I don't think I ever *could* deserve any of that, and I know this thing between us isn't a sure thing, but that's what I want to aim for with you. Because I know no matter how long I get to love you, it will be worth whatever comes after."

It was so close to the same thought I'd had earlier tonight, and before that, as we drove back from New Eden, our hands clutching each other against the gearshift, but now it sounded different, felt a little sour in my stomach.

"It will be worth it," he said again, more quietly, more urgently.

"You can't know that," I whispered. I stepped back from him slowly, swiping the tears from my eyes.

"Fine," Gus murmured. "I can't know it. But I believe it. I *see* it. Let me prove I'm right. Let me prove I can love you forever."

My voice came out thin and weak. "We're both wrecks. It's not just you. I wanted to think it was, but it's not. I'm a disaster. I feel like I need to relearn everything, especially how to be in love. Where would we even *start*?"

Gus pulled my hands away from my tear-streaked face. His smile was faint, but even in the cloudy light of morning, I could see the dimple creasing his cheek. His hands skated onto my hips, and he pulled me softly against him, tucking his chin on my head. "Here," he whispered into my hair.

My heart skipped a beat. Was that possible? I wanted it so badly, wanted *him* in every part of my life, just like he'd said.

"When I watch you sleep," he said shakily, "I feel overwhelmed that you exist."

The tears rushed full force into my eyes again. "What if we *don't* get a happy ending, Gus?" I whispered.

He thought it over, his hands still sliding and tightening and pushing against me like they couldn't sit still. His dark eyes homed in on mine. As I looked up at him, his gaze was doing the sexy, evil thing, but now it seemed less sexy-evil and more . . . just Gus.

"Then maybe we should enjoy our happy-for-now," Gus said.

"Happy for now." I tasted the words, rolled them over the back of my tongue like wine. The only promise you ever had in life was the one moment you were living. And I was.

Happy for now.

I could live with that. I could learn to live with that.

Slowly, he began to sway me back and forth again. I wrapped my arms around his neck and let his circle my waist and we stood there, learning to dance in the rain.

28

Nine Months Later

R EADY?" GUS SAID.

I clutched the advance copy of *The Great Family Marconi* against my chest. I suspected I would never be ready. Not for this book and not for him. Handing it over to the world was going to feel like falling headfirst out of an airplane, and I could only hope that something below decided to rise up and catch me. I asked Gus, "Are you?"

His head tilted as he considered. He had just finished the line edits phase of editing his book, so his manuscript was held together by binder clips, rather than the cheapo paperback binding used for the advance copies, which would arrive any day now.

In the end, my book had sold three weeks before his, but his had sold for a little more money, and both of us had decided to ditch the pen names. We'd written books we were proud of, and even if they were different from what we usually did, they were still ours.

It was strange not to see the little sun over waves, Sandy Lowe's logo, on the spine where it had been for all my other books. But I knew my next book, *Curmudgeon*, was going to have it, and that felt good.

Curmudgeon, my readers would love. I loved it too. No more or less than I loved *Family Marconi*. But perhaps I felt more protective of the Marconis than I did my other protagonists, because I didn't know how they'd be judged.

Anya had insisted that anyone who didn't want to *swaddle the Marconis in the softest silk and hand-feed them grapes is just swine with no need for pearls. Don't you worry.* Of course, she'd said that when forwarding the first trade review this morning, which had been largely positive apart from describing the cast as "unwieldy" and Eleanor herself as "rather shrill."

"I think I am," Gus answered and handed his stack of pages to me. He had no reason to worry, and I told myself I didn't either. In the past year, I'd read both of his books, and he'd already read all three of mine, and so far, each other's writing hadn't left either of us repulsed by the other.

In fact, reading *The Revelatories* had felt a bit like swimming through Gus's mind. It was heartbreaking and beautiful but very, very funny in some moments, and extremely odd in many.

I passed him my book and he grinned down at the illustrated cover, the stripes of the tent swooping down into curls at the bottom, tying knots around the silhouetted figures of the characters, binding them together.

"It's a good day," Gus said. Sometimes he said that, usually when we were in the middle of something mundane, like loading the dishwasher or dusting the front room of his house in our nasty cleaning clothes. Since selling Dad's house in February, I'd spent a lot of time in the beach house next door, but Gus came to my apartment in town too. It was over the music store, and during the day, while we were working in my breakfast nook, we could hear stray college students stopping by to test out drum sets they could never have fit in their dorms. Even when it bothered us, it was something we shared.

Truthfully, sometimes Gus and I liked to be grumps together.

At night, after the shop closed, the owners, a middle-aged brother and sister with matching bone gauges in their ears, always turned their music up—Dylan or Neil Young and Crazy Horse or the Rolling Stones—and sat on their back stoop, smoking one shared joint. Gus and I would sit on my tiny balcony above them and let the smells and sounds float up to us. "It's a good day," he'd say, or if he'd accidentally shut the balcony door with it locked again, he'd say something like, "What a fucking day."

And then he'd climb down the fire escape to the weed-smoking siblings and ask if he could cut through the store to the second stairwell inside the building, and they'd say, "Sure, man," and a minute later, he'd appear behind me with a fresh beer in hand.

Sometimes I missed the kitchen in the old house, that hand-painted white and blue tile, but these past few weeks as summer began anew, I'd heard the clamor and laughter of the six-person family that was staying in it, and I imagined they appreciated the touch as much as I ever had. Maybe someday, one of the four kids would describe those careful designs to his own children, a piece of memory that managed to stay bright as everything else grew vague and fuzzy.

"It *is* a good day," I agreed. Tomorrow was the anniversary of the day Naomi left Gus, the night of his thirty-third birthday, and he'd finally told Markham he'd prefer not to have the big party.

"I just want to sit on the beach and read," he'd said, so that had been our plan for the last two weeks. We would finally swap our latest books and read them outside.

I was, of course, surprised he'd suggested it. While we both loved the view, I'd seen in the last year that Gus wasn't lying about how little time he spent on the beach. He thought it was too crowded during the day, and at night, it was too cold to swim any-way. We'd spent much more time down there in January and Feb-ruary, walking out along the frozen waves, holding our arms out as we stood on the edge of the world, squinting into the dying light, our jackets rippling.

The lake froze so far out that we could even walk on it past the lighthouse my father had once ridden his tricycle into. And what was more, the water froze so high and the snow piled on top of it such that we could walk right up to the *top* of the lighthouse, stand on it like it was part of some lost civilization underneath us, Gus's arm hooked around my neck as he hummed, *It's June in January, because I'm in love.*

I'd had to buy a bigger coat. One that looked like a sleeping bag with arms. A fur-lined hood and rings of down-stuffed Gore-Tex all the way to my ankles, and still I sometimes had to layer sweat-shirts and long-sleeved T-shirts under it.

But the sun—fuck, the sun was brilliant on those winter days, glancing off every crystal edge sharper than when it had first hit. It was like being on another planet, just Gus and me, closer to a star than we'd ever been. Our faces would go so numb we couldn't feel the snot dripping down them, and when we got back inside, our fingers would be purple (gloves or no) and our cheeks would be flushed, and we'd flick on the gas fireplace and collapse onto the couch, shivering and chattering and too numb to undress and tangle up beneath blankets with any semblance of grace.

"January, January," Gus would sing, his teeth clacking from the cold. "Even if there aren't any snowflakes, we'll have January all year long."

I had never liked winter before, but now I understood. Sitting on a blanket on the sand tonight was nice, but we were sharing the sparkling waves with three dozen other people. It was a different kind of beauty, hearing shrieks and squeals rise between the crashing of water on shore, more like those nights I'd sat out in my parents' backyard listening to the neighbor kids chasing fireflies. I was glad Gus was giving it all a try.

We read for a couple of hours, then staggered home in the dark. I slept at his house that night, and when I woke, he was already out of bed, the burble of the coffeepot coming from the kitchen.

We went back to the beach that afternoon and sat side by side, reading each other's books again. I wondered what he would think of the ending to mine, whether it would feel too contrived to him or if he'd be disappointed I hadn't truly committed to an unhappy ending.

But his book was shorter and I finished first, with a burst of laughter that made him look up, startled, from the page. "What?" he asked.

I shook my head. "I'll tell you when you're done."

I lay on the sand and stared up into the lavender sky. The sun had started setting and we'd long since eaten our snacks. My stomach growled. I stifled another laugh.

Gus's new book, tentatively titled *The Cup Is Already Broken*, was nothing close to a rom-com, although it *did* have a strong romantic thread woven into the plot and *had* come extremely close to a happy ending.

The protagonist, Travis, had left the cult with all the evidence he needed. He'd even talked Doris into leaving with him. They were happy, extremely happy, but for no more than a page or two before the world-ending meteor the prophet had been predicting hit the Earth.

The world hadn't ended. In fact, Travis and Doris were the only two human casualties. It had missed the compound and hit the woods just off the road the two were traveling on. It hadn't even been the meteor to kill them—it had been the distraction of it, Travis's eyes skirting off the road he'd worked so hard to get onto.

The right tire had run off the shoulder, and when he'd cranked it back too hard, he'd hit a semitruck that was flying past in the other direction. Come to a screaming halt, crumpled like a stomped-on can.

I closed my eyes against the dusky sky and swallowed my laughter down. I didn't know why I couldn't stop, but soon the feeling hardened in my belly and I realized I wasn't laughing. I was crying. I felt both defeated and understood.

Angry that these characters had deserved better than they'd gotten and somehow comforted by their experience. *Yes,* I thought. *That is how life feels too often.* Like you're doing everything you can to survive only to be sabotaged by something beyond your control, maybe even some darker part of yourself.

Sometimes, it was your body. Your cells turning into poison and fighting against you. Or chronic pain sprouting up your neck and wrapping around the outsides of your scalp until it felt like fingernails sinking into your brain.

Sometimes, it was lust or heartbreak or loneliness or fear driving you off the road toward something you'd spent months or years avoiding. Actively fighting against.

At least the last thing they'd seen, the meteor streaming toward Earth, had distracted them because of its beauty. They hadn't been afraid. They'd been mesmerized. Maybe that was all you could hope for in life.

I didn't know how long I'd been lying there, tears trickling quietly down my cheeks, but I felt a rough thumb catch one and opened my eyes to Gus's gentle face. The sky had darkened to a brutal blue. Seeing that color on someone's skin would make your stomach turn. It was gorgeous in this context. Strange how things could be repellent in some situations and incredible in others.

"Hey," he said tenderly. "What's wrong?"

I sat up and wiped my face dry. "So much for your happy ending," I said.

Gus's brow furrowed. "It *was* a happy ending."

"For who?"

"For them," he said. "They were happy. They had no regrets. They'd won. And they didn't even have to see it coming. For all we know, they live in that moment forever, happy like that. Together and free."

Chills crawled down my arms. I knew what he meant. I'd always felt grateful Dad had gone in his sleep. I hoped the night before, he and Mom had watched something on TV that made him laugh so hard he had to take off his glasses and get the tears out of his eyes. Maybe something with a boat in it. I hoped he'd had a few too many of Mom's infamous martinis to feel any worry when he crawled into bed, apart from that he might not feel so hot in the morning.

I had told Mom this when I'd gone home to visit at Christmas. She had cried and held me close. "It was something like that," she promised. "So much of our lives were something like that." Talking about him came in fits and starts. I learned not to press it. She learned to let it out, bit by bit, and that sometimes, it was okay to let a little ugliness into your story. That it would never rob you of all the beauty.

"It's a happy ending," Gus said again, bringing me back to the beach. "Besides, what about *your* ending? Everything tied up perfectly."

"Hardly," I said. "The only boy Eleanor had even *thought* she'd loved is married now."

"Yeah, and she and Nick are obviously going to get together," Gus said. "You could sense that through the whole book. It was obvious he was in love with her, and that she loved him back."

I rolled my eyes. "I think you're projecting."

"Maybe so," he said, smiling back at me.

"I guess we both failed," I said, climbing to my feet.

Gus followed me. We started up the crooked, rooty path. "I don't think so. I think I wrote my version of a happy ending and you wrote your version of a sad one. We had to write what we think is true."

"And you still believe a meteor hitting the Earth is the best-case scenario in a romance."

Gus laughed.

We'd forgotten to leave the porch light on, but usually there was nothing to trip over. He'd never had porch furniture, and when I'd given Dad's to Sonya, we'd decided to save up and get our own, then promptly forgotten. Tonight, however, the porch wasn't empty. A cardboard box sat against the door, and Gus scooped it up, studying the shipping label.

"Must be the advanced copies," he said. He sounded a little nervous but didn't hesitate to balance the box against his hip and use his keys to slice open the tape along the top. He set the open box down, withdrew a copy of the book, and passed it to me.

"Don't you want to see it first?" I asked.

He shrugged. "You first. I'll just watch your reaction for signs that they accidentally printed it upside down, or with the wrong title."

But they hadn't printed it upside down or made any other ridiculous mistake. It looked gorgeous, with shades of blue swirling across its cover, the clean white lettering of the title so large I could read it perfectly even in the dim light of the stars and moon. "It's perfect," I said, running my fingers over the words. I flipped the flimsy cover open, and thumbed through the first few pages. "The typesetting is really wonderful and—" I'd just hit the dedication page, and whatever I'd been about to say dispersed from my mind like smoke on a breeze.

The bound manuscript I'd read hadn't had a dedication in it, or if it had, I'd somehow missed it. Which seemed improbable both because of how closely I had studied every word, as if each were a piece of Gus I could bottle up and keep, and because there was no way I could have missed those first two words.

For January, I don't care how the story ends as long as I spend it with you.

I looked up at him, his perfectly imperfect face obscured by the prickling tears in my eyes, the mess of dark hair turned jet black by the night, the soft gleam in those eyes I loved so much. "You just had to outdo the most beautiful dedication you'd ever read, didn't you?"

He smiled. "Something like that."

His hand found the side of my face, and his warm mouth pressed into mine. When he pulled back, my hair catching in his scruff, he said quietly, "And to answer your question about the best-case scenario for a love story, yes. If I were hit by a meteor while in the car with you, I would still think I went out on a high note."

My cheeks still heated when he said things like that. The lava-like feeling still filled my stomach.

"I love you, Augustus Everett," I said, and he didn't shudder at the sound of his name, just smiled and ran a thumb over my jaw. So much had changed in the last year. So much would change next year too.

In books, I'd always felt like the Happily Ever After appeared as a new beginning, but for me, it didn't feel like that. My Happily Ever After was a strand of strung-together happy-for-nows, extending back not just to a year ago, but to thirty years before. Mine had already begun, and so this day was neither an ending nor a beginning.

It was just another good day. A perfect day. A happy-for-now, so vast and deep that I knew—or rather believed—I didn't have to worry about tomorrow.

Acknowledgments

Behind every book that makes its way into the world is a whole village of advocates, and this book couldn't have had a better village fighting for it every step of the way. Huge thanks, first, to my amazing editor, Amanda Bergeron, whose skill, passion, and kindness have made every minute I spent working on this book pure delight. No one could have understood nor refined the heart of January and Gus's story quite like you, and I'm forever grateful to have had you in their corner. I'm still just starry-eyed over getting to work with you.

Thank you also to the rest of the inimitable team at Berkley: Jessica McDonnell, Claire Zion, Cindy Hwang, Grace House, Martha Cipolla, and the rest. Huge gratitude also to the whole team at Viking, especially the brilliant Katy Loftus, Vikki Moynes, Georgia Taylor, Ellie Hudson, Emma Rogers, and Holly

359

Ovenden, as well as to the teams at Droemer Knaur, Vulkan, Lavender Lit, Harper Italia, Le Cherche Midi, and The House of Books. I feel so ridiculously lucky to have found a home and family among you.

To the first person who read this book in any form, Lana Popovic, thank you so much for always, always believing in me and for inspiring the world's best fictional agent, Anya.

Thanks also to *my* perfect dream of an agent, Taylor Haggerty. You have been a guiding light to me through this whole process, and I know on a deep bone-level that *Beach Read* could not have made it here without you and the rest of the incredible people at Root Literary: Holly Root, Melanie Castillo, and Molly O'Neill. Huge thanks also to my ridiculously savvy foreign rights agent, Heather Baror, and the rest of Baror International, as well as Mary Pender of UTA, who has been an incredible support to me since the beginning of this journey.

I also must thank my dear friend Liz Tingue, one of the first people to take a big chance on me and my writing. Truly, none of this would have been possible without you. I'm forever grateful to both you and Marissa Grossman for being on my team since the beginning.

There are so many other people who have been essential to my growth as both a writer and person, but I especially need to thank Brittany Cavallaro, Parker Peevyhouse, Jeff Zentner, Riley Redgate, Kerry Kletter, Adriana Mather, David Arnold, Janet McNally, Candice Montgomery, Tehlor Kay Mejia, and Anna Breslaw for being such wonderful friends and giving me such a lovely, vibrant writing community. You are all sparkly, fierce, hilarious, and ridiculously talented. Not to mention, like, *really* pretty.

And of course, I couldn't write about family, friendship, and love if not for the spectacular family, friends, and partner that have been given to me.

Thank you to the grandparents, parents, brothers, sisters, and whole lot of dogs who have always surrounded me in love. To Megan and Noosha, the women whose friendship has taught me how to write about best friends. And to the love of my life, my perfectly favorite person, Joey. Every moment with you is the vastest, deepest happy-for-now I could have dreamt of. With you in my life, it's hard not to be a romantic.

Need another sizzling, laugh-out-loud love story?

Book Lovers

EMILY HENRY

**ONE SUMMER. TWO RIVALS.
A PLOT TWIST THEY DIDN'T SEE COMING . . .**

*Nora is a cut-throat literary agent at the top of her game.
Her whole life is books.*

*Charlie is an editor with a gift for creating bestsellers.
And he's Nora's work nemesis.*

Nora has been through enough break-ups to know she's the woman
men date *before* they find their happy-ever-after. That's why Nora's
sister has persuaded her to swap her desk in the city for a month's
holiday in Sunshine Falls, North Carolina. It's a small town straight out of
a romance novel, but instead of meeting sexy lumberjacks, handsome
doctors or cute bartenders, Nora keeps bumping into . . . Charlie.

**She's no heroine. He's no hero.
Can they take a page out of an entirely different book?**

'Her best yet'
TAYLOR JENKINS REID, author of *Malibu Rising*

'Sexy, funny and smart'
EMMA STRAUB, author of *All Adults Here*

'*Book Lovers* is *Schitt's Creek* for book nerds'
CASEY McQUISTON, author of *One Last Stop*

ORDER YOUR COPY NOW!